NO TURNING BACK

Also by Freddie P. Peters:

COLLAP$E
BREAKING PO!NT
SPY SHADOWS
IMPOSTER IN CHIEF
(Coming out in Winter 2021)

In the NANCY WU CRIME THRILLER series
BLOOD DRAGON

Don't miss FREE access to the backstories that underpin these
books as well as FREE chapters.

Go to www.freddieppeters.com

NO TURNING BACK

FREDDIE P. PETERS

HENRY CROWNE PAYING THE PRICE BOOK 3

Glossary of Technical Terms

Term	Meaning
ANPR	Automatic Number Plate Recognition
IDENT1	UK central database for biometric identification, fingerprints etc.
NCA	National Crime Agency
SOCO	Scene of Crime Officer
SO19	Special Firearms Command of the Met
SFO	Serious Fraud Office
UVF	Ulster Volunteer Force
INTERPOL	International Criminal Police Organisation

List of French Expressions
with English Translations

French Dialogue	English Translation
Absolument	Absolutely
Absolument mon cher	Absolutely my dear
Absolument, rebel de la gauche	Absolutely, left wing rebel
Andiamo	Let's go
Bien entendu	Certainly
C'est vrai	It's true
Dés que j'ai fini	As soon as I have finished
En tête à tête	Face to face (romantic and intimate)
Ha, voilà. Parfait	Ha, here we are. Perfect
Je le sais	I know
J'ai besoin de vous	I need you
J'ai besoin de vous parler	I need to talk to you
Je suis très flattée, mon cher ami	I am very flattered, my dear
Ma chère	My dear (female)
Ma chère amie	My dear friend (female)
Mais je n'en doutais pas moins	I had no doubt about it
Messieurs	Gentlemen
Mon ami	My friend (male)
Mon cher	My dear (male)
Mon cher ami	My dear friend (male)
N'est-ce pas	Isn't it
Très heureux de l'entendre	Very glad to hear it
Une proposition irrésistible	An irresistible offer
Vraiment	Really
Vraiment désolée	Really sorry

No Turning Back
First published 2019 by Freddie P. Peters
www.freddieppeters.com

Text copyright © Freddie P. Peters 2019
This edition published 2021

The right of Freddie P. Peters to be identified as the author of this work
has been asserted by her in accordance with the Copyright, Designs and
Patents Act 1988.

ISBN: 978-1-9993373-0-8

A CIP catalogue record for this book is available from
the British Library.

Cover design by Ryan O'Hara.
Typesetting by Aimee Dewar.

To Claude

Prologue

The blindfold sits heavy over his eyes. Henry fights the desire to adjust it and show his apprehension. He has been led down a series of long corridors; at least they feel that way. They must be underground judging by the lingering smell of damp and mould that had puzzled him at first. The floor feels smooth underneath his feet. Someone has used strong detergent on the floor but it hasn't managed to cover the smell of decay.

By his own estimation, Henry has been sitting on this small uncomfortable chair for fifteen minutes, perhaps longer. He spreads his long fingers carefully on his thighs. He does not want to fidget or, worse, show trembling.

"Hello Henry," says a voice that sounds familiar.

He turns his head slightly. To his surprise he is not sitting directly in front of the door but side on. He does not respond.

"Do you know why you are here?"

Henry still does not answer.

"Remove the blindfold."

A pair of hands pull at the material and his eyes hurt even more. The mask comes off but Henry keeps his eyes shut.

Should he open them? If he does he will know the man's identity and there will be no turning back.

"I am here to offer you a deal ... a one-off chance." The voice is smooth and convincing. It is what he has been wanting to hear since he walked through the doors of HMP Belmarsh. Henry inhales deeply and opens his eyes. The light blinds him

1

and he jerks his head sideways, raising his right hand to protect his face. A strong spotlight has been placed above him. He need not have worried about the man's face as it's hidden in the shadows.

"Do you know why you are here?"

"Because I'm – a City banker?" He still can't bring himself to use the past tense.

"Wrong answer."

Henry's head falls imperceptibly. He will not be defeated by the shame that eats him alive every day.

"Because I'm – a terrorist?"

"That's a much better answer."

The man moves his head, indicating to the guards still standing behind Henry's chair that they can now go. His handcuffs were removed when he was pushed down on the chair. How very confident of the men who have brought him to this place.

But what could he do, deep underground in one of MI6's bunkers?

"You're growing very close to Abu Maeraka?"

Henry shrugs. "You mean Kamal?"

"Who else did you have in mind?" The man is still in the shadows. But Henry can almost distinguish his shape. He is medium height but his shoulders are impressive. He has turned away for a short moment, enough to light a cigarette and its red dot now glows at his mouth. Henry almost wishes he had taken up smoking in jail. Only cigars, of course, to celebrate the obscenely large deals he used to structure and close in his investment banking days.

Henry does not answer the man's question. He has questions of his own. "Did you get him transferred to Belmarsh?"

"Does it matter?"

Henry's throat tightens. These fuckers have been playing him all along. Anger, his old friend, grabs him again. It swells in his belly, a rumble that is familiar and exciting. Henry exploited that feeling so often when he worked in the City.

But no more.

He must stay in control. He must push away the images that haunt him: the Paddington bombing, the bodies, the smell of burning flesh and above all his cowardice.

Inhale – Exhale.

The man has moved behind him. Henry feels his proximity. Two strong hands

2

land on his shoulders and the acrid smell of smoke assails his nostrils. The man is speaking in his ear. Henry does not understand what he is saying now … it is a foreign language, something throaty. Henry has heard it before, around him, Middle-Eastern – almost certainly Arabic.

"Have you told anyone of your plans with Abu Maeraka?" The hands have tightened and the breath in his ear becomes hotter, the fetid smell of cigarettes repulsive. Henry's fingers are digging into his thighs, his body stuck to the chair.

Powerless.

The door opens with a crash and men pour into the room: four, five – maybe more. They grab Henry's limbs; push him back into a contorted position. A damp cloth sticks to his face and water starts gushing over it. The wet cloth has become so heavy, it clings even closer to his nose, to his mouth. His breathing slows. His head is leaden. His mouth gasps desperately.

Breathe – Breathe.

His chest is about to explode and at the very last instant the man removes the cloth.

"What is your plan?" The voice is so calm.

The room has become hotter as more men come in. They jostle to tear Henry's clothes from his body and he can't move. He should run. He should resist but remains frozen.

Powerless.

The cloth comes over his face again. The water fills his nose, his lungs. This time he will drown.

He screams a noiseless scream that no one can hear.

Chapter One

Midnight, Inspector Pole stretched, moving his tall body gently so as not to disturb Nancy. He picked up his BlackBerry, scrolled down his emails. Nothing from Andy and no text either.

Promising.

He placed his hand over Nancy's and squeezed gently. She moved a little closer, rolled her face towards him slowly, "Mmmm". The music they had been listening to, a new Philip Glass piece Nancy had recently discovered, had just finished. Pole smiled. He looked at her slender body, the loose silk trousers and blouse that accentuated the curve of her waist and breasts. He turned sideways to face her more fully, resting his head on his bent arm. He squeezed her hand once more. Nancy's eyes fluttered open and she stirred with a smile.

"So sorry Jonathan." She moved one arm lazily over her head, stretched, bent her arm and facing Pole rested her hand on his shoulder.

"It's midnight after all," Pole replied. Nancy falling sleep in his company felt more like a sign of trust than boredom.

"Any news?"

"Nothing," Pole replied, placing a kiss on her hand. "In my profession no news is not always good news but tonight I —"

The unmistakable buzz of the BlackBerry interrupted him and Pole rolled his eyes. Nancy chuckled.

"Pole," he answered.

Nancy bent forward to grab the yellow notepad that now lived permanently on her coffee table and handed it to him with a ballpoint pen.

Pole started to scribble.

"Are you serious?"

The person at the other end of the phone confirmed a piece of information. Pole cast a quick eye towards Nancy. He did not like what he was hearing.

"Fine. With you in a few minutes."

Pole's interlocutor seemed in turn surprised.

"Yes, I said a few minutes. Yes, I know where this is." Pole hung up.

"Should I get ready too?"

"Body found at the entrance of the Regent's Canal – tied to a trolley."

"Is that reason enough to be calling you?" Nancy asked, dubious. "Someone's death warrants attention, of course but …"

"No, only the quirkiest cases go to your friend Pole."

"Do tell – the suspense is killing me. Metaphorically that is."

"The man has been identified as a well-known criminal, on the INTERPOL most wanted list."

"And?"

"I can't hide anything from you – he was a prolific art thief, Italian with deep mafia connections." Pole had finished tying his shoelaces. He stood up. Nancy had already sprung off the sofa and was running barefoot towards her bedroom.

"I'm grabbing a pair of shoes, be with you in two ticks. I am a consultant with the Met after all."

"But perhaps I should check first what this is all about?"

"Nonsense, Jonathan. If art is involved you know you need me."

"Do I?"

"*Absolument mon cher,*" Nancy said from inside her bedroom.

Pole put on his jacket, pocketed his BlackBerry and moved towards the door. Nancy caught up with him.

"*Andiamo.*" She closed the door of her apartment behind them. "Let's see what the Italian Mafia has in store for us then."

Islington High Street was teeming with people. Nightclub goers, restaurant goers, cinema buffs – an eclectic mix of age and culture that so characterised her neighbourhood.

A group of giggling girls was heading towards Camden Passage, dressed in black but each sporting angel wings on their back and headbands with flashing bobbles – a hen party going to The Ladybird Bar, no doubt.

Nancy was walking alongside Pole watching his determined pace. He had placed himself between Nancy and the pavement kerb as any gentleman worthy of the name would do. She recalled the first time one of her older colleague in Chambers had walked in this way and offered her an explanation.

In the days when pavements were either small or simply non-existent, a gentleman would walk between the lady he accompanied and the road, shielding her from the splashes of mud, soiled water or sometimes worse. Nancy smiled but said nothing.

She slowed down to let a couple of Punk men, complete with Mowhawks and safety pins, cross before her, losing a little ground to Pole.

He was already focused on the case. He had called the officer on site to request the pathologist he trusted and her team. Yvonne Butler might not be available but someone in her team would be. He stopped abruptly as they were approaching the canal from behind the Angel.

"I am sorry – was I going too fast?" Pole's face was hardly visible in the shadows of the night but Nancy could see the lines of his forehead gathered close together.

"Don't flatter yourself, Jonathan. You'll never be too fast for me."

Pole laughed softly and brushed a strand of hair away from Nancy's cheek.

"Are you ready for it? It won't be pretty."

Nancy rolled her eyes but smiled. "Jonathan, I am not the squeamish type. I could not have done all those years at the Bar if I had been. And in any case we ate our dinner some hours ago."

Pole did not move, for a moment unconvinced by this show of

bravado. But Nancy had seen her fair share of nastiness. She would somehow cope with whatever the canal was about to reveal.

The musty smell of all but stagnant water told them they were near. Nancy recognised the stairs that led from Colebrooke Row to the water's edge. Already a couple of police cars were parked near the steps. A few passers-by had gathered, together with residents concerned or curious about the latest disturbance.

Pole flashed his ID as he approached the uniformed police. "Good evening officer."

"Good evening Sir, PC Leonard, Sir," the young woman said, glancing a suspicious eye towards Nancy.

"Ms Wu is with me. She consults for the Met."

The young police constable moved sideways. She nodded towards the towpath.

"Not a pretty sight, Sir."

Pole stopped at the top of the stairs, looking down on the scene. He hesitated.

"How bad is it?" Nancy asked with an even voice.

"He has been – beheaded." The young woman shuddered.

"Is it your first time at a crime scene, PC Leonard?" Pole asked kindly.

"No, Sir, but I haven't come across one of these before," she said moving her head towards the canal. "And they left his wallet in his jacket pocket – nothing stolen."

"So not a robbery gone wrong then?"

"Doesn't look like it —" PC Leonard was interrupted by the static of her radio. "Yes, he has arrived, Sir."

Pole thanked her and turned towards Nancy.

"I'll be fine, really." Nancy's voice had lost a little of its assurance but she would not backtrack and let him down now. Pole nodded.

The body had been covered up with a blanket. Pole walked towards it and, crouching, lifted its corner carefully. He pulled back slightly but forced himself to inspect the corpse thoroughly. He let the blanket fall back and stood up, his tall body towering over the dead man. He looked at Nancy standing only a few feet away and shook his head.

"You don't need to see that," Pole said with kind determination.

Nancy hesitated; the protest she had prepared stuck in her throat. "This is butchery – an execution."

"And the fact that whoever has done this has not bothered to hide it, is what? A warning?" Nancy offered, relieved she could direct the conversation away from the body itself.

"Almost certainly."

"Who is the victim? You said he was on the INTERPOL most wanted list. Strange to be found in the middle of Islington, *non*?"

"*Très bonne question*, as ever."

"Good evening Guv. Good evening Ms Wu." Pole was interrupted by a young man in thick glasses.

"Nice to see you again, Andy." Nancy extended her hand and DS Todd shook it awkwardly. The light was bad but she could have sworn she saw reddening cheeks.

"Massimo Visconti, Italian from Venice, established a reputation as an inventive art thief, organised a number of high-profile heists, caught as the result of a tip-off and managed to escape before serving his sentence." Andy was reading from his notebook. Pole cleared his throat. "Sorry Guv, I thought Nancy, I mean Ms Wu, would want to know the details."

"I do indeed but I think your boss is more interested in what you might know already about the murder – weapon used, witnesses, that kind of thing."

"Right, right," Andy delved into his notebook again. "Got the name of the guy who found the body, he was walking his dogs; actually, the dogs found the body. As for the weapon, we are still looking – we have a team doing a fingertip search of the area —"

A series of calls interrupted Andy; something had been found.

The three of them moved swiftly towards a part of the towpath covered by undergrowth and empty bottles discarded thoughtlessly. An officer was flashing his torch in the direction of a piece of metal that shone in the light, his long stick pulling back branches to keep it in sight.

"It's a large knife," Andy said flashing his own light on it. "And there is a lot of blood on it."

Nancy moved closer and shone the small torch she had borrowed from Andy on the knife that had been dumped in the undergrowth.

"OK, well done: bag it, send it to the lab – you know the drill," Pole said, moving away to look in the opposite direction. "Forensics have arrived – Yvonne." Pole waved.

Nancy ran the beam up and down the part of the weapon that was visible. She gave Andy his torch back.

"Is it a knife? I'm not so sure ..."

Pole joined her and for a moment the pronounced features of his face in the shadows looked grotesque. "Let's see what forensics has to say. You remember Yvonne, don't you?"

Nancy smiled "Absolutely. No one would forget Yvonne."

"Come on, what's on that great mind of yours?" Pole asked before they reached the team in white protective overalls waiting for them at the bottom of the canal steps.

"It's not a large knife, Jonathan. It's a short sword, probably antique by the look of the decorations I saw on the hilt. And I think I have seen something very similar once before."

* * *

The laptop was still open on his coffee table. Brett cast an eye towards the ornate XVII century French clock sitting on the fireplace mantelpiece – it was gone 1am. He had almost finished the report he was writing for his minder. MI6-Steve had been clear: a report every time he met The Sheik.

Brett looked at his empty whisky glass, hesitated then shrugged. He only had a few words to add. A final glass of the amber liquid would do no harm. He stood up, walked to the small bar absent-mindedly swinging the elegant tumbler from the tip of his fingers. He ran his hand over a stylish bottle. His lips arched in the type of smile he had not had for a long while.

The unexpected outcome of dealing with the requests of his latest client was the ridiculously large sums of money he was prepared to pay. Brett opened the bottle and poured a generous measure into the thick crystal glass, enough to appreciate it, but not enough to be called greedy. At £2,500 a bottle, this forty-year-old Highland Park had to be savoured.

The ping of an email interrupted him. He screwed the top of the bottle back on with an irritated gesture.

An email at this hour, on his hyper-secure MI6 laptop, did not bode well. Brett moved back to the seat he had abandoned to recharge his glass, sat down heavily and opened the message.

"Massimo Visconti is dead – let's meet tomorrow, 8am."

Brett sagged back into his leather sofa, his throat so tight he could hear the laboured sound of his own breathing. He looked at his glass and pushed it away.

"Visconti dead," he murmured several times, forcing himself to hear the words. The Master of Thieves, dead.

Brett had entered the world of art theft, dealing with terrorists from the Middle-East knowingly, yet his sense of British superiority had convinced him he would always prevail.

With Visconti's death, the solid rock on which that certainty was built had just been chipped – a small but noticeable chip.

Chapter Two

The shrill sound of a bell interrupted his sleep. He tried to push it away but its persistence told him he could no longer ignore it. The memory of a nightmare surfaced. Henry opened his eyes and for a moment did not know where he was. He gulped in some air.

Yes, he could breathe.

The Belmarsh High Security Unit bell kept ringing. Henry moved his arm across his eyes, just one more minute to let the fog of his mind clear. He counted to thirty, turned on his side; just a few more seconds before he was ready to face the routine of washing in the small basin squeezed into the corner of his cell, collecting his breakfast from the prison canteen and starting Day 1,365 of his thirty-year sentence.

The countdown had started in 2008 and it was only mid 2012 … Henry ran his hand over his chin, the black stubble that, to his delight, had not yet started turning grey unlike his hair, had also grown rough and uncomfortable.

Henry stretched his muscly body. He craned his neck to look at the watch he kept strapped to the head of his bed. No time to dither. Kamal would have been awake for a while, rising for his first morning prayer and now he would already be on his way to breakfast.

Henry threw back the covers, jumped into his standard prison uniform, a sad-looking tracksuit, tidied his bed and left the cell. He had twenty minutes for the morning meal and would put this time to good use.

Kamal had already settled in front of his tray, at the agreed right-angle to the canteen's door. He barely moved his head when Henry arrived. Fraternising outside allocated times was not encouraged within HSU Belmarsh. It was with good reason that the High Security Unit, a prison within a prison, had a reputation for being the most secure in the UK.

Henry moved past Kamal towards a table in the opposite corner of the room. His spoon was balancing precariously over the edge of his tray. One move sideways to avoid colliding into another inmate and it fell to the ground.

Henry grumbled. Dumping his tray on the table at which Kamal was sitting, he bent down to retrieve the wayward item of cutlery.

Kamal lifted his foot slightly, enough for Henry to place a small piece of paper underneath it. Henry shot up again, dumping the spoon on his tray in a gesture of disgust.

The prison officers would be paying him attention by now. He carried his tray to the table he had chosen, cleaned the spoon on the small paper napkin he had collected with his breakfast and started eating his porridge. The guards' attention moved to Kamal. The young man stood up, his small frame almost childlike, his demeanour reassuring.

No one meeting him would have branded him as a terrorist: the strength of his beliefs betrayed only by the intensity of the large brown eyes that observed and never yielded.

The officers relaxed. Kamal moved slowly to the conveyor belt on which he placed his tray. It disappeared into a small opening in the wall, beyond which no inmate had access.

Henry looked at his watch, 8.25am. Another five minutes and he would be returning to his cell. Big K was nowhere to be seen, preferring most mornings to take his food to his cell – a small luxury he seemed to particularly enjoy.

Henry's gym time would be coming up right after bang-up time had ended at 10am. He would catch up with Big K then. Big K's activities and connections in drug dealing had earned him the privilege of spending time at HSU. He certainly was a flight hazard and Her Majesty's Prison services were not taking any chances.

"Man, I'm so dangerous they've locked me in here." A raucous laugh would always follow. But with the kudos HSU brought, also came boredom. In his more truthful moments Big K would sit on one of the benches in the gym, towel slung over his powerful neck.

"I tell you friend, I am out of here as soon as I can get parole. I am a reformed bloke." Henry never failed to nod convincingly but could a leopard, one of the mightiest big cats, ever change his spots?

His mind drifted to another tough prison in another county. Northern Ireland Maghaberry was a harsh place. Would Liam and Bobby feel as restless as he felt? Henry pushed the thought away. It would lead him nowhere to reminisce.

Perhaps.

Henry sought to change. No, he had changed. The terrible anger that had seized him for most of his adult life had started to be channelled differently. The shock of incarceration, of having to face his involvement with the IRA, had almost destroyed him.

His brilliant banking career, which had made so many of his colleagues envious, had been damaged without any possibility of repair. No one in the world of finance ever recovered from money laundering for a terrorist organisation and so it should be.

For his part Henry was done with that world of power and excess. He was looking for something different. He needed to prove to himself that he was not the monster he had been made to feel during his trial. He had come to understand his motivations but now this was no longer enough, he wanted more. Forgiveness might never be within his reach, but he could perhaps hope to atone.

Within the confines of his prison cell, within the rarefied atmosphere of the most secure prison in the UK, how could he achieve this?

Henry pushed his empty plate away and took another quick look at his watch – 8.29am. He stood up, following in Kamal's footsteps, and made his way to Cell 14. He walked past the officers with the same amount of disinterest he had shown them whilst coming in.

Would the small piece of paper that was stuck under Kamal's shoe make it all the way to his cell? A small amount of honey, used to sweeten the tasteless porridge served daily, might do the trick and keep it glued in place. A pang of anxiety ran through Henry, accompanied with the inevitable tinge of excitement.

13

So far, so good it seemed. The now familiar bell rang again. Inmates were returning to their cells and when their doors clanged shut the choking silence of HSU Belmarsh fell on them again.

* * *

Henry's letter rested on her desk. Nancy touched the paper with the tip of her fingers. It was not a letter really, more a rushed note, quickly penned in the tight handwriting she knew so well, the inclination of the letters always tilting to the right and the short paragraphs developing ideas with ease.

But Henry's note had brought a chill to her heart. Nancy read it again, trying once more to decipher the hidden message within it, not yet certain of its full impact.

Nancy, dearest friend

I could not miss this occasion to write a letter that I know will only be read by you and you alone. Writing to you has been my lifeline; thank you for never giving up on me.

There is not much time and though I feel there is so much I want to say I will have to be brief. I have been restless. Not about my sentence. I deserved it. But it is about going beyond it. If it was right to make me pay for what I did, don't I somehow deserve to be given the chance to show I can change – that despite everything I am redeemable?

You will hear or see things in the next few weeks that might make you doubt me; please give me the benefit of the doubt.

You will be asked to interfere or even stop me – I beg you, don't.

You may even be told that I have killed myself or been killed. I will never let this happen.

Trust has been at the core of our friendship – believe in me one last time. I know what I must do.

Henry

Nancy ran her slender hand over the letter and left it there for a moment. She could not reply to Henry's message. It had been placed abruptly in her hand as Henry was leaving Scotland Yard for Belmarsh, his time away from the HSU having come to an end. Nancy sighed and folded the letter. The flow of a constant correspondence that had passed between them had been broken. The feeling of unease that had started gnawing at her since she had first read Henry's words had grown stronger. She could not confide in Pole. Nancy had let Pole grow closer, intimate, but that intimacy had consequences. Should she choose between her allegiances?

"No," she said replacing the letter in its folder. "Not yet."

From the time she had organised, then joined Henry's defence team almost four years ago, her support for him had been unwavering. It was love of a very special kind, not one that called for crumpled sheets and intimacy. It was the love of deep friendship, that of two people who understood each other.

There were no excuses for what Henry had done. He too was adamant that he must bear the consequences of his actions. But perhaps it was the hope that some goodness still remained, untapped, ready to be given a chance, that made him a man one could not turn away from.

Nancy had been given that chance when she had decided to move away from the Bar and concentrate on the world of art. Perhaps Henry deserved that chance too? Her BlackBerry buzzed, the vibrations spreading into the wood of her desk and into the tips of her fingers.

"*Bonjour* Jonathan; don't apologise please." Nancy smiled at Pole's protectiveness.

"It is a sword – a Mashrafiya sword."

"Let me grab my pad." Nancy stretched to dislodge a yellow pad buried under a pile of opened documents and pulled it towards her. She pressed the speaker button.

"I am very impressed." Pole's voice tilted into the base register. "You did say it looked like an antique sword and it is."

"Very glad my hobby can be put to good use."

"Do not tell me you are a specialist in Arabic artefacts?"

"Alas no, I simply test my skills religiously with the weekend FT Quiz and this name crops up regularly. I am just a bit of a snob when it comes to general knowledge." Nancy chuckled.

"I had half wondered whether this was the result of one of your cases. I couldn't quite imagine that your other passion would have got you close to such a weapon and the countries where you might find one."

"You mean the contemporary art scene?"

"*Bien sûr.*"

"You would be surprised how prolific art is in the Middle-East, daring and irreverent too – Iran, Iraq, Lebanon. The Istanbul Biennial." Nancy could summon in her mind dozens of pieces by artists she had come to know well. "These artists risk their lives for their art. *Pardon* Jonathan, I am digressing."

"Not at all but perhaps a conversation over dinner?"

"And what a good idea that is." Nancy's voice was all smiles. "Still, let's talk about the Mashrafiya now. Has Yvonne come up with anything?"

"Too early for forensic results." Pole hesitated. "I am glad you did not see the result of its use though. I have seen quite a few cuts in my time, but this was one of the worst."

"In what way?"

"Deliberately brutal." Pole's voice lost some of its colour. "Not only to the victim but to the people finding him. It was meant to shock."

"Any theory about why?"

"Nancy," Pole's voice became softer. "I am not sure you need to be involved in this one."

"Jonathan, really? I have dealt with war criminals and various other unscrupulous individuals. I don't scare easily."

"Which is precisely what scares me," Pole carried on before she could protest. "I have some news that will interest you and it involves Henry."

Nancy's mouth dropped; for a moment she could not say anything. Her throat tightened as her eyes fell on the folder that contained Henry's letter.

Had Pole guessed or, even worse, seen it?

"The SFO has been in touch with me. One of their lawyers has requested help on a case involving a suspected high-profile banking fraud."

"You mean the Serious Fraud Office?" Nancy managed to say with enough composure.

"The very same."

"Pray, tell." Nancy inhaled deeply and pushed the folder away. "They have not said very much yet, but I gather the SFO hopes to use Henry's expertise in banking and financial structuring matters. They have heard about the way Henry helped with resolving the LIBOR scandal case."

"Ah. That case has done the rounds in well-connected legal circles."

"I know. It has at The Met too. Superintendent Marsh has not stopped talking about it. It's almost embarrassing."

"You're just too humble, Jonathan." Nancy teased.

"Anyway," Pole changed subject swiftly; his personal qualities were never his favourite topic. "I would of course have recommended that you be involved but —" Pole stopped for a short moment and Nancy's heart missed a beat. She could hear the rustling of paper. "— the SFO lawyer had asked for you already. Her name is Marissa Campbell."

"*Je suis trés flattée, mon cher ami.*" A little French helped defuse the anxiety of not telling the whole truth. "Both you and Marissa have thought of me." Nancy cringed. Was she sounding obsequious? "Do we need to adjourn somewhere for —"

"Lunch. *Absolument*," Pole suggested with enthusiasm. "Our favourite place, 12pm?"

"Our favourite place it is," Nancy replied without hesitation.

* * *

The drab little office smelt of over-brewed coffee and sweat. Mark Phelps stood up, moved to the small window that overlooked an outside wall stained with the dirt that pervaded Trafalgar Square.

There was little light in the room, the only thing he could see distinctly was his reflection in the window. The investigation team had left the room. He wrapped his long arms around his body and squeezed.

His body started shaking a little, a tremor that came in short bursts and ran from his neck down to his belly. Mark moved away from the

17

window. He had to sit down. The clock on the wall indicated 9.35am.

He had spent almost fourteen hours with the SFO team that Marissa Campbell was leading. They had offered to stop at 1am but he had too much to tell.

A draught of fresh air startled him. Marissa Campbell walked in with another two cups of bitter coffee, sugar sachets and small tubes of milk. She sat opposite Mark and pushed a cup towards him.

"You should go home," she said.

"I should. I should." Mark sipped at his coffee, eyes fixed on nothing.

"Why hesitate? You can say what's on your mind, Mark. It's only the two of us."

Mark inhaled a small gulp of air. "Is it all worth it?"

Marissa smiled a tired smile and nodded. "It's a valid question."

"Only time will tell, I guess but I'm glad I said it all straight away, otherwise I might have faltered. I still can't quite believe I'm accusing my employer of fraud. That bank is one of the largest investment banks in the City."

Mark dropped his gaze on his solid wedding band; the tan of his body made it look more noticeable. He had told Marissa his wife believed he was travelling on business.

Marissa picked up on where his eyes had fallen.

"Are you worried about your family?"

"How am I going to tell my wife I am almost certainly putting in jeopardy my lucrative career at the bank. A career I have been fostering for the past ten years?"

"Perhaps by explaining you could no longer stay silent about what you have uncovered … She must know you are an honest man."

"I'm not sure it will be much comfort when the papers start talking about me even if they don't mention my and I become Bank X's whistle-blower."

"It is not your fault if that bank has been caught the 2008 financial crisis. And if its management has decided to save its independence by not accepting the UK government bailout, over and about saving it from collapse."

Mark stretched his body, in a half-hearted movement that felt

18

tired. "Asking too many questioned about how far the bank was willing to go to preserve its autonomy and the method used did go down well. They'll know it is me."

"Your name will be protected. You know that?" Marissa's solid body was hunched over her cup. If she was tired, she did not show it. Her dark eyes rested on him with confidence. Mark nodded.

"Did you ever see this film with Russell Crowe ... The Insider?"

"It's the UK ... not cut-throat America."

"I'm not so sure it will make much difference. I doubt a whistle-blower in the financial sector is ever going to find a job again." "Have you spoken to Helena yet?"

The name of his wife spoken within the confines of this horrible little room took the wind out of him. He ran a weary hand over his face.

"I haven't told her yet."

Marissa nodded. She knew how hard it would be and she was not going to judge him. Mark looked grateful for her patience.

"Today. I'll tell her today."

"It is a brave decision to report your employer Mark. Remember that."

Mark nodded and moved away from the subject to one that gave him some confidence.

"How soon are you going to launch the case?"

"You mean prosecute?"

Mark nodded.

"You know how this works; it will take time, a long time."

"And what should I do in the meantime?"

"Go back home. You're tired and making a decision now is not a good idea." Marissa's broad shoulders had moved across the table a little more.

Her hands stretched over the table, reaching out to him to give Mark strength. She was there for him, an able person, a decision-maker who could keep hold of the rudder in a storm and never let go.

Mark looked out of the window, trying to gauge what the weather was like outside.

"It's fine out there; you'll be fine." She had moved away from the table, calm. Mark finally stood up, gathered his small rucksack, now empty of the folder, USB keys and CDs he had brought with him the day before.

The lightness should have been a relief, yet his hands gripped it tightly, wary. Marissa moved closer, ready to grab him if he fell.

Mark managed a smile and pushed his chair against the table. "And you are telling me you can get help from someone who understands the City well? An ex-banker you said?"

Marissa nodded.

"Oh yes. And I also know the right person to make sure he co-operates."

* * *

The taxi dropped him at the top of a small alleyway in St James's. Brett paid and left a small tip. He could not be bothered to collect a few pennies. More importantly he was keen to hear what MI6-Steve had to say about Massimo Visconti.

Brett was, for once, eager to meet his minder. That thought irritated him. Still, he had played his hand rather well so far with his latest assignment, and there was more, much more to come.

He barely acknowledged the doorman, walked straight through the club to the smoking room and let himself drop without much ado into one of the armchairs. Steve was late.

Did it mean anything?

Could The Sheik have discovered he was with MI6? Could he have discovered Steve was his minder? Could he? ... Ridiculous.

Brett steadied himself. He was a Brit and Brits did not succumb to absurd paranoia; now was not the time to lose one's cool. He looked at his watch for the umpteenth time – 9.11am.

One of the waiters he knew well offered him a selection of newspapers, but he waved him off impatiently: 9.15am.

Another five minutes and I am leaving, Brett muttered, fidgeting with one of his cufflinks – 9.19am.

Brett stood up, hoping that his impatience would summon Steve. He looked in the direction of the door, hopeful.

Nothing doing.

A couple of members had stopped their conversation to give him a curious look. Brett ignored them and they quickly went back to their business. Brett sat down again abruptly. He was safe in the club and certainly less so outside. What would he do if Steve did not turn up? He had been given specific instructions to follow in this eventuality. He was trying to recall what the process was. But when Steve had spoken about the possibility, Brett had dismissed it.

Arrogance today was not his best friend.

His mobile buzzed.

Delayed, wait at Club, must speak urgently.

Brett shuddered, grateful that he had stayed. He waved at one of the waiters and ordered his usual breakfast: two eggs, boiled, two pieces of white toast, marmalade and the club's special English Breakfast tea, with whole milk. (Brett did not believe in drinking milk that did not taste like milk).

"Eggs runny, marmalade thick cut, toast slim cut. I do not like doorsteps." The waiter didn't hesitate, reassuring Brett that he was indeed among like-minded people and that his breakfast instructions would be, as ever, followed to the letter.

Steve finally arrived, sinking into the armchair opposite Brett's as Brett's breakfast was served. He waved at the waiter. "The same," he said not bothering to greet Brett nor acknowledge the man taking his order.

"That bad, is it?" Brett always enjoyed needling MI6-Steve whenever he could and yet he was relieved to see him this morning.

Steve's podgy face looked a little leaner than usual. His receding hair stood in small clumps sticking out in all directions.

His expensive suit looked out of place on his body. No doubt MI6 had indulged him with a handmade, Savile Row suit. After all, he could not meet his contact Brett in one of the most exclusive London clubs dressed in a Marks & Spencer's outfit, even a three-piece.

"I have spent the best part of this morning – and it is only just after 9am – trying to find out about Visconti's murder." Steve bent forward, elbows on knees. "All this is on account of you because —" He stopped to let the waiter serve him his breakfast. "Actually, could I also add bacon to my order?" Steve said, turning towards the gloved man … no need for please or thank you he had been told. "Not the streaky stuff but crisp."

Brett started tapping impatiently on the arm of his chair. Steve ignored him. "Where was I?" Steve added another spoonful of sugar to his tea. Brett remained silent. He ran a couple of fingers slowly over his slim moustache and waited. Unbearable, but the well-bred English gentleman in him knew how to endure pain.

"Yes. I would not want to lose one of my best assets."

"And why would you lose me?" Brett asked, slowly moving his hand towards a fresh cup of tea. His fingers rested for a moment over the delicate handle of the bone-china cup.

No, they were not shaking.

Steve grinned, uncovering a neat row of white teeth. "I am so glad you knew it was you I had in mind. Still, back to Visconti, we are now certain it was an execution, mujahideen style. So, some questions for you, old chap." Steve cracked the top of his egg open; pieces of shell scattered over his plate. He ignored the mess he had just made.

Brett inhaled deeply.

How could Steve be British and not know how to open a boiled egg with civility?

"You had some questions?"

"A couple." Steve carried on whilst buttering his toast. "First … Any inkling from your latest acquaintance?" Steve hesitated … cut his toast into two triangles and started munching.

"And the other question?" Brett asked, having not yet touched his own breakfast.

"Do you feel exposed?" Steve had been concentrating on a perfectly crisp piece of bacon until then. He put down his knife and fork and looked at Brett with unusual graveness. Brett opened his mouth, closed it again. He pushed his lanky body into the back of the comfortable leather armchair.

"Are you concerned? And for that matter should I be concerned?" His desire for humour at Steve's expense had vanished.

"Why don't you answer my first question?"

"Well, I have absolutely no idea. I might be of use to The Sheik, but I don't think he sees me as one of his buddies."

"Fair enough." Steve moved on to a second piece of toast. "There was a third photograph when you met him to arrange for his sniper to enter the Royal Exchange in London."

The bluntness with which Steve had mentioned the Royal Exchange marksman, conjuring images that even Brett had found hard to stomach, unsettled him. "There was, but as I told you he never showed me who or what it was."

Steve finished the second piece of toast, chewing the last mouthful thoughtfully. "Did you know Visconti – well, I mean?"

"You mean, rather, did I ever do business with him? Before …" Brett cleared his throat. The thought of how MI6 had managed to secure his services still rankled him. The name Henry Crowne surfaced as a bad memory linked to Brett's MI6 recruitment; it was almost nauseating.

"Yes, yes, before we got you to work for us." Steve replied with a small wave of his hand.

"His business was a little different from mine. More paintings, some of a classical nature, old masters … then a lot of modern stuff." Brett waved his hand dismissively. "But his greatest successes were in the Middle-East. When he started in Iraq, he was the first to handle antique pieces looted from the main historical sites back in the early nineties, even the Baghdad museum – very daring and lucrative, but well before my time."

"Glad to know the thieving community benefits from its specialists too. What are you going to tell me next? You had business cards indicating that as well."

Brett ignored Steve. He was just an undiscerning East-End boy. "In short, I have not seen Visconti for years. His reputation in the market has suffered since he was caught, of course. Then again, you are the guy in the intelligence service. I am surprised your various snooping operations have not been more effective."

Steve grumbled.

"Park that question then. How about question two?"

"If you had not called me in the middle of the night to tell me about Visconti, I would have said all is well."

Steve cocked his head. "Then again, we are talking terrorists."

23

"So you think there a but?" Brett held his cup in mid-air.

"The very question I have been asking myself since last night. I can't think of any." Steve rested his cup of tea on his lips before taking a sip. "... And zero contact since the Royal Exchange and the transfer of Clandestine X."

"None," Brett confirmed, his jaw clenching.

Steve finished his second egg. His plate was empty and he was eyeing Brett's. Steve poured a little more tea in his cup.

Brett wondered for a short moment what it was Steve wanted to ask and yet seemed reluctant. The realisation of what it was hardly surprised Brett ... he was not done with MI6 by a long shot.

"You want me to get in touch with The Sheik to offer my services again, don't you?" Brett said calmly. He should have known that MI6 would not let the trail go cold so readily.

"Yes." Steve pushed his squeaky-clean plate aside. "We have an idea about what might draw The Sheik out."

Chapter Three

Henry had left the letter half-finished. It languished on his small desk since he had abandoned it. It was the first time that words did not come easily when writing to Nancy. Had it been a mistake to be so truthful – at least as much as he could be with his feelings? He did not fear betrayal. That she would never do.

Never.

But she might guess; she might decide – despite him asking her not to – to interfere in order to save him. Henry shook his head, a slow soulful movement.

"You've saved me already," Henry murmured.

He rolled his pen across his thumb and caught it back with his index finger before it fell off, repeating the move in a rhythmic fashion.

The decision he had made had taken hold like a plant taking root and ensnaring a tree, spreading inexorably over the many months he had spent at Belmarsh. It had felt foolish, daring, stupid, the only way, impossible: a merry-go-round of emotions.

But now he had decided he would apply his immensely skilled mind to the task. Redemption would never be found within the sterile walls of a prison cell, let alone in a unit like HSU Belmarsh in which the inmates were so well guarded that absolutely nothing could happen to them. Or so it seemed.

The arrival of Ronnie Kray had changed the balance of this rarefied world though. As crazy as it may sound, a certain Reginald Murphy had decided to change his name to Ronnie Kray by deed poll.

His ambition to emulate or even surpass the deeds of his idol seemed well on track from what Henry had gathered.

Henry had started to find out at his own expense that Kray was not a man to cross. A bad joke about what Henry considered a ridiculous tattoo on Kray's back had almost cost him dear.

Today Henry, the once ambitious banker, bent over backwards not to be noticed. He wanted to blend into the crowd of HSU inmates so as to further his master plan.

Escape.

No one had ever achieved this feat before, no one – from the most notorious gangster to the most wanted Russian spy. But Henry had a plan, the first building block of which he had laid securely.

Henry pushed the letter away. He was not in the mood. He reached for his legal file and extracted from it a list he had been assembling since he had last visited Scotland Yard, the compilation of possible scandals financial or political or both, that the regulatory authorities or the Serious Fraud Office might want to investigate.

Being allowed out once more was essential for the plan to work. He must find a way, through Nancy or perhaps Pole. Henry ran his hand over his short hair. Could he stomach using his friend to achieve his purpose?

No, it would have to be Pole.

What was the price he was prepared to pay to show he could rejoin the human race? And what was the point of showing there was goodness in him if it had to be done by exploiting Nancy?

Henry stood up, irritated that the thought had entered his mind. He crossed his cell in one long stride, leaned against the wall, his back pressing against the cold surface. He needed to exercise, to burn the tension in his body, control the fire that raged in his belly.

Only thirty minutes to go before gym time. Henry removed the top of his tracksuit. The heat of exasperation had spread to his entire body. He reached his desk again and looked at the list.

– Manipulation of foreign exchange rates, also known as FX
– Insider trading; Henry had spotted some interesting movements in the stock market

– Circumvention of sanctions directed at countries on a restricted list: Iran, Iraq, North Korea
– Bribery linked to sales of armaments in the Middle-East, most likely Saudi Arabia

Henry dismissed the first two, perhaps too obvious and an overkill for the use of his remarkable mind and his knowledge of the financial markets as well as its players. The last two on the other hand were promising.

Doing business in the Middle-East had always been a complex issue for Investment Banks. Most countries in the Middle-East that respected Sharia Law would never consider interest-bearing investments such as loans or bonds but instead purchased equities, without hesitation.

The idea was to introduce an element of risk sharing between investor and client and remove the risk of punitive high interest rates. Not an entirely ridiculous idea after all: at least these investors had not been involved in the subprime market that so very nearly crashed the world markets in 2008.

Henry would be manning the HSU library for a couple of hours in the afternoon. Could he risk logging onto the computer there to access the Internet? He was allowed computer access but only to operate it as a word processor. The Internet was out of the question and so of course was email.

The prison officers, however, had different log-ins that allowed them more freedom in order to fulfil some of their duties. Henry had never even asked about Internet access. He had simply observed the place the officers' hands landed on the keyboard, the slight hesitation before entering their passwords.

Henry had spent most of his career as a banker, almost twenty years, on the trading floor of large investment banks. He had not only memorised the very special keyboard that traders used, the Bloomberg keyboard, but he also operated the standard one effortlessly. A great advantage in deciphering the passwords of the guards.

Fraternising with prisoners was discouraged within HSU Belmarsh and this suited Henry fine. The most innocent of questions might have aroused the suspicions of the highly trained officers. Courteous but distant was Henry's motto. He had cracked the last two passwords, but he was under no illusions; one day he would hit the wall either by being discovered or by not being able to good guess the passwords.

He stood up, stretched one long arm over his head, then the other and moved once more to the only part of the cell wall that was free. He stood with his back against the cool surface and let his body slowly slide down to the floor into a squat. Then he sat on the floor, crossed his legs and started breathing slowly and deeply, his latest discovery for relaxation.

His well-exercised muscles released gradually, his mind rested in stillness, thoughts floated in and out, ephemeral. A new skill that eased the anger and harnessed it, this time perhaps for good. He emerged on the other side of this ocean of stillness, rested. His mind came to and started measuring the impact of what he would need to do next – the permutations, possible outcomes – discarding what would not work in the process. His focus was complete, yet his body was relaxed. He would do what he needed to do to achieve his goal and the plan that he had honed looked solid.

Henry's mind now moved in another direction. Why had Kamal been sent to Belmarsh? Unquestionably for his terrorist's activities, but why on the same spur?

Kamal, the man who had masterminded the Paddington bombing, the very event that had almost cost Henry his life. His back tensed, his knees trembled. Henry could hear the sound of the bomb again – the barely human cries of the wounded ripping the silence of the cell apart.

Breathe in. Breathe out.

There was nowhere to go in his six-by-ten-foot box. Unlike Paddington, there was no escape, no running away.

Breathe.

Henry slowly rolled his head around. His mind floated over to a new question. One part of the equation had not revealed itself yet but his progress with Kamal meant it almost certainly would soon.

* * *

A few drops fell on her head and Marissa cursed. She had started to walk towards Scotland Yard. She needed some fresh air after an exhausting night with her key witness. Whistle-blowing was no small beer. No matter how much the law sought to protect him, Mark's life would never be the same again.

She accelerated her pace. Her umbrella was safely tucked away in one of the drawers of her desk. No chance it would get wet, unlike her.

How many years since she had left Barbados? Twenty? No, twenty-one at the end of this month. A black student attempting the impossible – to become a barrister in London. She smiled at the picture forming in her mind: the tall, almost masculine frame of a young woman arriving at Heathrow Airport, uncomfortable in the heavy clothes she had purchased for a fresh life in London.

One suitcase and one designer leather bag, brand new, purchased by the family as a farewell present. The brand was nothing too ostentatious, Mulberry, and yet instantly recognisable. It was by now well-worn but still she could not bring herself to discard it. The rain asserted itself and Marissa started to run – only a few yards to go. The pun almost made her laugh.

She entered the offices of Scotland Yard, shook herself, releasing the beads of water that had formed on her cropped hair. She no longer tried to straighten her unruly mane. Her style was clean cut, close to her skull. The security guard gave her a disapproving look. She ignored it and presented her work badge.

"I have an appointment with Inspector Pole."

The guard scrutinised her badge for longer than was necessary, switching between the photo and the face in front of him but there was nothing to be done about it – she was indeed Marissa Campbell.

"Take a seat. I will call Inspector Pole's office."

Marissa moved to the reception area where seats were arranged in a semicircle. She did not sit but instead turned towards the large bay window to watch the rain lash down in large sheets of water, almost tropical. She had never worked with Pole before but knew Nancy Wu well, a woman she admired greatly.

Despite her high-profile career Nancy had always found time to mentor students from her *alma mater*, King's College, and Marissa had been lucky enough to be one of them. Nancy had offered her pupillage when no other chambers would give her a chance; more recently, Nancy had been the only person she could confide in. The only one who knew how to listen to Marissa's anxious calls about a large case she was dealing with, without asking questions that might compromise her integrity.

Exceptional, Marissa nodded.

The outline of a tall man materialised in the window, his reflection only a dark silhouette. Marissa turned to face him.

"Inspector Pole. Pleased to meet you." Pole extended a friendly hand. Marissa shook it, firm but warm. His intelligent eyes were already at work, but his smile was no fake, a man she could do business with.

* * *

"I looked at the file that HMP Belmarsh sent me. I can see why he might be a good resource," Marissa said, flicking through a large set of papers she had spread over their meeting table.

"Boredom is the worst enemy of someone doing time within the confines of Belmarsh's High Security Unit and Henry is doing thirty years," Pole said.

"That level of security risk?" Marissa asked, her large dark eyes resting on Pole with calm. The delicate features of her face had a benevolence that didn't match the strength of her voice.

"With his IRA background he is at the top of the list. Although some would say the IRA has been decommissioned."

"What about the New IRA or whatever they care to call themselves these days?"

"Well observed," Pole replied raising an approving eyebrow. "Henry's friends were certainly part of that so, yes, HMP needs to keep an eye on him."

"Then it will be good to work with Nancy." Marissa grinned. She enjoyed speaking to Pole, a perfect stranger, and recognised his skill of putting her at ease.

He must have done his research and knew she and Nancy were close. But she felt obliged to ask questions she had not yet had time to clear with her former mentor.

"She is part of his legal team …" Marissa let her sentence hang hoping for additional information.

"And she is keen to keep her client a law-abiding con," Pole carried on with the flash of a smile.

Marissa nodded. She spread her hands over the open pages of the HMP document, still assessing its content. "I can't hide it from you. I am delighted Nancy has agreed to be part of the team."

"Then I won't hide it from you either, so am I. I have worked with her on some pretty high-profile cases, much to my benefit."

"You mean the LIBOR scandal involving the Bank of England?"

"The very same. And Crowne went straight to the heart of the matter, by the way. As much as I don't like to admit it, he is a very *smart arse* to quote the man himself."

"I gathered that. The additional advantage, of course, is that he no longer works in the City, yet remains perfectly knowledgeable about the way it operates."

Marissa moved a few pieces of paper around, replacing them neatly in the file in a different order. She extended her firm hand, brought her coffee cup to her lips, and drank in small cautious sips.

"I presume you can't yet share the details of the background of the case?"

"You know the rules as well as I do, Inspector. But perhaps I can ask a few questions about what you estimate Henry's skills are and you might get a sense of what is going on."

"Fire away."

"How much does Crowne know about the Middle-East?"

"He has done business there," Pole replied, lifting the file that he had compiled. He went straight to a couple of pages at the back of the folder and started reading.

"He worked on certain investment funds specifically designed for that region called Sukuk funds. Those investments are compliant with Sharia Law." Pole kept reading. "Crowne specialised in equities which were key assets in those funds."

"Which countries?" Marissa asked. She put down her cup. Her eyes had turned a shade darker.

"UAE, Oman, Qatar and Indonesia."

"Indonesia is irrelevant," she said. Pole stopped reading. "Apologies, I should not have interrupted."

"He took a trip to Saudi Arabia. Not sure what the outcome was on that occasion. It was just before the takeover between HXBK and GL, the bank he worked for, was announced."

"You mean he had to stop working on this deal because of the takeover announcement?"

"So I understand."

"I hope you won't mind if I borrow your file?"

"That's the reason I brought it with me."

Marissa raised the cup to her lips again, realised it was empty, crushed it in her hand and dumped it in the wastepaper basket. She moved slowly and deliberately as if continually aware of the impact she might have on her surroundings.

"Was he closely involved with the rescue plan for GL during the financial crisis?"

"No. He was excluded from the merger team."

"He was never tasked to find finance to rescue the bank or a bailout solution?" Marissa moved her body forward, leaning over the neatly arranged papers lying on the table.

"No."

"That must have been painful," she observed neutrally. If she was going to work with a hotshot from the City, she wanted to know how to manoeuvre him to her advantage.

"I will speak to the SFO director." Marissa picked up Pole's file and her own.

"And I will speak to Superintendent Marsh." Pole ran his solid hand over his goatee. "He will be keen on this new high-profile case."

"In the meantime, I will organise a meeting with Nancy if you don't mind." Marissa's eyes lit up for a moment. She would relish being involved with her former teacher, mentor and friend on a par.

What a thrilling prospect.

Chapter Four

The brightness of the light always made the contour of each instrument sharper. Pole recoiled from the smell. Invariably the mortuary had the same effect on him.

Yvonne had been working on Massimo Visconti's body since she had arrived at 8.00am. She had been swabbing, bagging meticulously and was about to start the heavy work on the cadaver's internal organs when Pole arrived.

She stopped working for a moment and Pole was grateful for it.

"Morning Jon. Want a preliminary on my findings?" Yvonne said lifting the visor of her protective headpiece. "I don't need to tell you what the cause of death is. Serrated blade to the throat."

"I can see that very well thank you, a severed head is usually a good indication," Pole grumbled.

"Yeah. But you will see that the jaggedness of the cut means that the perpetrator took his or her time."

"Could the perpetrator in fact be a woman?" Pole asked with a frown.

"Well, it might explain the structure of the cut. It is not a clean slash either because of the desire to inflict pain or because it was difficult, perhaps both."

"And the sword we found?"

"Almost certainly the instrument used. It all seems to match but I will confirm this with final tests, blood etc."

Yvonne moved to the sword that had been placed back in its

evidence bag. She opened the bag carefully and drew the blade out with her gloved hands.

"It's old, very old, perhaps even an antique, well preserved though, and sharp. In fact, it has been sharpened recently probably with the intention of killing. I have swabbed the victim to check for metal residue."

Pole was leaning against the wall, his tall body braced against it, his arms crossed. He craned his neck to see what Yvonne was pointing towards. She lifted her head and smiled. Pole took his time to walk over to her, eventually coming to stand over the beheaded body.

"I see what you mean about the cut."

"If you look at his wrists and ankles, you can see he was in shackles. He was not killed immediately after his abduction. These bruises have taken time to set and the skin is badly damaged."

"You think he was locked up for a while. Any idea for how long?"

"He had lost weight, I think; the skin is slack in places. And he was severely dehydrated so I would say over a month, perhaps longer."

"Any other signs?"

"Apart from the fact that he was probably starved, and not allowed to shave or wash. I will tell you more when I have finished the examination of his internal organs."

Pole moved slowly around the body, taking in the details as Yvonne was pointing them out to him. His breathing had slowed down to a minimum, little gulps of air that prevented him from smelling the only too familiar odour of decomposition.

"For what it's worth," Yvonne carried on, slamming her visor back down, "I think it's a warning."

She selected a scalpel and started on the Y shape incision. Pole willed himself to move steadily back to his place against the wall. But Yvonne shooed him away with a wave of her hand.

"Don't need you here," she said without looking at him. "I'll let you know as soon as I have some meaningful results."

"Good," was all Pole managed to say.

"And I don't need you fainting on me."

* * *

The gallery had just opened its doors. A simple white cube with a small recess, large enough to house a select number of art pieces. Phillippe Garry emerged from the diminutive office nestling at the back of the gallery, balancing two cups of Sichuan tea on a small tray. Nancy smiled as he advanced towards her, always attentive to her needs.

"Here you are Nancy. You converted me to Sichuan. I hope you like my choice."

"So kind of you Phillippe but I don't need the VIP treatment really." Nancy chuckled. "Although I am very appreciative of it of course."

She took the delicate bone-china cup and saucer and sat down on the wide windowsill alongside the pamphlets describing the gallery's latest show.

"I have gathered as much information as I could on the Chinese name you mentioned but I haven't had much luck. I also have the feeling my contacts are not being forthcoming."

The cup wobbled in Nancy's hand and a little tea spilt into the saucer.

"How clumsy of me," she said.

Her elegant hand put the cup and saucer down on the floor to look for a tissue in her bag.

"Please don't worry," Phillippe hurried back into the tiny kitchen. He took a little while to find the required paper towel.

Nancy was grateful. The emotions rising in her chest were not yet ready to be witnessed. He might have sensed it, giving her time to compose herself before he reappeared.

Phillippe mopped up the spilt tea carefully and threw the paper into the wastepaper basket in a perfect arch.

"Once a cricketer, always a cricketer," he smiled kindly.

"Thank you for taking the time but don't worry if you can't find more. I was not expecting there would be much in any case."

Phillippe nodded. "And I very much appreciate your involvement with the Ai Weiwei crisis. Strong support from high-profile collectors and friends, especially with your legal background, can only help."

Nancy drank a little tea before she replied. The warm liquid with its delicate fragrance helped to soothe her choking throat.

"I am always glad to help." Nancy took another sip. "Thank you for being discreet and for not prying."

"For you, Nancy, any time."

She attempted a smile. "What else is happening in China that is worth noting?"

Phillippe launched into a passionate description of the younger, subversive artists he supported. The challenges they faced from the state that was by no means ready to hear dissent.

The lines on his forehead moved, arched, settled again, expressing admiration and anxiety in turn. Nancy sipped her tea in silence, occasionally nodding, but despite her desire to listen she couldn't concentrate.

She could no longer leave the task of finding the artist she was looking for to Phillippe. It was too complicated, perhaps even dangerous. She needed to speak to Pole. A warm ripple moved through her body. Was he not the man she most trusted, whose affection she was finally learning to accept?

Phillippe's voice had stopped in mid-sentence. His iPhone was ringing. He pulled a face. A client. Nancy nodded smiling and was glad to let him take the call. She was in no fit state to have a decent conversation about art. Her mind was elsewhere.

When he came back, she rose slowly, put on her coat and moved to the door.

"I hope I have not chased you away," Phillippe said in a sorry voice.

"Not at all. I need to get on with my work." She smiled a reassuring smile and bade Phillippe goodbye. She stopped as she was about to leave the gallery.

"Mo Chow was my father. Under his artist's name. I should have told you earlier. I'm sorry … It's a complicated story, perhaps for another time."

She smiled again and drew the light coat close to her chest, clasping the collar tight with her hand. Phillippe nodded, stunned by the revelation. He simply raised his hand to say goodbye.

Nancy walked out and across to Central Street, took a sharp right. Her pace accelerated. Her chest was tightening and she hated the sensation. She would not be helpless or tearful for a man who had left his family behind and never told them why. She crossed another street; a car sounded its horn. She ran to avoid it.

"Get a grip," she muttered between gritted teeth after waving the driver an apology.

She closed her eyes and remained motionless for a moment.

Yes, she would speak to Pole.

* * *

The metal steps responded to his weight. Henry's light jog reverberated through the stairwell structure. He turned right when he reached the ground floor. Time for Association.

Kamal had already settled in his favourite chair. A couple of the other inmates, all of them sporting beards of various shapes, were assembled on the few chairs next to him. Their conversation was animated but Kamal stayed silent. He listened.

As soon as Henry arrived in the room, a couple of them walked away, not rushed, a natural enough looking move to go to speak with other prisoners. Henry had been struck by the need other people had, including the worst of offenders, to congregate.

People from completely different backgrounds, who would have never spoken in the outside world, conversed regularly, exchanged tips on how to make the suffocating atmosphere of HSU Belmarsh a bearable living hell.

Henry took his time.

He spoke briefly with Big K, the striking giant who was doing time for drug dealing on such a large scale he was deemed a flight hazard. They had a little banter about the latest rugby results.

Henry moved to the water cooler, poured himself a glass and finally reached Kamal's corner. He sat down in the armchair opposite, reached for the paper that had been left on the chair and started reading, his back turned to the people in the room.

"Got your message," he said.

Kamal gave a small nod. His eyelids fluttered. Henry turned a page, the paper now resting on his crossed legs, his foot beating an irregular rhythm.

"No one has ever escaped from HSU Belmarsh," Henry said, his head bent over the newspaper. He did not look at Kamal; he did not need to. The convention to discuss this explosive matter was clear. Whoever was doing the talking had their back to the room.

"People get transferred out. Usually after having spent a long time in here." Henry turned another page.

"You and I haven't done enough time." He drank some of his water. "Or rather you and I do not want to wait for that long."

Kamal had picked up the novel he was reading. He broke the spine of his book slowly. It cracked gently, a small sigh of relief.

"Three ways of doing it. Become seriously ill. Attempt suicide or ..." Henry pushed his tall body into the back of the chair. His muscles felt like iron against the worn material.

"Take the opportunity of a trip outside Belmarsh."

Kamal had started reading. He turned a page and smiled.

What did Henry want him to do? Betray his brothers, pretend that he had changed his mind, that the Jihad no longer meant anything to him?

"I know what you are thinking," Henry said, moving to another section of his newspaper, "but look at me. If you can convince them they need you and they do —"

Kamal closed his book and looked up. Someone was coming their way. Henry kept reading an article about the impact of the banks' financial rescue package. "The UK government bailed out these idiots back in 2008 and for what?" Henry said as a shadow spread over his paper. He half turned his athletic body towards it.

"Interested in the ramifications of the enduring financial crisis?" Henry asked, still holding his newspaper open.

"You're turning the pages of that newspaper awfully fast, Henry," Prison Officer MacKay said.

"I am a fast reader," Henry replied folding the paper out neatly. "You will find that the analysis of the banks' exposure to the subprime market on page four is still a great underestimation and that the one on LIBOR fixing on page six is barely scratching the surface. That's the *FT* for you. I didn't bother after page ten." He handed over the paper to MacKay with a broad smile, finished his glass of water in a couple of gulps and stood up.

38

"Terribly thirsty today. Must get another cup." Henry took his time to reach the water cooler. MacKay had taken the paper and skimmed through the articles. Kamal had returned to reading his book.

The familiar bubble of anger had swollen in Henry's belly as soon as MacKay had spoken. He let it rise without responding to it. In a few minutes he would be using the rowing machine that was permanently available in a secluded corner of the room.

Patience that had eluded him for most of his career in banking was becoming an essential ally. Henry crushed the paper cup in one swift gesture and dumped it with the others in the rubbish bin.

Henry turned to survey his surroundings. Big K was in a conversation with an ex-FSB agent, the intelligence service that had replaced the KGB after the USSR was broken up in 1991. They had discovered a common passion: chess.

And Big K had assured Henry he was receiving prime information about the Russian mafia and their appetite for cocaine. So much for being a reformed con.

"You are doing a market survey inside HSU Belmarsh?" Henry had laughed.

"Man. If the guy has got info."

"Yes, but nothing comes for free in this world. You told me that. What will he want in return?"

Big K had punched Henry's shoulder in slow motion.

"My man Henry is learning the ropes," Big K had chuckled.

Henry turned towards the small enclosure with the rowing machine inside. He checked the book. No one had reserved the slot starting before his but there was someone using it.

He waited against the wall for the inmate to finish. The grunts that came from inside the enclosure stopped. A few swear words for good measure. The gulps of someone drinking water, *no Lucozade at HSU Belmarsh – Lord knows what a sugar rush would do to some of the inmates,* and the man was out.

The rowing machine was free.

Henry entered the enclosure, adjusted the seat and bent forward to lock the resistance in position. He straddled the centrepiece, sat down and started pulling on the handlebar. Someone was leaning against the partition separating the room from the enclosure.

Henry recognised the overpowering scent. The sickly smell of Ronnie Kray's skin made his stomach heave. Kray's skin condition after covering his body with tattoos required special ointment, the smell of which followed Kray like a warning.

No matter, he was proud of those tats, a celebration of his idols: the famous Kray Brothers. Henry had first noticed the twins' heads inscribed on Kray's back at the gym.

"Minnie-me is pushing it a bit far," Henry had quipped. "One head perhaps but two – the guy who did his tat must have had a stutter." Big K had liked the joke and his laugh had bounced off the walls of the gym. But there are no secrets in prison and Henry's little joke had got back to Kray's ears.

Breaking Rule 101 of remaining unnoticeable in jail had been a stupid thing to do and Henry was starting to feel the brunt of it.

Kray stood silent, running his eyes over Henry as he started his session.

Henry stopped, adjusted the seat and started to pull again, a slow and rhythmic action that made the machine groan under his effort.

He looked straight ahead. Henry had had plenty of similar intimidation attempts when he worked on the trading floor and would not allow Kray to get under his skin.

Kray had started humming a low tune that could hardly be heard, a wasp buzzing around, looking for an excuse to sting. Henry accelerated the pace, the machine groaned louder.

The hum grew a little keener. Kray had dropped his hands across the low partition. He was slowly moving them inside the space, a progression measured and unstoppable. Henry's body was now covered in sweat, yet the hum had not stopped. His heart was pumping fast.

Could he push himself one notch up?

Should he push himself one notch up?

He increased the cadence, his muscles screamed, the machine protested but Henry did not care. Oxford's rowing team might have been impressed, not Kray though. The humming gained in intensity. Until suddenly it stopped.

"Have you booked a slot?" Officer MacKay asked.

Kray's hands had slid back outside the partition wall. He turned slowly towards the guard. "Thinking about it."

MacKay opened the book and pointed to a slot.

"15:30; put your name down." He handed a pen to the other man.

"Too late." Kray turned around, resuming the hum of his little tune. He took his time to walk away.

"Do you have beef with Ronnie Kray?" MacKay asked Henry as he was wiping his face dry of sweat.

"Not that I know of."

"Good. I don't want to have to separate you two and send you to the box."

Henry nodded. The box was not part of the plan.

* * *

"Are you taking the car? Helena shouted from the bottom of the stairs. She waited for a reply before climbing up a few steps and standing on her tiptoes to shout again.

"Mark? Are you taking the car?" She enunciated each word and waited again for a reply, her slender hand resting on the banister for balance.

A door opened and Mark called down.

"Not sure, why? Do you need it?" Mark's latest acquisition, his last folly before he decided to become a pariah of society, at least the society they were both involved in, was Helena's favourite car.

They had always wanted to drive a Jaguar and now they did. Mark waited with a faint smile for a reply. Helena was looking for an excuse to deprive him of his – their – favourite toy.

"It's going to rain, and I'll be on the motorway. Going to visit Mum," Helena said less convincingly than expected.

Mark moved to the top of the stairs. His wife was waiting; a full head of blonde curls brushed her shoulders. Her face lifted towards him with an irresistible smile. How could he say no?

He had another meeting at the SFO, going over his account of events one more time. His face darkened at the thought and Helena read the change in him immediately.

"Doesn't matter."

Mark darted down the stairs and caught her before she had turned away. He put his arms around her, a gentle, folding embrace.

"You can drive my car," he said brushing a kiss on her forehead. It was the least he could do.

Since he had told his wife about the whistle-blowing case the mood in their relationship had changed. Perhaps predictably it would take a little time for her to accept what was going to happen.

Helena returned his kiss, a quick peck on his lips, a smile, another peck, a little more insistent. She pushed him away gently.

"I need to hit the road before the traffic builds up."

Mark lets his hand slide away from her waist, helping her with her coat. The keys lie in a large ashtray, a souvenir from a trip to Mexico they took so many years ago he can't quite recall the date. He has always resisted her attempts at getting rid of it. Helena opens the door and waves a quick goodbye, with final instructions about food, kids, pets. Mark leans against the frame of the door, watching Helena slip into the car, a schoolgirl walking into her favourite sweet shop. A rush of cold air makes him shiver and he prepares to close the door.

The burst of heat and its force are staggering.

It propels him to the bottom of the stairs. His head hits the wall. The gale that has burst into his home stops him from breathing. It all goes black.

Chapter Five

His faded navy slacks felt tight around the waist. Brett pulled his stomach in, his chest out and took a glance at his image in the full-length mirror of his bedroom. He disliked this shabby look and even more what his trousers' waistline was telling him. He was putting on weight.

He released his breath and walked away from the mirror, unstrapping his Patek Philippe watch. He laid it carefully on a small table he used to arrange the necessary items a gentleman should own: cufflinks, lighter, leather wallet and cigarettes.

He would not be wearing or carrying any of these on his trip to North London. The Sheik had asked to see him after a couple of months' silence. Brett had not needed to find an excuse to see him after all. A good state of affairs but a worrying one too.

Brett sat down on the Louis XV bed, his hands stretched over his thighs, the material absorbing the film of moisture that was forming on his palms. Since accepting the deal The Sheik had offered him a few months ago, Brett had been operating well outside his comfort zone.

True, MI6-Steve had been surprisingly supportive. And the deal Steve had in turn offered to Brett for his continued involvement with The Sheik's terrorist organisation had been too good to ignore.

"You pull this one off and you will never have to hear from us again."

Now that Brett had had time to think about it, he was not certain that day would ever come. One did not deal with the head of a new UK terror cell with impunity. Brett had enough contact with the Middle-East to realise that.

A new organisation was growing in strength and might well surpass Al-Qaeda in the region. MI6-Steve would know that too. Still, the idea that he might *pull it off*, as Steve had put it, excited him. The assurance that he would keep the cash he had made from art trafficking and more recently the money The Sheik had paid him, persuaded him too.

How long would that money last? Brett would cross that bridge when it eventually came. He had been born into money and the aristocracy – a rare combination.

The money had evaporated but the title had remained, a useful tool for a skilled fraudster. Brett clasped his hands, cracked his knuckles and stood up.

He grabbed his old, shapeless jacket, pocketed the new burner phone he had just activated and made his way to the tube station. He sent a text to Mohammed, his London contact, as he was walking towards Hyde Park Corner. His phone pinged back. Mohammed had replied.

Brett did not bother to check the text. It was clear that the usual routine for meeting The Sheik would be repeated and he could expect the same treatment as before.

A large SUV with blackened windows waiting for him a few streets away from Finsbury Park Station. A couple of bulky men in black leather jackets shoving him into the back seat. A blindfold.

A journey that circled around the same area a few times in an attempt to make him lose track of his surroundings. The rough frisking on arrival and then The Sheik.

Every time another house, another room but the same figure clad in white robes, a crocheted white hat on his close shaven head and a jet-black wiry beard.

The phone pinged again. Brett squeezed the phone in his jacket pocket and muttered an insult. "What does this moron want?" He was on his way and would be, as ever, punctual. Or had the meeting been cancelled?

Brett found himself torn between the relief of deferment and the excitement of wanting to know what The Sheik had in store for him.

44

He yanked the phone out of his pocket and started reading.

New meeting location: Manor House tube.

He should have known, a last-minute change of location to destabilise him, perhaps to frighten him too. Nothing would ever be predictable with this lot.

Fear was the trademark of all Jihadi groups and he could feel it even in the heart of London. Brett acknowledged the text and hurriedly climbed down the steps leading to the platforms.

* * *

Pole accelerated, using the siren on the roof of his car to attempt to move the traffic out of the way. He went through a red light and DS Andy Todd sitting in the passenger seat closed his eyes. Pole might have smiled were it not for what he knew he would find at the end of his journey.

His mobile, placed in its holder on the car dashboard, was relaying with difficulty his conversation with Marissa.

"When did you last speak to him?" Pole was asking, changing gear again to slow down, blocked this time by a lumbering bus.

"Last night. No, this morning. It was around 3am when he left the SFO office." Marissa's voice was barely audible over the screams of the siren.

"I need to join you." She said several times as the message began breaking up.

Pole increased his grip on the steering wheel, banged his horn and moved up a gear again. "Let me find out first what has happened exactly. Are you on your own?"

Marissa's voice became garbled again. "No. With —"

"Can't hear you."

"In a meeting with Nancy."

Pole slammed on the brakes in front of the first police cordon at the top of Kensington Park Road. Andy lowered the window, showing his badge to the PC on duty.

"I'm nearly there," Pole said, killing the siren. He moved his car more cautiously along the street into which he had turned. There was another police cordon ahead, a couple of officers with dogs and paramedics being held back until the zone had been secured.

"Where are you?" Marissa's anxiety was real and Pole could not pacify her. For all he knew Mark Phelps could be dead. A dreadful situation the SFO would never have contemplated and for which Marissa alone now shouldered the responsibility.

"First I need to speak to the Counterterrorist Commander on site." Pole was not ignoring her but trying to assess the situation.

"Your call," Marissa said. "I am not going to lie to you. I don't want to have to handle this on my own if Mark …" her voice trailed.

"I'll let you know as soon as I can." Pole jumped out of his car and moved quickly towards the site of the blast. The unmistakable smell of explosive and burnt metal almost choked him. He covered his nose with his hands briefly. The memory of another explosion flooded his mind.

Paddington.

He could see the bodies strewed around, hear the moaning of the victims and picture the police van that was transporting Henry Crowne to the Counterterrorism Command Headquarters cracked open like a discarded nut. Henry had been lucky to survive.

"Guv," Andy materialised at Pole's side. "I think it is Commander Ferguson," Andy said adjusting his heavy glasses.

"Yes, and for once I am not going to grumble at being involved with someone I know at the Squad."

"Was it the Commander who responded at the Royal Exchange?"

Pole nodded and moved forward. A couple of heavily armed officers moved towards them and were about to stop them when Commander Ferguson's voice pulled them back. "Let them through."

"Pole, you again," Ferguson said waving him in.

"Car bomb?" Pole asked without bothering to greet the other man.

"'fraid so, with someone in the car unfortunately." Ferguson was moving towards the vehicle, the SOCO team was also moving towards it from the other side of the road, some of them still kitting themselves up for the task ahead.

"We have just cleared the area and allowed the paramedics to enter the house. Some poor bugger is trapped under the door it seems."

"Is it too early to know who the driver is?" Pole asked, the hand in the pocket of his raincoat squeezing his BlackBerry.

"We have just arrived. But the car is registered to a Mr Mark Phelps." Ferguson waited. If Pole was involved, he had details on the case that were relevant to it.

"Is he the person in the car?" Pole asked instead. Ferguson gave him a dark look but volunteered. "Not sure it's a man."

Pole nodded, relieved at the thought that Mark Phelps might still be alive and yet dreading to find out the identity of the dead person. It was likely to be a relative: wife, sister, daughter? Pole ran his hand through his greying hair. No matter who this was, the life of the Phelps family had changed forever.

"What's your involvement in all this?"

"Let's go into the house. I don't want to speak to you about it in the open." Pole was already moving towards the home.

Pole was already moving towards the home as voices came from inside it. A man was lying on the ground, dragged it seemed by one of the paramedics.

Someone was shouting, "He's stopped breathing." One of the paramedics was already doing CPR. A young woman rushed to the ambulance, returning with a defibrillator.

Another woman cut open his T-shirt exposing a bloodied chest. The paramedic applied the pads; the man's body arched up. The young woman took the pulse.

Nothing.

The paramedic rubbed the pads, applied them to the man's chest a second time. The body arched again, hanging suspended in mid-air for a few seconds and dropped back onto the ground with a thud. The young woman felt for the pulse once more. She nodded.

Everyone on the scene had been standing stock still, frozen, joining together in hope for the life of a man they didn't know. Mark Phelps was transferred onto a stretcher and moved into the ambulance.

Pole and Ferguson walked quickly to join the paramedics as soon as they realised Phelps was alive.

"Where are you taking him?" Pole asked.

"Are you family?" The young woman pushed back at the intrusion.

"No. Police," Pole produced his ID card.

"St Thomas's emergency."

Ferguson spoke into his radio. The victim couldn't travel unaccompanied.

Pole let Ferguson organise Mark Phelps' secure transfer to hospital. Andy had already started gathering information, speaking to the SOCO team inside the house.

Pole was happy for him to take the lead on this. He has a call to make.

* * *

The clunk of the lock shutting automatically was for once welcome. Today Henry greeted bang-up time. For an hour, he would not be expected to interact with other inmates or be disturbed. He walked to the small bookshelf he was allowed in his cell, evidence of his good behaviour, chose a large art book and moved to his bed.

He removed his trainers, placed his flimsy pillow behind his back and sat cross-legged in what had become a comfortable position. The book had been well thumbed and yet handled with care.

He opened a page at random and started reading. The prison officers were having their lunch but there was always a possibility that one of them, still on duty, might open the latch of his cell door.

The spine of the book cracked with the soft sound of a crisp waffle and Henry pushed the hard cover slowly apart. It came off to expose pages that had been glued together. Henry felt along the ridge with his finger and dislodged a small piece of cotton wool. It came loose and a small object slipped out of it.

The netsuke rolled into his hand, no bigger than a walnut. He turned the small piece representing a dog with pups around his fingers a few times. He let it rest in his palm and suddenly squeezed it hard. Its ridges pressed into his skin.

He inhaled and slowly let go of the breath. The exquisite piece of art represented everything Henry longed for and what he had lost.

He rolled the netsuke around his hand, stroked his fingertips along the back of the dog, appreciating the delicate carving of its nose and ears, the intricacy of the tiny pups suckling their mother.

A voice in the corridor made him jump and he hurriedly replaced the object in its cache, squeezing the cotton wool back into position. The book sat in his lap and he waited. A few minutes elapsed. Henry relaxed and started reading *Art & Today*, one of the best introductions to modern and contemporary art he had read so far.

Henry smiled at the picture that his random opening had selected, an installation in New York's Central Park called *The Gates* by Christo and Jeanne-Claude, in 2005.

His smile dropped. He had seen this extraordinary piece on one of his trips to New York that winter. The pictures in the book did justice to the power of the piece: red gates, thousands of them organised into two rows, meandering around a frozen Central Park, where snow lay on the ground, trees were bare of foliage but clad in ice.

He had agreed with a contemporary review then, that their installation made you see a place, a landscape, differently. That day, it had made him notice the beauty, vastness and fragility of Central Park.

Henry shut the book and closed his eyes. An unfamiliar sense of peace had settled on him since he had made up his mind about what he must do next – a sense of peace but also a sense of purpose.

It had taken him four years since he had been thrown in jail to formulate what had been haunting him, from his responsibility for Anthony Albert's death to his involvement with the IRA.

Even though the reconciliation process had started and decommissioning had been ordered, he had continued helping the IRA with their finances, so keen was he to belong, to repay Liam and Bobby for their unwavering friendship when he needed it the most and also perhaps to find a connection to the father he had lost so young.

But he could no longer excuse his behaviour – nor did he want to. He needed to prove if only to himself that he could be better than what he appeared to have become.

Henry threw the pillow away with one hand and lay back on his small bed. The frame creaked a little underneath his weight. He held the book against his chest, heavy. Henry opened his eyes and lifted the book over his head. He felt free from a heavy burden. He knew what it would take. Something that might perhaps cost him everything.

Kamal had plans for him. He had suggested as much during their coded conversations. Henry did not need to be a genius to work out why he wanted his involvement.

Henry had been a banker, a brilliant banker. He had managed to keep the finances of the IRA hidden, inaccessible to the most extensive of investigations. Something new was happening in the world of terrorism in the Middle-East.

Kamal, or Abu Maeraka – his warrior name – had convinced him that something more powerful, more extreme was afoot. Another new organisation that needed someone to help with the money they were already amassing. Would they trust a non-believer though?

Perhaps not, or perhaps for as long as they required his services and then … But it was all part of the yet-to-be-revealed master plan and, if Henry was right, also the reason why Abu Maeraka had been transferred to Belmarsh on the same wing as Henry.

Henry stood up in one jump. His well-trained muscles responded to the command instantly. He replaced the art book on its shelf and lifted out a much smaller one he had recently been lent. The *Holy Qur'an* in Arabic with an English translation. Kamal had not told him about the book.

Henry had simply one day found a little parcel of green silk on his chair. Kamal had not bothered to give Henry a simplified text. It was a Qur'an with a translation but no commentary.

The perfect way to lure a man of Henry's calibre, whose intelligence was his greatest asset and his biggest downfall. Henry replaced the Qur'an on the bookshelf too. There was nothing wrong in trying to understand the way of thinking of the people he wanted to join – at least for a while – but now was not the time.

His watch indicated he had another few minutes before bang-up time was over. He returned to his bed, stretched out again and reviewed the status of the financial market in his mind.

He had succeeded in cultivating his good reputation as a model inmate, keeping himself to himself in the hope that the next fallout from the 2008 financial crisis would provide him with a get-out-of-jail card of a more permanent nature.

The world of banking was still far too messed-up not to produce yet another spectacular outrage. His involvement in the LIBOR scandal had proved decisive. Even Pole had given him due credit.

He sensed that the next shocking incident was around the corner, and he, Henry Crowne, was ready for his next move.

* * *

"What did Ferguson say?" Marissa asked, a small muscle at the edge of her mouth twitching with nerves. She straightened up, her solid frame shielding the back of her chair. Nancy nodded. She too wanted to know.

"It will take some time to analyse all the components of the bomb but from what has been gathered so far it was motion activated: it detonated when the car started to move." Pole pushed his chair back.

"Can we tell the origin? I mean I've heard it's possible to trace the maker of a bomb." Marissa clasped her hands so hard that the knuckles had turned white.

"It will be given top priority, no doubt about it, but my guess is that we will find most of the components originated from within the UK – such as the timing device and the motion sensor. Our best hope of finding something that helps with more specific identification rests with the explosive itself —"

"But the bomber?" Marissa interrupted.

"If we can trace the origin of the explosive it will tell us something about who is involved and possibly who the bomber is, assuming he is known to the Counterterrorist Squad."

Marissa remained silent. Her face had frozen. She absorbed the information, trying to make sense of what it meant.

"Does Mark Phelps know?" Nancy asked.

Marissa nodded, took a deep breath. "He is in shock but, surprisingly, he remembers everything."

She broke out of her frozen stance and spread her hands over the table.

"He knows about his wife?"

"That she didn't survive the blast ... Yes." Marissa held her breath for a moment.

"It's the hardest thing I have ever had to do." She dropped her hands into her lap. "I have prosecuted dozens of cases and yet …"

Pole glanced at Nancy and stood up. "I'll get us some fresh tea, shall I?" She blinked in acknowledgement.

"If you are blaming yourself, don't," Nancy said as soon as Pole had closed the door. "It won't help in any way. More importantly, how could you have predicted this?"

"But I can't help wondering whether there were signs I missed."

"Because of who is involved in the case?"

Marissa stood up, went to the window and leaned her head against it. "That is what I like the most about you Nancy, always going straight to the point. I liked it very much during my pupillage years, but it is tough to bear when you are on the receiving end of it."

"I'm sorry Marissa," Nancy said, coming alongside her and extending a friendly hand. "I didn't mean to be insensitive."

"But you are right, this is no time for self-pity. The best thing I can do now is help you find the frigging bastards who did this." Marissa spoke with feeling, the attitude of someone who understood injustice and who would not shy away from tackling the cause of it.

There was a rasp against the door and Pole entered with a tray bearing some appetising looking biscuits – no doubt snatched from the tin of one of his colleagues – and some freshly brewed tea. Pole placed a cup in front of Marissa and Nancy. Everyone drank in silence but the biscuits remained untouched. Marissa waited.

"There is no immediate rush to decide what your next move is going to be." Nancy's voice was calm, hoping it would help.

"Mark came to us, I mean the Serious Fraud Office, about six months ago." Marissa had sat down again. "He had been working for HXBK for ten years as a very senior compliance officer, so he saw a lot of privileged information. About a year ago his boss was taken ill. Something sudden, a heart attack I believe. Anyway, he had to step in."

Marissa drank some tea. "To cut a long story short, he came across documents that his boss hadn't had time to file. During the 2008 crisis the UK government offered a bailout programme to enable the banks to escape bankruptcy. I am sure you remember the likes of RBS and Lloyds accepting the offer. Of course, no government pulls together a programme like that without wanting shares in the institution they intend to salvage and taking some level of control at board level."

"You mean government officials on the board of these institutions, complete scrutiny, reducing the risk profile of the deals done by the bank?" Nancy asked.

"That's right." Marissa nodded appreciatively. "HXBK had found an alternative solution. A private investor."

"Someone out there was willing to invest enough money to salvage them, despite their involvement in the subprime market?" Pole asked incredulous.

"That's correct." Marissa nodded again and this time her stiff shoulders relaxed Nancy remarked. She had found a team that was more on the ball than many of her colleagues and the light in her eyes said so.

"Were the terms of the share purchase commercial and who was the investor?" Nancy asked.

"A state in the Middle-East. I can't say more at the moment and no, not at all, the terms of the share purchase were reasonable bearing in mind the circumstances. It's what happened subsequently to the money HXBK received that has become an issue."

Marissa opened the file she had been guarding closely and handed them each a copy of a short document. "A sum of money representing a large portion of the original investment has been lent back to a fund registered in Panama."

Nancy speed-read the document, still listening to Marissa.

"In itself a fund registered in Panama is legal," Nancy said.

"Very true but the question is who is the Ultimate Beneficial Owner of the fund? So far we have not been able to determine who the UBO is."

"And you suspect this UBO is someone representing the Middle-Eastern State that lent the money?" Pole had finished reading the document too.

"That's right."

"Mark thought it was the case too. Otherwise he would not have contacted you?" Pole turned his BlackBerry face down as several messages kept appearing on its screen.

"Mark had a conversation with senior management, at CEO level, and the answers he received were less than convincing."

"How so?" Nancy frowned, drawing her elegant eyebrows together.

"A final document was issued confirming the verification of the identity of the UBO, but that identity was never made available to Mark and the excuse made that the identity was politically sensitive complete non-sense. The complexity of the structure of the fund's ownership was not particularly transparent either." Marissa finished her tea. "When Mark's boss returned, he told Mark in no uncertain terms to close the file and stop questioning a transaction that had already been finalised."

"In other words, don't ask the awkward questions," Pole added.

"Mark's involvement in high-profile transactions almost completely dried up at that point."

"If you don't have the identity of the UBO you don't have a case." Pole handed the document back to Marissa.

"No, not a chance."

"This is the reason why you need to speak to Henry Crowne," Nancy said also handing the document back.

Reluctantly, Pole nodded. "We do need Henry."

Chapter Six

Andy was pacing up and down in front of Pole's office. He was speaking to someone on his mobile phone and waving a sheaf of papers.

"What's all this extra activity about?" Pole asked with a faint smile.

"Got some results on the Mashrafiya, Guv." Andy looked disappointed as Pole's face remained blank. "The sword that was used to behead Massimo Visconti."

Pole slapped his forehead. "That sword, the Mash ... whatever."

"Rafiya," Andy's mind was already on the next piece of news. "I have managed to find out where it came from."

"You mean it has some special origin?"

"It was stolen from a museum in Iraq during the last Iraqi war. But this particular piece is very important. It is supposed to have belonged to the man who fought alongside the prophet Mohammed."

"Go on," Pole said opening the door of his office and waving Andy in.

"The museum in Baghdad was ransacked a number of times but very thoroughly after the fall of Saddam Hussein."

"I see what you are getting at," Pole said dumping the file Marissa had prepared for him to a dangerously high pile of papers. The pile wobbled. Andy held his breath. Pole sat down hardly noticing. "You think Massimo Visconti had something to do with the theft of this sword?"

Andy sat down in slow motion, a wary eye still on the pile of documents. "Yeah, Guv, I do."

"And? You can't hide anything from me you know." Pole leant forward, elbows on his desk, hands clasped together over another bundle of papers.

"I also think …" Andy took his time to speak the words, "…he might have known his assailant."

"That is a pretty big assumption. From having possibly stolen the Mashrafiya to being slaughtered with it and by whom – the person who asked him to steal it in the first place?"

"I know, Guv, so I spoke to DCI Grandel." Andy waited for Pole's reaction.

"That's a good idea. With his long experience in stolen art he must have a view. What did good old Eugene have to say for himself then?"

"He confirmed that Visconti was heavily involved in art trafficking out of the war zones in the Middle-East. He was on the ground way before anybody else dared chance it according to DCI Grandel."

"Who were his contacts in the region? Do we know?"

"According to DCI Grandel, Visconti had already realised that he had to work with the fighters on the ground, get very close to the local people. In particular the rebels in Iraq who needed funds for the war against the US and the government it supported there."

"You mean Al-Qaeda?"

Andy nodded.

"So after nearly ten years of playing happy families with a number of terrorist groups, looters and so on Visconti comes to a sad end. But why? What changed?"

"That's what I'm trying to find out. He was arrested, remember."

"But he escaped." Pole had started to fiddle with a rubber band and stopped, keeping the elastic fully stretched.

"You don't seem convinced."

"It's not that, Andy. It's what comes next if your theory is right."

"You mean …" Andy's chubby face dropped.

"Yes, what does it mean if we prove Visconti was murdered in the middle of London by a terrorist cell?"

Andy's blue eyes darted from Pole to the papers he had prepared for his boss, attempting to articulate a response to the chilling question.

56

London. Terrorism. Last bomb from the IRA, 1993. Then 2007 the Al-Qaeda bombing happened.

"So no, I am not saying you are wrong," Pole released the elastic band. The car bomb that had just killed Mark Phelps' wife could well validate Andy's findings.

Superintendent Marsh would shortly be addressing the press. The Home Secretary would almost certainly chair a Cobra meeting to discuss the event. But Pole did not want to overreact. Andy needed to find proof.

"Shall I go back to DCI Grandel?"

"That's a good plan. Get all the information he has available on Visconti. Do we know what he stole? Do we have the names of people he dealt with? You know the drill."

"On it, Guv." Andy adjusted his thick glasses, leaped out of his seat and left Pole's office, already dialling Grandel's number on his mobile.

* * *

The blindfold had been knotted too tight. Brett could feel the pressure against his eyes but did not dare loosen it.

He gathered the car that was taking him back was not the one that had driven him to his meeting with The Sheik. It had been cleaned recently, the smell of detergent mixed with an overpowering rose-scented air freshener almost made him throw up.

Brett had known that a tough meeting would happen one day but perhaps not so quickly and not so openly brutal. There was nothing physical, at least not yet, apart from the tight blindfold and the rough way he had been frisked when he had got out of the car that had picked him up from Manor House tube station.

The change of pick-up address had already unsettled him. But again, it had been intended to. The journey had taken longer than the usual thirty minutes or so. The pattern of the journey had also changed.

Brett had relied on his training, spotting the turns that indicated the car was going around in circles. This time though there was very little circling around the same area. By his reckoning the drive had taken a little more than forty minutes in a straight line. He was taken deep into the suburbs, the heartland of a community he knew nothing about.

The blindfold had only been removed when he was in the meeting room. The place was dilapidated, the floorboards bare, the wallpaper had been torn down, taking with it pieces of plaster. The house had no heating and the cold seeped through his body as he stood wondering once more whether this was a meeting or an execution.

Should he sit down on one of the mattresses that were lying on the floor? Perhaps not. He had been brought here as a warning. He was intended to be scared and he was, but more importantly he should show that he was.

Someone walked through the open door. Brett jerked back. The Sheik waved to him to sit down. His eyes focused on Brett with a coldness he had not yet witnessed.

The Sheik sat down on a mattress opposite Brett's, drew a photograph from a brown envelope and threw it at Brett's feet.

"Do you know this man?"

Massimo Visconti's face, the unmistakable large brown eyes, the slightly hooked nose and strong jaw – a charm that seduced all. Brett held his breath for a few seconds. Should he deny it? But it would not make sense. Visconti was too well known in the art-trafficking world. He had nodded hesitantly.

The Sheik's face relaxed slightly. Brett saw he had passed a test.

For now.

"It's been in the news," he mumbled. Perhaps he could glean more information?

The Sheik threw several more photos onto the floor. It took almost a minute before Brett could make sense of what he was seeing and when he did he scrambled to his feet and stumbled to the back of the room, reeling in horror.

He coughed and reached for a handkerchief in his trouser pocket. He wiped his mouth and face with it.

The Sheik had not moved, terrifyingly patient.

"Why?" Brett mumbled, immediately regretting the question.

The Sheik invited him back onto the mattress Brett had left so abruptly.

"I reward well but I punish harshly."

The Sheik had pulled another photo out of the brown envelope. Brett's eyes closed.

"Please, no more."

"This one has his head still very much on his shoulders." He handed Brett the picture.

Another attractive face was looking at Brett from a photo that had been professionally shot: dark blue eyes, furrows that cut deep into his face, a decisive chin and a mane of dark hair. It was a man Brett once knew well.

Brett fidgeted in the back of the car. They were a good thirty minutes into their journey back. The car had turned in a direction he was not expecting, taking another route to deliver him back to a tube station.

Brett kept his mind occupied, replaying the second part of his meeting with The Sheik. Yet the pictures of Visconti's mutilated body kept appearing in front of his eyes. He pushed away those images to concentrate on the face of the man who was very much alive.

Henry Crowne.

* * *

The drip bag would need replacing soon. Marissa wondered whether she should call the nurse. Mark was asleep and she felt awkward at the thought of waking him up, at the thought that the woman at his bedside should have been his wife, not her. Never had she had to face a threat to the life of a key witness or the devastating consequences a case might have on a family.

She had organised protection under the witness protection programme, but it had always been a successful pre-emptive move.

Pole had been efficient without being overbearing. Mark's children had been collected from school on the basis of an emergency, taken to Mark's parents and the police were guarding the house. At least they were all safe.

Mark stirred, perhaps disturbed by Marissa's intense gaze. She stood up carefully and placed her large, heavy hand on his.

"Mark," her voice cracked a little.

He turned his face slightly and opened the eye that was not covered by bandages. His mind was adjusting, extricating itself from the fog created by medication and pain.

"Hi," he mumbled. He turned his head a little more towards the glass of water on the bedside table. "Thirsty." Marissa brought the plastic tumbler to him and helped place the straw in his mouth.

She wanted to say something meaningful, but she could not think of anything. What could she say to the man who had almost lost his life, lost his wife and would almost certainly spend the rest of his existence looking over his shoulder?

Mark took a few long pulls of water and let his head fall back again on the pillow, eyes closed.

"Shall I leave and come back later?" Marissa asked.

"No." Mark remained silent and Marissa thought he might have fallen asleep again.

"Children?" Mark asked, opening his good eye again and fixing it on Maria with a look of anxiety.

"Yes, they are fine. They are with your parents under police protection."

It was excruciating, Marissa's stomach was a lump of lead in her midriff. She could not let him down. He had trusted her when he came to the SFO. "Mark, if you want to stop?"

"No." The same determined word surprised her.

"No," Mark repeated. "She can't have died," he slurred, "for nothing." The bandage restricted his jaw. "Catch the bastards."

Marissa squeezed his hand. "I promise."

* * *

"Enter."

Marsh was in a foul mood today, Denise, his PA, had warned. He had asked her to rearrange an entire week of meetings to fit in an interview with *The Times* on a prickly subject.

60

Pole straightened his tie and gave Denise a wink. She gave him the thumbs up. He walked into Superintendent Marsh's office.

"Good afternoon, Sir."

"Pole. Good afternoon." Marsh was now on the charm offensive it seemed. Pole had barely told him about the SFO request for a contact to be found that could both speak to HMP Belmarsh's governor and the Home Office but Marsh's well-trained ear had picked up the tone.

Another high-profile case.

"What does Counterterrorism Command say about the bomb?" Marsh asked, settling deep into his chair. His eyes glinted with interest. Pole cringed. The body of Mark Phelps' wife had scarcely reached the mortuary and Marsh already wanted something he could deliver to the Press.

"A motion device triggered the explosion, Sir. CT Command is being very cautious in making assumptions." Pole sat down before being invited to. Marsh would have to wait until Ferguson, the commander in charge, gave him more information.

"Right, right. Of course, we would not want to jump to conclusions, would we?"

"We certainly would not, Sir."

Whatever the conclusions about the bomb and the Mashrafiya, they would hit Marsh's desk only after they had hit Ferguson's and Nancy's.

"The SFO has confirmed they intend to request assistance from Crowne, I presume?" The very large piece of news Marsh was savouring.

"They have indeed, Sir. I have prepared a draft request on their behalf to be sent to Belmarsh and the Home Office. Assuming your backing of course."

March gestured consent as if Pole did not need to ask.

"Understood. However —" Marsh moved his body forward in an abrupt fashion, forearms on his desk. "I will want to know all of the details and I mean *all* the details of this operation."

Pole nodded, with pursed lips. "Absolutely Sir, as ever."

His omission in the last case involving Henry Crowne and Nancy, an attempt on the life of one of Whitehall's most senior civil servants, had irritated Marsh greatly. Pole had managed to plead urgency and he had had a point. Marsh knew it. Nevertheless, he was the man in charge and Pole had better remember it. Pole remained impassive as Marsh scrutinised him for a sign – anything indicating he was already not quite as transparent as he was intended to be.

"Good," Marsh finally said. "Take me through the SFO case and why they want Crowne."

If Marsh thought Pole would make any mistakes when explaining why they needed Henry, he would be disappointed. Marissa and Nancy had done a superb job of briefing him and, much to his surprise, he was getting the hang of all the City jargon too.

"You must have read that during the financial crisis in 2008 the UK government offered a bailout facility to UK banks." Marsh nodded; so far so good, he was following.

"However, one of the banks that could have benefited from such an offer decided to go elsewhere to find the necessary capital." Pole sat comfortably in his chair, legs crossed and moving his hands as he spoke. "Bank X – the SFO is seeking to avoid disclosing the name – was funded by a Middle-Eastern country and therefore raised enough capital not to need the UK government bailout."

Marsh wriggled on his chair. Mentioning the Middle-East always had an effect on senior Met officers.

"What the SFO has discovered through a bank employee who contacted them is that a large part of this cash has been lent back to a fund in Panama. The structure of the fund is complex. This means that the SFO has been unable to determine who the Ultimate Beneficial Owner of the fund is."

"Is this illegal?" Marsh asked, arching his mouth in a doubtful fashion.

"It is not, Sir, unless the fund is structured/designed for illicit motives or the money is used for illegal purposes." Pole was enjoying himself. Marsh, an intelligent man despite his voracious ambition, was starting to struggle.

Pole 1 – Marsh 0.

"How illegal then?" Marsh rearranged his collection of Montblanc pens on his desk, each received after a new promotion no doubt.

"The whistle-blower, Mark Phelps, has information indicating illegal activity."

"Which is what? Drugs. Weapons. Human slavery?"

"None of those, at least as far as we can tell, but rather the very fact that the money received by Bank X has been lent back to the Middle-Eastern country that invested it in the first place."

Marsh opened his mouth, closed it. No, he would not ask the question that was burning his lips. Was this illegal too? "Is this whistle-blower reliable?" Marsh asked instead.

"Very. The SFO is convinced of it and Marissa Campbell, an experienced prosecutor, as well." Pole briefly locked eyes with Marsh. "And by the look of it the bombers thought as much too."

Marsh pulled away from his desk. "Clearly." Marsh remained silent for a minute or so.

"If Mark Phelps has been targeted, I assume Bank X is his employer?"

"That's correct, Sir." Pole kept his countenance.

Blast. Marsh 1 – Pole 1.

Marsh grinned, satisfied. "So why call it Bank X still?"

"As far as Crowne is concerned, the documents he sees will be redacted. The SFO does not want the case to be contaminated. If he finds the UBO, his findings will be based on the Panama fund structure only, no other inference."

The Super pursed his lips, pondering the validity of the argument. Not that the SFO director would take any notice of his opinion but it was good feeling one could perhaps present a different opinion.

"I see the point," Marsh said slowly. He was formulating his next question in the most neutral fashion he could think of. Pole was expecting it but he would be damned if he was going to make it easy for his boss.

"Are you using your consultant, Ms Wu?" Marsh avoided Pole's eyes. He sounded almost innocent.

Pole suppressed an ironic *Certainly Sir, shall I also organise dinner?* and simply shrugged. "Unless you have any objection to it."

"No, not at all," Marsh volunteered, perhaps a little too keenly.

Pole coughed, a feeling he was not familiar with rising slowly in his chest, a shade of jealousy perhaps.

"Although I still have to receive formal confirmation from the SFO, they are likely to be comfortable with our arrangements." A little disingenuous of Pole since Marissa had specifically asked for Nancy to be involved with the case. Marissa almost certainly had more confidence in Nancy than she had in Scotland Yard.

Nancy had been a brilliant QC before she gave it all up, and an even better mentor. It was clear to Pole that Marissa would never forget the time she had spent as Nancy's pupil.

"Let me speak to the SFO director – only if that would help, of course." Marsh's keenness must have been clear even to him.

"I am sure it will be perfectly fine, Sir," Pole rested his crossed hands on the side of the chair. He was not prepared to facilitate another meeting between Nancy and Marsh. The last time had almost soured his relationship with her. Even though Pole had made much progress with the delightful Ms Wu since then, he was not taking any chances. The little bubble of jealousy burst into a sense of joy.

Marsh was talking again and Pole caught only the end of the sentence.

"Call the governor, now."

"Absolutely," Pole said, hoping he was not committing to some ridiculous requirement for The Super.

Marsh sent him a quizzical look but started dialling, switching on the loudspeaker.

The deep voice of HMP Belmarsh's governor answered.

"Phil. Superintendent Marsh here. How are you?"

Marsh was on the offensive again. Another high-profile deal that would further his career.

* * *

The seventh door had just clanged shut. Henry stretched his arms and legs to be frisked once more before being allowed out of High Security Unit Belmarsh for time with his visitor.

Nancy had left a message that she would see him during the early afternoon visiting slot. It was not her usual day and Henry was excited. Something was afoot. He had scanned the news bulletins on his small radio in search of a clue. There was nothing he could put his finger on. Frustrating.

Had he been on the trading floor he would have browsed through Bloomberg and Reuters and almost certainly had a good idea. He could have tried the library and attempted to log in, bypassing the restrictions imposed on inmates, as he had done successfully a few times now. But he judged it was not worth taking the risk. He needed to keep his powder dry for when he knew exactly what he was looking for.

The door to one of the inner yards opened. Henry hesitated. Confinement in HSU sometimes made him shy of walking outside the compound. The urge for freedom he then felt was often unbearable.

The fresh air hit his face. The weather had turned bitterly cold. He had felt it even from within the stuffiness of his cell. He walked over the threshold slowly, closed his eyes and inhaled.

Gusts of wind brought with them smells of cooking: mutton, onion and something else he could not quite define. He called it the Belmarsh smell, a smell one recognised just the way one recognised the smell of one's own home when walking in, with perhaps something particular to a prison: fear, despair, anger mixed with an infinitely small grain of hope for those who could find it.

Henry arrived in front of the next set of doors without noticing. The clunk of yet another set of locks reminded him that he had to keep moving. He turned his head briefly towards one of the yards reserved for HSU prisoners and noticed the small silhouette of a man walking slowly on his own around the perimeter, two guards in attendance.

"Henry?"

"Yep, sorry." Henry moved quickly inside the warm building and along the corridor. He did not know who the inmate was but had heard from Big K that several prisoners were deemed such high-risk that they were never allowed to mix with the others.

Henry had smiled. He was not deemed such a high risk and neither was Kamal.

A mistake? Or a plan?

Nancy was already sitting at a table in the meeting room when Henry entered. She had brought newspapers with her that she was arranging in front of her. Her briefcase was underneath the desk, neatly aligned with the legs of the table. Henry stopped, smiling.

They were allocated an hour and a half which often was too short but surprisingly had also proved too long on several occasions. It was almost always a shock to meet someone from the outside world: the clothes, the scent of freshly washed laundry or simply soap, a new hairstyle – and with Nancy, the fragrance of Issey Miyake.

She lifted her head, aware that someone was watching her and she broke into a smile.

"Do you have some good news?" Henry asked with a wry smile whilst bending down to put a quick kiss on her cheek.

"Perhaps." Nancy pushed a few papers towards him. Henry read the headlines in a low voice.

The UK government bailout – an update was RBS too big to fail?

Barclays says choosing Qatar as investor perfect decision … TSB rescued by Lloyds. Will it work?

"OK, these banks have all been exposed to the subprime market in London. Nothing very new here." Henry said as he speed-read the papers. Nancy nodded but said nothing. Henry ran his hand through his short hair, irritated.

Could it be that his mind was becoming rusty? It had been over four years now since he had left the trading floor and four years since the banks had been offered a bailout. He scanned the papers again to find a common denominator.

"Aha. The UK government bailout programme," Henry said, a cheerful look on his face. "That's the point, isn't it?"

Nancy smiled in acknowledgement.

"Exactly right." Her face looked kindly amused, the almond shape of her eyes a little more pronounced, her lips gently arched upward.

Henry pushed the papers away and crossed his arms over his chest, ready for more.

He was needed again.

His breathing had become faster, hope bubbling up in his gut. Yet he did not want to acknowledge what he was hoping for, a little Celtic superstition perhaps.

"I won't keep you guessing," Nancy said. "The Serious Fraud

Office is proposing that you assist them with a particularly complex investigation."

"The SFO?" Henry frowned. His heart was now beating fast, the short hairs on his neck standing up.

"That's right. They are preparing a request to go to the governor of HMP Belmarsh as well as the Home Office."

"Wow, I'm speechless," Henry said. It was an honest answer. He would have never dreamt the SFO would need him, but hey, why not?

"Same conditions as previously?" He asked. It almost felt routine.

Nancy leaned forward, arms on the table, hands crossed. " Absolutely. I am to be appointed consultant to the SFO and Inspector Pole will be the official liaison between The Met and the SFO."

Henry rolled his eyes but broke into a smile.

"Pole, I would never have guessed. Still, I shouldn't grumble, better the devil you know."

"You were almost friends the last time you two worked together."

"Of course, we were trying to save you."

They both fell silent as the scene unfolded again in front of their eyes. The gun's discharge, Pole and Henry rushing into the room to rescue Nancy and her friend, glass shattered all over the floor, a man down, blood … so much blood.

Nancy had turned pale and Henry extended his hand, squeezing hers.

"I'm sorry, I didn't mean to bring back those memories in such an uncouth fashion."

"I know." She cleared her throat, squeezed his hand in return and slowly let go. "I can tell you a little more about the case; not much though, but perhaps enough to get that impressive brain of yours ticking."

"Am all ears."

Nancy summarised what Marissa had told her: the investment in Bank X by a Middle-Eastern country; the fund and its complex structure. Henry's focus was absolute, taking in every detail until Nancy had finished.

"Where is the domicile of the fund? Can you at least tell me that?" he said after a moment.

"Panama."

Henry grinned, uncovering a set of regular teeth. He crossed his arms behind his head, nostrils flaring.

"Panama, hey. I was wondering when the issue of fiscal paradises would surface. It seems it now has."

Nancy arched her eyebrows. "Really? Let's hope the governor will agree to let you out then."

Henry's smile broadened even more. "He will. Your good friend Pole will make sure of it and, if not, I can guarantee Superintendent Marsh won't hesitate to assist."

"But before I agree to support the SFO too, I want to have a little chat with you about something." Nancy opened her briefcase and placed an untidy piece of paper she had taken out of it in front of Henry.

"Would you care to elaborate please?" Nancy asked, her eyes on Henry. "If it means what I think it means … I will not be walking through these doors again for a very long time."

"I know – a bit melodramatic – very Irish. I get some strange ideas within the confines of HSU. It always passes." His smile had become rueful. He had known the question about the note he had written to Nancy a few months ago would come up. He did not regret writing it and simply hoped he could be convincing enough now.

"So just a bit of the blues nothing more dramatic than that?"

"Absolutely." Henry's smile did not falter. His heart raced a little. He didn't like lying to Nancy, but it was the only way.

"Escape out of HSU is not an option, you know that." Nancy leaned forward and placed a hand carefully across her mouth so that no one could lip read what she was saying to Henry.

"I know – the most secure prison in the UK." Henry's shoulders sagged sightly. "I am convinced of that."

Nancy searched his face. He felt his smile drop but she pulled back. He thought she was convinced.

Now the game was on.

Chapter Seven

The frisking was done professionally. She was glad however when the heavy prison door closed shut, leaving her outside and Henry still inside.

Nancy was only half convinced by Henry's explanation. The HSU was an impressive environment, a smaller community of inmates imprisoned within the main body of Belmarsh prison itself.

The prison officers too were different, better trained at identifying problems early and under strict instructions not to fraternise with the prisoners. But even if Henry dreamt about freedom, no one had ever escaped from HSU Belmarsh.

She felt reassured. Her experience of visiting Henry regularly had convinced her that no one would ever change that.

The bus arrived. She climbed on board and found a seat at the far end. She had been followed by a couple of other women. She recognised one of them, also a regular visitor. Her son was doing time for GBH, assault on his girlfriend and mother of his unborn child.

The younger woman was talking to the older one animatedly. The meeting with the prisoner she was visiting must have gone well, leaving a small glimmer of hope that he might change his ways and that there could be happiness once he came out.

The two women would leave the bus at Hackney Central and take a tube that would deliver them into the heartland of gangs' territory: high-rise estates riddled with drugs, weapons and abuse, a place where few policemen would ever venture. It looked cliched and yet sadly too familiar.

Nancy sighed; poverty in a country like the UK was a disgrace. What was the excuse in this place of abundance? It was not India. Or China with 1.4 billion people to feed.

Her body shuddered; she pushed away the memories of China. Nancy looked at her watch, almost 4pm. She could be with Pole in half an hour if she got off now and hailed a cab. Would it be unprofessional to distract him in the middle of two murder investigations? Nancy rested her forehead against the window of the lumbering bus.

The words of Phillippe, the young gallerist who had kindly agreed to help her with her search for her father, came back to her. "The trail goes cold after 1989." She opened her bag, fumbling with the zip, grabbed her BlackBerry and sent a text to Pole. She could hold back no longer. She had to know.

Pole replied within minutes. Nancy smiled. She sat back in the taxi she had been lucky to find quickly. How much more was she prepared to tell him about her childhood and her greatest fears?

The taxi swerved wildly, the cabbie banged his horn and lowered his window to give the cyclist a piece of his mind. He had barely avoided a man on his bike with a child seat at the back complete with a small passenger.

Nancy was thrown to one side, causing a searing pain in her right shoulder. The pain grew in intensity going way beyond what the impact should have provoked. Memories of another bike flooded her mind, uninvited.

Her long hair has been braided in an equally long plait that has not been undone for days. She wants to scratch her scalp but she is too frightened to let go of her father's back. Her father is pedalling fast. She is barely holding on. The small child seat on which she is perched has been built by him, a rackety affair that has done a good job of carrying her this far but now is threatening to collapse at any moment. She hears her mother call after them. They must reach the safety of their next stopover before it is dark, before the roads are deserted and the red guards prowl the streets. Nancy sees that they are in a city, people moving like ants, relentless, unstoppable. Her father slows down and a few people stare. Her mother is a foreigner and easily recognisable despite the scarf around her hair — just a little effort and they will be safe.

They turn off into another street, away from the main road, then take another turning into a smaller lane. Her father stops and takes her into his arms. He is almost running. Nancy sees her mother move her bike alongside her husband's, as she clasps her father's neck. Her mother catches her satchel on the handlebar of the bikes; they collapse with a loud clatter. Her father drops Nancy in front of a wooden door and runs back towards his wife. Out of nowhere four young men in uniform have appeared ... red guards.

A door opens and shuts. She is in; they are out. She wants to cry but one hand covers her mouth, and another grabs her shoulder in an iron vice, "Don't say anything." The use of English stuns her.

Nancy heard another voice in the distance. She had taken hold of her shoulder trying to ease an overwhelming pain. The cab had stopped, the cabbie was speaking to her from the car's open door – "All right? Hurt?"

Nancy opened her eyes. She could hardly hold back the tears. She managed a breathless, "Don't worry – it's fine; an old wound."

* * *

Pole had once again arrived before her. She slowed down and spent a few moments observing him. His tall body was bent over a small coffee table. He had managed to secure their favourite spot, a couple of comfortable small sofas alongside the bay window, secluded from the rest of the cafe and its clusters of armchairs and couches.

She sometimes wondered whether he used his police ID card to secure the spot. He had ordered pastries already. Her latest favourite, introduced to her during a trip to France, the Ile de Ré, a little island close to La Rochelle.

These chaussons aux pommes, a kind of apple turnover drizzled with coarse granulated sugar, had awoken her taste buds and she was delighted she had found them in the middle of London.

Pole had a knack for knowing when he needed to be there first to welcome her; perhaps he heard it in the tone of her voice. This simply reflected the skill of a successful DCI and yet his ability to read human feelings always impressed her. It was one of the things which made him so immensely attractive.

Nancy started walking towards him. Pole had just finished rearranging one of the small sofas when he saw her. She was now all smiles and so was he.

"Jonathan, *mon cher ami*, always full of thoughtful attention when I need it the most," Nancy said putting one hand on his shoulder and standing on tiptoe to kiss his cheek.

"*Très heureux de l'entendre*," Pole kissed her cheek in return and bent forward to help her with her coat. "Did it not go as well as you expected with Henry? I would have thought —"

Nancy pressed his arm to interrupt him. "No, he is raring to go, just as we expected." She sat down, inhaled deeply. Pole sat opposite her, patient. He was there, as always. ready to give her all the time she needed.

Nancy looked into Pole's face, his intelligent eyes that creased ever so slightly near the temples when he paid attention, the famous goatee, now more salt and pepper than when they first met, and one immense quality above all.

Truthfulness.

"I have been thinking about this for a while now," she finally said whilst pouring the tea that had just arrived. Pole nodded encouragingly. He was pouring his own tea, a slow careful movement, mindful of not disturbing the atmosphere of confidence.

"It's about —" Nancy hesitated. Did she really want to do this?

"The past?" Pole ventured.

Nancy felt her lips tremble. "Thank you, yes, it is, very much so." She took a sip of tea. "It's about someone from my past." Hesitating once more, she looked into Pole's eyes. He let her gaze deeply into them. Her right hand started shaking ever so slightly but she could only see immense kindness in front of her.

"It's about – my father."

* * *

The cab almost felt comfortable. It was an old model, the cushioned upholstery had seen better days and so had the scuffed floor. Marissa pushed her body into the left-hand corner, squeezing herself between the window and the backrest. It was oddly cosy.

She spent a few moments observing the driver. He too had seen better days: short white hair barely covering his skull, hunched over the wheel, hands knotted with arthritis and yet smoothly weaving his taxi through heavy traffic.

She closed her eyes and rested her head against the window. Mark's bandaged face and hands sprang to mind, interrupting her train of thought. She buttoned up her coat, shivering. Was it truly what he wanted to do – carry on with the case? He was still so raw and shocked. She had never hesitated in prosecuting even the most tedious of cases. But today was different. Her large dark eyes felt moist. She opened her handbag, fished out a couple of tissues and ran them over her face.

She was about to arrive at the Serious Fraud Office where the director was waiting for her. Under his leadership the SFO had regained much of its lost reputation. He was unlikely to let the human factor interfere with the decision to follow through.

"David is going to want to prosecute. No matter what," Marissa whispered. David Black had made it his mission to restore the agency's relevancy.

He had reopened the LIBOR case after his predecessor had decided not to prosecute bankers, consequently revoking the previous decision. If there was sufficient evidence, he would want to forge ahead.

She asked the cabbie to drop her at the bottom of Trafalgar Square, paid and stepped out into the cold. She raised the collar of her coat and brought it close to her face. The wind was pushing mercilessly into her.

She moved at a slow pace, each step making ground against the gusts and sudden squalls of driving rain. She was getting wet, but she would not hurry, wanting to gain a few precious minutes before having to face a decision she did not want to make.

She entered the SFO building, greeted the receptionist with her usual nod and took the lift to the third floor. She ran her hand over her thick short hair, brushing off the raindrops.

She almost smiled: the advantage of African hair … it was hard for it to get wet. Her mobile phone buzzed, reminding her why she was back in the office. David was waiting for her and his texts made it clear.

Marissa was sitting in a narrow chair in front of the director's desk.

He was pacing down the length of his office, rehearsing the speech he would deliver to the Attorney General, his boss. The LIBOR scandal was at the forefront of his strategy to charge the bankers who had manipulated the benchmark. LIBOR served to fix interest rate levels not only in the UK but also around the world, a $350 trillion scandal.

Even he had gasped at the figure. How far could he go in holding the banks and the bankers to account? And now this new scandal, another bank to prosecute. This was exactly what the SFO needed after years of lacklustre performance.

Marissa shifted a little. The wretched chair made her self-conscious of her size, and yes, it was not supposed to be comfortable to be in the director's presence. David stopped and peered over his narrow, blue-rimmed glasses.

"Your view, Marissa."

"I think he has decided to carry on."

David looked puzzled. "You sound unsure."

"He has barely recovered from the shock of the blast and from losing his wife, of course." Her voice trailed.

"I am not talking about Mark Phelps; understandably, his decision isn't final yet." He moved to his desk and sat down heavily. "I am talking about you. Your views on the case. The evidence looks solid so far."

"We still need to demonstrate that the Ultimate Beneficial Owner of the fund that received money from HXBK originates from the same Middle-Eastern country that invested in them in the first place."

"A circular transaction of the worst kind." The director smirked. "You've found a banker that can help, haven't you? I read Crowne's résumé. This case should be a walk in the park for him."

"Perhaps." Marissa's large hand moved a few sheets of paper around the file she had laid open on the desk.

David leaned back in his chair, one hand swinging the glasses he had removed.

"Marissa, we can't afford another BAE Systems failure. Surely, out of all people, you know that too."

Marissa froze for a few seconds. She had been expecting a reference to the case that still haunted her but perhaps not so soon.

Not being able to properly prosecute BAE Systems for bribery in the sale of armaments to the Saudis had been the worst moment in her career. What amounted in her view to a mere slap on the wrist for BAE and a pardon granted by Tony Blair to the Saudis, who had invoked national security, had been a severe blow.

"I know, Sir; how could I forget?" Marissa straightened up.

"You were not helped by the previous director, of that I am aware. But I am here to give you all the backing you need."

"It is very much appreciated."

"Come, come. What is it?"

"What if he changes his mind?"

"I presume we are back to Phelps. It is your job to convince him otherwise."

"He has two children. He may not want to risk their lives too." Marissa rearranged the papers again, meticulously aligned them in a neat pile. She could feel the heavy scrutiny of her boss's eyes. It was almost impossible to escape his astute and prodding attention.

"Are you reluctant to prosecute because you fear more lives will be lost?"

"I think that is correct, Sir." Marissa lifted her face and looked at him calmly. She was glad he had prised the question out of her.

He stopped the rhythmic movement of his hand. The glasses stood still in mid-air. His icy gaze rolled over her like water over a duck's back. The lady was not for turning, at least not yet, but she knew he would keep trying.

"They will benefit from the witness protection programme if they need to."

"Which has had mixed results," Marissa answered.

"If we give up now and he yields to intimidation, others will follow suit. These people will use the same techniques again and win."

Marissa held her breath. Of course, he had a valid point. But what was she expecting from such a seasoned lawyer?

"He is under armed protection, the Counterterrorist Squad is in attendance, and from what I can tell, Inspector Pole is a man who gets results." The director had resumed swinging his glasses from the tip of his fingers, round and round they went.

"His wife is dead," Marissa spoke without conviction, trying to find the argument that would perhaps stop or at least delay the wheels of the SFO from moving forward inexorably.

"It's a tragedy, an abomination but not prosecuting will not bring her back. More to the point, her murderers will have achieved what they wanted."

Marissa felt her tense body give a fraction. Her shoulders had been braced since she had started the conversation and her feet were itching to leave.

"I know you have a point, Sir, but I need to be absolutely sure that Mark will not change his mind and cave in at the last minute," Marissa said. Perhaps an argument that was giving her a little more time to assess her own feelings about the impact of the case on Mark's family.

"And it is also your job to make him feel secure enough not to want to cave in, as you put it." The director put down his glasses and stretched his hands over the desk's surface. "I understand it was a shock. You may not believe it but I understand. You know though that the only way to do the wife justice is to find and prosecute the bastards who did it."

Marissa locked eyes with the director for an instant – manipulation or compassion? She didn't know.

She slowly closed the file.

"I will speak to Mark."

* * *

Sotheby's Cafe was buzzing with a fauna that Brett hardly noticed. Afternoon tea was being served and much champagne being consumed, Brett could tell.

He navigated the tables, managing to avoid the long legs and Louboutin high-heeled shoes of an ultra-chic brunette. His eyes lingered a little too long over the legs that had almost tripped him. She did not mind the look nor did she move away – ruffians, plenty of money but little education.

Brett recognised the stocky frame of MI6-Steve. It was the first time Steve had arranged a meeting outside Brett's club or some facility regularly used by the agency.

It felt rushed or perhaps it was just that Brett did not like the fact that his ability to anticipate the moves of his associate had been thwarted.

Afternoon tea had arrived, a mountain of cakes and finger sandwiches into which Steve was tucking hungrily. Brett sat down without a word.

"It's a good table, relax. We can speak without being disturbed."

"If you say so." Brett was in no mood for risk-taking.

"Care for tea?" Steve was already pouring Brett a cup. He was almost jovial.

"Was it part of the plan?" Brett asked as calmly as he could muster. He so wished he could turn the plate of cakes onto the little rat's head.

"Which part of what plan?" Steve had wolfed down what must have been a coronation chicken sandwich going by the look of the yellow stains on his fingers. He wiped them on his napkin, scrunching it in the process.

Brett stopped Steve when he tried to finish pouring him tea. Afternoon tea was served with lemon. He waved at one of the waiters who was too busy serving a group of Asian women to notice.

Brett stood up, made his request known and came back to the table.

"I saw the pictures of Visconti's body." Brett had decided on another tack. His stomach felt queasy. He took a sip of tea, forgetting altogether about the lemon slice he was so eagerly awaiting.

He cleared his throat discreetly. MI6-Steve's face lost some of its glee. Brett had not mentioned this when reporting on his meeting with The Sheik. Steve put down the sandwich he had just grabbed.

"You should have said." It was not a reproach; an indication rather that MI6-Steve could have been better prepared. "And no, I didn't think The Sheik would show you the photos."

"Yes, well. I don't think I wanted to speak about it then. But this is not the reason we are here. As much as I dislike Crowne, I need to speak to you about him. And I find it easier to speak to you about him face to face." Brett took another mouthful of tea. He so wished they had met at the Club; he could have ordered a much-needed glass of whisky.

Steve bent forward. He would wait for Brett to be ready to tell his story. He had seen too many of these executions not to know the effect it would have on someone who saw a beheading for the first time – even in a photograph.

The slice of lemon arrived, a little slim but it would have to do. Brett refilled his cup, dropped the lemon into it and stirred.

Almost acceptable.

"You may not believe it, but in all my years dealing with these people, selling their looted artefacts and art pieces, I had never seen a Jihadi execution." Brett closed his fingers tightly over the handle of his cup.

"The slaughter of the kafir, the infidels." Brett stopped. The pictures materialised in front of his eyes. His stomach heaved. He brought his napkin to his lips for control.

"You don't need to give me the details," Steve said. "I have seen enough myself. I understand." He moved his glance away for a moment, stirred too by the dread the photos were meant to inspire.

"The question that matters now is why?"

"A warning." Brett tried to gather his thoughts. "I don't know why though. Everything has gone smoothly so far and," Brett stopped in mid-sentence. "You don't think they know about …?"

Steve shook his head.

"You would not have made it out alive otherwise, no matter how much they need you. And if they had wanted you to deliver something for them and then execute you, they would not have warned you."

"Right. Right."

"How much do you know about Visconti's business?" Steve asked.

"In my art business —" Brett started.

"You mean your trafficking business," Steve replied, glad of the diversion.

"No need to be crude." Brett frowned. "Visconti was known to be one of the best at supplying almost any piece his clients wanted. He was connected all over Europe, in particular Eastern Europe, the Middle-East, of course, and Asia."

"OK, so you know he was a crook who stole art from anyone but in particular from museums and war zones."

"Well, some of his thieving, as you call it, has saved some exceptional pieces from destruction."

Steve rolled his eyes. "Not going to argue with that one. What else?"

"It all went very badly when he was caught with a stolen piece from one of the best-known museums in Venice."

"And after that?"

"He escaped. But you know that already." Brett put the cup he was holding back on its saucer abruptly. "Then I assumed he had retired, but perhaps not." Brett pursed his lips in a dubious pout.

"Would he have started the old business again?"

"I don't think so." Brett wiped his mouth slowly. "There would have been a buzz in our community and my contacts would have told me."

"You've heard nothing?"

"Not a word." Brett felt genuinely puzzled. "Are you testing me?" He had no time for Steve's games.

"I'm not trying to trick you. Visconti was up to something, that much we know."

"What? The great MI6 lost track of a well-known art trafficker – shocking." Brett looked suitably distressed.

"No need to rub it in." Steve grumbled. "Not our pad anyway; we're not the National Crime Agency."

They both fell silent. The leftover sandwiches and cakes looked unappetising. Brett called for a fresh pot of tea.

"Still," Brett said, playing with his cigarette pack. "I don't understand why the photos."

"There is perhaps an explanation," Steve mused, toying with a piece of uneaten bread. "If Visconti worked for them and he did not deliver they may …"

"Ask me to deliver instead." Brett shook his head. "Shit, what have you dropped me into?" Swearing was not part of Brett's education but at that very moment he no longer cared. "Some crappy weapon deal, Lord knows?"

"Very possibly," Steve replied, his bulldog face more serious than ever.

"You mean, almost certainly,"

"Whatever you need, we can provide."

"Don't be ridiculous – you mean bodyguards, a bulletproof jacket and a change of identity?"

"Well, remember what we agreed."

"A clean slate to start again and a fat bank account. As long as I live long enough to enjoy it, which at the moment is starting to look rather unlikely."

"You don't know what The Sheik has in mind and Visconti didn't have the backing of MI6."

"So. Anything I need, hey?" Steve was onto something big and Brett could feel it. Brett waited.

"Fine," Steve grunted. "Anything you need."

Brett poured a fresh cup of tea. "I meet The Sheik again in a couple of days." He took a content sip.

"Glad to hear it." Steve poured himself another cup of tea in turn. "And to accompany this excellent cuppa, how about the topic that brought us here in the first place?"

Brett shot a dark eye at Steve. Did he really have to be such a tiresome arse?

"You mean Henry Crowne?" The name almost stuck in his throat.

"The very same." Steve grinned.

Chapter Eight

The library was empty, and today's librarian was taking his time, checking the cards he had taken out of the filing box. These showed the names of everyone who had either borrowed or returned a book.

Henry was sharing the job with a strange-looking man, thin as a wire, an equine profile and an unusually high forehead. The Doc had a reputation. He had been convicted for prematurely terminating the life of several of his patients; to him, euthanasia did not only apply to cats and dogs.

Yet, the Doc was incredibly well read and at times Henry almost forgot why he had been convicted in the first place.

Almost.

"Library shutting in fifteen," The Doc said, his nose still stuck in the cards.

"Just finishing a letter to my lawyer. Won't take five." Henry sat down in front of the computer and moved to the right screen.

The Doc raised one eye and finished replacing the cards in the box. He did not care what Henry was up to as long as it did not impact him.

Henry started typing on the keyboard. He had once more cracked the password that allowed him access to the Internet, access reserved only for the prison officers. The PC provided for inmates was designed to facilitate writing to their solicitors and other officials.

Two icons to choose from: a cat and a dog. The corny humour of assigning a cat to the cons and a dog to the officers still made Henry smile. Today he had clicked on the dog and the little pet had responded to its master's voice; Henry was in.

The password was complicated enough but Henry had taught himself to touch type. A skill he deemed essential for a man who prided himself on his quick and error free email replies.

Henry had also noticed that although the screen was shielded from viewers its reflection could be seen in the shiny surface of a steel cupboard behind it. He simply had to be patient and keep an eye on the guards' fingers when they typed. The password was changed fortnightly and Henry had kept up with the change.

He was searching for articles on Serious Fraud Office lawsuits. The SFO had had mixed success in prosecuting high-profile cases. The BAE Systems debacle must still have been rankling badly.

In 2004 the SFO had started litigating against the company for making illegal payments to government officials to win deals relating to armaments. It had made payments to several governments in Africa and the Middle-East.

The allegations covered payments handed over to an unnamed Saudi official in relation to the £40 billion al-Yamamah arms deal between the UK and Saudi Arabia. However, the case had been dropped after the UK government argued the enquiry might upset the UK–Saudi relationship and threaten national security.

BAE paid a record UK fine of £30 million in 2010, "for failing to keep reasonably accurate accounting records relating to its activities." The SFO confirmed there would be no further prosecutions, including of the individuals identified in the fraud. BAE had taken measures to implement a better ethical and compliance culture.

Henry smiled a knowing smile. Could any arms deal be done without a large backhander? He doubted it, or perhaps he was too cynical. Henry continued reading.

The US Department of Justice had also pursued BAE and had received almost the entire amount of the final fine – over £400 million. Well done the prosecutors of the DOJ, Henry thought. The conclusion of the case had not ended well for the previous SFO director, Robert Wardle, who had narrowly escaped being charged with perverting the course of justice.

Henry looked at the clock on the wall. He did not have enough time left to finish his research. The Vincent and Robert Tchenguiz case looked embarrassing, but the discovery of its details would have to wait.

"The SFO needs to score," Henry murmured.

The Doc pushed his chair back noisily. It was time to leave. Henry closed the article he was reading, erased his browsing history, printed the letter he was supposedly writing.

One of the prison officers had arrived and was doing a circuit of the library. He checked what Henry had printed without reading it, a quick glance showed it was harmless. Henry left slowly. Bang-up time would start shortly, an hour back in his cell, followed by free time for dinner and then lock-up for the rest of the night.

Henry's mind was buzzing despite his nonchalant pace. He had to mine the SFO story further. He had also started browsing Panama in the hope he would find snippets of information telling him what the interest was in this particular fiscal paradise.

But nothing obvious had come up. He knew the place well from numerous trips and had looked up the name of the law firm he had worked with there in the past, Mossack Fonseca. There was nothing relevant on their website apart from the usual corporate ads detailing how easy their shell companies were to set up and maintain.

Henry left the long corridor that led from the library. Another officer was waiting for him whilst the first guard was locking up. He found himself in the common room where the inmates socialised during the day.

They were allowed twelve hours outside of their cells, not a bad ratio. Henry slowed his pace further, scanning the perimeter for troublemakers. To his relief Kray was not around. Big K had also disappeared and so had Kamal.

Perfect timing.

He did not want to have to face anyone, including Big K. No matter how much he enjoyed the banter with the Jamaican giant, Henry needed to put down on paper what he had learned. Try to find a pattern and get an angle, anticipate why the SFO sought his expertise.

It had worked superbly well in the LIBOR manipulation case. He just needed to pull another similar trick out of his hat and he would get closer to his goal.

The door clanged shut behind him and Henry felt almost free in his cell. His heart had not sunk as it usually did at the sound of the bolts closing, a regular reminder of where he was. In one step he reached the little table he called his desk. The word gave him hope that when he sat down at it he could still produce work worthy of that name. He pulled a pad from underneath some books and started writing.

A list of all the countries he had used to structure complex transactions: Europe, the US, Asia, as well as all the small jurisdictions that offered legal advantages. Nothing ever illegal when working in banking.

But a clever understanding of the differences in the laws of each place had allowed him to take advantage of discrepancies. There was however one noticeable exception – he placed a star next to the place he had used for structuring the funds and accounts the IRA once used.

Now those were illegal – good old-fashioned money laundering. His hand stiffened and he stopped. There it was, in black and white, his commitment to what he thought had been his father's cause. He put his pen down for a moment.

The pain of betrayal surged into him like a tidal wave, threatening to drown him. He pressed his hands over his trembling thighs and the spasm going through his body eased off. It had become easier not to succumb, to let the feelings course through him and then be released.

Was it the passage of time or the faith in the plan he was meticulously pulling together?

Perhaps both.

The plan was shaping up as he had hoped it would. The word that had been haunting him no longer felt fantasy but reality.

He would escape the most secure prison in the UK: HSU Belmarsh.

* * *

Low tide on the River Thames had dropped the waterline of its banks. Nancy had walked for a while along the path that led to the water's edge. It was not a route she knew well nor one that would take her back to the safety of her apartment. Pole had been full of attention. She had never felt surrounded by so much kindness and, dare she say it – love. He had patiently waited for her to tell the story of her father, questioning seldom but always with tact.

Nancy leaned towards the water, her forearms resting on the stone wall. The colour of the Thames had turned icy grey, the swells within it giving the river an occasional silvery glimmer. She pulled up the collar of her coat and fished out from its pockets the gloves she had forgotten to put on.

She had allowed Pole to jot down a few notes, mainly dates and names. Early memories of her childhood in China – the visits to her mother's family in the UK, their escape during the Cultural Revolution since her father had become one of the artists the Chinese government wanted to "re-educate" – had come flooding back.

"I never speak about it," Nancy had said to Pole.

"In your own time." Pole had extended his strong but elegant hand, wrapping it around Nancy's fingers and she had almost cried. She was not yet ready for this ultimate show of trust.

"My father left us – after almost ten years in Paris." Nancy had taken a gulp of tea to dissolve the lump that had swollen in her throat.

"You mean he left to go back to China after the Cultural Revolution was over?" Pole had helped by putting it into words for her.

"That's right. He had great hopes for China once Deng Xiaoping took over." Nancy struggled to continue, and Pole pressed her hand gently again. Nancy squeezed back so hard she thought she might hurt him.

"I'm sorry," she said releasing Pole's hand and withdrawing in shame. Pole captured her wrist loosely.

"It will take a lot more than a tight pinch to hurt a well-weathered DCI like me." His smile was reassuring, his eyes a mixture of affection and gentle tease.

Nancy groaned. "I have to know, Jonathan." She raised her wounded eyes towards him. "Oh God, sorry. I am not very good at giving you the right background."

"This is not a Scotland Yard case. It is you and one of the most important events …" Pole's voice trailed off.

"I need to know whether he is still alive," Nancy had spoken quickly. She felt exhausted. She let her body drop back into the small sofa she had been sitting on. For a moment she closed her eyes and when she reopened them Pole had moved next to her. She rested her head against his shoulder and for a while there was nothing left to say. Pole's BlackBerry buzzed and he sent the call to voicemail with a click. Nancy straightened up slowly.

"I need to gather some proper information for you. I have an old file." Her voice still sounded uncertain. Pole's phone rang again, another click. He would not be rushed. Nancy managed a smile and gently cupped his cheek with her hand.

"The great DCI Jonathan Pole is needed."

Pole kissed the palm of her hand and returned her smile.

"I am sure they can wait a little longer."

Nancy had sighed. "Thank you."

Nancy was now on her own. She turned her back away from the river. She leaned against the wall, facing the Globe theatre. She wondered whether she was right to dig up the past. Her father had left France for China in the early eighties. He had written a few letters but then silence. Whenever he wrote it had always been about the new government, hope for the future, the artist's role at the centre of the people's revolution. He never asked about her, never wished her mother, his wife, well.

The anger sizzled within her. She would not surrender to it though, not any more. Still, she was unsure what the result of a confrontation with reality would be. She thought about Henry. His own anger had led him to where he was, a grubby prison cell and a thirty-year sentence to go with it. Could it have been her?

Perhaps.

She had, after all, worked with the famous Jacques Vergès when he had defended Klaus Barbie for crimes against humanity. He had called her back when he was hoping to mount the defence of Saddam Hussein.

A vicious gust of wind made Nancy shiver. It was time to head home. She decided to leave the heart-aching questions for another day. Another case demanded her attention and she was glad of it.

* * *

"Slow down." Pole broke into a slow jog towards the lift doors on the ground floor of Scotland Yard, pressing his mobile against his ear "I'll be with you in less than five minutes."

Andy had received news from the Counterterrorist Squad and Commander Ferguson was agitated. He had delivered the information to Pole's DS as, "the Inspector was nowhere to be bloody seen," quoting the man verbatim.

Pole did not regret the time spent with Nancy. He had devoted enough years to The Met; his personal life, for once, would come first. Andy was pacing outside and almost rushed into the lift as Pole walked out.

"That important, hey." He could never be cross with Andy, who was sometimes puppy-like but so goddamn bright.

"Ferguson says that the material used for the bomb underneath Phelps' car matches the Paddington bomb."

"Let's go into my office." Pole pushed the BlackBerry deep into his pocket. Perhaps he should have answered the call after all.

They both walked in silence. Pole closed the door of his office and sat behind the desk. Andy moved the pile of documents occupying the only other chair in the room and sat down.

"OK, what do we know?"

"Ferguson is categorical. Same components used for the Paddington bomb. The one that almost killed Henry Crowne—" Andy stopped abruptly. Pole knew all about the bomb that had exploded near the train station four years ago. He had been called to the scene as it had just happened and witnessed the carnage it had left behind.

"Two possibilities," Pole said. "Either the same person built the bomb, or we have the same explosives supplier." Pole started playing with a large paper clip he had found on the floor. This was not the news he wanted to hear.

"Ferguson's conclusion exactly."

Pole remained silent. Loose connections were coming together forming a web of improbable links. The bomb that had targeted Mark Phelps the SFO witness, the explosion that had almost cost Henry his life and Henry being dragged out of Belmarsh to work on the SFO case. What of the Islington canal execution?

"Guv." Andy was waving tentatively.

"Sorry, just thinking…" Pole didn't yet have a theory. "Never mind, I need more time to elaborate. What does Ferguson want to do next?"

"He would like to speak to you about Mark Phelps and the witness protection programme."

"Has he spoken to Marissa Campbell?"

"No, he wants to speak to you first."

Pole was about to call Ferguson, his hand hovering over the phone.

"How about Visconti links to the Middle-East? What did old Grandel say?"

Andy looked lost for a second. "You mean —" as if answering his own question, he carried on. "DCI Grandel confirmed that Visconti was very well connected with a number of looters in the Middle-East. Well-known terrorists raising money by selling artefacts – particularly in Iraq."

"Does Grandel think that could be a motive? One of his deals going wrong?"

"Not sure, Guv. Visconti was arrested in Italy and had been serving time until he escaped."

"How long did he serve?"

"A year and a bit."

"Hardly any time then. Was he caught for trafficking Middle-Eastern pieces?"

"No, he tried to organise the theft of a well-known painting in one of the main museums in Venice. He managed to steal it but got caught with it in his possession.

"DCI Grandel thinks the buyer got cold feet because of the publicity and Visconti didn't have time to shift the piece before the police found him."

Pole sat back in his chair. Was the old link between Visconti and the Middle-East relevant or was he trying too hard?

"And does Grandel think Visconti tried to reconnect with his previous contacts?"

"That is his assumption. Visconti was sighted in Geneva shortly after he escaped and then nothing."

"Good work. Keep digging. What about INTERPOL?"

"Nothing yet."

Chapter Nine

A distant sound of locks opening, the cell flooded with light.

"Hello Mr Crowne." The voice was far away. Henry could not quite place it. He squinted into the harsh neon light overhead.

"Hello Mr Crowne; you don't mind if we check your cell, do you?"

Henry rolled over on his side, threw the sheet and blanket to the bottom of the mattress in a slow and uncertain move. He swung his muscular legs over the edge of his diminutive bed.

"Sure," he mumbled, rubbing his eyes.

It was a good sign. The governor of HMP Belmarsh had decided, once more, to allow him outside the compound; the downside – impromptu checks of his cell.

Henry had undergone a few of these searches when he had been asked to assist Pole and Nancy on the murder enquiry linked to the LIBOR scandal. He was ready for what came next.

However, one of the new prison officers on his wing was keen to show he could do the job to an exacting standard and Henry had been a little anxious – all right, very anxious. His small art piece, his netsuke, could have got him into real trouble and, worse, it would have cost Nancy a lot too. But no one had outsmarted Henry Crowne on that day. Complacency meant mistakes and he was not about to let himself down by being smug. Gone were the days of investment banking.

His legal file marked in bold letters LEGAL & PRIVILEGED was sitting on his desk. An irresistible decoy for any prison officer worthy of the name.

The three guards moved noisily. Henry stood up and donned his tracksuit bottoms. He moved to the head of his bed, waiting for instructions.

John, a short stocky man, was in charge. Not a bad chap, but all officers appointed to HSU Belmarsh were discouraged from befriending inmates. No small talk, which Henry regretted.

He had always been good at it, creating an atmosphere of trust in which people enjoyed working. He had struck the right tone, though, courteous without being obsequious, but detached. He did not seem to want anything from anybody.

The file did the trick. Officer number two, tall and wiry, a man whose name he did not know, was already moving towards the desk. He had been brought in on the task from another wing within HSU. Henry waited a few more seconds before protesting.

"Hey, that is a privileged document," he said raising his voice.

"So you say," the tall man replied. He had picked up the file from the desk, not opening it but threatening to.

"That's the law and I know my rights," Henry replied, crossing his arms over his chest.

The other guards had stopped searching. No one wanted a confrontation. John took the document away from the other officer, looking at the outside before putting it down again. "It's the same one I saw last time we searched."

"And the one I take when I see my legal representative."

The search resumed. Henry cursed himself. He should have pulled back a little. The guards were now moving around his bookshelf. Some books were opened and thumbed, then came the turn of the heavy art book that hid the netsuke.

The spine cracked. Henry held his breath. The guards would have to look into the spine to see the little bundle and even if they did the small clump looked like paper.

"You like your art don't you, Henry?" John asked. He was still perusing the book, looking through the images.

"Are you saying I could start a collection?" Henry shot back. Shit, what am I saying? he thought. A small film of perspiration formed at the back of his neck. Henry tried to look amused. He hoped the sudden tension in his body would not betray him. John kept going through the pictures. The sound of an object dropping on the floor almost made Henry jump. His legal file had been left on the side of his desk and it had now fallen to the floor, its contents lying on the ground.

Henry almost burst into laughter. It had all been about this goddamn file after all.

"Sorry," the tall officer said with a grin, already gathering the papers together. Henry moved towards them quickly. "I'll do it." He knelt and bunched the papers together in a disjointed move, pushed them into the folder and hugged it to his chest. He looked suitably annoyed and the guards took note.

An excellent decoy indeed.

Any information worth remembering he would never store on paper but rather in a place no one else could access – his brain.

The search lasted another ten minutes. The art book had been left on his chair, pushed around every time the officers moved to access another part of his cell. Henry's back was now resting against the wall, his eyes in the distance.

He forced himself not to look at the book precariously balanced on the seat. One of the guards bumped into the chair and this time the book almost fell. John caught it with one hand. "I wouldn't want your collection to get damaged." Henry felt the punch in the gut.

Had John guessed?

The officer threw the book onto his desk, gave the other two a nod.

"Very funny," Henry managed to mumble.

He collapsed on his bed as soon as they had left and did not move. What if they came back? His cell was a mess and he was now fully awake. He waited in complete stillness for a while.

Finally, he stretched and a small bubble of contentment burst in his chest. The decoy had worked. Wheels were in motion and he was once more allowed outside HSU Belmarsh. Kamal would be aware of it and yet Henry was not entirely sure what the other man's plans would be. Would he attempt to escape at the same time as Henry? What Henry was sure of was that Kamal and his group wanted him for his knowledge of banking and finance. He had built an impenetrable maze of companies and bank accounts for the IRA. The money that had been taken to finance the IRA decommissioning had never been found and its origins would remain unknown for ever. Someone with such capabilities was invaluable to a new ambitious Jihadi splinter group.

Henry started tidying his room. It did not take long and once done he sat on the floor, back against the wall, knees to his chest. He dropped his head back, resting. The last piece of the puzzle was still missing. What if it never came?

Henry groaned. He must trust his instinct. It would. It had to.

Henry did not believe in coincidences. Kamal Al Quatari known under his battle name as Abu Maeraka had been transferred to HSU Belmarsh on Henry's wing the minute he had been found guilty of terrorism.

There were three wings in HSU but the man who had almost cost Henry his life had been transferred to his wing. Henry's jaw tightened. He pushed away the images that were trying to force their way into his mind.

The smell of burning petrol filled his lungs. He stood up abruptly. He needed to walk away from the scene. He took off his T-shirt and, lying on the ground, he started a series of press-ups: thirty, fifty, one hundred.

Henry collapsed face down. His heart pumping in his chest, his throat on fire. He turned on his back and let the cool surface of the floor calm him down. It helped. The images of Paddington receded. The bomb exploding near the police van that was taking him for questioning had been the turning point he needed. The driver of the police van had died and his colleague had been trapped in the vehicle. Henry had not had the courage to help.

He sat up, grabbed his T-shirt and wiped the sweat from his face and his body. He bunched up the garment into a ball and threw it into the corner of the cell. He knew why he had joined the IRA.

He had wanted to believe his father belonged. Wasn't it better to think he had died a partisan's death rather than a drunk's? Liam and Bobby had given him a sense of belonging. And perhaps their cause had been just, but nothing justified the killing of innocents.

Nothing.

Henry walked to his washbasin and ran his hands underneath the cold water. Whose blood was he trying to cleanse? He splashed his face, moved his fingers through his greying hair. Atonement would only come one way.

A life for a life.

The thought pacified him somewhat. After the months of agony during his trial and the early days at Belmarsh a glimmer of hope had emerged. A flicker of light he had learned to kindle.

His need for redemption had astounded him. He had realised he would never be fully forgiven for what he had done but he could perhaps show he could be a better person. The plan he had slowly elaborated was bold, perhaps as bold as the one that had brought him down four years ago. But unlike the man who had wrecked Henry's future, Henry was willing to risk his life and face death. The lies and manipulation that had sent him to prison had only been devious at best.

Henry lay down on his bed again. He had a couple of hours before breakfast. And he needed a sharp mind for what was coming next.

* * *

The piece of toast popped out of the toaster with a small mechanical click. The smell of warm bread made Brett's mouth water. He started buttering his toast and checked the tea had brewed long enough. He opened a jar of his favourite marmalade. It was all looking appetising and yet something essential was missing, a butler.

Brett could not help smiling at his own delusions of grandeur – gone were the days of *Downtown Abbey*, an absolute tragedy. He moved to his lounge, placed the buttered toast on the table and activated the screen of his laptop, special edition, MI6 encrypted.

Steve had sent additional information that might help him with The Sheik's request. Brett had acquired a reputation for gathering information and in particular information of a sensitive nature on his clients. It had helped him to cut deals, to know their tastes and how far they would go for a piece they truly desired.

The Sheik wanted everything Brett had on Henry Crowne. Brett had looked a little puzzled but he was not prepared to argue after having been shown Visconti's pictures. He had assured The Sheik he would do his very best. It was a balancing act, neither too much nor too little or his own head would be next.

The file was extensive and Brett was surprised. This was not a last-minute cobbling together of information. It had taken time, perhaps years, to gather. Some parts were blanked out. Still Brett could see considerable effort had been used in finding out who Henry Crowne truly was.

Brett bit into his toast, white of course, none of that wholemeal rubbish. The idea of delving into Crowne's life rather changed his mood.

The family history was unexpected. A mixed marriage forty years ago in Belfast was unheard of. There had been speculation about Henry's father's IRA affiliation. It looked likely despite the lack of evidence. The puzzlement was Henry's father's marriage to a British woman.

Perhaps it was a cover-up. Henry's father's death attributed to a UVF assassination reinforced the idea. This part of the document was heavily redacted, and Brett's curiosity was piqued. Steve might one day indulge him.

Brett kept reading.

As for Henry, outstanding academic results, a move to London with a career in law then investment banking – a UK bank, a Swiss bank and finally GL, one of the most successful American banks before the 2008 crisis. Brett hated to admit it, but Henry was a very clever man.

Then entered Brett Allner-Smith, his good self, into Henry's life. All the pieces of art and antiquities he had sold to Henry – listed, with prices, provenance whether legal or illegal. Brett felt almost nostalgic. But not quite.

Henry was only an Irish peasant trying to look the part. He chuckled at the news that Henry had taken elocution lessons to rid himself of his Belfast accent. And yet Brett could never forgive Henry for leading him straight into the claws of MI6. Brett poured some fresh tea. The little coward had recanted on a deal involving a stolen Iraqi artefact that had almost cost Brett his life.

Brett had offered Crowne, the man whose deals earned him millions in bonuses, an exceptional piece, a piece every museum would want to own. Henry had been keen; so many of these pieces went missing. It was almost his duty to salvage one of them. Brett had been cautious to start with but eventually trusted Henry's desire to own something no one else could. At the eleventh-hour Henry got cold feet.

"One million dollars," Brett said aloud. It was the sum he owed his Al-Qaeda contacts for the artefact and these people did not accept credit.

Brett drank his tea and pondered. Now Crowne was in prison and he, Brett, was involved in a potentially lethal operation that far exceeded his appetite for risk. No time to feel sorry for himself though; if he played his cards right he would escape the clutches of MI6 and the money he had made would go a long way towards restoring his past standing.

Brett resumed his reading. The dossier was now dealing with Henry's involvement in money laundering for the IRA. The fund structure Henry had used had never been completely uncovered, essential pieces of the puzzle were missing and by the looks of it Crowne had not been willing to cooperate.

Brett read through all the documents in one sitting. He kept sipping his tea and whenever his cup ran dry he poured more without stopping his reading. It was riveting and almost – creative. He put his cup down and started putting together a sheet of information for The Sheik. The Sheik would be impressed. He pulled towards him the notepad that already lay on the table and started writing.

Out of nowhere the images of Visconti's body resurfaced. He stood up, feeling giddy. Brett leaned forward against the table. The moment passed.

Never feel complacent; that was the only way to stay alive.

* * *

The black and white photos had turned yellow around the edges. An elegant young man in a three-piece suit, yet sporting a Chairman Mao collar shirt, a young woman with long dark hair, a short dress with broad stripes and insert pockets that interrupted the lines – she could remember the dress, she thought.

Both are all smiles. He has wrapped his arm around the young woman's shoulders and she has her hands on the shoulders of a little girl called Nancy. Nancy turned over the photo and looked at the date. By then her parents had left China as the Cultural Revolution was biting hard.

They had just arrived in Europe after months of travelling through the Chinese countryside to escape the communist regime and finally reached Hong Kong, then France. Nancy shuddered. She had kept very little that could remind her of that era but somehow this faded picture of three happy people had been hard to let go of.

She had gathered together the few documents she had kept that related to her father. She adjusted her dressing gown, drawing it tighter. Her hands were freezing despite the pleasant temperature of her apartment.

She was still somewhat puzzled by her renewed desire to find her father. It had started a few years ago when she had decided to give up the law after a remarkably successful career as a QC. She paused at the thought. Any regrets?

None whatsoever.

Having more time to think about the direction of her life had perhaps allowed her to let her true emotional needs emerge or perhaps her aversion to being attached despite the keen attraction she felt for Pole had caught up with her.

She could no longer argue that her busy job was taking her away from possible relationships or that men do not like to date a woman of keen intellect in a position of power. Her intellect was certainly intact, but she had become a philanthropist, patron of the arts and collector. Nothing very scary about that.

Nancy moved to the kitchen, a modern and aesthetic space – wood, steel and stone – with plenty of room to cook and enjoy a gathering of friends or entertain a single person. She smiled at the memory of her first dinner "*en tête à tête*" with Jonathan Pole, both a little nervous and both trying to be humorous about it.

The gurgling of the kettle was interrupted by a sharp click. It snapped Nancy out of her reverie and she started preparing a fresh pot of tea. She always took pleasure in this simple ritual but today it had become a little less enjoyable.

She saw her mother, so very English yet so very carefree, making the same gestures. But this time the attractive young man of the photo has disappeared. Her mother looks tired, sleep deprived through lack of news. Silence tearing at her soul every day. The ghost of her father floating over them both since his departure for China, ever since the letters he had promised stopped coming.

By then Nancy had decided to push memories of her father away, push them to a place they could no longer be reached and could no longer hurt. Nancy, the rebel who dissented as a matter of course at The Sorbonne, was merely dealing with her loss.

She knew that now more clearly than she had known then. But she also understood that her indecision, her reluctance to commit to a man, was rooted in this pain she had ignored for so long.

Nancy was back in her lounge. She was drinking tea. She didn't quite know how she had got there.

A few months ago she had almost lost her life and the chance to respond to Pole's affection. Her stomach tightened at the thought.

"It is time." She must move on. It was somehow ironic though. She, who had been so instrumental in helping Henry come to terms with the rage that had almost destroyed him, was now on the same journey. Harrowing, laborious but worthwhile.

She hoped.

Nancy returned to the photo, the old documents; she started on her yellow notepad to do what she had done best all her life, to ask the hard questions.

Chapter Ten

A crust had started to form on his bowl of porridge. He laid the tray carefully on his small desk, opened the salt sachet and sprinkled it over his breakfast. He always preferred eating porridge the Scottish way.

He began eating, taking his time. Henry had rarely eaten in his cell since he had made contact with Kamal. He was careful not to break the pattern of his daily routine. Anything out of the ordinary would attract the attention of the prison officers. Today was different. He was once more allowed outside HSU. The guards would understand he might not wish to show his excitement or apprehension to the other inmates.

Kamal would also know that Henry was on his way to Scotland Yard. He had assured Henry that, God willing, he would organise an escape. Henry's goal had been set. Even if his outings became a regular occurrence he would never feel he had given enough until his life was in danger.

Henry finished the porridge, moved to his bed and sat down cross-legged with his mug of tea. He had expected Kamal to have a crack at the rhetoric about "the fight", "the Jihad", but he had been remarkably silent.

He had simply demonstrated to Henry how other Muslim inmates were devoted to him. One of them was sent to the box, a room with nothing inside apart from a Perspex window, for instigating a fight. A couple of other inmates had tasted the segregation unit, a place where prisoners spent at least twenty-three hours in their cells every day, for breaking HSU rules. Kamal or Abu Maeraka, always affable, always discreet, was slowly building his army within HSU and perhaps outside.

Henry suspected that the guards were not fooled by his manners but knew could they do nothing about someone who was polite and did not seem to cause trouble. He was a true leader of the kind that inspired total devotion.

Henry had mentioned the Qur'an, after finding the small book in his cell. It had been clever to say nothing beforehand, to let Henry wonder why it had been put there. "You might want to understand how my brothers think," had been Kamal's reply when Henry had questioned him about it. It was unobtrusive and clever. Would Henry be asked to join the faith once he was outside?

Henry drained his cup. He pushed the thought aside. For now, he needed to anticipate what Kamal had in mind for their escape.

He had never entered a deal in his City banking life without having the upper hand or at least without having an ace up his sleeve. This situation was different though, more fluid. He needed to think on his feet, to be prepared for all eventualities and also to be physically ready.

He had trained his mind ruthlessly for more than twenty years in investment banking and on the trading floor. Today he would train his body, pushing himself to the limit alongside Big K. Henry might even regret leaving Big K behind.

Henry stood up, grabbed a small towel which he slung over his well-developed shoulders and walked out of his cell. His porridge would give him plenty of energy since, after all, it was a decent breakfast.

"What's happened to your taste buds?" Henry murmured with a sigh. Gone were the days when he would have returned a boiled egg to the kitchen because it was not cooked to perfection. Henry prepared himself to run the gauntlet of the gates he had to cross before arriving at the gym. He would be frisked a few times in the process. Nothing so strenuous ever happened in a standard prison compound, even on the Category A wing, which housed the most dangerous criminals. But this was HSU Belmarsh and no measures were spared to ensure maximum control over the inmates.

Henry entered the gym where Big K had already started his routine. He had his back turned against the wall facing the door. Henry had never thought about it before but realised now that none of the machines had their backs turned to the door – so no one could sneak up from behind.

Big K was in full swing. The rowing machine was moaning under the strain of his efforts. Henry set himself up a couple of machines away, arranging the weights tray. He added to the set left behind by a previous inmate. Henry stretched against the wall and when he was done started exercising. One of the officers at the far end of the room observed them for a moment, then looked elsewhere.

"Not at breakfast this morning?" Big K asked as he slowed down the pace.

"Nope, felt like a little bit of privacy in my deluxe three by nine suite." Henry replied as he pushed hard on the traction bars.

"You're out again?" Big K slowed down a little more, the machine now purring comfortably.

Henry exhaled loudly. "Can't hide anything from you."

"Lucky bastard, man; you're gonna breathe some proper fresh air." Big K shook his head.

Henry smiled. "You mean the shitty fumes of the van that's going to take me to the Yard and the crappy air of the crappy room in which they are going to squeeze me?"

"At least that's proper kinda pollution, right?"

"As opposed to what?" Henry pressed on the traction bars harder and heard the weights hit the top of the machine.

"The BO of all the guys who don't shower after exercise. Man, I don't get it; show some respect." Big K replaced the handlebar in its holder, wiped the sweat from his face and drank from the plastic cup he had brought with him.

The guard looked in their direction again. Big K had moved towards the wall at the back of Henry's machine and started stretching.

"Any news about Ronnie Kray?" Henry asked before his next move.

"Zippo. He's been unusually quiet after he tried to piss you off. Think John had a chat with him." Big K groaned as he changed legs. "That guy is a real nut job – unpredictable, know what I mean?"

Henry started quick repetitions, pumping hard and unable to reply.

"Got news on Kamal." Big K was almost hesitant.

Henry squeezed the traction bar and pulled a couple more times on the weights. "What's the word on the street?"

"You know he was transferred straightaway to HSU after being sentenced?"

The officer stood up and started walking around the room. Henry replaced the traction bar. He added to the weights tray again and restarted his routine.

His muscles screamed under the pressure. The guard walked past them and returned to his seat. Henry stood up, walking behind the back of Big K's machine to start stretching. "And?" he said, running the towel over his face.

"Kamal got busy during his trial." Big K detached every syllable, "Radicalisation."

"You mean he radicalised some of the other detainees?"

"Yup. And he got others to do it too, recruiting guys like you and me." Big K paused. "The guy is real bad news, man."

"Thanks for the tip." Henry was almost at the end of his weights routine. "How do you know that anyway?"

"'Cos he got his guys in the main prison units and so have I."

Big K had moved away from the machines for a final set of stretches. He was clocking up a lot of goodwill which he would want to cash in sometime. Nothing came for free. But if Henry was smart enough, he would be out of here before he found out what Big K's price was.

* * *

The police officers at the door checked her ID, three of them, wearing body armour, heavy weaponry and earpieces plugged in.

They looked the part and Marissa was almost reassured. She walked into Mark Phelps' parents' home. Another police officer, a middle-aged woman this time, in civilian clothes, greeted her. Mark and his children had been moved to the back of the house. The terraced property in Holland Park was not dissimilar to the one Mark had just left. After the explosion the house had been boarded up and forensic specialists were still working their way through the crime scene.

The smell of cooking surprised Marissa and it made her mouth water: a mixture of vanilla with a hint of cinnamon, her favourite spices. Someone was preparing comfort food for a family in distress. Marissa gingerly entered a spacious room, photos in different shapes of frame on every shelf. Mark was sitting on the sofa with his arms wrapped around his children, huddling together in silence. The pieces of cake that had been placed in front of them were barely touched. Marissa stopped, her imposing frame intruding on their intimacy.

"Hello Marissa," Mark said in a tired voice, his face still partially bandaged and his bruises shading from yellow to blue.

"Hello Mark," Marissa took one step forward, undecided. "If this is not a good time ..."

"It won't be a good time for years to come," Mark replied. He kissed his girl and his boy of the top of the head. "Come on guys, perhaps you could check whether grandma needs your help."

The little girl wriggled away but the young boy clung to his dad even tighter.

"We'll watch a Disney movie a bit later. OK, big guy?" His son nodded and slid off the couch, fingers still stuck in his mouth.

Mark's mother appeared in the doorway. She brought Marissa a cup of tea and poured a fresh cup for her son. She gently squeezed his shoulder and as she turned away he squeezed her hand in return.

"Any news?" Mark asked as he was taking a sip of his tea.

"Nothing new yet, I'm afraid. At least nothing that's been communicated to me." Marissa sat down in the armchair closest to him.

"You said someone would help with the case." Mark shifted a cushion that no longer felt comfortable against his back.

"That's right. A woman called Nancy Wu; someone I know and respect hugely. She is a former QC. She practised criminal law for years and has a lot of experience in white-collar crime." Marissa would not mention Nancy's representation of war criminals. Why muddy the waters?

"Her name sounds familiar," Mark said. "How do you know her?"

"I was her pupil when I trained as a barrister."

Mark nodded. Marissa was expecting more questions but instead he closed his eyes and let his head rest against the back of the settee.

Marissa waited. Perhaps it was too soon. She put down her cup silently. Mark opened his eyes again.

"Mark?" Marissa moved her body forward as much as she could, whispering.

"Mmm?"

"I have to ask." Marissa inhaled. "Are you certain you want to carry on with the case?"

Mark arched his unbandaged eyebrow in surprise. "I would have thought that the SFO would be very happy."

"Of course, the director is ecstatic, but I am not the director and I will support you in whatever you decide to do." Marissa's face was smooth and open. She meant what she said.

"I don't think I will change my mind, Marissa, but thank you for giving me space." Mark moved his body again trying to find a more comfortable position. "Besides, they will crucify you if they learn you haven't secured my participation."

"That's my problem." Marissa tightened her mouth, determined.

Mark ran his hand mechanically over his bandages. "Unless you're not confident of a successful prosecution."

"No, it's not that," Marissa interrupted, placing a hand on the sofa next to Mark. "I will fight for this, believe me, but I will not push you to do what you do not want to do."

Mark nodded.

"Anyway, maybe it's time for me to go back to where I come from."

"Barbados."

Marissa smiled, a beautiful broad grin that shone like the sun of her own country.

"Don't you have family in the UK though?"

"Oh yes; some of them arrived in 1948. Have you heard about the Windrush generation?"

"Should I have?"

"Don't worry, not many people have unless they're part of that community or deal with immigration issues for those who didn't think it necessary to have papers. The policy of the current Home Secretary, Theresa May, means there's a hostile environment."

"Tell me." Mark winced as he moved forward to replace his cup on the table. Marissa hesitated but then why not? It was an important part of the UK's history that was seldom talked about.

Marissa spoke about the first wave of people from the Caribbean who had arrived after the Second World War to help rebuild the country. The first boat that carried them was called HMT *Empire Windrush*. It was the beginning of waves of immigration between 1948 and 1971.

With the continuing labour shortage in the UK many of them settled. "Many of those people have been here for decades, have families. But, unfortunately, often have no official papers."

"Surely, they must be entitled to something?"

"Strictly speaking, no – unless they have applied successfully for leave to stay." Mark was about to question her again. "A story for another time." Marissa smiled.

"Will you find someone on the banking side to help with the case? You said you would since it is important." Mark asked after a moment.

Marissa froze. Until now she had not thought about it, but how could she explain to Mark that the man about to work with him on the SFO case had been condemned for financial terrorism?

"We are looking at options," was the best Marissa could think of, off the cuff. Not entirely false. Crowne had not been confirmed yet. She would work out later how to break the news to Mark.

* * *

With a croissant stuck in his mouth, a cup of coffee in one hand and a couple of files under his arm, Andy was struggling to retrieve his pass from his trouser pocket.

A hand holding an ID materialised in front of him and Pole opened the door of the large open-plan room in which his team worked. Andy shook his head and mumbled something that sounded like thank you.

Pole rolled his eyes and smiled. "Have your breakfast, then we can talk."

Pole moved to his desk, dumped his mac on a pile of documents, sat down and booted up his computer. He was expecting results from forensics yet anticipated no surprises. He picked up the phone and dialled Yvonne's number.

"Analysis confirmed," Yvonne said by way of greeting.

"Blimey, bad day already?" If Yvonne was abrupt, something was up.

"A partial set of prints is giving me trouble."

"Relevant to my case?"

"Possibly, I'll tell you tomorrow – and don't ask me whether I have run them through IDENT1."

"I wouldn't dream of it," Pole teased. No point in badgering Yvonne further.

Andy had materialised in front of the desk, his files still under his arm and a few crumbs of croissant scattered on his pullover.

"Good news, Guv," he said moving files from the chair that stood in front of Pole's desk so he could sit down. Pole extended a hand and took the files from his DS. "That would be useful as we have nothing new from forensics."

"Eugene, I mean DCI Grandel —" Andy grew a little pink and Pole laughed. "Don't worry, half of the force calls him by his first name. A couple more meetings and he will ask you to call him Uggie." Andy nodded and carried on in a rush of words.

"Well, the thing that is interesting about Visconti and his trafficking is that he uses – I mean he used to use – the Libyan route."

Pole pulled a face. "OK, backtrack a little."

"Yes, sorry Guv. I've been wondering who and where his connections were in the Middle-East and how he would go about doing his smuggling." Andy waited, his large glasses almost down to the tip of his nose.

"Don't hold back. This sounds good."

"Visconti knew his way around and he had never had trouble smuggling art before."

Pole nodded to indicate he was listening.

"Then he gets killed – worse, it's a proper barbaric slaughter. So there is a message, a message really worth sending to whoever."

Pole moved his chair to get closer to his desk. "You think it's got nothing to do with art."

"Exactly." Andy clicked his fingers. "What if he decided to change tack. He'd been burnt on the art scene with his arrest. He was done on the art market front but ..." Andy's face had turned pink again and the dimples in his cheeks made him look mischievous.

"He has a trafficking route he can use."

"Maybe he tried to find another market, using that route?"

"Keep going."

"If he knows the Libyan route well because it's the one he's used for years, perhaps he wants to be part of the other trafficking that happens on that route.

"Don't you think he would have known he was going to piss off the other traffickers?"

"But maybe he was desperate or —" Andy smiled. "He had a new source from a different place?"

"You mean not coming from Africa? I assume I am right in saying that Libya is mainly used for trafficking out of that continent."

"I'll check it out."

"But you already have an idea about the alternative "market" don't you?" Pole stopped fidgeting with his BlackBerry.

"My guess – either drugs or armaments." Andy waited for the effect the last word would have on his boss.

"Armaments? You mean supplying weapons to people in the UK?"

"I think so, Guv."

"And I think the Visconti case is seriously hotting up, if you can find more to substantiate your theory. Call the NCA. I'll speak to Ferguson at Counterterrorism Command."

* * *

The trees had almost completely lost their leaves. From the vast windows of her lounge Nancy could look out on the gardens surrounding her apartment block. The sky was low and heavy. She rubbed her arms vigorously with her hands and shivered. It was barely 10.30am but she felt exhausted. The road back to China, to her past, was proving long and hurtful.

The buzz of her BlackBerry took her by surprise. She turned away from the window, hesitant.

It could be Pole.

She crossed the space to the coffee table quickly. Marissa was calling;

another ring and it would go to voicemail. "Just this once," she murmured.

The voicemail kicked in. Nancy waited. Her finger hovered over the button that allowed her to access her messages. She shook her head. The bitterness of her past was encroaching on the work she enjoyed doing but she had to allow it to surface.

The art book she had left open on the table, begging to be read, was calling her back to China. Ai Weiwei's desire to reconnect with ancient techniques of production, praising handcraft associated with Imperial China, had unsettled her.

She is sitting at a table, a piece of paper, a pot of black ink in front of her and a brush in her hand. Her father is teaching her calligraphy. He is both patient and demanding. She has repeated the same movement to create the same ideogram so many times she can't count any longer.

He has told her about the pressure of the brush on the paper, the inclination of the hand, but above all, the intention – the moment of stillness that precedes the act of creation, the slight hesitation and the movement that gives life to a word.

Her father is a modern artist yet the skill of the old helps him to conceive and execute. He won't compromise – no matter how much the new Maoist thinking is trying to compel him.

Nancy muffled a cry with her hand and dropped the pen she had been holding absent-mindedly since she had sat down on the sofa. The Chinese ideogram for girl was staring up at her from the first page of her notepad – the first word her father had taught her because it is simple and because it is her.

She turned the pad over gingerly, as if it was burning her fingers, torn between the desire to rip out the page, destroying it with a crush, or let the memories of her father flood back in.

Marissa's message was now awaiting her, the buzz of her BlackBerry telling her so. Nancy brought her chin down to her knees, huddling them with her arms, it was all too much.

Marissa's call would have to wait. Her artist friend, Susan, had offered to give her lunch and today this is what she would do. To escape once more the echoes of her past.

* * *

Marissa had started on her report for the SFO director. She had penned its outline on a sheet of paper and was about to type a new document when she went back to her mobile phone again. She had left a message for Nancy half an hour ago: no reply. The numbers displayed on the screen told her it was lunchtime already. She hesitated – perhaps a little more work before she joined her colleagues in the queue for sandwiches? She checked her messages again as if it might make a text from Nancy materialise.

Marissa sighed. She pulled together the documents that had spread over her desk during the course of the morning into a well-ordered pile.

Her unfinished conversation with Mark was still hanging uncomfortably over her. He had to trust her and to foster that trust she had to be transparent. But how could she release the information about Crowne to him in one go without jeopardising the case?

"Hello Mark, you are about to work with a terrorist."

She extended her arm and reached for another file, on which the title Henry Crowne/HXBK was written in bold letters. She lifted the cover but did not start reading the documents she almost knew by heart. She needed a chat with Nancy and she also needed some air.

Marissa stood up, approached the window and spotted a faint glimmer in the sky. The sun was trying to pierce through the clouds: she could do with a few rays, even if they were weak, on her skin.

Trafalgar Square was surprisingly empty. Even the street artists in their Yoda or Pokémon outfits, hovering in mid-air, had given today a miss. She gave her scarf another twist around her neck and turned her face towards the sun, seeking its warmth.

She spent a couple of minutes with her eyes closed, trying to imagine she could feel the meagre rays on her skin. A cold gust of wind reminded her it was time to start walking again. She crossed the road and entered the St Martin-in-the-Fields Crypt Cafe. The place looked busy. It was lunchtime after all.

Marissa bought a bowl of soup and some bread. It would be enough as she was not particularly hungry today. If she hurried, she could sneak upstairs into the main body of the church to hear one of their free lunchtime concerts. The programme included Debussy's Clair de Lune, a piece for piano she could play herself.

The front pews were almost full, a mix of students who had come to support their friends and family members eager to make sure the church was not empty for the performers' first recital at St Martin's. Marissa sat in a quieter back row, near one of the great stone pillars that supported the balcony. She lowered her eyes, leaning against the uncomfortable stiff wooden frame of the seats.

St Martin's was a good place for meditation she had found, a quiet space to turn within and seek guidance, so very different from the vibrant church she used to visit with her family on Sundays, and yet a place where she could experience the same joy.

The music almost startled her, but the meditative calm of Debussy's piece took her over instantly, her fingers moving with each note the young pianist was playing. She liked his touch, evocative of a breeze – speeding up and slowing down the tempo of the piece following his own inspiration, just the way Debussy had instructed.

More Debussy pieces followed, and Marissa was transported – the young artist's playing was so fluent. She wished she could be sitting there in front of an audience, playing the instrument that had always inspired her the most, the piano.

A vibration in her bag reminded her suddenly that it was midweek, and she had an urgent case to go back to. She discreetly slid along the pew and disappeared through one of the side doors. She scrolled down her messages to discover a text from Mark.

I need a chat and need to do this outside my home – I'm on my way.

The words punched her in the stomach. She checked the time. The message had been sent forty minutes ago. If she rushed back, she might just make it before Mark arrived. She ran down the steps that lay at the entrance to St Martin's. The crossing light had turned red.

She waved frantically towards the car that had started coming her way so she could cross. Her pace accelerated even more once she was on Trafalgar Square; she ran towards the rotating doors of the SFO offices. People were exiting the premises, slowing the doors down, and she had to match their unhurried pace.

She heard the receptionist call her name. "You have a visitor."

When Marissa finally walked into her office, she saw Mark standing over her desk, a file open in his hands and through his fingers she could read the name Henry Crowne penned in large letters.

Chapter Eleven

The studio space was beautifully peaceful and yet busy with creativity. Susan had not bothered to tidy up for her friend's visit and Nancy liked it that way. The colourful and almost tactile drawings her friend was working on had had a soothing effect.

Nancy sipped her coffee, almost ready to listen to the long list of calls that queued for her attention. Her phone buzzed again, a text message followed, and a sense of guilt sent a small shiver along her spine. She apologised to her friend, moved to the back of the studio and listened to what Marissa had to say.

Mark had discovered Henry would be the financial expert helping on his case … he knew who Henry Crowne was … Mark's reaction had been fury and disbelief.

"No," Nancy blurted. She ran her hand through her thick jet-black hair, hardly able to wait until the end of the message. She dialled Marissa's number – engaged. She left a voicemail of her own. She was going to the SFO to see her.

Her friend smiled kindly when Nancy made her excuses. It was urgent and she believed her. Nancy dashed into the first cab she could find. Less than thirty minutes later she was arriving at Trafalgar Square.

Marissa was waiting for her in the lobby of 2–4 Cockspur Street.

"Let's go for a coffee," Marissa said.

"The Crypt, St Martin's?"

"Good idea. We may need a miracle."

They both walked in silence. This time the Crypt Cafe was almost empty with plenty of tables to choose from.

"This is a disaster," Marissa sighed, collapsing on a chair.

"Is he determined not to speak to Henry?"

"He went mad – almost literally – when he realised who Henry Crowne was."

"Had you not mentioned to Mark you might involve someone like Henry beforehand?"

"I did but I didn't want to release Henry's name until we had the all-clear from the Belmarsh governor ..." Marissa's voice trailed. "And then there was the bombing and after that I was not sure it was a good idea altogether."

"Is there something else?" Nancy prodded a little.

Marissa hesitated. "No."

Nancy did not pursue the matter. She would return to it later though.

"What did Mark exactly say if I may ask?"

"First an incoherent explosion when I entered my office. I have never seen him like that. Months of tension, then the raw grief coming out all in one go. My colleagues almost called Security."

"What then?"

"He refused to work with a terrorist, a coward who kills innocent people, who targets decent folk like him and his family."

Nancy fell back in her chair. "I can't say I blame him for his reaction," she eventually said.

"I hadn't done a great job in preparing him either." Marissa's long fingers were pushing a couple of forgotten breadcrumbs towards the centre of the table.

"We have all been shocked by what happened."

Marissa kept playing with the crumbs, not meeting Nancy's eyes.

"Is he still prepared to go ahead with the case?"

Marissa raised her head, surprised. Her large brown eyes lit up and she managed a smile. She recognised the Nancy Wu QC she had known and admired in the past.

"You're always prepared to go to the point and never shy away from the hard questions."

"Always. And I am glad you remember." Nancy gave her friend

a kind smile. "So, yes, does Mark Phelps still want to testify in this whistle-blowing case against the large UK bank he works for?"

Marissa swept away the crumbs with the back of her hand. "He does."

"Then, I'm afraid, we need Henry to work with him."

Marissa remained silent.

"I understand your reservations. You don't know Henry and you have never worked with him, but I assure you, if you want to unravel this complex financial structure, he is the best."

"Perhaps if you were to speak to Mark," Marissa ventured.

"That's a good idea. You need to remain the person he trusts in all of this. And I am expendable."

"It's settled then."

"It is indeed."

* * *

The radio was chattering in the background. Bang-up time had started at 12:45pm sharp, allowing the officers to have their lunch.

The news bulletin he was listening to was interrupted. Henry's attention focused a little more on what was being said. A couple of words made him hold his breath.

Explosion. Bomb.

The radio presenter on BBC4 was describing an explosion that had happened less than twenty-four hours ago in Notting Hill Gate. Henry sat on the edge of his bed, rigid. The story unfolding on the radio was punctuated by flashbacks. "The Metropolitan Police acting in conjunction with Counterterrorism Command have confirmed that the bomb was planted underneath a car."

Henry hears the deafening noise of the explosion that rocks the van in which he is sitting.

"Speculation about the target."

His body hits the ceiling of the van; everything goes black.

"The identity of the victim has not been confirmed."

The glazed eyes of the dead officer who looks at him but can no longer see.

Henry stood up in a jump, grabbed the radio and squeezed so

hard he heard it crack under his grip. He threw it on the bed. The radio station was almost lost and he could now hear only a few jumbled words.

He must know what had happened though. His fingers fumbled with the wavelength button, tuning in and out – "act of terror". The presenter had moved effortlessly on to the next topic. Henry's body went limp. The question that had been haunting him for years surfaced unexpectedly.

Was he up to it? Could he join them and defeat them the way he had planned?

Behind this new bombing was Kamal's cell. When bang-up time was over, Henry could go and find him and finish him off. He could snap Kamal's neck like a twig. He knew how to do it. The images played in front of Henry's eyes, mesmerising.

Kamal's face contorted.

Kamal's eyes emptying of life.

Kamal's body going limp.

Henry's breathing had become short, his fists squeezed so hard they hurt, but in that moment pain felt good. He slammed his fist against the wall.

It was all fantasy, though, for Henry Crowne was no killer. He had learned that on the day of the Paddington bombing but perhaps he could be taught?

Henry dropped to the floor and lay on its cold surface. He must learn to pretend if he was to fulfil his plan. He must learn to pretend to share Kamal's belief. But was it too crazy? HSU Belmarsh was stifling but also safe in a strange sort of way. Once he was out on his own, there would be no one to look after his back.

No Liam, as there had been in Belfast.

No Nancy, as there had been during his trial.

No one.

Henry heard the bolt on the cell door being released and for once wished it had not come so soon.

* * *

"I'm on my way to see Mark." Nancy was walking towards St James's. The traffic was solid and she would only catch a cab when on Piccadilly. Pole had listened to her account of the latest development without interrupting. He would never say he was enthusiastic about facilitating Henry's second trip out of HSU Belmarsh but he had seen the results previously and there was no denying it – Henry was impressive when it came to banking expertise. Nancy understood his point of view. If something went wrong during Henry's transfer, Pole and The Met would be in the firing line.

"I agree, this is going to be difficult." Nancy waved down a taxi. She accelerated her pace to reach the place where it had stopped. She was glad she had chosen a pair of comfortable Chanel pumps. She kept speaking to Pole in between giving the cabbie directions. Pole would have to speak to Superintendent Marsh.

"Give me some time before you speak to The Super. We don't know yet whether Mark will change his mind."

Pole seemed undecided and reluctant to formalise Henry's trip out of HSU Belmarsh if Mark was refusing to work with him.

"I am not going to force the issue, Jonathan. I don't want to get Henry out of Belmarsh at any cost."

Pole had hit the nail on the head though. A gentle or perhaps not so gentle reminder that her friendship with Henry could not blind her.

"I understand the risk to your reputation, too." She wished she could have had the conversation with Pole in person, though perhaps he would have seen her unease, or perhaps he could hear it in the tone of her voice?

"The point I really want to make to Mark is that if he is serious about unravelling the financial structure that underpins Bank X's money flows between it and the Middle-Eastern state in question, he needs an expert."

Pole was agreeing, albeit reluctantly.

The cab was now well on its way to Holland Park and Nancy told Pole she had to go. It was time for her to gather her thoughts for what would be a very uncomfortable conversation.

She took her yellow pad out of her satchel, started listing the points she had made to Pole and added one she had not mentioned.

What did Henry's letter mean?

Despite Henry's best attempts at reassuring her, Nancy was still grappling with the feelings that the letter had elicited. Henry was not someone who rambled on paper. For all his faults, Henry was solid, and she doubted he had written something to her that was devoid of meaning.

He had brushed the letter off as the after-effect of the life-threatening situation they had found themselves in. Nancy was not convinced. She wished she had spoken to Pole at the time but it had felt like a betrayal of Henry's confidence. And now it was even more difficult to speak to Pole about it.

The taxi slowed down, and Nancy replaced the pad in her satchel. The three armed police officers looked suitably impressive from a distance. Pole had called Commander Ferguson. She was expected. She paid the cabbie and moved at a slow pace towards Mark Phelps' parents' home. She kept telling herself that if Mark really was serious about the case he needed Henry's help.

If.

Nancy stopped for a moment. The terraced house looked peaceful, the small front garden well-kept and welcoming, a typical prosperous family home. Nancy crossed the road and presented her driving licence to the two policemen guarding the house gate.

She was allowed through the garden gates and presented the document again to the other armed officer before ringing the doorbell. The chime of the bell sounded cheerful and out of place. This was not a home that invited drama or pain, but a cosy place built for the joys of family life.

A plain clothes policewoman appeared at the door and let Nancy in. She asked Nancy to wait in the hallway, no doubt checking Mark was up to receiving a visitor. Nancy's eyes scanned her surroundings. Photographs had been hung all over the walls: African animals, foreign landscapes, Masai warriors with their beaded necklaces and spears.

"Mark will see you."

The policewoman's voice made her jump, its neutral tone felt almost like a rebuke. Had this man not had enough? Nancy fought the desire to turn back.

She entered a large lounge, warm and welcoming. Mark was facing the bay window. In the garden, despite the cold, his children were playing football with their grandfather. Nancy paused. She could see Mark's face in the glass's reflection – bruised and scared.

"Good afternoon Mr Phelps, my name is —"

"I know who you are," Mark interrupted. He moved with difficulty towards the couch. Nancy waited. She looked at the broken man taking a seat and her throat tightened. The conventional "I am sorry for your loss" felt inadequate and unseemly.

Mark indicated she should sit down.

"Thank you for seeing me." There was a genuine feeling of sympathy in her voice. Mark nodded and for a while they both sat without saying more. He was observing her, and she let him take time to speak first.

"So?" Mark's face barely moved when he spoke, his lips hardly pronouncing the words.

"You have been told, I'm sure, that I consult with the Metropolitan Police as a former QC."

Mark nodded.

"I have been asked to assist in the supervision of a person, a former banker, who can help with the case the SFO is preparing against the bank."

Mark closed his eyes. His hands tightened on his knees.

"Are you not forgetting one essential detail?" he managed to articulate. His good eye opened wider and fixed Nancy with anger or perhaps even hatred.

Nancy sat still. She understood suffering, the need to inflict pain in return. Her calmness was compassionate rather than detached.

"I'd be a fool not to mention it."

"Then why have you come here?" Mark's voice was trembling, any minute now he would unleash his fury.

"Because I understand that you have chosen to keep going with the case despite what it has already cost you."

"Find someone else," Mark replied without hesitation.

"We could try." Nancy paused. "Yes, we could, but I am not sure we will find the person we truly need."

Mark attempted to laugh. His face twisted instead in pain, his throat almost choking.

"The person we are talking about —", not mentioning Henry's name seemed less provocative – "used to be one of the best financiers in the City but also —", she took her time to formulate the last limb of her argument – "but also someone who understands how criminal organisations operate. He knows how to put together a fund structure that is opaque enough —"

"Find someone else," Mark interrupted.

"The people who are good at mounting these structures are seldom caught because they do not implement them."

"Must be someone else ... arrested?" Mark had hesitated for an almost imperceptible moment.

"And because very few financiers behind bars will share their knowledge to unravel these funding structures, unless they can cut a deal. If we are talking about those who are free – how many will have the courage to do what you have done?" Nancy's voice had lost a little of its composure. She too was passionate about exposing the truth.

Mark's face dropped onto his chest so that Nancy could no longer read his expression. "I want you to leave." Mark had raised his head just enough so he could speak.

Nancy gathered her belongings, taking her time. Perhaps he did not mean it? She had detected a shift, she thought. She finally rose and moved towards the door. Her heart sunk in her chest. It was as much Mark's defeat as hers. He would never unravel this conundrum without Henry's help.

"Goodbye," she said as she reached the door.

Mark rose slowly and made his way to the bay window to resume watching his children play. Nancy walked all the way to the main road at a slow pace. Could she have been more convincing without appearing manipulative? She pulled her scarf tighter around her neck, the cashmere felt warm and comforting against the bitter cold of the wind.

She had reached the main road. It was time to speak to Pole again.

A small patisserie looked promising with plenty of empty tables at the back of the shop. She ordered and settled in the far corner, secluded. She took out her BlackBerry and paused. Hesitation was not helpful when it came to running a case – she could be measured, considerate, open-minded but today she felt the flux of the situation, a situation she could not control.

Pole and Marissa needed to know she had failed and yet she felt she had made a connection with Mark. For an instant he had seen her point of view. She dialled Pole's landline number. The voicemail kicked in. She switched to his BlackBerry.

"Pole." His tone sounded formal. She was interrupting.

"Sorry Jonathan, I will call back later."

"No, please – tell me."

Nancy gave him the details of her meeting. He did not interrupt. Unusual.

"Have I stunned you into silence, *mon cher*?"

"It is disappointing, I must say – is there anything that could make him change his mind?"

Pole now seemed keener to facilitate Henry's involvement. Perhaps he had spoken to Marissa again.

"I'm not sure. I thought he hesitated. Something happened fleetingly but then he asked me to leave."

"He needs to think it through. We should not have hoped to convince him that fast. Let's give him more time."

"I like your optimism. His emotions are very raw. He needs to let reason speak, but it is too early."

"Will you tell Marissa?"

"I will. And will you inform Marsh?" Nancy was expecting one of Pole's humorous remarks about Marsh's keen interest in Ms Wu.

"Let's wait a little," Pole replied. Nancy said her goodbyes and returned to a tasteless cup of tea. At least it was warm.

* * *

Pole dropped his BlackBerry on the small table.

"Mark Phelps is not budging."

The young man opposite bent forward, elbows on the plastic top.

"That's a shame but I have the impression that that is not the end

118

of it?" His light brown eyes read Pole in an uncomfortable fashion. Pole was not used to being on the receiving end of interrogations.

"We'll have to see."

"Crowne has to help on this case."

"I understood you the first time around." Pole's eyes locked briefly with the brown eyes.

"I know you understand, Inspector, but you need to do more than understand; you need to help."

"As long as 'help' does not mean breaking the law, I am good."

The young man shrugged. "A little accommodation with the truth perhaps?"

"What about Marsh?"

"Not your problem."

"Are you joking?" Pole crossed his arms over his chest.

"I am doing anything but joke, Inspector."

Pole stood up. "Unless Marsh is in the loop, I am not doing anything."

The young man pulled away from the table; his chair screeched.

"You might," he said stretching his arms over his head, "reconsider. Ms Wu, a very attractive woman I have to say, is looking for her disappeared father?"

"How do you …?" Pole's shoulders dropped slightly.

"Know? Never mind that. But how about a good old-fashioned you scratch my back and I scratch yours?"

Pole did not reply. He could have clocked this arrogant little arse.

"You know your way back out The Cross, Inspector."

Pole grabbed his raincoat and disappeared through the maze of corridors.

* * *

The car had stopped abruptly. The driver swore in what Brett recognised was Arabic. His third meeting with The Sheik had yet again been arranged at the last minute. Brett had grumbled about it and Mohammed, his contact, apologised profusely, but what could he do? It was The Sheik asking. Brett had known Mohammed for years and he would not have believed him to be a Jihadist. But Mohammed had been recruited to serve The Sheik and there was nothing he could do except do as he was told.

The car gained speed once more, driving through the streets of North London. Despite the blindfold, Brett knew they were going around in circles.

The underground station at which he had been picked up by the man in the leather jacket had changed once more. More precautions, more checks, his burner phone had been switched off and the battery removed – all this could mean only one thing.

A large operation was in the offing.

The car went over what he thought might have been the threshold of a garage door, or onto a pavement, and stopped. Brett was manhandled out of the vehicle, roughly without being violent, just enough to instil fear.

Brett played the part, suitably scared, but still with it. The scared part was becoming increasingly easy to act, whereas being with it …

The blindfold was removed and the large man who had been leading him by the arm through the corridors of the house they had entered indicated a door with a movement of his head. Brett stepped in and found to his surprise The Sheikh already there.

No greetings necessary.

The Sheik indicated that Brett should sit. The mattress on the floor was thin and had seen better days.

"What have you got for me?"

"As much information as I could gather in the amount of time I had." Brett handed over his dossier: printed documents, photocopied news articles, photos. Everything he had gathered on Henry Crowne over the years Crowne had been his client and everything MI6 had allowed him to disclose without arousing suspicions.

The Sheik grabbed the file and started leafing through it, taking his time to read the parts that seemed important to him. A faint smile moved across his serious face.

"Do you have a USB key with these documents?"

Brett fished the key from his jacket pocket and placed it on the floor.

A woman in a niqab entered noiselessly. She placed a tray carrying two glasses and a large brass teapot on the ground. She poured the liquid and disappeared without a sound, invisible. The Sheik extended his hand and took a glass; he was still reading. Brett took the other glass and pulled a face, his fingers scorched by the searing liquid inside. The Sheik was still holding his – immune it seemed to pain.

"How did you get all that information?" The Sheik asked taking a sip of tea.

"It's taken time – almost ten years' worth of work. I ask a lot of questions and I work with people who can find information too."

"Who are these people?"

"People who specialise in identity theft." Brett wriggled on the mattress; it was uncomfortable more ways than one.

"I want names."

"It is unlikely the names they operate under are their real names. It might not be very helpful."

"That's for me to decide."

Brett squirmed. The Sheik raised his eyes for the first time since he had started reading the documents, the cold stare of a man who had killed many times, without giving it a second thought.

Brett took a pen out of his inner jacket pocket and started jotting down names on the envelope The Sheik had discarded on the floor. He handed it over and as he did The Sheik's body relaxed a fraction.

How interesting, Brett thought, you too are under pressure. This was more than just a terrorist cell seeking to wreak havoc in London.

"One last question." The Sheik finished his tea. Brett waited.

"Would he join the Jihad?"

Brett's mind went blank for a short moment. Surely he could not mean?

"Crowne." The Sheik's eyes drilled into Brett.

"I don't know."

And that was an honest answer.

Chapter Twelve

Marissa had spoken to Pole. Marissa had spoken to Nancy. She now needed to speak to Mark or perhaps it was too soon. Tomorrow the SFO director would want to hear about "progress".

If Mark persisted in refusing Crowne's help and yet was still determined to be the SFO's main witness, he had to measure the impact of his decision. Maybe she could convince Mark he did not need to meet the man or perhaps she could simply not tell him of Henry's involvement.

She discarded the latter idea the minute she formulated it. Mark had to trust her and she had to trust herself.

"I need a walk," she spoke aloud, an affirmation. Marissa stood up, grimaced and arched back a little, hands on her waist. She looked at the piles of documents neatly arranged on her desk: read with annotations – read, needing further comments – to be read (the largest pile).

She hesitated. She could take some papers to read at home. She could take a cab to Battersea and walk the rest of the way. She could log in from home. She could …

"I need a walk."

Marissa logged off, dropped a loose paper clip into the stationery holder on her desk, shrugged on her coat and walked towards the bank of lifts. She caught the reflection of her body in the large windows of the SFO office, a tall form stooped with tiredness.

Trafalgar Square was impossibly clogged up with cars. She did not bother to wait for the pedestrian light to turn green and moved across the road towards Parliament Square. She took a woollen cap out of her coat pocket, a cosy hat she always carried once the winter had started and adjusted it on her head. Marissa gathered pace. She thought about which route she would take today, turning towards Victoria; once there she would jump on the 344 bus.

The walk had loosened her body a little and her mind felt more alert. Marissa had given Mark her word he could choose not to go ahead with the case. The SFO director would never accept this though, not after the string of disappointments (the politically correct term) the SFO had encountered.

For her there was the BAE Systems case – yes BAE had been charged a heavy fine. $450 million was a considerable sum but most of it had gone to the US Department of Justice. And what of the employees who made illegal payments on behalf of the company – nothing.

The UK had invoked national security and Saudi Arabia was pardoned by Tony Blair whilst he was prime minister. The sale of armaments in return for bribes – a practice supposedly rampant in the industry – was a case worth fighting for and yet she felt it could have gone so much deeper.

She was already on Parliament Square and stopped at the traffic lights, close to the kerb, her feet ready to move the second the little man had turned green. She felt the pressure of the crowd behind her, as eager as she was to reach their destination. Marissa stepped back a little. The traffic that was whizzing past felt somehow too close. The pressure on her back surprised her. There was no space left to move. She pushed back more decisively, a couple of men protested. She apologised. She looked around. No one was paying attention to her.

She was now turning into Old Queen Street and the flow of people eased off. She looked behind her. A couple of women, chatting and crossing the road. Marissa slowed down and her mind drifted back to Mark. Mark in his hospital bed, Mark at his parents' home, with his children – the images kept coming but did not provide her with any answers.

She turned around again – fewer people still. In the distance, a car turned into the street, drove slowly past and disappeared around the bend of the road.

The Counterterrorism Command offer of protection popped into her mind. What would murdering her achieve? Someone else would take the case.

Marissa broke into a slow jog. She thanked her American friends for convincing her to wear running shoes on her commute. Her bag was now rhythmically banging against her back. She was only a couple of streets away from one of the main roads.

Once at Buckingham Gate she would hail a cab. A car drove past again at a steady pace. Was it the same car? Marissa accelerated her jog into a run, crossed the street as the lights turned red, the sound of car horns following her. She kept going and, as she reached the other side, put her hand up, dashing into the taxi that had stopped.

The cabbie looked at her in the mirror. "Are you OK, luv?" She nodded, too shaken to speak. She turned and looked through the back window.

The SUV she thought she had seen driving past her was a few cars away. No, this was ridiculous, the black SUV looked like any other black SUV. She took a tissue from her bag and ran it over her face. The black SUV had moved up and was now stopped alongside her cab, one lane away. She moved forward towards the intercom.

"We're going to Scotland Yard," she shouted, her eyes wide open.

The cabbie turned down the radio.

"What's that luv?"

"Turn around, turn around; we need to go to Scotland Yard."

"All right, all right – calm down," the cabbie grumbled. "I need to get out of the one-way system first."

Marissa sat back and squeezed herself into the corner of the cab furthest from the SUV. Her mind was racing. She could get out again, could try to get a cab going in the right direction but what if they were after her?

No chance of escape.

The SUV was stuck in traffic too; if they were going to attempt anything they would have to wait until they could move away safely, surely?

Marissa fumbled in her bag, found her mobile phone, hesitated, and then called Commander Ferguson's number – engaged.

The traffic was moving in her lane; the SUV was still stuck. The cabbie moved to cross into a new lane. He managed to squeeze between two undecided drivers – there were now two lanes between her and the SUV. The SUV was moving now, also trying to change lane but with less luck than the taxi. Marissa tried Ferguson again – still engaged.

"Shit, shit." Marissa could see the SUV pushing against the traffic despite the protestations of the other drivers. It would not be long before it would be level with her cab – then what?

"Can we try to go a little faster please?" Marissa asked. Her voice must have sounded desperate and the driver registered.

"You've got a problem?"

"Perhaps. I really need to reach Scotland Yard."

The cabbie opened his window again and indicated he needed priority, another cabbie let him in and they started to move faster out of the traffic jam. The SUV was stuck again, and Marissa felt hope. Her body now half turned, looking through the rear window.

"No. No," she cried raising her hand to her mouth.

A figure had jumped out of the SUV and was crossing the lanes that separated them. The gun was pointing in her direction, the gunman running towards her cab.

"What the fuck?" The driver blurted as he looked in his rear mirror. The cabbie sounded his horn; the traffic moved faster. He turned into the Embankment to the sound of gunfire being discharged. He did not stop until they reached the Yard.

* * *

"Ferguson is on his way." Pole put a cup of tea in front of Marissa. His gesture was slow, not wanting to scare her, knowing she needed time to recover. Marissa nodded, the tissues she had used to wipe her face still in her hand.

"The cabbie is fine by the way; a bit shaken but fine."

"Good," Marissa barely managed to utter. Pole sat down as well, drank some tea and waited. She stretched a quivering hand towards her cup, wrapped her other hand around it. Her mouth opened and closed.

Her eyes were moist, but she recovered and cleared her throat.

"You need a statement from me?"

"Let's wait for Ferguson. There's no rush. You're safe here."

Pole's voice was reassuring. There was nothing wrong with being scared.

Pole and Marissa drank their tea in silence. Pole didn't need to fill the time with meaningless words. If Marissa needed to talk he would be ready.

When Commander Ferguson arrived Andy Todd also joined them.

"You think you were followed?" Ferguson asked as soon as he had finished greeting Pole and Marissa.

"I think so. I had not given my safety much thought, even after Mark's wife." Marissa was still struggling with each word. Her face strained with the effort of concentration, of trying to remember and to be accurate.

"The SUV drove past you twice?"

"I think so."

"The shooter?"

"Small man." Marissa covered her eyes to still herself. "Small person. Five foot two or thereabouts, dressed in black – balaclava or hoodie."

"Anything else that springs to mind?" Ferguson asked.

"It was so quick..." Marissa's jaw clenched. "There was something unexpected..."

"In your own time." Pole cut through Ferguson.

"The gunman raised his weapon as soon as he was out of the SUV as if he wanted everyone to know he could do this."

"These guys are not afraid of dying..." Ferguson shook his head.

Pole waited to hear more but Marissa looked spent. Perhaps this particular individual had more to prove.

Andy was taking notes in his notebook. "We need to have access to all CCTV cameras in the area and around Buckingham Gate."

Ferguson nodded. "Can you deal with it?"

Pole did not have to ask. Andy had stood up and disappeared the moment the request had been made.

"I doubt we'll find them by tracing the vehicle. It was probably stolen and will've been set on fire and completely trashed by now," Ferguson said.

"But people make mistakes."

"Not these guys." Ferguson moved to the window. He looked outside. It was dark and blustery. "In the meantime, we need to get you home safely," he said to Marissa. "I'll send a team to secure your flat. If it's too complicated, we may need to move you to somewhere safer." Ferguson commanding voice softened a little. "Does that work for you?"

"Yes, fine. I'm fine. Thank you for asking." Marissa's rigid body sagged a little.

"Perhaps a friend or family member could stay with you?" Pole's voice, warm and comforting, somehow made it worse.

"I hope you find these fuckers and you have no mercy," Marissa said, stunning both Pole and Ferguson into silence. "I need to powder my nose and I'll follow you."

"Tempting instructions," Ferguson said once Marissa had left. Pole nodded. He had joined Ferguson at the window.

"Something bothering you?" Ferguson asked. "Apart from also being tempted to follow Ms Campbell's instructions?"

"Yes, but I'm wondering," Pole ruffled his goatee with his knuckle. "Who might be next?"

* * *

The doorbell buzzed a couple of times. Nancy moved swiftly to the intercom to let Pole into her building. She left the door of her apartment on the latch and ran to the kitchen. She had decided on a good old-fashioned blanquette de veau for their supper later on. First a private view at one of the contemporary art galleries she supported in Islington for the opening of her favourite sculptor, Bernard McGuigan, followed by *dîner a deux*.

Pole knocked and entered.

"I'm in the kitchen, Jonathan," Nancy's cheerful voice called.

"You shouldn't leave the door on the latch you know," Pole said walking into the kitchen with a bottle of red wine and a bunch of white lilies.

127

Nancy had donned oven gloves. The smell of slow-cooked meat filled the room with a delicious aroma when she opened the Le Creuset casserole lid. She stirred the stew with a wooden spoon, lifted it to her lips – perfect.

"It's not been a good day, I think?" Her smile had disappeared. She took another spoonful and presented it to Pole.

"Sorry, I shouldn't bring it home. Good evening Nancy," Pole blew on the spoon's contents and took a bite. He smiled at what was good old comfort food. He put the wine and flowers on the table. He hugged Nancy gently, kissing the top of her head and pulling back.

"What's happened?" Nancy asked taking off her oven gloves in a sharp move and placing her hands on his shoulders. "Another —"

"No, no," Pole interrupted. "But it was a close shave."

Pole sat down at the kitchen table. Nancy opened the Nuits-Saint-Georges he had brought, poured out two glasses without tasting the wine first and listened carefully to Pole's account of Marissa's near miss.

"How is she taking it?" Nancy took a sip of wine, ignoring how good it was.

"Very shaken to start with, of course, but she's bounced back pretty quickly."

"You mean she is damned pissed off?"

"That's a good way of putting it." Pole smiled. "But she won't be put off that easily from working on the case."

"Quite the contrary. I've known Marissa a long time and I'd say missing their target is the worst these people could have done." Nancy raised her glass to her friend. "Courageous is definitely Marissa Campbell's middle name."

Pole swirled the wine around his glass, more in a meditative gesture than to let it breathe. He finally took a sip. "The question now is, what next? Or perhaps who's next?"

Nancy stretched her hand over Pole's. "What are you worried about? That these people are on a murder spree?"

"That's a possibility. If the intention is to intimidate or murder key witnesses, in a case that is not even a full case yet, they will target whoever it is they feel they need to target."

"It would be almost impossible to reach Henry in HSU Belmarsh," Nancy said.

"I'm not worried about Henry."

"You think I might be a target?" Nancy pulled a dubious face.

Pole drank a little wine. "You are the go-between connecting Henry and Marissa."

Nancy squeezed Pole's hand again. "For all we know, Mark may not want to work with Henry and Marissa may have no other choice but to agree to that."

They had moved to Nancy's lounge whilst talking, sitting close on the sofa. Pole looked absorbed in something he seemed to have recalled.

"Jonathan? Is there anything else?"

Pole shook his head. "No, you're right. Let's go to this art preview you've been raving about." Pole finished his glass, forgetting to comment on the excellent Nuits.

He was keeping something from Nancy. She couldn't figure out what.

* * *

The small gallery nestling in Islington's back streets was already packed when they arrived. Nancy pushed the large silver globe serving as a door handle, and she and Pole entered Phillipe Garry's gallery.

Philippe welcomed Nancy with a warm hug. He shook hands with Pole and insisted on bringing them a glass of wine. Pole looked around at the diverse crowd only contemporary art could produce.

He felt immediately at ease amongst this eclectic mix of bohemians and collectors. Nancy greeted a couple of artists she knew well and introduced Jonathan. "Jonathan Pole, a friend".

They smiled, inquisitive, but before they had time to launch into personal questions, Pole started to comment on the quality of the pieces displayed around the gallery.

"Bernard's craft is truly impressive." Pole had picked up a thing or two about art, to Nancy's delight, and she joined in the conversation.

"My favourite piece remains Ecstasy."

The other artists argued; perhaps the latest abstract pieces Day and Night or Ode departed from the well-known McGuigan figurative work but they were inspiring. Phillippe joined the debate. If they could wait until seven-thirty, Bernard would be arriving from the countryside then. He was finishing installing a large piece in the garden of one of his main collectors, but he would arrive later.

Another younger artist she had not seen for a while came to say hello to Nancy. Pole started a conversation with a seasoned collector, Audrey.

The room buzzed with opinions, news about current work being conceived or art pieces being purchased. A young man in a hat perched on the back of his head and dressed head to toe in black was gesticulating in front of the largest sculpture on display, elaborating on the technique, the material used and the impact the piece would have on the art market.

"This is crazy, have you seen the latest figures? Frieze Art Fair was again a complete success. The galleries sold eighty per cent of their art stock by the end of the first preview day."

"I heard they had done so even before that," a young woman in a vintage Alexander McQueen dress replied.

Pole moved towards the small office and casually consulted his BlackBerry.

"Any news?" Nancy asked as she presented him with a fresh glass of wine.

"Sorry." Pole took the glass and gently tapped Nancy's.

"Don't apologise. I am very impressed you have spent almost a whole hour without looking at it."

"I am glad my efforts at being civilised have borne fruit." Pole smiled.

"In fact, I am impressed full stop." Nancy raised her glass to him. She saw a little warmth rising to Pole's cheeks.

"I'd told you I can talk the art talk too," Pole teased.

The rumble of voices changed, suddenly turning to an acclamation. The door opened and a man with a mane of thick grey hair and a friendly smile entered. The artist had arrived.

Time to go back to the party.

* * *

Henry heard the bolt of his prison cell door releasing. Another visit before he was due to leave the compound, normal procedure. He would be expected to be ready before the inmates were allowed out for breakfast and would return after night lockdown had started.

The most senior of the prison officers came in. Henry was sitting on the bed, reading a book he had borrowed from the library, something of quality but not contentious, *A Brief History of Time* by Stephen Hawking.

"Change of plan, Henry. Your trip has been postponed." The guard withdrew without further explanation.

"Wait." Henry jumped from his bed, but the door had already closed. "Wait." Henry slammed his hand against the door. The small window latch opened. "I don't have any more information. I'll let you know when I have some news." The latch closed again.

Henry lifted his fist to bang against the door once more. It took all his determination and more to stop. If the guards were toying with him it was not the time to rise to the bait. Henry spread his hands on the door. He needed to scream.

What had happened? Why had Nancy not contacted him?

His mind was fluttering, a bat caught in a confined room, bumping into the walls and never finding a way out. His cell closed in around him. He needed space but there was none.

The desire for self-harm returned. He had never succumbed to it when he was a teenager in Belfast. Always fighting the temptation to test his resistance to pain. The street fights alongside the O'Connor brothers gave him enough deep cuts and bruises, sometimes broken bones, to satisfy his thirst for torment.

Prison was a new form of slow-burning torture. Henry was the first one to recognise he deserved his sentence but going through with it was another matter.

Henry's body was now trembling with anger. The old foe had returned, summoned by the unexpected outcome of the officer's visit. He needed to speak to Nancy. But there was no mobile, no phone he could use at this time of night. He would have to wait until the morning, queue at the telephone booth and finally place a call.

Henry returned to his bed in one step, threw the sheet and blanket to the floor and yanked the mattress from its base in a vicious move. The chair hit the desk. The carefully arranged books and papers shook, some fell to the ground. Henry did not care. He rolled the mattress, sat on the impromptu punching sack and started pummelling it with blows. He kept going, hitting, swearing, hitting again. A painful memory hit him

He can only hear the shots. The short sharp burst a gun makes before it hits its target.

It is August. The weather has been pleasant since the beginning of the month. Henry's mother is visiting a friend in Ballymurphy. She does not know that the British army is about to launch Operation Demetrius. It is holiday season so she has decided to spend time with her friend whose son is Henry's age. The house overlooks the green. The day has started like a normal day, breakfast with Henry and Patrick running around the house before they finally sit down to eat toast and fried sausages. Henry's mother and her friend are sitting at the window, smoking cigarettes.

Men run past shouting. Everybody goes quiet. Even at the age of four, Henry knows when he must stop talking. Men in uniforms of the Parachute Regiment run after them. There is no shooting at this stage, just running. His mother moves away from the window and asks the boys to go upstairs.

And then it starts – the gunfire. The shots are coming from somewhere on the left, from high up. His mother freezes at the bottom of the stairs. She calls them to come down now. Where is safe? They huddle in the kitchen. His mother's friend is still at the window. One man is down on the ground. She screams.

Another man with arms over his head moves slowly towards the body. He is shot as well. A few moments later a man in a white collar, a priest, takes his handkerchief out of his pocket, moves it over his head. He is looking around, hoping the marksmen will see his white flag. He walks steadily; surely, they wouldn't dare. A few minutes later Father Hugh Mullan collapses; death is instantaneous.

Henry couldn't feel his fists. The past refused to let him go. The sweat was pouring from his body; it soaked his T-shirt, his tracksuit bottoms. He rolled onto his side, banging his back against the leg of the bed. He could hardly breathe.

He no longer knew whether he remembered the actual killings or whether he recalled the story told by adults around him. Ballymurphy had rarely been spoken about. Henry's eyelids fluttered open.

His cell was in a mess. He did not care. He had until the morning to make it look presentable again, to keep up appearances. But for now, he wanted to stay with the violence that burned within him.

Henry sat up and shuffled towards the only part of the wall that was wide enough for him to lean his back against. His mind had quietened down somewhat. Lashing out in the privacy of his cell was the only way to control his anger.

Nancy had not called. There must be a delay that could be overcome. Henry had done good research on the topic of fiscal paradises and he knew the people well.

He knew the countries that sell passports – real passports – to the Russians, the Middle-Easterners and others in search of a new identity. He knew that Cyprus and Malta are used extensively to launder money. He knew these people open bank accounts, create companies, trusts, structures with so many layers that the Ultimate Beneficial Owner of the funds will never be found. Unless you are Henry Crowne, of course, because he knew all the tricks.

Henry stood up warily. The cell had been plunged into darkness. He fumbled towards his desk and switched on the wall light. Time to clean up the mess.

I just need to speak to whoever is running the case. I can make a difference.

When he had finished, Henry ran a wet flannel over his body, washing away the rest of the anger.

He moved to his bed and lay down. He must prepare for a day of waiting and hoping.

Chapter Thirteen

Nothing had managed to lift Marissa's spirits this morning. She had made herself a cup of her favourite Jamaican coffee, a couple of pieces of crunchy toast with guava jam – nothing doing.

The images of the shooter aiming at her kept coming in front of her eyes as soon as her mind stopped thinking. She had called the SFO director late last night; she had explained the interference as she had decided to call it.

An attempt on her life sounded too grand or perhaps too scary. The long silence that had followed her account of events had said it all. It was up to her to decide whether she wanted to go ahead. "I'll support you in whatever you do," he had said.

No "your life matters more than a bloody case", not that the SFO director would have sworn in front of his staff.

Marissa was ready for work and time was moving on. She could not quite bring herself to go out and make the call.

"It must be shock," Marissa grumbled.

The intense determination she had felt last night had been replaced by a sluggishness she did not know herself capable of. Her mobile rang. Nancy's name flashed on the screen. Always there when you needed her.

Marissa held back a sob. The mobile went to voicemail. But as Nancy's name disappeared from the screen Marissa felt the urge to speak to someone. She rang back.

Marissa didn't have to say much to Nancy before her former mentor suggested coffee and a chat. As she was about to leave, a young woman stood in the hallway. Marissa had almost forgotten the presence of the young police officer who had been dispatched for her protection. She stopped Marissa, reminding her she would be calling for a car to drive her to wherever she needed to go.

The car arrived and Marissa was asked to sit in the back. She did not know what to say to her police escort. The young woman was now speaking to the driver about the best route to take, avoiding traffic or slower roads. Marissa turned her face to the window and absent-mindedly watched the scenery go by.

The Groucho Club was buzzing at breakfast time: artists, TV producers, aspiring young and not so young actors, were huddled into groups, joking and whispering in a conspiratorial manner. It certainly was colourful. Marissa felt a little out of place with her plain black suit, white shirt and severe haircut. Nancy waved at her from a table in the Brasserie.

"Thank you so much, Nancy; you're always here when I need you." Marissa said as she sat down.

"The least I can do. How are you holding up?"

"I'm not sure." Marissa hunched over the small table. "Last night I was so certain; now I'm not so confident. I'm not frightened, which is odd too."

"You're still processing what happened." Nancy laid her hand on Marissa's arm and squeezed gently. "We can simply have breakfast without talking about it."

"No. Well, I'd love a coffee, but I also need to discuss options."

"You mean yours as well as Mark Phelps'?"

Marissa wriggled on her chair, a direct question but to the point. She waited for the coffee to be served.

"These people won't stop at anything." Marissa's eyes had darkened, and her voice had acquired a new hard edge.

"I agree, but the real question is – will the fact that you stop working on the case make any difference to the outcome?"

Marissa stopped stirring her coffee and looked at Nancy in surprise. "Are you saying Mark will remain a target for the rest of his life?"

"That is part of the problem. We can't be sure, but can we take the risk?" Nancy said.

Marissa liked the collective "we". It was her and Nancy very much together on this case.

"If it were the mafia, we would know what to do, but here we are in uncharted territory."

"I'd say these people are worse than the mafia."

Marissa's hand wobbled and she put her cup down. "Mark has been outed anyway as a whistle-blower. He is protected but the harsh truth is that he will lose his job. Bank X is probably shredding documents as we speak."

"He is almost certainly past caring about his job by now. It is more a question of survival." Nancy's calm and ability to dissect a case had always impressed Marissa.

"The only hope is to find out quickly who is behind the Panama structure. Then enrol Mark and his family in the witness protection programme."

"And we are back now to the thorny question surrounding Henry Crowne's involvement."

"Mark has not made contact by the way."

"But does he know what happened to you?"

Marissa drank some coffee; her face lit up, a little bit of goodness in a cup.

"Not yet. But I will tell him," she said, unhappy at her own procrastination.

"It might —" Nancy shook her head, "No, I think it will make a big difference."

"Don't you think he will be even more reluctant?"

"Mark hesitated when I spoke to him – only once, but he did. I think the rational part of him wants to use Henry."

"But why would the incident ..." Marissa drank a little more coffee, "...of last night, convince him?"

"The only way to take some pressure off his family is to find the ultimate owner of the funds and even, perhaps, the people who are also funding the terror cell."

"Nancy, that is the huge leap. Do you really think he will think about it?"

"My guess is he has been spending all this time thinking of the permutations. He will not rest until his wife is avenged. He trusts you and needs you to help. With this latest attempt the pressure has escalated. He can't afford to make the wrong call and I think he knows it."

"Even if Mark is concerned about me, I am not so concerned about myself."

"This is why he trusts you. He also knows you will respect his decision."

"The SFO director will bypass me. I realised this last time I spoke to him."

"I can imagine." Nancy topped up her cup of tea. "Does Mark really need to know you are working with Henry?"

"Of course, I could keep it from him." Marissa frowned. "It wouldn't be honest though."

"Mark only needs to see the outcome of Henry's findings. He has already given us all the information Henry needs. So what difference does it make if Henry works on it without Mark knowing?"

"I suppose it could work."

"As long as you still want to take the case on." Nancy said with a kind smile.

Marissa sat back in her chair, drinking her coffee in small gulps.

"The time for hesitation is over. I'm in. I won't let the bastards get away with it."

"Quite positive?" Nancy asked, her face now serious.

"It won't be another BAE Systems." Marissa finished her cup. Time to resume her work at the SFO.

* * *

The small queue for breakfast moved rhythmically: tray, plate or bowl, eggs or porridge, toast with a very small piece of butter wrapped in foil, marmalade or jam. Gone were the days of luxurious breakfasts at the Four Seasons Hotels or the Shangri-La, an endless choice of foods catering to international tastes.

Henry shuffled with everybody else. Kamal would want to speak, he thought. Henry had not given any dates confirming when he was meant to be let out, but a substantial delay would alter his credibility

137

or, worse, affect Kamal's plan. Henry scooped a couple of greasy eggs onto his plate, chose two pieces of toast that seemed edible. He poured tea into a plastic mug and sat down at a table from which he could watch the crowd moving in and out of the canteen.

One of Kamal's latest recruits appeared at the end of the line. He started shuffling too: eggs, toast, tea. He walked to a table close to Henry's and sat down so that he was facing him. He ate his breakfast slowly, observing the other inmates who chose to sit away from him. This seemed to suit him. The young man glanced at Henry a few times.

A couple of officers sat in the room. There was never any privacy at HSU Belmarsh. Henry was just about finished and expected not to hang around. He saw the young man drop the flimsy paper napkin that came with the cutlery to the floor.

Henry stood up and moved towards the conveyor belt for trays. As he walked past, he told the young man about the napkin; he bent down to pick it up, thanking Henry. This is what the guards saw.

"When does he want a chat?"

"Library, this afternoon."

It was all Henry needed to know.

* * *

The library had just opened. Henry had taken a seat at the small desk, opened the box containing index cards for books borrowed and returned using a key the officers had given him. He was waiting. The library opened every day for a couple of hours with a rota of librarians picked from a list of "suitable" inmates.

Henry was alone for the first fifteen minutes. He stood up, went around the bookshelves. No new books had arrived. He went on to a small window, the pane of glass was opaque and thick but it was the closest he would get to daylight. He had not heard from Nancy although the post was late yet again and had not arrived before he had to leave his cell.

A couple of inmates entered. Only a limited number of people were allowed into the library at any one time. It was all very efficient; inmates wanting to use the library would take a number and wait until their number flashed up on a board. They were allowed fifteen minutes inside, no longer.

"Cashier number five," Henry murmured with a tired smile. The anger of the previous night had sapped his energy. He just wanted to have a quiet day, but Kamal might have other plans.

Inmates picked up books. Henry filled in the cards. They left. Uneventful. Perfect.

The clock was moving forward; a few more inmates came and went.

Henry walked out of the library to pour himself a glass of water, looking down the corridor in a nonchalant way. Only twenty minutes left before the library closed. Irritation had been replaced by anger and, more worryingly, doubt.

Did Kamal know something Henry did not?

Henry slumped into his chair, then straightened up and checked the cards one more time. He would let off steam with a workout on the rowing machines after the shift had ended. He needed to stay calm. If the Jihadi group Kamal belonged to was serious about building a financial empire, they needed him. Didn't they?

The soft steps of someone walking in refocused his mind. Kamal had put down a couple of books on Henry's desk without a word. He was now browsing the bookshelves. Henry could hear the soft movement of books being taken out, the cover being opened, the pages turned, the slight effort of returning the book to its place. Kamal emerged from the row of shelves with one book, a biography of Richard Wagner – intriguing.

The guard had popped out for a minute, ready to close the library for the day.

"How is life treating you Henry?"

"Not bad?" Henry replied whilst filling in the card.

"Ready for a change of scenery I understand." Kamal's face was soft, his long beard left uncut, a sign of rebellion that made him look more like a poet then a murderer.

"And you?"

"Always ready for what God presents me with."

"God and I are not on speaking terms," Henry replied, miming the need for a signature on the card.

"Not yet, not yet." Kamal signed and pushed the card forward but did not let go of it when Henry tried to pick it up. "Be ready."

"For what?"

"Be ready."

Henry let go of the card. It was not good enough. But Kamal simply left the card on the desk and walked out.

Henry stood up abruptly and fought the desire to follow Kamal, slam the door of the library shut and punch him in the face. Instead he stretched.

Patience. Henry consulted the clock on the wall, ten minutes to go. He walked to the window again, turned his back to the door and pretended he could see through the frosted glass.

He heard him before he saw him walking through the door. The low whistle that preceded him everywhere he went. It was not a tune, or at least not one Henry or anybody else had ever heard before. It was animal-like, a warning the way a dangerous creature might announce itself.

Ronnie Kray walked through the door.

Henry turned back in a flash.

"We're shutting down," he said walking back to the desk and closing the box of indexed cards.

"Still five minutes mate," Kray replied with a wink. He walked straight to the far end of the library and started browsing through the shelves. The whistle had started again, covering the noise of books being moved around.

The officer came in, banged his fist against the open door. "Five minutes. Make your choice." He was standing outside the door.

What could happen now?

Henry relaxed and took out the card with Kray's name on it. What a ridiculous idea. Change your name to emulate some fucked-up bloke, who did, after all, spend more than twenty years in prison.

"Bloody idiot," Henry muttered. He looked up to find Ronnie Kray standing in front of him.

The fist that flew in his face was barely a surprise to Henry. Henry threw his body to one side, but Kray's blow caught him on the edge of his head. The chair screeched and bounced against the wall. Neither man had made a sound.

Henry stood up before Kray could come around the table and throw his second punch. Henry had hunched forward, fists at the ready. Kray launched into him head first, trying to catch Henry in the stomach. Henry swirled to his right too late. The knock propelled him against the wall. He contained a yelp, rolled sideways on the floor to find that Kray had caught his shoulder against the bookshelves. He had fallen on one knee.

Back on his feet Henry took a defensive position again. The scream of a whistle did not stop Kray. He took the chair that was now lying on the floor and hurled it with all his might at Henry.

The back of the chair caught Henry's shoulder and threw him against the row of books. The lot collapsed with a clap of thunder.

Other guards had arrived, running through the door, sticks at the ready, and then slowly approached the two men.

"Come on. You don't want to do this." One of the officers was doing the talking. The others advanced steadily towards Kray. Kray ignored them.

Henry had retreated between the other shelves. He could see Kray's face, intent on inflicting damage, eyes crazed, a mix of hatred and glee. Kray had been waiting for this and there would be no reasoning with him. All Henry wanted to do now was to be his victim. He could not be sent to The Box.

Could not.

The guards were at each end of the bookshelves. Kray lunged forward with a scream that stunned everyone. Henry braced himself for impact once more.

The Kung Fu leg kick propelled him against another lot of bookshelves, books tumbled again. Kray dashed forward, slipping on the books and falling to the ground. The guards threw themselves on him, four of them. Their sticks came down on his back, arms and legs. One of them managed to pin him to the ground with an armlock.

It was over.

Henry had not moved. His face was throbbing. His chest burning with pain. Two officers grabbed him by the shoulders, stood him up and handcuffed him. They would sort out later who had done what.

Henry wiped the blood coming out of his mouth and nose on the side of his shoulder.

Henry's mind was working fast. Damage limitation was essential to avoid The Box. "Bloody idiot" had been directed at himself. He thought he had made a mistake. The story might hold. In the distance he could still hear Ronnie Kray, yelling, swearing, spitting.

One of the guards opened the door of the corridor leading away from the main area of HSU. Henry found himself in front of a room he did not know. The cuffs were removed and he was pushed into it.

"Wait in here, Crowne." The door closed shut and Henry limped to one of the chairs. He sat down slowly.

"Fuck, fuck, fuck," Henry mumbled. He lifted the bottom part of his T-shirt and wiped the rest of the blood that had started congealing on his chin. "It can't be happening now."

* * *

"These are my conditions," Mark said, a calm voice that had not lost its determination. He had insisted he wanted to see Marissa at the SFO offices after she had told him about her own brush with death.

Marissa looked at the sheet of paper listing Mark's conditions in neat yet rather large handwriting. She nodded.

"I agree with most of them."

"But?" Mark asked somewhat surprised.

"About Crowne?"

"The IRA banker," Marrisa's voice tightened.

"I am not sure this is entirely practical?"

"I don't care, Marissa. I can see he is the right man for the job and this is my demand for working with him."

"I've thought about it too. I have no desire to work with this – monster either but I need to squeeze every bit of information from him, and I mean everything. I am not letting these —" Marissa stopped herself from swearing, "these other monsters get away with it."

"How about this Nancy woman?"

Marissa hesitated. How much was she prepared to tell Mark?

"She is a very smart woman. I have worked with her before. She is an extremely good lawyer."

142

Mark waited. It was not what he wanted to hear.

"She does know Crowne very well, too."

"A little too well?"

"I'm not saying that."

"What are you saying, Marissa? That perhaps she might not be objective?"

Marissa hesitated for a fraction of second. She had not asked herself that question.

"I don't think so," she replied slowly. Mark picked up on it.

"Why are you hesitating?"

"Because so far I have had no cause to doubt her." Marissa's mind had been made up. She needed to steer Mark away from the dangerous waters into which he was wading. "In any case, I will be the one dealing with her directly."

"And with Crowne as well, as agreed?"

"Agreed." Crowne was a terrorist but at least he was behind bars. To her the IRA felt dated but somewhere, very deep, in the darkest part of her soul, she understood what being the conquered people, the underdog, meant.

Marissa focused on Mark again. He had dropped his chin against his chest, a sign he was reflecting, she had learned. She gave him the space to think. She poured some water into two glasses; the gurgling of the bottle emptying sounded almost too loud.

"Are you sure you want this confrontation?" Marissa pushed a glass towards him.

"No, I'm not sure. But even if I never see him again, I need to ask him why."

Marissa nodded. "Then I will ask him whether he agrees to meet you."

* * *

HMP Belmarsh's doctor shone a light into Henry's eyes with a small torch, left right, left right. He inspected his nascent bruises.

"Quite a fight, wasn't it?"

"More an aggression than a fight." Henry grumbled.

The doctor kept prodding Henry's body for other signs of damage. "Why did you have this fight then?"

"I told you this is not a fight...I didn't start this."

"But you must know why Ronnie had a go at you?"

"It's Ronnie we are talking about. here I've got no idea what goes through this guy's head." Henry's anger had risen into his belly. Did this idiot not know Kray was a nutjob?

"Still, you've received quite a pasting."

"It's only because I protected myself and didn't retaliate."

The doctor raised a quizzical eyebrow. When did inmates not relish a good fight?

Henry inhaled deeply. He did not need to be rattled by this little asshole, Kray had done a good enough job of that.

"In my experience there is always a trigger."

Henry managed to shrug, wincing as he did so.

The doctor moved back to his desk. "You'll live."

Henry nodded and started to slowly get dressed again.

Why Henry had not kept his mouth shut was a question that would come later in the privacy of his own cell.

The doctor looked at the two officers.

"I don't think he needs to go to the hospital. I'll come back tonight to check him over again."

"Come on, Henry." One of the officers nodded in the direction of the door. Henry dressed in the standard Belmarsh tracksuit still covered in blood and followed them. He had not asked where he was going. At the bottom of the stairs one of the guards started climbing towards Henry's cell. Henry limped in the same direction. They were taking him back. Henry stepped into Cell 14.

"Get changed," said the officer he knew. "The governor wants a word."

Chapter Fourteen

From a distance Pole could see Andy standing at his desk and gesticulating, whilst talking on his mobile. He stopped abruptly and bent down to jot some illegible note in his notebook.

Pole smiled. Working with his newly promoted DS was a treat. There was something almost childlike in the way Andy engaged with his job so enthusiastically. Pole's DS hung up but kept talking at the screen as if reprimanding it for not delivering the answer quickly enough.

"I am not sure it will take any notice," Pole said.

"Guv," Andy turned around with a small jerk, but Pole's amused face gave him confidence. "I've got some really interesting news."

"Very good, shoot." Pole leaned against the desk, arms crossed.

"I confirmed, well I think I confirmed, the route that Visconti was taking to smuggle the art pieces and artefacts out of the Middle-East war zones."

Pole nodded, "Go on."

"I am ninety-nine per cent sure he's been using the African route: Libya, Malta then Italy."

"What's the alternative?"

"From Tunisia to France or sometimes Southern Spain."

"Are there no direct routes? I mean from the Middle-East?"

"Not really. The most direct route would be to Turkey or Greece."

Andy had brought a map of the countries surrounding the

Mediterranean onto the screen. He had drawn the routes in different colours, making them easier to distinguish.

"What leads you to believe Visconti was taking the African route?" Pole said. "Choose a less obvious route to avoid detection?"

"That's one of the reasons I think, but it may also be that it is where he had the best contacts for smuggling."

"Who else is using that route for trafficking?"

"The Narco unit told me that drugs are smuggled along a completely different route. People trafficking drugs established their routes before any of these were mapped and they don't like to mix."

"Armaments, as you suspected?" Pole bit his lip. This case was getting bigger by the minute.

"That's much more interesting because that's where the lines are getting blurred and Libya is in such a state of flux that weapons transit through it all the time."

"To where, do we know?"

"The whole of Africa. CT Command was pretty adamant."

"Nowhere else?"

"Nope." Andy moved his mouse and new lines appeared on his map of the Mediterranean and Africa. Pole moved to the back of Andy's chair to take a better look.

"How about migration?"

"You mean people?" Andy turned around surprised.

"Why not?"

"That's an interesting idea, Guv. I'll dig around."

"How about INTERPOL?"

"Haven't had much luck."

"Let me make some calls too. In the meantime, take me through the chart."

"As far as weapons are concerned, African trafficking goes through the Libya–Tunisia route then moves to Malta and Italy. The Middle-Eastern trafficking goes through Turkey; they have various entry points through the Arabian Peninsula."

Pole was following the various colours on the chart with his fingers. "That's a pretty good map you've put together." Pole straightened up and resumed his previous position, leaning against

Andy's desk. "Visconti departed from the norm. He took the risk of taking a much longer route for the trafficking of his goods, I presume to avoid detection."

"Overland that's got to be true, but I'm not sure it holds when it comes to sea transfer."

"Which is why he would probably have stopped first in Malta?"

"A short stop to secure the goods and then carry on to Italy." Andy nodded approvingly.

"Hey, I too am a bear of some brain." Pole grinned. "What's next?"

"I need to find out whether Visconti changed any of his MOs and I need more evidence to prove that he moved from art to armaments."

"Or people," Pole added. "Anything else?"

"Well." Andy adjusted his thick glasses. "I've got the feeling —" Andy stopped, hesitant about how to put his idea across to Pole.

"I don't care about diplomacy. Come on, say it how you see it."

"I'm not sure CT Command is telling me everything."

"I'm sure they're not."

"I asked whether they had Visconti on their radar and they were pretty vague."

"Vague is good." Pole clicked his fingers. "They can't say categorically no, or they might be misleading us."

"What if it's national security and all that?"

"Then they need to tell us Visconti is off limits."

"Would someone else be leaning on them?" Andy asked, candidly.

Pole hesitated for a second. His DS had just raised a tenuous link he had not yet considered. "What do you mean?"

"Other agencies."

"Let's first see what Ferguson has to say before we jump to any conclusions." Pole patted Andy on the shoulder. "Doing a really great job. Keep it up."

Andy beamed a smile and went back to work.

Pole's face darkened when he crossed the threshold of his office. He closed the door and pulled a brand-new phone out of his pocket. Time to call MI6.

* * *

The smell of bland meat, boiled cabbage and mashed potatoes made him retch. Henry had taken his lunch to his cell and left it on his desk. He was not hungry. The bruises on his face had started to change colour: pus yellow and dirty blue. He touched his cheek gingerly. It had almost doubled in size despite the pack of ice the doctor had given him.

Henry looked at the plate that was getting cold. He fought the urge to throw it into the toilet. He reached for a small tin of herbs stashed away on his shelves and sprinkled a pinch over the dish; perhaps it would help.

He sat down and put a forkful of mash in his mouth. At least he did not have to chew any of it, for once overcooked was a good thing. He kept going until his plate was empty. It was fuel for survival. Whilst eating, Henry was mentally going over the meeting he had just come back from.

HMP Belmarsh's governor had not been happy. He had spent half an hour being lectured about fighting, privileges to be reconsidered and, of course, was he fit to be released to help with the SFO case? Henry had remained silent, contrite, repeatedly making the point that he had been attacked. The CCTV cameras would tell. But no fight ever started unprovoked. The governor dismissed him; he would be told later what his ruling was.

The familiar clunk of the cell door's bolts told Henry it was bang-up time. He stretched his arm towards the biscuit tin. Another clunk surprised Henry. He pushed the tin back and turned around painfully. Someone had just released the bolts and would enter his cell in a few seconds.

"Hello Henry, put your shoes on and bring your coat."

Henry's mind went blank. Shoes. Coat. He was leaving the compound. Was it so cold outside that he needed a coat? He could not quite tell. The temperature in HSU was almost constant, hospital-like, a temperature that made you limp and comatose.

He remembered – the segregation unit was at the other end of the large structure that made up HMP Belmarsh.

"Hurry up, I haven't got all day." The officer moved his hand in the direction of the landing.

Henry sat on his bed, fished out his shoes from underneath it and fixed the Velcro into position. There were no shoelaces allowed in prison. From a small wardrobe Henry pulled a duffel coat Nancy had hurriedly purchased when he had been sent to HSU. It was not the place where an inmate should be wearing an Armani camel coat.

He started walking, one officer in front and one at the back. He did not want to ask where he was going. He did not want to show he cared or that he was scared.

Henry went through the fourteen checks it took to exit HSU:

- body checks
- name checks
- metal detectors

As Henry approached the small reception area within HSU his stomach somersaulted. True, he went through the same area when he was out on exercise. But today he was turning left towards the governor's office again. He would be told he had instigated the fight with Kray. No matter how much Henry had argued, he had lost the argument.

He would now be told how long he would spend in the segregation unit. He would almost certainly lose some of his privileges as well. All this for two small words: "Bloody idiot". He could scream at his stupidity. Who was the bloody idiot now?

Henry stopped beside the door leading to the outside.

"Sit please," one of the guards asked. Henry did as he was told. He could not give up so close to his goal. He had to argue his case again: self-defence, never had a scrap with anyone before, a saint – by HSU standards of course. At six foot three and with four years of solid gym training he could have inflicted damage on Kray but the only injury Kray could show would have come from the guards. But would they want to admit they had savaged him?

This was hopeless.

"It's cold outside," one of the guards warned. Henry nodded and slowly moved his arms into the sleeves of his coat. He adjusted the collar and stepped inside the yard where another two guards were already waiting for him.

A large van was parked outside. He almost ignored it until one of the guards opened the back door. "In you go."

Henry could not hide his surprise and he caught the amused look on the guard's face. He limped for a few seconds towards the open door and before he could take it all in the handcuffs were put on him and he was pushed inside.

There was already a guard sitting in the van, a man he had not met before. The second guard sat down in silence opposite his colleague. The van lumbered out of the gates. Henry let his head fall against the cold metal of the cage in which he had been locked up. He was leaving Belmarsh.

The plan was still on track.

The excitement was so intense he needed to calm down and chat. "Any chance of some water?"

The officer he did not know grabbed a bottle from underneath his seat. He stood up, walking cautiously and hunched forward to avoid falling when the van suddenly hit a pothole. He slid the bottle through the bars without a word and went back to his seat.

Henry opened the bottle and drank the water in one go. He closed his eyes and tried to quieten his thoughts. It was an astounding outcome. Who could have cut a deal of that magnitude with Belmarsh? The SFO needed him badly. A reassuring thought.

Henry brought his mind back to the last time he had left HSU. The LIBOR scandal had been about to explode, and he certainly had been instrumental in its uncovering. He smiled at the memory. The UK government, the Bank of England and quite a few top executives in the City were about to feel the pain.

His smile broadened at the idea of working with Nancy and Pole again. He had almost enjoyed working with Nancy's *favourite inspector* as he liked to tease her every so often. Henry stretched. His mind now felt alert once more. He thought about the case that Nancy had outlined. It would take no time to help them find out who the mysterious ultimate beneficial owner of the fund was.

The van slowed down and stopped for a little longer than Henry would have expected at a set of traffic lights. It took a sharp right and went over what felt like a ridge. The angle of the van tilted forward.

They were no longer following the road but going underground. The van was moving slowly. It took another sharp turn to the right and stopped altogether. For a moment everything was silent and almost peaceful.

The door of the van opened with a metallic thump and both guards got out, leaving Henry alone in the cage. He had forgotten his watch and could not tell how much time had elapsed since they had left Belmarsh. Twenty minutes perhaps, half an hour at most.

The heating in the van had been turned off and the cold was seeping through the metal frame. Henry moved around. He leaned his back against the part of the van that connected with the driver's seat. He stretched his long legs and waited.

The door of the van opened again, a small gap to start with. Henry stayed put. His heartbeat had risen, and he started breathing slowly, ready to deal with whatever life was about to throw at him.

A squat young man entered. He was wearing a sober blue coat and a pair of black leather gloves. He sat as close as he could to the cage, crossed his legs, one foot in the air. "Hello Henry." He spoke with an imperceptible smile.

His voice did not try to disguise a faint East-End accent. "I'm glad we finally get to meet." He uncrossed his legs, moved forward, now elbows on knees. "And I feel certain that you've been expecting the call." The smile broadened, uncovering a neat row of teeth, sharp and dangerous.

"What makes you say that?" Henry asked folding his legs under the bench.

"Experience. And the help of the few people who know you well."

"There aren't that many of those around." Henry's face expressed certainty, perhaps a hint of irony.

Contact, at last.

The young man ignored this. "I have a deal for you."

"How about an introduction first?" A negotiation; finally, something Henry knew he excelled at.

"OK then, you can call me Steve for the time being."

"And later on?" Henry pushed.

"We're not there yet," Steve said, his small eyes drilling into Henry, searching for the weak spot and finding it already. "You're an angry man, Henry."

Henry fought the desire to tell the little chap to bugger off. He smiled instead. "It's a good asset on the trading floor."

"But it's something that gets you killed in my world."

"And what is your world?"

"Intelligence." Steve's amused eyes were roving over Henry again, gathering much more subtle information than the police had ever done.

"OK, intelligence about what?"

Steve laughed, a resounding don't-give-me-that-bullshit laugh. "You have spent four years at HSU Belmarsh with some pretty high-profile characters and you have befriended Kamal, sorry Abu Maeraka, so what do you think?"

"Cards on the table straightaway, hey." Henry was almost impressed.

"No time to lose, mate." Steve leaned against the side of the van.

"What do you want, information?" Henry was not going to make it so easy. Cards on the table but one ace up his sleeve.

"That's rather obvious." Steve looked disappointed.

"What's in it for me?"

"Need a bit more; you tell me what you can give me, and I'll tell you how much it is worth."

"No." Henry had pursed his lips. He moved to sit next to Steve on the other side of the cage. "I'll tell you what I want, and you tell me what I need to do to get it."

"Ambitious. I like it." Steve nodded with appreciation.

"Get me out of Belmarsh." Henry locked eyes with Steve.

Steve stood up, walked to the other side of the van but did not walk out. He was thinking.

"Hypothetically, if I said yes, *if*, you'd have to deliver something pretty big to me, something no one else can."

Henry had stood up too. He leaned against the bars of the cage, casually so.

"How about the financing structure of a new terrorist organisation?"

Steve moved closer. He was much shorter than Henry, but he did not feel threatened. "Now we're talking."

Steve moved away. "I'll contact you again."

"Is that it?" Henry hands now clung to the bars of the cage.

"Yup. I need to organise a few things before the next step."

"How do we make contact?"

Steve took a small picture out of his jacket pocket, on it the face of a man, looking serious, taken to fit an official badge.

"He will be your contact." Steve moved the photo so that Henry could see. Henry squinted. His eyelashes batted a few times.

"You're not serious, are you?"

"Couldn't be more serious, mate." Steve replaced the picture in his inside pocket and grinned.

Chapter Fifteen

The same dingy room, the same smell of sweat and bad coffee – Henry recognised it immediately. He loved it. It had been fun to work on the LIBOR case with Nancy and Pole here, despite the dramatic twist that could have cost them their lives.

Still, it had been a breakthrough for Henry, a way to consolidate his plan, to see how to move forward. Today the stakes were even higher. He had had no time to take stock of what Steve had said and what his proposition meant. MI6 needed him. Now he knew why.

Henry rolled his head from side to side a few times, inhaled deeply and exhaled slowly counting from ten to one. The palms of his hands had gone moist. He rubbed them on his thighs. So much was riding on this meeting. He was about to meet the SFO prosecutor, Marissa Campbell.

He dragged a chair across the floor away from the small table that would become his desk. It screeched, sending a shiver along his spine. He sat with an effort at the main table. He stretched his hands over its top, fingers spread to the limit. He was not ready the way he would have liked to be.

A soft noise startled Henry. He rotated his body with a wince to face the door. Friend or foe? He shook his head in relief at the sight of her.

Nancy had walked into the room carrying two cups of Benugo coffee, his favourite.

"Good afternoon." She smiled.

"Good afternoon Nancy." Henry stood up and bent forward to give Nancy a kiss on the cheek. She almost dropped their coffee as she spotted Henry's bruises and swollen face. She hurriedly put the cups on the table and dragged him into the light. "Who has done that to you? I need to report —"

Henry lifted his hand. "No need to panic. It's under control."

"What do you mean?"

"The nutcase who did this will be spending a lot of time in the segregation unit."

"Are you certain?"

"Positive."

Nancy looked unconvinced. "Positive." Henry repeated, bending forward and finally kissing her cheek, a gentle human touch that almost felt awkward. This was one of the other punishments he had to endure in prison. Human contact was either violent or non-existent. Nothing in between.

Henry handed her a coffee, they sat down and started drinking in silence.

"Inspector Pole is on his way," Nancy changed the subject.

Henry's jaws clenched and his look darkened.

"Surely, you can't be that annoyed at working with Pole again?" Nancy said surprised. "Henry? I thought you had made your peace."

"So sorry Nancy; getting out of HSU makes me nervous." It was the best he could do. Pole's involvement in the case had taken on a new meaning. A pang of sadness shook him. He had to lie to her.

She looked at him still in doubt. "Are you sure you are OK? Is something troubling you?"

Henry shook his head. He felt a distance opening between him and Nancy, a small gap but a break, nevertheless. He had not thought about it but now, in her presence, he understood how much he had felt included, encompassed in a field of friendship that was seamless. And the fact that he was about to lose it wrecked his heart.

"I'm fine working with Pole, really." Henry forced himself to smile.

"I'm sorry," Nancy said laying a friendly hand on his shoulder. "You had plenty of time to prepare last time you were allowed outside Belmarsh; today has been very rushed."

155

"Why was that?" Henry's hopes lifted; perhaps she knew about MI6?

"The attempt on Marissa. The bomb that was meant for Mark Phelps delayed the procedure to approve your helping us, but this time —"

"What do you mean? Another bomb?" Henry had turned to stone.

"Have you not been told?" Nancy said surprised. She gave Henry the details of what she knew. He listened in silence. First Mark Phelps, now Marissa Campbell's unsuccessful shooting. The implications almost overwhelmed him. After all, he had been branded, no – he had been a terrorist too. Would these people still want to work with him? The thought hit him square in the chest.

He took a gulp of coffee. Something to keep his throat from closing. His focus went for a moment. He pushed away the question that was crushing him.

Who would be next?

Their coffee was almost finished. Nancy started taking documents out of her satchel. Her yellow legal pad and unassuming biro came out as well. Henry welcomed the disruption. He picked up the pen between his thumb and index finger and inspected it.

"What on earth is that?"

"It's called a pen I believe." Nancy smiled coyly.

"Don't you have anything more decent to work with?"

"You mean a Montblanc pen, Cartier?"

"Or even a good old Parker. With proper ink, I mean."

"And it has taken you four years to realise that I cannot abide writing with any of those. Tut, tut, tut. Where has your sense of observation gone?"

"Ouch, point taken." Henry was still holding the pen the way he would a piece of junk.

"We do not receive tombstones or ridiculously large corporate presents when we close a case. Unlike you bankers."

"Ex-banker if you please. And Pritchard QC did have a very large collection of excellent pens if I recall." Henry was enjoying the light banter.

"Indeed, a point on which Pritchard and I strongly disagree – my rebellious nature and my old communist upbringing," Nancy replied, equally enjoying the tease.

"You, a commie?" Henry arched his eyebrows in genuine astonishment.

"I did tell you my father was a communist; remember I am half-Chinese from the mainland of China not Hong Kong."

"Of course, you did say. And the years at The Sorbonne."

"*Absolument, rebel de la gauche.*" Nancy nodded.

A knock on the door stopped them in their tracks. It opened and Pole entered followed by a tall black woman.

Henry stood up, uncertain whether she would want to shake hands. He thanked Nancy mentally. She had helped him once more to feel he was human after all.

Pole extended a firm hand towards Henry. Their eyes met and Henry knew he had been told not to make his life difficult. Pole introduced Marissa Campbell as the SFO prosecutor dealing with the Bank X whistle-blowing case.

She extended an equally firm hand and shook Henry's. Her broad face was amiable, the face of someone you could confide in. Perhaps wrongly. Her willingness to shake his hand after what she had gone through impressed Henry. She sat herself in front of him, impassive. She was here to do a job and a job she would do.

Marissa took over and started by recapping the facts of the case. By 2009 Bank X had refused the UK government bailout programme. It had instead received funding from a state in the Middle-East. So far, so very good; nothing wrong with this.

However, a large proportion of the funds raised had been subsequently lent to a Panama fund, the ownership structure of which was complex. It had been impossible so far to establish who the ultimate beneficial owner was.

The suspicion was that the same Middle-Eastern state was benefiting through some of its government's officials. And this was a circular transaction UK legislation did not allow, in clear contravention of the law.

Mark Phelps, the whistle-blower, had had access to information that supported the suspicion, and he was ready to speak up. But the documents he had been able to collect were insufficient to bring about a conviction. The SFO needed the details of the Ultimate Beneficial Owner, the UBO.

157

Henry nodded a few times. He could already think of a number of ways in which he could disentangle the fund legal structure and find out the name of the UBO.

"How much do you know about Panama?" Marissa directed a first question at him.

"I understand how the system works." Henry moved nearer the table and spread his long fingers over a set of documents Marissa had just put in front of him. "May I?"

"That is why you are here, right?" Marissa shot back.

Henry ignored her tone and started going through the file, speed-reading the details it contained. "I'll need more time to digest the information, but I can see already that complex layering is going to make it very hard to find the UBO."

"Yes, we gathered that."

"You would like me to disentangle the ownership structure and trace the individual or individuals at the top."

"That would be helpful." Marissa blinked. It would be bloody marvellous. Henry made a metal note of her tic.

"What do you need?" Pole asked.

Henry tapped his fingers on the side of the table. "I need a couple of Bloomberg terminals. Like last time, set up to access live market data. Access to the web." Henry locked eyes with Pole again. If he wanted to facilitate he needed to provide the right tools for data mining. "And, a burner phone."

"Shall I also provide you with the keys to your cell?" Pole shot back.

"That would be really nice. However, the governor at Belmarsh may not be that forthcoming."

"Let's calm things down a little." Nancy moved her arm across the table to separate the parties. "Perhaps we should remind ourselves why we are here."

"Well put," Marissa added. "We are hoping to unveil significant criminal activity."

"Why the phone?" Nancy asked.

"Because I need to make a call to a former contact. He won't talk if he knows the call can be traced."

"And you won't give us the name, I presume." Pole looked unhappy. Henry's contact was outside his jurisdiction. Henry understood why Pole would rather focus on finding out who the relevant person was at the end of a long line of connections but this was not the way it worked in the murky world of tax evasion.

"Spot on, Inspector," Henry replied, giving him the thumbs up.

"Ms Campbell, would you agree to my suggestion?" Henry's voice almost trembled. It was her he needed to convince.

"I will support it to the extent you can demonstrate it is necessary and I can see progress in the unravelling of the structure of the Panama fund." Marissa had relaxed suddenly. Perhaps she had seen enough of Henry to sense that she could trust him to deliver the information needed. Perhaps it was something else altogether. Henry did not care. All that mattered was that she was willing to work with him.

"Which countries are you intending to call?" Pole asked.

Henry sat back and thought for a moment. "I may need information along the way from Malta, but my first port of call will be Panama."

"And in Panama?" Pole was not letting go.

"Mossack Fonseca, the largest law firm in the country."

Marissa nodded. "If you can get something out of them, I'll be very impressed."

"Then prepare to be amazed." Henry almost smiled.

* * *

"Your guest has arrived, Sir," the porter said, whilst taking Brett's trench coat and trilby hat.

"Has he?" Brett would have been annoyed at the news in other circumstances, but MI6-Steve's early arrival could mean only one thing.

Trouble.

Brett walked without stopping through his club. A few people he knew were reading their newspapers, expecting to be greeted, but Brett had no time for common courtesies.

Steve had selected a suitably secluded corner. Brett caught the young man unaware as he moved towards the chairs, a first since Steve had become his minder. He was observing a couple of men speaking loudly about their views on the current government. A lot of posturing and very little depth. Steve might have been amused by the shallow conversation. Instead he seemed to survey the people Brett frequented. His small beady eyes, roving in their direction unnoticed. Brett resumed his walk.

"It is unusual to find you here before me." No need to be civil with Steve. He might even have been disappointed if Brett had been polite.

"Thought I might pick up some intel." MI6-Steve grinned. "But I gather you also have some important info for me."

Brett sat in the armchair opposite Steve's. He did not want to face into the room whilst discussing his findings about The Sheik. A gloved butler took Brett's order – Glenfiddich, no ice – but no need to specify – the butler already knew.

"The Sheik is contemplating turning Crowne into a Jihadi." Brett barely contained a smile. How was that for a piece of news?

"Good," Steve replied, swilling his glass of whisky in slow motion to dissolve the ice that swam in it.

"Are you being flippant for the sake of it?" Brett's nostrils flared. The East-End boy was annoying him more than usual today. His glass of whisky appeared as if from nowhere and Brett almost thanked the waiter. He took a large mouthful hoping it would help.

"Nope, just very happy to hear they think they can do that."

"Enlighten me then."

"It means they are starting to trust him."

"And what if he gets —" Brett looked for the right word, "turned?"

"Don't worry about that. That's my problem, not yours."

"Not so. I need to know whether to encourage The Sheik or not."

"Do you think they will listen to your opinion on a matter like that?"

"He just did. So why would he ask if he didn't want to know the answer?"

"To test you. To see whether you have an agenda; whether you want to place Crowne."

Brett stopped for a moment to consider Steve's point. True, he had not thought about that.

"You did good by not lying about your opinion by the way. He would have guessed in any case. Which is why the less I tell you the better."

"You're looking after my interests now?" Brett sniggered.

"No, looking after my interests, but since you are part of my interests ..."

"And here I was, hoping."

"You need to keep your powder dry for what comes next."

"Are you intent on talking only in riddles today?" Brett drummed his fingers a few times on the arm of his chair.

"Be patient, I am coming to it." Steve took a mouthful of whisky. "I believe you are about to be asked to arrange the transfer of another consignment out of the UK."

"You believe or you know?" Brett sat back in his armchair.

"Let's say we are ninety per cent certain."

"That sounds pretty certain to me. Anyway, I presume the next request from The Sheik will be armaments."

"Have you been told already?" It was Steve's turn to sound miffed.

"No, my dear fella," Brett savoured his small success. "I might be a toff but I do have a brain, as you yourself remarked a few months ago."

Steve whistled softly and grinned. "Go ahead, and ...?"

"When The Sheik asked me to bring Clandestine X into the UK, he didn't mention armaments and I was keen to stress that suited me fine. And it does." Brett took another sip of whisky. "Then, there is the shooting – the one that caused the death of the young man at the Bank of England. And the other – execution." Brett felt strangely queasy. He did not do emotions but the latest development had been a little too much even for him. MI6-Steve nodded encouragingly.

"A couple of days ago, The Sheik saw me and produced the photos of Visconti, as you know."

This time, Brett felt sick. He braced himself and a bead of sweat rolled down the side of his face. He quickly wiped it away with a white cotton handkerchief.

"You think it's a way to 'incentivise' you to do the things you don't want to do. Like armaments?"

"That's what I think," Brett gulped down more whisky to clear the nausea.

Steve finished his glass and looked at the small lump of ice still dissolving at the bottom. "Possible."

"What if it is something – lethal?"

"Brett, all armaments are lethal. That's the point."

"I may only deal with antiquities, but I know what a gun is for," Brett replied dryly. "I mean extreme weapons: chemicals, nuclear?"

"We will be tracking the parcel. You know the route; that is all I need. Just keep The Sheik on board."

"Do I have a choice? Unless I want to finish like …" Even Brett couldn't bring himself to be sarcastic about Visconti's death.

"We are getting deeper into this project."

"You mean I am."

"No, we are. You have just become one of our top priorities. You should be flattered."

"No, I should be mightily scared."

Brett finished his glass and put it on the table. Time to leave the comfort of his club.

162

Chapter Sixteen

Pole and Henry were walking alongside each other, the prison officers who accompanied Henry walking a few steps in front of them. Pole slowed down a fraction, Henry matched his pace. The distance between them and the officers increased a little, then a little more until Pole felt able to speak.

"You spoke to Steve Harris?" Pole murmured.

Henry nodded. Pole glanced at him. Henry's body had tightened. He was on the alert, looking straight in front of him.

"Why you?"

"Convenience and …" Pole hesitated. There was not enough time to speak about Nancy. He was not even sure he wanted Henry to know about the quest for her father. Should he trust Henry and tell him about the deal he had cut with MI6 to gather information on China?

The officers stopped in front of the lifts, in a few seconds they would turn around and see the two men lagging behind.

"Past history." Pole added swiftly before quickening his pace.

It was too late for Henry to ask another question. Pole noticed the clenched fists in the tight clasp of his handcuffs. They had entered the lift and Pole still could not quite read Henry's mood.

Anger – as ever. He was not surprised or even concerned about it but could the essential ingredient their relationship needed to work together be found? He did not know. Pole would have to work a little harder than he had anticipated.

Trust would not come easily.

They reached the end of the long corridor at the back of the Scotland Yard building. A high security reinforced door opened onto a small inner courtyard. The back door of the prison van was already thrown open. Henry got into the vehicle without looking at Pole. The van door slammed shut and Henry was on his way back to HSU Belmarsh.

Pole almost felt sorry for him. He ruffled his goatee and stayed in the yard to watch the van pass through the heavy gate that led to the street. An icy gust of wind made him shiver. He walked back through the corridor and towards the room where Nancy and Marissa were debriefing about what Henry had said.

Pole had noticed a nascent shadow on Henry's face. Henry did not seem the sort to grow a beard. A silly idea, of course; why should he not?

No, Henry was close shaven, clean-cut, the blade doing its job close to his jaw and close to his throat. It seemed important and yet Pole could not make it out yet.

* * *

The door had shut behind them. Nancy had barely said goodbye to Henry. It felt inappropriate to demonstrate their closeness in front of Marissa.

Marissa had been outstandingly controlled. Not a hint of nerves or anger, after what she had just gone through. Remarkable. Her eyes had followed the two men leaving the room, her heavy frame tilted forward, ready to follow them. Nancy cleared her throat. Marissa's body twitched, awoken from her concentration.

"What do you think?" Nancy asked, moving to the chair Pole had occupied next to Marissa.

"Very bright. Not what I expected – intelligent of course; I thought he would be – but not as brash or arrogant as I had anticipated."

"You think you can work with Henry, despite …" Nancy hesitated. Should she bring terrorism into the conversation? She, who never shied away from the hard questions, was uncertain.

"Despite his IRA connections?" Marissa asked. "You look surprised Nancy. Wasn't it you who taught me to ask the tough questions?"

"It seems the pupil has exceeded the master." Nancy laughed, joining fist and outstretched hand in the sign of a Kung Fu master. Marissa hesitated and joined Nancy in a giggle; it was nice to be a little less serious.

"I'm not so sure about that but I'm glad you feel that way nevertheless." Marissa carried on smiling. "And to answer your question, I can't deny it, it is unnerving to be working with a former IRA operative. But now that I've met him ..."

"I'm glad of it. He will deliver what he has promised."

"I have no doubt about it. He is – on a mission." Marissa's face became thoughtful.

Nancy nodded. Henry was dedicated, almost obsessed with the idea of redemption. A subject he spoke regularly about. But Marissa had put her finger on something new. Something had moved in Henry's attitude. Nancy could not quite fathom what, unless she took his letter at face value.

Marissa's voice came back into focus. "... burner phone might be difficult."

"But we won't leave the phone with him all the time and we may even be able to limit his access."

"You mean narrow it to a specific country?"

"For example."

"A good idea. Still ..."

Pole knocked and walked in. Nancy smiled as she turned in his direction. He had stopped inside the door frame, making sure he was not interrupting an important conversation.

"Come in; it is your interrogation room after all." Marissa said.

"Just making sure I'm not intruding on something essential." Pole smiled. "You may have been talking fashion or hairstyles."

"That is so not PC." Marissa chuckled. Her smile broadened to uncover a small gap in the middle of a set of otherwise perfect teeth.

"Then what? Henry's long list of must-haves?"

"That's more like it." Marissa kept smiling.

"Superintendent Marsh is going to have a fit," Pole mused. "I like it."

"Perhaps I should be the one asking?" Nancy's eyes sparkled, teasing him.

"Not a chance." Pole crossed his arms. "I am keeping my powder dry for a better occasion."

"You mean there will be a better occasion than asking Marsh to let Henry have a phone?"

"Absolutely. No doubt. Obvious." Pole replied almost serious.

"Am I missing something glaring?" Marissa questioned, amused.

"Hardly." Pole gestured dismissively and came to sit at the table. "Going back to the case, how much are you prepared to disclose to him?"

"I'm not sure yet. Let's see how he gets on with what he's been given so far."

Pole dropped his head forward a fraction. Considering.

"What if he needs to meet with Mark Phelps?"

The room stood still for a moment. Nancy felt her stomach drop at the memory of her meeting with Mark.

"I've spoken to Mark myself. He's had time to think." Marissa aligned a paperclip on the wad of documents in front of her.

"Has he changed his mind?" Pole sounded dubious.

"Somewhat. He can see that Henry is the right person to help deliver the evidence for the case."

Nancy felt almost relieved but there was a chill in Marissa's tone. "If he simply does not want to deal with him directly it should be workable, but is there something else?"

"There is. Mark wants to meet Henry, just once, to talk about his involvement with the IRA."

A deep intake of air came from Pole. Nancy was mildly surprised. How strange? Perhaps this is what she had felt when she had spoken to him. The need to make sense of it all. The need for a confrontation with his tormentor. It brought victims some release, made it easier for them to move forward.

Nancy felt two pairs of eyes on her waiting for her reply. She was Henry's principle contact. What would he say?

Accept? Refuse?

"Maybe this is a good way for Henry to atone?" Pole said, serious. No banter about Henry's famous need for redemption. Something he liked to tease Nancy about every time she brought the subject up.

166

"Maybe." Nancy could genuinely not decide.

Henry's desire to make amends was to be on his own terms, he would choose how and when to do so. Would the Henry-in-control-of-his-destiny agree to see a victim – not his victim, but nevertheless a victim of terrorism? A terrible reminder of the depth of his failure.

"I need to think about how I approach him about this." She spoke slowly, beginning to gauge what it would take.

"Otherwise …" Marissa let the sentence hang. It was not a threat, simply fact. It was Mark Phelps' price for assisting with the investigation.

"We understand," Pole said.

Marissa stood up, wincing as she did so. She rubbed her back and opened her satchel, methodically pushing her papers into it.

"Henry is due to come back tomorrow morning first thing. Belmarsh likes to get him through their gates before the other inmates are allowed out."

Marissa nodded. "I'll be here."

* * *

He stood arms stretched, legs apart – a vulnerable position he had learned to cope with. The prison officer frisked him, ran a metal detector up and down his body. Henry turned around to complete the check.

He was only through gate three. Another five to go before he reached the inside of HSU Belmarsh where he could move a little more freely. The journey back from Scotland Yard was always a deflating experience – as he had learned the last time he had been allowed out. Today had been particularly testing. The guards that had been around when MI6 first made contact were the same and yet they had behaved as if nothing had happened. Henry's mind was racing. He had to find a way to deliver the Ultimate Beneficial Owner of the Panama fund structure. He had been restless through the entire return trip at the thought of the plan coming together, at Kamal – Abu Maeraka's – words. He was also concerned. Henry would be allowed only minimum contact with inmates from now on.

Still, he could not be denied a shower or gym time. And he needed to have the conversation, not about Abu Maeraka's ploy for escaping, but about Nancy – no one must target her or the deal was off.

The usual metallic sound almost startled him. It was another door being opened. The routine checks started all over again. How many times did you need to frisk someone to be sure he was not carrying anything on his body?

The thought of smuggling something inside his backside had felt repulsive to start with but what would he now accept should his freedom depend on it? Suddenly the idea did not sound so distressing after all. Henry almost smiled. Give him another ten years and he might consider it a perfectly good option.

Henry stopped before the final door. It was almost 7pm and dinner was now available. He was asked to move into a small room; he would be brought some food, almost certainly cold and barely edible. But, hell, he had been allowed out, yes … out. He would gladly eat a piece of cardboard if it meant he could keep visiting the outside world.

The officers had left him on his own. He started shaking again, a tremor born from excitement and danger. Henry stood up and stretched his tall body. It felt heavy and muscular.

"Be ready," Abu Maeraka had said. He was. He wanted to shout the words in his throat building up to a roar.

Henry stretched again. Could he ask to go to the gym? The concern for Nancy stole most of his enthusiasm.

The small spy window carved into the door opened and closed almost instantly. Another inmate stepped in carrying a tray. Not someone Henry knew, even by sight. There was no eye contact; the guard was surveying the young man's every move. As he placed the small tray on the table, the young man brushed aside the small paper napkin that had been hurriedly placed on top of a plastic spoon. The paper towel dropped to the floor.

Henry froze. The young man mumbled an apology, picked up the napkin and disappeared as quickly as he had come. The door banged shut after him.

Such a clumsy gesture and yet such an important one. Was Abu Maeraka speaking? Be ready.

Or could it have been a genuine mistake? Henry replayed the scene in his mind. The very slow movements to place the tray on the table, the young man's hand trembling as he brushed the napkin away, his back hiding his movements from the guard – too deliberate. Big K had warned Henry. Abu Maeraka was building an army, his influence growing stronger every day. But wherever the young man came from, HSU or main compound, the message was clear ... Be ready.

Henry looked at the unappetising-looking pizza on his plate – a piece of cardboard, hey. He wolfed it down. It was fuel for a purpose.

* * *

Nancy and Marissa had left. Andy wanted a word. Marsh, The Super, wanted him – now. But he would have to wait his turn. Pole locked the door of his office and actioned the security pad that required a code to open it. The latest in security measures.

His second mobile phone was ringing. He hesitated, but what was the point in delaying. He needed to speak to Harris anyway.

"Harris," Pole kept his voice bland, no sign of anger, none of anticipation.

"Inspector Pole." Harris was waiting. He held all the cards, at least for the time being. Pole clenched his jaw.

"He has made a number of demands. In particular, one for a mobile phone." Pole elaborated further and gave Harris the details.

"A phone, good. Just make sure you limit the range and we will do the rest."

"Right," Pole replied. Harris seemed to have anticipated Henry's request, or had he suggested it?

"How has Marsh reacted?"

"I am about to have that conversation." Pole's voice took on a stubborn edge. He would not be pushed to discuss every step of the enquiry whether Harris liked it or not.

"Don't worry, Marsh is far too keen on his new high-profile case and he will be delighted to know Ms Wu is involved." The tease was hardly bearable.

Pole did not reply, torn between giving Harris a piece of his mind and terminating the call. "My secret weapon. Marsh will never say no to her."

Pole could hear the smile in Harris' voice, good shot it said. "I gather."

"How far are you with Crowne?" Pole asked.

"As much as I would like to show you the big picture, Inspector Pole, I am afraid I can't discuss with you the —"

Pole interrupted bluntly. "Harris, don't give me that bull. This is not the first time I've worked with MI6 so don't piss me off unnecessarily."

"I genuinely can't tell you." Harris sounded serious. "But I can tell you that I will keep Ms Wu and Ms Campbell safe."

"Now somehow that does not give me the warm glow it is supposed to," Pole replied. "Since you have mentioned Ms Wu perhaps you can tell me where your investigation into her father's disappearance is at?"

"It is China, and it was thirty years ago – very little has surfaced so far, a few cuttings on him as an artist and that is about it, and yes, before you ask, I am trying."

"You are trying, Agent Harris, I am glad even you admit that." Pole had moved to his desk, pleased with his pun. "Any timeline?"

Harris sounded interested enough in finding out more about Nancy's father. Pole asked a few more questions. Harris replied patiently and Pole wondered …

"Do you have any particular interest in Mr Wu?" Pole was unexpectedly direct. He was listening. There was a short intake of breath, a slight hold and release. Harris' voice remained even.

"None that I can think of, but I will let you know if that changes," Harris carried on. "Before you go, Inspector Pole, it would be good if you could arrange for Crowne to be on his own tomorrow between eleven and noon."

"I'll see what I can do." Pole hung up and threw the mobile on his desk. He slumped into his chair. Dealing with MI6 meant that he would never be one step ahead. There were too many moving parts he could not see, was not told about. As for being kept safe – Pole's experience told him otherwise. He was certain Harris would choose the security of his asset over and above that of Nancy or Marissa.

Pole's mobile rang. He grunted.

"I'm on my way Denise."

"The great man is waiting for you. Impatiently."

"I am walking as we speak."

"No, you are still at your desk wondering how to get what you want from him." Denise's voice had a cheerful tone that Pole trusted. She had been Marsh's PA for as long as Pole could remember. How she had delt with The Super for so long was a mystery.

"Can't fool you, can I?"

"No. You have two minutes to materialise in front of his door."

"Now, I am walking."

* * *

Marsh was outside his office speaking to Denise, when Pole arrived. Pole slowed down in the hope The Super would walk into his office without noticing him but was out of luck.

Marsh straightened up and looked towards Pole over his half-moon glasses. He waited for his DCI to approach and walked into his office without a word. Denise rolled her eyes. Pole moved an eyebrow up but there was no time for pleasantries. The great man had been waiting.

"The latest please?" Marsh asked as he sat down behind his desk. Pole resisted the urge to ask him which case he wanted to discuss; he needed to convince Marsh about the phone.

"The first meeting with Crowne was a success. I think the SFO prosecutor is impressed and convinced he can help."

"You think or she is?"

"She is."

Marsh shot Pole a look. "Timetable?"

"A series of daily meetings for the next three days. There is a lot to go through and the SFO needs to speed up the information gathering phase. They are willing to support Crowne in facilitating his requests."

Marsh suddenly moved forward in his leather chair. "What does Crowne want that is contentious then?" His voice showed that he was weighing up the impact of a dangerous situation. No matter how much Pole disliked Marsh for his brusqueness and political ambition, his mind was sharp.

"Top of the list – a burner phone." Pole gave it to Marsh straight, there was no need to be subtle with him.

Marsh's eyebrows rose and stayed like that until he had sat back in his chair.

"I see. And the SFO is willing to support this?"

"As long as we limit the range of the phone."

Marsh nodded. "Which destination?"

"Panama."

"I don't like it but you and the SFO are going to tell me that there is no other way, right?"

"Right."

"What does Ms Wu think?" Marsh's eyes moved away from Pole for a short moment. Pole straightened up a little. "She also believes it is not ideal —"

"Of course," Marsh interrupted. "Perhaps we can discuss options."

"I am not certain you will —"

"I'll ask Denise to arrange a meeting," Marsh interrupted again. "Please let Ms Wu know."

"Shall I tell the SFO we have a delay?" Pole made a final attempt.

"No. But let them know I need a second opinion."

Pole left a few minutes later. Perhaps Nancy could pretend she had a headache. A permanent one at the thought of meeting The Super.

172

Chapter Seventeen

"I suppose it would be too much to ask to be allowed gym time or even fifteen minutes on the rowing machine?" Henry asked as he was walking alongside one of the officers.

The small podgy man smiled. "Don't push it. You've been allowed out, right?"

"That doesn't mean I was able to run a marathon along the banks of the Thames, John."

"A good set of press-ups in your cell should do the trick." John was still amused. He had been working in HSU Belmarsh for almost two years. His time was due to end soon, much to Henry's regret. John had managed to be pleasant without compromising the *Sacro Saint Dicta* of HSU – "Thou Shall Not Fraternise With The Cons."

"Perhaps a shower after the set of press-ups, then?" Henry twisted his nose. "I don't want to offend my Scotland Yard colleagues with a good dose of BO and give Belmarsh a bad reputation."

John laughed outright. "It'll take more than a pongy con to give HSU Belmarsh a bad reputation. It's got one already."

"Still, I am meeting with two ladies tomorrow." Henry pleaded jokingly.

"I'll see what I can do."

Henry nodded and prepared to enter Cell 14. He slowed down a little, crossed the threshold and stood there until the door was shut. He could feel the metal against his back. Henry's body swayed gently, an oscillation that gradually pushed him inside the room. He forced himself to move slowly to his bed, two steps. He sat down, using his breathing as control.

Inhale – exhale.

Adrenaline was still coursing in his veins – everything was now possible.

"Everything," Henry murmured.

He let his mind drift, coming back to one word in focus. He had lived a boring but sheltered life since he had started his sentence. He hoped the four years spent in an environment in which hardly anything happened had not blunted his mind and his ability to anticipate danger. He would very soon find out.

Kamal was ready. Henry was still puzzled at the thought. Be one step ahead of the competition had been his motto and he had never failed. Today he was prepared to let someone else make a life-changing, even life-threatening, decision on his behalf but it was the price he had to pay.

Henry relaxed into the thought. Kamal and the new Jihadi group he was helping to build needed Henry Crowne. He certainly could construct a financial empire, unassailable and capable of churning out hundreds of millions. But a new idea was forming in his mind. Kamal had another motive perhaps.

Henry scratched his nascent stubble. He had always hated the idea of growing a beard but needs must. He would have to fit in and look dedicated. He picked up the small book wrapped in a delicate silk scarf. It was only 9pm. Time to read a few verses of the Qur'an before sleep.

* * *

Yvonne's phone rang for a while before someone picked up. The mortuary was not a place where matters were rushed. A young voice asked for a name. Pole replied he was returning Yvonne's call and the next minute the pathologist was on the line.

"I have something to cheer you up. Perhaps."

"How did you know I needed good news?" Pole's voice sounded almost offended.

"'Cos you're having to deal with The Super."

"How did you know? Never mind. What is it that is so cheerful in the middle of explosive devices, cadavers and other forensic paraphernalia?"

"I sent the bullet that was recovered from the taxi carrying Marissa to ballistics and there is a bit of forensic evidence on it."

"The suspense is hardly bearable."

"I have a partial print."

"OK. That could cheer me up. I can hear there is something more."

"Yup. That partial fingerprint is pretty close to the one I found in a previous case."

"Go on."

"The Royal Exchange sniper."

Pole's entire body tensed. Images and sounds jumble in his mind. The noise of a bullet shattering a window and the thud it made when it hit its target, Nancy and Edwina barely sheltering from the shooter, the man dead on the floor.

"Jon, Jonathan, are you still there? Hello …?"

"Yes, sorry. I'm back. I mean I'm listening." Pole's voice sounded faint. He leant against the desk.

"Flashback," Yvonne's voice was professional but considerate. "Happens a lot."

"Right. Thank you." Pole cleared his voice. "Would someone have been that careless?"

"More often than you think. In particular with bullets. And this is only a partial print, don't forget. I don't have enough to identify the person, but I have enough to establish a connection between the print on the bullet that almost killed Marissa Campbell and the one which exploded Gabriel Steel's head."

"And I presume the same gun."

"Correct."

"And how about …?"

"Visconti? Lots of prints on the sword and zero matches on IDENT1 so far, but I haven't finished."

Pole remained silent.

"I agree entirely," Yvonne said.

"What now? Can you also mind read?"

"You were thinking so loud I couldn't fail to hear. All this could be connected. I'll focus on the fingerprints."

"Thanks Yvonne, good to know we are on the same wavelength. My intuition —"

"Intuition! I'm a scientist. If I ever even whispered the word intuition I'd be branded a hysterical woman."

Pole managed a laugh. "I promise I won't mention it to The Super."

Pole hung up and looked at the long list of calls he had to return. Nancy had suggested a late dinner. He sat down and started his round of calls. He would be damned though if he missed an evening with the woman in his life.

* * *

"Will we see you at the wedding, old chap?"

Brett lifted an eye from his newspaper. He replied without asking the other gentleman to join him.

"Almost certainly, the young Earl of Coventry is finally tying the knot. I wouldn't miss it for the world." Brett barely smiled. He had no time to waste on such pleasantries. A few more words were exchanged, and the intruder retreated.

Brett resumed reading his paper, barely managed a few lines and checked his watch again. MI6-Steve was late, very late. Brett tried to pay more attention to *The Telegraph* article speculating about the death of Massimo Visconti: mafia – Sicilian or Russian? It was all about art smuggling – perhaps Italian old masters or even antiquities from further afield.

The paper had taken Visconti's death as an excuse to lament the theft of art in war-torn countries. "Better that than letting it be blown to pieces," Brett murmured with contempt. He dropped the paper and ordered a second whisky. He was meeting The Sheik again the next day, another request at short notice for a conversation in which he would be asked to deliver an impossible deal. Armaments of some horrendous nature. Antonio, his reliable Italian smuggler, wouldn't like it. Then again, if the price was right …

MI6 had promised back-up and he needed it, preferably now.

Steve was over an hour late. Even by his casual standards when it came to timetables, this was alarmingly late. Had something happened to him? Brett pushed the idea away but as time passed it kept creeping back into his mind. His handler was not a man he would have chosen to mix with – still, he was his protection, as his link to the agency.

The whisky arrived. Brett inspected the amber liquid through the thick crystal of the tumbler, an elegant Victorian Royal Scot Diamonds piece. He took a mouthful and closed his eyes.

Surely, if something had happened to Steve, he would have been contacted by now – although there were no mobiles allowed in the club.

Surely, they, whoever they were, would have sent a note.

Brett straightened up; this was ridiculous. The whisky was not helping, and he resented it. He would finish his glass and make a plan – back at home he could activate his emergency code.

The sound of a body dropping heavily into a chair startled Brett.

"Did you miss me?" Steve asked with a grin and a wink.

The tumbler shook in Brett's fingers and a few drops landed on his immaculate trousers. Brett brushed them off with the back of his hand and suppressed a curse.

"That much, hey." Steve turned towards the gloved waiter who had appeared noiselessly at his elbow. "The same thanks."

Brett would have liked to summon outrage at the way Steve was being so matey – name your drink, don't thank the waiter for crying out loud –but he was too relieved to indulge in his favourite pastime: correcting MI6-Steve in the ways of the upper classes.

"The reason why you are late had better be a good one."

"It is but ..."

Brett pursed his lips. "You can't tell me."

"At least not yet." Steve nodded. "We're picking up a lot of activity outside the UK. Too early to give us a lead."

"So that's it – no intel I can use, nothing." This was not the support Brett had been waiting for.

"Not quite. It is almost certainly about movement between countries."

"Really, I would never have guessed." The sharpness of Brett's voice amused Steve.

"You may want to prep Antonio up."

"Let me handle Antonio as I see fit."

"I reckon it will be armaments this time around," Steve interrupted Brett. His face had turned serious.

"I thought you had no idea."

"Not enough details though."

"Is that supposed to be reassuring?"

"It's not. Don't care whether you're reassured, Brett. I care whether you're still alive at the end of this deal."

"I don't believe one word."

"And to make matters even better, I think you've just been promoted by your Jihadi pal."

"To state the obvious, he is not my Jihadi pal. And what do you mean promoted?"

"You're about to replace Visconti – again unofficial." Steve emptied half of his whisky in one gulp.

"Was Visconti one of your – assets?" Brett's eyes had locked with Steve's.

"Nope. I don't even know whether anyone tried to recruit him."

"Let me rephrase the question. Is the fact that someone tried to recruit him what got Visconti killed? He was one of the best operators —"

"Hold your horses," Steve interrupted. "When it came to stolen artefacts, paintings and the like, perhaps, but armaments is a different matter altogether."

"And why would I fare better?"

"You got me." Steve raised his glass and drained his whisky.

Brett tapped his fingers on the arm of the leather chair. "Do I facilitate anything?"

"We've had this conversation before, yes. Anything goes."

"But before, it was hypothetical; today …" Brett let the sentence hang. He could not quite believe what he was letting himself in for.

"What matters is that we track the payload."

"But Antonio does not tell me the route he takes. That is the deal. I only see the merchandise when it arrives."

"And that is what we want."

"So, you don't care that some ridiculously dangerous item – nuclear, chemical, whatever – transits through Europe."

"I didn't say that but if it's the price to pay for dismantling this terror cell ..."

Brett had bent forward towards Steve as the conversation progressed. He now sat back in his seat. "Anything else?"

"Try to find out more about Crowne."

"You're not serious?"

"Extremely."

"And what am I supposed to find out? Whether they are going to get him out of jail?" Brett sniggered. His fair complexion had turned a shade of pink, making the roots of his hair almost look white.

"That would be ideal." Steve replied. He was not jesting.

Brett put the glass to his lips, realised it was empty. Another one? What the hell, it might be his last. He looked in the direction of one of the waiters.

Brett remained silent for a moment. Was MI6 genuinely expecting Crowne to escape? The answer seemed straightforward after all. Yes, they were.

"You want to recruit him, don't you?" Brett asked suddenly.

"You don't expect me to answer that question?"

"The idea of sending the peasant to the hell that is the Middle-East war zone has some appeal."

"Whether it has some appeal or not, it's off limits."

Brett sat back again. He had scored an unexpected point against MI6-Steve and he savoured it.

"If you know what is good for you, Brett, just let it rest." Steve's biting voice slapped Brett out of his mood.

"Fine, I'll see what information I can gather tomorrow."

* * *

The warm smell of food made Pole's mouth water. The small restaurant's top-floor room was packed, yet Nancy had secured a corner table that commanded the entire space and felt cosy. She was reading a book, her head slightly tilted forward, a pair of Chanel glasses shielding her eyes. Pole reached the table in a few long steps. Nancy lifted her face with a broad smile, small lines creasing the corners of her almond eyes.

She removed her glasses and lifted her face to Pole. He bent forward and kissed her cheek. Nancy closed her eyes. The brush of his lips on her skin felt delicious.

"Sorry I'm late." Pole sat down on the banquette next to Nancy.

"Don't apologise, Jonathan. The book I am reading is keeping me excellent company."

"Which book am I competing with?"

Nancy laughed. "Nothing can compete with you, *mon cher*, but, if you must know, Murakami."

"*Kafka on the Shore*," Pole added smartly. "Even a copper like me has read the man who is tipped to be the next Nobel Prize winner."

"*Mais je n'en doutais pas moins.*" Nancy pressed her fingers into his hand. "Let's order, I'm famished and so must you be."

The menu looked appetising and they chose a mix of peppery lamb, seabass cooked in lemon and herbs, okra fritters and roast aubergines. The waiter brought a tasty plate of beetroot hummus with freshly baked lagana bread for starters. Nancy and Pole enjoyed the first dish, sharing their impressions of the food they were eating. It was good to take pleasure in having dinner together.

The conversation drifted onto the latest art show they had visited together. Pole had been enthusiastic about the artist he had not known before, Bernard McGuigan. He spoke about his grandmother, her art galleries in London and Paris, opened in the fifties. "She would have loved his sculptures," he said animatedly.

"She must have met some of the biggest names in modern art. And so must you."

"She did, although she had a preference for the quieter, more obscure artists. Or artists that once were famous but have somewhat faded from memory; although she was a great fan of Kupka or Dubuffet."

"You own a Kupka, *n'est-ce pas?*"

"*Absolument*, although I have a few more on loan to museums."

"She had a very avant-garde taste, right until she sold the galleries, you mentioned before."

"She was fond of videos and installations way before they became popular; Joan Jonas in particular was a favourite. And we are talking early seventies."

"I am impressed. I can't quite get to grips with some video installations, I must say, but Jonas, she is a giant of that medium."

Pole spoke about the artists he had met. Nancy was listening but at the same time her mind was wandering towards another time. Pole gently took her hand. "What is on your mind? I'm talking about art which you always find uplifting but somehow I feel it is dragging you down today."

Nancy sighed. "I'm sorry. It's just bringing back some memories; Paris, artists in the seventies ..." She squeezed Pole's hand back and left hers in his, safe.

"Your father?" Pole's voice was cautious, only murmuring the words. Nancy nodded and her face changed. Her radiance had disappeared; it was sad and overcast. The memories of China rolled back like thundering clouds.

"I can't hide anything from you. Well, I'm not trying to anyway."

"I know it's not easy. I'm afraid I've not made much progress since we last spoke about it." Pole had moved closer, his shoulder almost touching hers. She ran her elegant hand over her hair and tugged a strand that had escaped from the clasp behind her ear.

"I'm not expecting you to find anything significant this early on. It was over thirty years ago, and I haven't heard from him for almost as long."

"Still, it's important to you. I don't want to let you down."

"Jonathan, *mon cher ami*, I can't ever imagine you letting me down." Nancy had tilted her head towards him. "And I also hope you won't do anything you shouldn't to get the information."

"*Moi. Jamais*," Pole said mockingly offended.

"*Vraiment*, Inspector Pole. I know what you are capable of." Nancy squeezed his hand once more. Pole remained impassive. Being involved with MI6 to solve her father's disappearance fell squarely into that category.

"May I ask a question?" Pole became more serious.

"Of course." Nancy drank a little wine.

"Why now? After so long."

Nancy pulled back slightly and considered her answer.

"Maybe because I feel ready. It would have been impossible – too difficult – when I was working." Nancy's eyes focused in the distance, conjuring images that did not speak of happiness.

"You needed to hold it together when you were a QC, emotionally." Pole ventured.

"That is a good way to put it."

"I can understand," Pole said.

"Time to move on. I can't spend the rest of my life hesitating." Nancy's voice wobbled a little. Pole moved his shoulder even closer and she rested her head on it lightly. They stayed silent for a moment before Pole murmured quietly.

"Shall I take you home?"

"Please."

Chapter Eighteen

The coffee grinder made its crunching noise, its small vibrations rippling through her fingers. Marissa opened the lid and closed her eyes. She inhaled deeply the rich aroma of freshly ground coffee beans. She poured the coarse powder into the cafetière, an old-fashioned two-part affair. The water had boiled and reached the right temperature. She poured it over the coffee in small doses, making sure it was wetted through.

Marissa touched her face gingerly. The bump on her forehead she had got diving to the floor to avoid being shot, had come down and the bruise near her eye had darkened. At least a black eye on a woman of colour might be less noticeable. Marissa chuckled at the thought. Finally, a small advantage.

She was wearing her usual black suit, white shirt uniform. She was allowing herself a quick cup of coffee before the police car came to pick her up. Crowne would already have arrived. She had left it to Pole and Nancy to speak to Henry about his proposed meeting with Mark Phelps.

Against all odds, Marissa had decided to trust Henry. His rebellious nature chimed with her own, although she was grateful, she had never been dominated by it and plumbed its depth. She dropped a lump of sugar in her mug and drank in small sips. She never stirred her coffee, enjoying its bitterness being gradually replaced by the sweetness of the taste once she reached the bottom of the cup.

Marissa understood only too well the temptation to seek revenge. Black and female in the legal profession, let alone the judiciary, had not been easy. King's College London had been a bedrock of support, helping her assuage her frustrations. With Nancy as a master and mentor during her pupillage, she had learned to gain in confidence. She could not have hoped for a better role model: similar experience, equally ambitious and above all the same determination to preserve their integrity.

It was still early, and she had absent-mindedly moved to the lounge whilst drinking her coffee. The space was dwarfed by the grand piano she had positioned beside one of the bay windows, not too close though to avoid exposing it to the sun.

She lifted the keyboard lid and ran her fingers over the white and black keys. She placed her cup on the floor, leaned over a little. Her hands moved quickly, playing the first bars of Debussy's 'Clair de Lune'. The melody brought back the unhappy memory of her meeting with Mark. Music was her sanctuary. It should never have been violated in that way.

The doorbell rang. At the same time her BlackBerry buzzed with a new text. The police car was waiting for her. She gently closed the keyboard and finished her coffee, enjoying the sweetness of the last gulp. She moved back to the kitchen, looked around: everything was in its place, tidy and organised. The doorbell rang again. She hesitated; a wave of anxiety surprised her.

"I'm outside." Marissa recognised Pole's voice.

Her knees wobbled and she grabbed the door handle for balance. "Is everything all right?"

"Yes. Don't be alarmed. I was just on my way to work and thought I'd give you a lift and use the official car as an escort."

Marissa opened the door, struggling with the bolts.

"Sorry, I didn't mean to worry you." Pole's tall frame loomed in the hallway.

"I'm going to be a bit jumpy for a while." Marissa closed the door behind her, secured all the bolts. She tested the door handle. Pole called the lift but when it arrived, she could not quite remember whether she had switched on the alarm. She cursed between gritted teeth, went back to check whilst Pole held the lift doors open. She hurried through the same ritual. When they reached the ground floor, Marissa slowed down. "Did you want to speak to me about anything in particular?"

Pole smiled. "Direct in your questions, just like Nancy taught you."

"No point in beating around the bush with you, Inspector."

Pole led her to his car and opened the passenger door to let Marissa in. She nodded an appreciative thank you. The escort car's engine was running. It moved alongside Pole's. The officer in the passenger seat lowered the window.

"I've checked traffic around the bridges across the Thames. Battersea is our best option."

Pole had also lowered his window. "OK, you're in the lead. I'll tune into your radio frequency in the car to follow your route."

"Fine by us." The officer closed the window and the car moved forward at a measured pace. Pole checked his rear mirror. No one behind him. He pulled out.

"Going back to *your* question about *my own* question Marissa," Pole said with a smile that did not reach his concentrated eyes. "I wanted to know what you thought about Henry."

"Off the record?"

"Off the record."

"As financial criminals go – and I have seen my fair share of them – I like Henry Crowne. Before you choke, I know this isn't what you were expecting me to say."

Pole shook his head in disbelief. "What is it with you lawyers indulging a criminal like Henry —"

Marissa interrupted. "I said financial criminal. I did not say terrorist. As far as that is concerned ..." Marissa stopped. She was about to condemn Henry for his IRA affiliation but before she could continue the police radio interrupted.

"Inspector Pole, change of plan. There's an accident on Wandsworth Bridge, all traffic re-routed to Battersea. We are re-routing to Lambeth Bridge."

"OK, your call," Pole answered. He looked again in the rear mirror. The traffic behind was still light. Nothing out of the ordinary. Marissa had stopped talking, observing him as he drove.

"You were saying," Pole asked. "Terrorism is a no-no."

"Surely, you don't think I'm condoning it?" Marissa feared her voice sounded somewhat forced. Could Pole have read her hesitation? Or was he simply trying to put her at ease during the ride?

"There are quite a few barristers who try, genuinely, to understand why people resort to violence. Any form of violence, including terrorism." Pole indicated, turning right into a maze of smaller roads. The police car was still comfortably close.

"That's true but it's also part of their job. I don't deal with those people."

"Even money laundering?"

"Point taken."

"What about the BAE Systems case? Bribery paid to Saudi Arabian officials." Pole kept an eye on the lead car and one on Marissa. "I too read the papers."

"And I presume you did a bit of digging around before you agreed to work with me."

Pole chuckled. "Once a copper, always a copper. Got to know the background." A small moped had come alongside the lead car. Its basket bore a Deliveroo sign and the driver was checking his watch. Pole's attention switched to the bike , Marissa noticed. It seemed well used. The driver's jacket was bulky, enough to hide a weapon. The traffic light went amber, then green; the driver swerved in front of the lead car and disappeared into the distance.

Marissa fell silent as well. Pole relaxed, the lead car moved on. It picked up speed again. Pole accelerated, ensuring no car moved in between. They were on the approach to a large roundabout. A few cars were already waiting in an adjacent lane. The lead car indicated right, accelerated then veered to the left, almost turning back on itself. Marissa heard an unfamiliar noise that did not bode well.

* * *

Pole hears it again, the noise of tyres exploding on impact.

"Marissa, brace position," Pole shouts.

He looks into the rear view mirror, reversing – a bullet hits his windscreen, the glass cracks but holds. Pole picks up speed. Marissa muffles a scream, head on knees, hands over ears.

The police officers in the other car jump out, taking up position. Pole hears retaliatory shots. A van moves to block Pole's retreat. Pole changes gear, moving forward towards the crowd of police officers advancing towards them under the cover of cars parked along the street. Another shot hits the car from behind. Men in balaclavas get out of the van. Pole counts at least two. He increases his speed and brakes furiously sending the car sideways, his flank exposed to the shots. The men fire rounds in his direction.

"Stay down," Pole shouts. "The car can stand this."

The glass of his window takes a bullet; another one and it will explode. An officer is running in the direction of Pole's car. Pole manages to manoeuvre his tall body onto the back of the car. He opens the door as the officer arrives. The officer starts firing, giving Pole and Marissa cover to leave Pole's stranded vehicle.

Marissa has opened her door but she has to be coaxed out of her seat. Pole helps her to crawl towards other officers who have just arrived. Pole crouches behind another vehicle. Marissa has been extracted from the danger zone.

Pole glances in the direction of the shooters from behind the bonnet of the car protecting him. He sees a small rucksack moving rhythmically with the blast of gunshots. Pole hears a cry of pain. He retreats to check none of the officers have been hit.

One of the gunmen is limping between two cars, takes another bullet and rotates with a jerk. Pole loses sight of him.

The rucksack he had spotted keeps moving away from the scene. He waves at the officer closest to him.

"Another shooter, five cars down."

The officer nods, starts inching slowly towards the spot. The rucksack has stopped.

The officer yells. "Drop your weapon." The gunshots start again. The rucksack has moved behind a large tree. The officer has moved into position. The rucksack suddenly moves backwards, in a flurry of gunshots.

The attacker has reached a small alleyway and disappears into it. Pole stands up and starts running after him. The gunman picks up speed. Pole accelerates. He can't see a gun. Pole can only hear the pounding of his feet on the pavement. They reach a main road. The shooter doesn't stop, effortlessly avoiding the cars.

Pole follows but is less nimble. He slows down, almost hit by a car. He does not stop to apologise when the driver angrily sounds his horn. The gunman increases the distance between them. He now turns left, running along the central reservation of the road. Pole swears. He needs to cross the road before he can follow.

Which is the closest tube? *Lambeth North.*

Pole races across the road again. Cars barely avoid him. The shooter is now on Kennington Road. He jumps over the protective railing and runs between the cars almost in a straight line, fearless.

Pole climbs over the rail further down the road. He pushes himself as hard as he can. A mass of people is coming out of the tube station. The attacker jostles his way through. Pole makes a final effort and bursts down the stairs of Lambeth North.

The crowd is too dense. He slows down and when he reaches the corridors, looks around and tries to spot the man he has been chasing. Pole does not want to create panic or, worse, a hostage situation.

For all he knows the shooter still has a gun and bullets in it. He scans the tide of people: a young woman fiddling with her mobile, two men in baseball caps. Pole vaults over an entrance gate and considers the direction of the tube line. He can hear the rumble of the next train approaching. He reaches the bridge that straddles the two platforms.

People have started to gather towards the edge of one of them. He must make a choice. He climbs down the stairs two by two as the train appears. He thrusts his tall body forward. And he sees it, the small rucksack at the end of the platform. The doors have opened, people pushing through to get out, people jostling to get in.

The warning beep sounds, the doors about to shut. In a final effort Pole reaches for the rucksack with one hand and the hoodie with the other. The rucksack comes loose and slides along thin arms; a plait of thick black hair escapes from the hoodie – a scarf – a woman. Pole freezes. The doors close and the train lumbers away. She never looks back.

Pole gathered himself together. Had he been chasing the wrong person? But surely the owner of the rucksack would have resisted it being pulled away? He unzipped the bag impatiently. It was empty.

"Shit," Pole blurted. "Shit."

He ran back up to the concourse and knocked at the window of one of the ticket booths. The man looked up, taking his time and putting down a newspaper. Pole shoved his ID onto the glass and indicated he needed to come in. The man adjusted his glasses, suddenly jumping to attention and moving quickly to open the door.

"What can I do for you, Officer?"

"Do you have access to CCTV cameras and can you call Waterloo?"

The elderly man looked blank.

"I'm in pursuit of a suspect."

"Right. Right." He grabbed the phone and dialled promptly. "What does he look like?" Pole clenched his fist. The description was ridiculously bland: small build, black trousers, black hoodie and scarf – and a plait of dark hair.

"Where is your CCTV camera access log?"

The phone was ringing.

"Do you still want me to call them?"

"Yes, tell them I am looking at CCTV footage to get a better description."

The old man waved Pole towards the back of the ticket booth. Pole walked into a small room, smelling of food and coffee. A weary young man stood up. Pole showed his warrant card again.

"I'm in pursuit of a suspect, direction Waterloo. The train left three minutes ago."

The controller keyed instructions into a portal he had called up on his monitor. A number of screens appeared, replaying the event. Pole could see himself holding the rucksack, stupidly stunned.

"Go back a couple of minutes." Pole was searching. "There. There," he shouted, pointing at the screen. He looked at the small figure, weaving her way through the crowd towards the far end of the platform.

The other man came into the room. "They're waiting for you on the phone." Pole nodded. "Can you send these images to Waterloo Station and the British Transport Police?"

The young man nodded matter-of-factly.

"Hello, this is Inspector Pole. I am following a suspected attacker in a firearms incident. Your colleague here is sending you a picture of the suspect. "He …" Pole hesitated. "I'm not sure whether it's a man or a woman, but this person is armed and certainly dangerous."

The woman who had taken his call responded immediately. The trace was in motion. Pole went back to the weary young man.

"Can you roll forward and switch to the train itself?"

"Sorry mate. Can't do." The man shook his head. "You have to ask the LUCC to see the footage of what's happening on a train."

Pole shook his head, exasperated. He should have remembered; only the London Underground Control Centre had access to the camera footage from trains.

"Not my fault mate." The young man had become almost animated.

Pole ran his long hand through his salt-and-pepper hair. There was nothing he could do at his end for the moment. He gave his contact details and walked out of the station towards the site of the shooting. He called Andy. The images gathered at Lambeth North were on their way to him and he would call the LUCC. Pole broke into a jog. Marissa was unhurt when he left. He hoped it would still be the case when he returned.

* * *

Pure luxury. Henry had been allowed a proper coffee from the Caffè Nero close to the Yard. Andy had obliged and he would be eternally grateful. The same arrangement of screens had been set up as the last time he helped Pole, together with a Bloomberg terminal and a printer. No mobile phone yet but it would come. Henry just needed to be patient and start impressing them as he had before.

A very large wad of papers had been left for him to go through. It looked disproportionately big on the small desk where it lay.

Henry smiled, cracked his fingers in a ready-to-tackle-anything gesture and started keying in instructions on his BBG keyboard. He liked the colour coding of its display, specific to traders or research analysts.

He called up the names of several law firms he knew that could put together complex legal structures of the type Marissa had mentioned. Mossack Fonseca was still at the top of the list.

Their website deceptively plain but effective, the four-branch logo that represented them a well-known trademark distinguishing them from the other Panamanian firms. Henry checked whether the website listed the contact names and telephone numbers of people working there.

But no, only one enquiry number, just as it had always been. The reputation built on forty years of servicing the world with legal, yet obscure corporate structures had to be preserved. Henry pondered. His contact would probably still be working there, but if not, he knew how to trace him. Mac would be aware of Henry's fall from grace, but that eventuality had been thought through and worked out a while ago. Henry also suspected Mac would not want to be the subject of an international search warrant.

Henry seized upon the pile of documents and went through them methodically, underlining the details he needed to commit to memory.

For Bank X, the rescue package extended to UK banks by the government had been unpalatable. Treasury representatives sitting on the board meant an unwelcome intrusion of civil servants lacking the understanding of risk taking in the international banking sector.

The offer from the Middle-East on the other hand had been much more appealing. Henry grinned a wicked grin. The name of the Bank and the Middle-Eastern state had been blanked. Who did they think he was? Some newbie who did not know his way around banking?

He had heard the news at the time of the offer and could still remember it clearly. HXBK was the bank which had bought his previous employer GL for almost nothing. The press had been all over it for days.

What the press had not been told about was the arrangement between HXBK and an obscure Panamanian structure that was soon to receive a substantial amount of the money diverted from the cash injection HXBK had received.

Speculation had been high that Saudi Arabia would once more increase its exposure to the financial sector in the Western world. But the Saudi Sovereign Fund had made their fair share of investments and Henry had discounted them immediately.

The two remaining candidates were the UAE and Qatar. Qatar was the most interesting. It had started to show interest in building up its Sovereign Fund investments and HXBK was an ideal candidate.

The stock was depressed. Henry went to his Bloomberg screen and dropped HXBK's share reference into the BBG search engine. The stock had dropped by seventy per cent at the beginning of the 2008 crisis.

"Shit a brick," Henry blurted. "Time to buy."

And this is what Qatar had done four years ago.

How far would a bank go when its management had been grabbed by the throat or possibly somewhere even more painful?

Henry nodded. "Far – very, very far."

Chapter Nineteen

Brett had hoped The Sheik would want to see him at a reasonable time when he had been told the day before they were having a meeting. But a text he had received on his burner phone had simply said instructions would arrive at 6am. The promised instructions duly arrived at 6am on the dot, giving Brett scarcely two hours to get to the meeting place at Tottenham Hale.

The old navy-blue slacks and the faded jacket would be the first clothes he wore today. Brett checked his MI6 laptop as he ate a quick breakfast. No further news from Steve. Where was his minder when he needed him?

Typical.

Brett made his way to Knightsbridge tube station. It was far too early for the shops to be open, but a few staff were already starting to arrive. At 7am it seemed Belgravia was only just waking up. Brett's burner phone buzzed. What now? The sound raised his hopes – perhaps a cancellation.

Further instructions had come through. Mohammed would be meeting him at the station. The game was on.

Sitting in one of the deserted carriages, Brett tried to occupy his mind. His nervousness had increased in recent days and the last meeting with The Sheik had been, well, frightening. Brett did not like to admit that he had been scared. It was fine to be fearful in the Middle-East, constantly on one's guard. He had taken many trips to countries close to war zones to meet his trafficking contacts. Even in countries like Egypt, the UAE or Qatar he had remained careful.

But Brett objected to being frightened on his very doorstep in London. Granted, Tottenham Hale was not exactly his neighbourhood. Still London was his stomping ground and he wanted to roam around it freely. He checked the cheap watch he had bought the day before.

He might arrive early. No matter, Mohammed would be there early too. Brett liked Mohammed, a cultured, mild-mannered man who had become embroiled in the trafficking business to clear debts he could not repay otherwise.

The Tottenham Hale sign appeared through the window. Brett disembarked and walked towards the tall escalators. On the concourse he looked around him. The once white tiles on the walls looked filthy. Brett moved around the large open space that lay in front of the station.

Trees bare of leaves seemed strangely petrified. The few concrete benches were mostly empty. Mohammed was there, hunched over a cardboard cup bearing the name of the local caf. Brett walked towards him and sat down abruptly, making him jump.

"You're early." Mohammed looked startled.

"So are you," Brett replied. Mohammed took his own burner phone out of his pocket to send a quick text. "They're just around the corner. Waiting."

"Well, it seems everyone's early then." Brett's stomach rumbled quietly. He did not want to think why. *Focus, focus on what's coming. That's all.*

The heavy SUV pulled up alongside the pavement. The door opened and the same ritual started: eyes blindfolded, burner phone confiscated, bundled up in the back of the car between two large bodies.

It took them more than half an hour Brett estimated. A thick-necked man pushed Brett into the corridor. The place was different again. How many people were willing to let The Sheik use their properties?

Brett snapped back to the moment. Focus.

The frisking was rougher than usual. Brett let his body go. He hated being touched but he had learned not to resist. Somehow the feel of a relaxed body that seemed non-responsive to the intrusion discouraged the intruder.

Brett had entered a large room that looked more lived in than the places where he had been taken before. Rugs, thick mattresses covered with colourful throws and large cushions to sit on. The smell of spices and a sweet aroma Brett could not define. He was left alone and stood in the middle of the room waiting – five minutes, ten minutes.

Brett finally moved to the mattress that faced the door and sat down. The door opened and a black figure entered, full niqab, hands gloved, bringing tea in a glass silver pot and two glasses. She did not look at Brett, simply laying the tray on the low table in front of him. She poured the tea and left.

The silence with which she moved was remarkable, almost gliding, her feet barely touching the ground. Her long dress rustled with a faint noise, yet her manner felt familiar.

The smell of sweet tea made Brett's mouth water; steam rose from the glasses in long lazy coils. A couple of minutes passed. It was excruciating and intended as the perfect way of preparing Brett to succumb to the demands that would be made of him.

Brett stretched his hand towards the glass; he was not ready to admit defeat yet. The door opened and Brett hurriedly withdrew his hand. The Sheik entered and sat down without a word.

"You do not drink?" he asked with a faint smile.

"I would have, but you arrived." Brett's face remained smooth.

The Sheik nodded, took his tea and sipped the burning liquid. Brett followed in silence.

"Visconti was a great disappointment." The Sheik refilled his glass. Brett's gut tightened, the horror of the pictures he had seen only too fresh in his mind.

"I have a deal that needs to be delivered quickly."

"Armaments?" Brett's voice sounded wooden.

The Sheik lifted an eyebrow and broke into a broad smile.

"I thought you did not do armaments?"

Brett's mind snapped back into action. "You mentioned Visconti."

"Only that he had disappointed me." The Sheik's eyes scrutinised Brett, his posture, his face.

Brett shrugged. He could feel the sweat gathering at the back of his neck.

"Visconti had given up on art; arms seemed the next thing to try, I assumed." Brett moved towards the teapot and refilled his glass. Was this credible?

"Why would you assume it, and why would that be of interest?"

"He was a competitor; it's always good to know what a man like him would do." The pitch of his voice had risen. He sounded on edge.

"You have not been a disappointment so far."

"I'm not certain I feel reassured." Brett sounded scared; at least he did not need to fake the way he felt.

"What do you know about armaments?"

"Very little." Another honest statement.

"Unfortunate."

The panic rising in Brett's gut made it gurgle again.

"But I am not in need of arms. I will need to move two of my people out of the UK, very soon."

"Two people?"

"Very soon," The Sheik added.

"How soon?" Brett was almost happy, people not armaments and out of the UK – good riddance.

"I will let you know. Be ready."

Brett straightened up. It was time to speak about his favourite topic – money.

"Two million." The Sheik had read his mind.

"That sounds reasonable," Brett managed.

The Sheik stood up. He moved towards the door and repeated before he left, "Be ready."

The door remained open. Brett rose unsteadily to his feet and stood for a moment. Who would be worth that amount? He did not have time to think about the answer. Much to his annoyance he had to use the lavatory.

* * *

"Too severe, too funky, too short." Nancy was standing in her walk-in wardrobe, flicking through the clothes rack. She was meeting Marsh in a under two hours. "This is ridiculous." She chuckled. "Pole can't think I am dolling up for The Super and I'm not. Still a good bit of power dressing can't hurt."

She kept going through her outfits, shifting the clothes hangers rhythmically.

"*Ha, voila.*" Nancy smiled. "*Parfait.*"

Grey pencil skirt, just above the knee with a discreet black and white line woven into the material. She took it off the rail and held it against her. To go with it, she chose a black jacket, with black leather lapel and cuffs, over a simple pearl grey silk top – Vivienne Westwood at her best.

She dressed quickly, the way a busy professional woman learns to. She walked to the bathroom, applied some light make-up, fastened her hair with a simple clasp. The final touch was a pair of Chaumet white gold earrings. She was ready to do battle. Marissa was counting on her.

She heard the ring of her BlackBerry from within her bag and moved swiftly to her bedroom.

"*Bonjour* Jonathan," Nancy's voice had a smile in it until Pole interrupted.

"Where are you?"

"I'm about to leave."

"I'm sending a car, a police car, to pick you up."

Nancy closed her eyes and dropped onto the bed. "What's happened?"

"Another attempt on Marissa's life." Pole's voice was rasping. "I'm on my way back from the scene."

"Is she …?" Nancy felt her eyes prickle.

"No, sorry. I should have said. She is all right but very shaken though. It was close."

"You think I'm in danger?" Nancy inhaled slowly. She cared less about her safety than that of Marissa.

"You're working on the case. I'm not taking any risks." Pole's voice shook a little.

"Fine, I'll wait for the car and I'll let Marsh know I might be delayed." Nancy's voice changed tone. "Were you in the car too?"

"Well …" Pole hesitated.

"Bastards – find them."

"I intend to." Not in the mood to tease Nancy for using strong language, Pole continued, "Let me know when you are done with The Super."

"*Dés que j'ai fini.*" French always made Nancy feel closer to Pole, a language that was not the first they had learned as children yet which bound them together.

* * *

Marsh was on the phone when she arrived at Scotland Yard. The ride in the police car had been uneventful. Nancy had rehearsed what she would say to The Super to convince him to accept Henry's demands. She doubted though that he needed much convincing in the first place. She let her head roll back against the headrest. Memories of William Noble's hit-and-run surprised her. Another friend who had almost lost his life in one of the cases she was involved in – a chilling thought.

She pressed the release button of the window and let some fresh air into the car. The sharpness of the cold struck her face and made her shiver. The female police officer in the front passenger seat turned around. "Are you all right, Ma'am?"

"Absolutely. But it's kind of you to ask."

Nancy returned to the question that was preoccupying her. Did Henry have a plan? She was increasingly sure he had. The letter had said it all along no matter what he now pretended.

There was no doubt in her mind that he needed to be able to telephone his contact to deliver the UBO in the Panamanian structure. It was vital to the success of the case and if the range of the mobile could be restricted then … She sighed. The female police officer looked at her in the rear mirror. Nancy attempted a smile. So be it – if Henry needed a phone, she would help him get it and perhaps be more circumspect. Something she had hoped she would never have to do with Henry.

It was Pole she wanted to see now. If he was concerned for her, she was concerned for him. How close had it been for both him and Marissa?

Marsh's voice had tailed off. He was finishing his call to another member of his reporting line it seemed. Marsh's voice had risen too many times to remain polite and Nancy was sure she had heard the F word being used almost as often as it would be by the gangs of Hackney.

Denise, Marsh's PA, had kept her company until the great man appeared on the threshold of his office. The Super, in full uniform, as was to be expected, greeted Nancy with profuse apologies, but no, it was she who was late she replied. The exchange of playful courtesies irritated Nancy. It was hard to smile. She felt her face freeze when she first tried. She tried harder and the result must have worked. Marsh was almost blushing.

"I hear the latest development could affect you?" Marsh said putting a hand behind her back, almost touching her. The gesture was intended to be considerate without being invasive, protective perhaps.

"I have asked Inspector Pole to make sure you have the required protection."

"How very kind." Nancy thought she would lose it. Pole did not need to be told when people who worked with him needed protection. She quickly sat down, keen to come to an agreement with Marsh about the subject of her visit.

Denise entered with a fresh pot of tea, one of Marsh's quality brews that he prided himself on offering his visitors.

"I'll pour. Thank you Denise." Marsh sat himself in front of Nancy in the chair he had the habit of choosing when they met. Marsh remembered how she took her tea – how very charming. Nancy took the cup, proper china, that he was extending to her. Her patience was in short supply but needs must.

"So you have come to suggest I allow Crowne some additional liberties." Marsh's tone was as sweet as his tea, two sugars – in Nancy's view it spoilt the taste of a perfectly good cup.

"Not exactly." Nancy drank a little tea and extended an elegant hand to put her cup down. Marsh raised a quizzical eyebrow.

"I am here to make sure we measure the impact of his request and perhaps only then acquiesce."

"You're not convinced we should allow him to have a mobile phone?"

"That's correct. I don't have the technical skills to determine how securely we could monitor his phone or limit its range."

"I'm pretty certain that can be done. But, of course, I'll seek confirmation from my technical people in trace and make the suggestion."

Nancy nodded. "The other question is, why does he need a phone?"

"To make contact with someone who can deliver the required details relevant to this Panamanian structure, I presume."

"I agree, but is there any other way it could be done?"

"You mean, for instance, use a local contact to take a statement?"

"For example."

Marsh shook his head. "It wouldn't work because the informer would have to disclose his identity and even with guarantees I doubt they would take the risk."

"How about other social media? Opening an account solely for that purpose?"

"Possible, but then again, for it to work it has to be untraceable. I mean the contact would have to be established using an anonymised PC not on the grid."

"So it's tricky." She drank some more tea, pausing for Marsh to consider the impact of his own analysis of the situation.

"And it is much more difficult to circumvent the security protocols surrounding an account than to simply use a burner phone."

"I'm sure you are right." Nancy managed another gracious smile.

Marsh leaned back in his armchair. His gaze appraised her for a second. "What does he intend to achieve by contacting this person?"

"The answer to the SFO question lies with the UBO, the Ultimate Beneficial Owner, of the complex Panamanian structure and without that —"

"They cannot prove the circularity of the transaction between Bank X and a certain Middle-Eastern state."

"Exactly right." Nancy had finished her tea.

It was already decided, and Marsh must have known it but appeared to indulge by detaining Nancy a little longer. "What else could he do with the phone?"

"Get in touch with his former IRA contacts. But if the range of the phone is limited it will make it difficult. He could try to persuade his contact to get in touch with the former IRA on his behalf. But with the decommissioning going ahead I doubt they would respond. In any case HSU Belmarsh is the most secure prison in the UK."

Marsh's face dropped, struck by the directness of her answer – no frills, no trying to argue Crowne's case, a no-nonsense statement unusual in the realm where he operated.

His nascent smile said it all … he liked it.

Nancy adjusted a lock of hair that had come loose. Marsh found the gesture surprisingly seductive.

"Right, yes, well." He straightened up in his chair. "You're right. HSU Belmarsh's security record is impeccable."

"Precisely."

Marsh allowed himself one more minute of what seemed intense cogitation. "Provided my tech team can limit the range of the phone, I shall authorise it."

The exercise of power motivated by ambition. Nancy sighed, the downfall of most driven men.

* * *

The lift doors had just closed on a so very courteous Marsh. Nancy had given him a slightly rigid goodbye, thanking the great man for his enlightened decision. As soon as the lift started moving, she plunged into her bag, fishing out her BlackBerry. Reception was patchy and she kept trying to dial Pole's number. When she reached the ground floor, the call went through. Pole's line was engaged. She sped towards the next bank of lifts, leaving a message that she was on her way.

A mass of people walked out of the lift she was hoping to board. She gave way then squeezed in before the doors closed. On reaching her destination she dashed out but a tall figure stood in her way.

Pole was waiting for her. She barely resisted the urge to throw her arms around him. Pole grabbed her hand and held it tight.

"I could have slaughtered Marsh," Nancy's voice trembled. "You are fine though."

"All in one piece." Pole's voice was also shaken. "And Marissa is fine too, although she could do with a friend at the moment."

"I'll go to see her in a minute but …" Nancy hesitated. People had just walked out of the lifts. Pole reluctantly let go of her hand. "Let's have two minutes to ourselves."

Pole smiled. They stopped at the coffee machine in silence, walked into Pole's office and, with the door closed, stood alongside each other at the window. It was good to simply be together.

A quote by Saint-Exupéry came to Nancy's mind: "Love is not to stare at one another but to stand side by side."

Chapter Twenty

When Nancy entered the room, Marissa was still in her coat, her right hand clutching her collar up to her chin. Nancy slowed before moving towards her friend, startled by the dread she could see in her eyes. Marissa tried to articulate a few words but her chattering teeth made the sentence incomprehensible.

"I'm so sorry." Nancy moved quickly to her friend, arms outstretched. She hugged Marissa for a moment, her slender arms surprisingly comforting. Marissa nodded and sat down, still wrapped in her coat.

"It was awful," she eventually managed, eyes in the distance.

"Pole has spoken to Commander Ferguson. They've increased the security around Mark Phelps' residence," Nancy said as if reading her mind.

"Good," Marissa managed to articulate. A knock at the door startled them both. It opened gingerly and Andy popped in his head with an apologetic smile.

"Can I bring you anything?"

Both women shook their heads with a thanks. The door closed with a small creak.

"Do you know what I really need?" Marissa said in a recovered voice.

"A bar of Belgian chocolate? A nice French patisserie?" Nancy teased gently.

"No. I need Pole and Ferguson to catch those bastards and make them suffer."

Nancy stretched out her hand and squeezed Marissa's shoulder.

"I'm not quite sure about the suffering bit but Pole will catch them — he won't rest until he does."

Marissa stood up, still uncertain on her feet. She grabbed the edge of the table. "I'm fine," she said responding to Nancy's concerned look. She closed her eyes, inhaled and released the air slowly.

"Let's go and meet Crowne. We have business to do."

* * *

Henry had considerably advanced his review of the new batch of documents that had been left for him. The first instalment of files had given him a broad understanding of the construction of the fund that was receiving cash from HXBK. The second was giving him more details about the transaction itself.

He had started sketching out diagrams of the corporate ownership, reconstructing the multi-layered levels of companies, partnerships and funds that made the structure challengingly opaque.

A draught of fresh air. Henry recognised Nancy's scent and lifted a smiling face. His smile dropped almost instantly. Nancy looked grave and Marissa at her side, awful.

Henry's stomach tightened. He did not want to ask the dreaded question. "Have the Jihadists managed to —"

"Everyone is fine," Marissa simply said.

Henry stood up, hesitating. He arranged chairs around the table so they could all sit down. Nancy picked up the diagrams he had left on the table.

"These are looking encouraging." She nodded appreciatively.

Marissa picked up the pages. "Let's go through them together." Henry gathered it was all about being business-like.

"Good idea." Henry clapped his hands and moved documents around, fishing out a piece of paper stuck at the bottom of the pile.

"First of all, Bank X is one of the banks that did not join the UK government rescue programme. It found other means to survive its capital crisis and to buy another competitor that was defaulting, namely GL, my previous employer.

Marissa lifted an eyebrow. "You know who Bank X is?"

"I know which banks needed rescuing back in 2008. I know, or rather know what was, their management style. I can narrow down the number of banks that would have looked elsewhere to two – Barclays and HXBK."

Marissa gave a small laugh. Her eyes searched Henry's face in open amazement. Henry had received the files barely twenty-four hours ago. He had been locked up for the past four years in Belmarsh. "Did you already know about this?"

"Nope … but I still read the news and I spent twenty years in that business."

"You think Bank X is …?"

"HXBK of course. Their management team would never have stomached what RBS and Lloyds had to accept in order to receive the rescue package. The thought of having to agree to change the board composition to include government officials – never."

Both women remained silent, but Nancy gave a small, content nod. "HXBK had to raise cash, first to survive and then to hoover up competitors that went under, as I said previously. They raised cash from their existing shareholders – about nineteen per cent. I checked this morning on Bloomberg. The rest was raised by selling shares to a number of financial institutions and sovereign wealth funds."

"You were still at GL when it happened?" Nancy asked.

"Just about." Henry shrugged. He had not known at the time his downfall was imminent. A pang of regret came and went. "I do recall the terms of the UK government's rescue package."

"You think the terms were not generous enough?" Marissa asked

"It's not that, but HXBK wanted to buy the competition on its own terms, not to be dictated to by the government who to buy or not buy. They needed that deal."

"Though the price for GL was not astronomical. All is relative, but in investment banking terms I remember the price was around £700 million?"

"Wow, Nancy, spot on." Henry clicked his fingers. "On the ball as ever."

Marissa smiled. "Nancy is always on the ball."

"I'm flattered," Nancy returned the smile, "but I still don't see what difference it made. That is not such a large sum after all."

"Correct but remember HXBK acquired GL because of the large losses GL had suffered buying subprime assets." Henry waited expectantly.

"It needed to raise further capital to absorb the GL losses and satisfy the regulator." Marissa was nodding her head.

"Absolutely and remember, it did raise an additional £7 billion from its Middle-Eastern friends – namely the UAE and Qatar."

"That is your working assumption – UAE and Qatar as UBO?" Nancy asked.

"Yup. I think we are going to find someone in one of those countries at the top of the complex corporate structure we are trying to unravel."

"Have you made any headway with that?" Marissa's expression had livened up. Talking about the case she so wanted to bring to court energised her.

"I have." Henry closed the file that was open in front of him. He placed it on the floor, next to several other files he'd organised in his own way. He picked up another folder.

"The loan by HXBK is not in itself a problem," Marissa's voice was trailing.

"But it's who the ultimate recipient of that money is – I get it," Henry replied. He picked up a few pieces of paper, checked the data briefly and presented them to the two women.

"The company that received the loan was incorporated in Panama. Nothing wrong with that as such but the disclosure rules when it comes to ownership are far less stringent than in the UK."

"That's right." Marissa moved towards the table.

"The company's shareholding is split between other companies and foundations by using nominee companies." Henry was pointing towards numerous boxes he had drawn on his diagram. "The foundation that holds shares in the nominee companies is formed in Lichtenstein."

"And we are not going to know who the actual person is who holds the shares in the foundation because Lichtenstein does not disclose either," Nancy added.

"Correct." Henry nodded. "If we find that person, I'm certain it will be yet another company."

"How could HXBK have run this through their compliance department successfully?" Marissa asked.

"I think the Ultimate Beneficial Owner must have been disclosed but only to a very small number of senior people. The identity of that person is sensitive. Hence the limited disclosure, justified by the need to protect that individual," Henry replied.

"That is precisely what Mark said." Marissa ran her hand over her face. "When he asked the question about the UBO, he was told to mind his own business. Senior management had given their approval."

Henry leaned back and crossed his hands behind his head, thinking.

"I wonder." He changed his mind and moved back towards the table. "I wonder whether Marsh will let me have a mobile phone?"

"He'd better." Marissa looked up. "Otherwise I'll get the SFO director on his back and Marsh won't know what's hit him."

Henry's reserved manners had registered with Nancy and she kept her eyes firmly on him. He met her gaze reluctantly. She wanted an honest conversation. Something Henry was not prepared to have – at least not yet.

* * *

"From Lambeth North to Waterloo then he disembarks and leaves the underground system." Andy and Pole were following the slim silhouette in a dark hoodie which exited the tube carriage, walked up the stairs in no great hurry and left Waterloo Station, merging into the mass of passengers. Pole had kept his suspicions about the gender of the attacker to himself.

"And then ..." Andy switched to another CCTV camera installed on Waterloo Bridge roundabout. "He reappears along the embankment towards the National Theatre." Andy switched to a CCTV camera near the IBM building. "I think I can pick him up again going towards Bernie

Spain Gardens. Same hoodie but slightly different colour I think: he could have changed if the hoodie's reversible. Then I completely lose him in the Gardens."

"How many cameras around the Gardens?" Pole was hunched over the back of Andy's chair.

"Not many, two." Andy pushed his chair back and Pole moved out of his way. He grabbed a chair, sat down and rolled it towards Andy's desk.

"What did you see after he entered the Gardens. I mean around the area?" Pole had taken out his BlackBerry, spinning it around his hand.

"Well." Andy pushed his glasses back up the bridge of his nose and speeded up the images: an old man with his dog appeared, a couple of youngsters fooling around, a woman with a pushchair.

"On the other camera – a couple talking, finishing a shared cigarette —"

"And having a snog." Pole added with a smile. Andy's cheeks had become a little pinker. He kept moving the images forward; more pictures danced their crazy bop. Pole had almost given up.

"Then twenty minutes later a group of women, in niqab, leave together."

Pole straightens up. "Did you see them arrive?"

Andy scrolled back to the time he had lost the gunman, then back a couple of hours before. "No, I can't see them come in. At least not up to a couple of hours before the incident and not from the cameras we have."

Pole scratched the back of his head. "Are there other entrances to the Gardens not covered by CCTV?"

Andy moves to another screen, a map of the area. "Yes, Guv – the lane from OXO Tower."

Pole nodded. "And where is the group of women going to?"

Andy moves the images forward. "Towards Blackfriars – shall I ...?"

Pole's phone buzzed. "Yvonne, what have you got for me?" He pulled his notebook from his jacket pocket and scribbled a few words, at an uncomfortable angle.

"Great news, thanks. I'm with Andy; can I call you back in a couple of minutes?" He ended the call and turned back to Andy.

"This is what I would like you to do please – track the women back, find out where they came from and how many of them there were when they arrived in the Gardens. How many of them left?"

Andy was already working the cameras.

Pole disappeared into his office, already on the phone to Yvonne again.

"Well done Jonathan Pole." Yvonne sounded genuinely impressed.

"How did you know?"

"I didn't think Jihadists wore long hair, even plaited."

"You mean you nearly got her?"

"Nearly is unfortunately the word."

"You must tell me more next time we meet." Yvonne voice was ringing with excitement. "And you're right, there is a difference in fingerprints between male and female, ridge density is indicative of gender difference. It's not one hundred per cent but pretty close and is irrespective of origin or race."

"So, the partial prints you found on the bullets at the Bank of England and in the cab that was driving Marissa are both female?"

"Spot on. It didn't cross my mind to check to be honest, since they were only partials, but hey."

Pole sat down at his desk, still processing the news. Despite what he had seen at Lambeth North Tube, he was amazed.

"The shooter is a woman."

"Don't be so shocked. Women can be pretty lethal too. I open up cadavers all day."

"But at least they are dead, right."

Yvonne laughed. "Think about the Peshmerga too."

"You mean the Kurdish fighters?"

"Yes, they are some of the most feared fighters in the region and they are all women. They fought alongside the US marines in Iraq in 2003."

"How do you know that?"

"A story for another time."

"Aren't the Jihadists different? I didn't think Al-Qaeda used women, not as fighters."

Yvonne pondered. "That's a point. Perhaps they are changing their tactics?"

209

"Anyway, thanks for that. It gives me something to go on."

Pole ended the call. He was about to go back to Andy with a new set of instructions when he stopped. He stood at the door of his office and reached into his inner jacket pocket for Agent Harris' burner phone. He took it out and looked at it, considering.

Ferguson at CT Command would need to know. Harris could not ask him to hold back that information. But Harris had been clear – anything new about the terror cell was to come to him first. Pole swore and closed his door.

He moved to the window and placed a call to the only number entered in the phone's speed dial. The reply was almost instantaneous.

"Pole here. You told me you were working on an Al-Qaeda cell presence in London?"

Harris simply confirmed.

"How likely are they, would you say, to use a woman sniper?"

The silence at the end of the line pleased Pole.

"What do you mean? A woman?"

"Chromosomes XX. I'm sure you have heard of them."

Pole did not wait for a reply. He gave Harris the details of his discovery. The chase down to Lambeth North, the tracking to Waterloo Station, the long plait of dark hair, the fingerprints. As he spoke Pole could sense a deepening feeling of unease in Harris' silent attention.

"Keep me posted, even the smallest details, but particularly if you manage to track her location."

"What do you think it means?" Pole asked, doubting he would get an answer.

"Give me a few hours – if there's anything important, I'll let you know."

Harris hung up. Pole sat down on the only free chair in his office. He was starting to see where this case was heading, and it took the wind out of him. He thought of Nancy with a chill. He could not discuss this latest development with her, a great pity. How was he going to keep her safe without telling her everything?

Andy knocked at the door, gesturing urgently.

Pole waved him in.

"Guv, I know where the women went."

Pole would not give Harris a few hours after all.

210

*** * ***

"Another burner phone," Henry teased.

"What do you mean another?" Nancy was still holding the much-coveted device.

"I seem to recall you lending me something very similar a few months ago."

"Certainly not – not the same make or model, and hardly any roaming facility."

Henry laughed. It was a happy moment. In this dingy meeting room, situated underground, with prison officers waiting for him outside, all that mattered was that he was allowed time alone with Nancy.

"They've limited the range to Panama?"

"That was the deal. I tried to call the UK – engaged tone."

"No worries. All I need is Panama." He was still in a good mood. He did not want to think ahead. Just live in the moment: a good cup of coffee, a close friend, possibly even his best friend, and doing what he excelled at.

"I presume you will want to be on your own when you call your contact?" Nancy's voice was kind.

"Afraid so, yes. I need to make my contact feel comfortable and I don't expect he will want to speak to me immediately."

"You have an agreed process for this type of …" Nancy was looking for the right words, "emergency contact."

"That's the sum of it." Henry nodded. He had always appreciated Nancy's way of asking questions. Soon he would no longer have the benefit of her wisdom. He felt a cold trickle of ice run along his spine and shivered.

"It's almost 12pm in London and 7am in Panama. A little too early but not by much though. Another half hour and I'll make the call."

"What makes you think he will talk?"

"Because he will not want me to give his name and details to the UK police. He wants to stay anon – the John Doe of the Panamanian Legal System."

"So, what's next?" Nancy wanted to be clear about Henry's strategy.

"I get enough information to enable me to go back through

the chain of ownership until I find the UBO." Henry was rocking slowly on the back legs of his chair, a rhythmic motion that seemed to help him think. "I guess it will be a convoluted business that will eventually lead me to the Middle-East."

"Is that the reason why they have pursued Mark and Marissa?" Nancy sat on the chair next to Henry, her legs crossed at the knee. It was an inexplicably seductive pose and Henry could not help but smile. Pole was a lucky bugger.

"No one knows what that money is used for and I guess someone wants it to stay that way."

"Strangely, I don't feel threatened." Nancy pouted; it sounded odd, she should.

"Pole will be looking after you." A shadow crossed Henry's face that he hoped Nancy had not noticed. Pole would certainly do his bit, but Henry had given an unequivocal message to Kamal. *Whether Marissa or Nancy are kafir or in your way, do not touch them – otherwise the deal is off.* Henry meant every word. If anything was to happen to Marrissa, let alone Nancy he would never work for Kamal's organisation even though it would cost him his way to freedom.

"Do you think the case will go through?" Henry changed the conversation away from the danger zone that emotions always were for him.

"You're thinking about the BAE Systems debacle?"

"Yup, not the SFO's finest hour, despite the large fine."

"Marissa is doggedly determined. She will see this through – even more so now."

Henry looked up at the clock on the wall. He smiled an apologetic smile at Nancy.

Time to make the call. It was all down to him now.

Chapter Twenty-One

"The Sheik wants you to extract people?" MI6-Steve could not disguise his surprise.

Brett had settled in the cab that had just picked him up outside Green Park tube station. A new initiative from Steve to avoid meeting yet again at the club.

"That's what my email said, I believe." Brett remained stony faced.

"Names?" Steve ignored Brett's patronising tone. His ability to ignore Brett's comments made Brett furious. Steve was well in control of Brett's life.

"What do you expect? It's far too early." Brett took a sip from a bottle he had bought before boarding the cab – though water was not what he needed to soothe his battered ego.

"Did he give a number?" Steve unwrapped a piece of gum and popped it into his mouth.

Steve's jaws masticated the gum nervously. Brett cringed.

"Yes. I did also mention that in my email. Why do you insist on making me repeat myself?"

"Al-Qaeda does not extract people."

Brett frowned. For the first time since he had started working for Steve, MI6 was giving him important information. He did not have to grovel, beg or get annoyed as he usually did.

Unexpected and worrying.

"What are you saying?"

"I'm not sure yet – we're picking up some activity on social media; recruitment attempts on a large scale that have a different slant to the usual guff."

"How different?"

"More radical, more organised."

"Than Al-Qaeda?" Brett pursed his lips, incredulous. "Is that possible?"

"Why not? Splinter groups happen all the time. The question is whether they can turn into something new that will be successful."

"They feel organised and established in North London. The Sheik never meets in the same place, but I always have the same driver and contact meeting me."

"Exactly my point?"

Brett nodded. "True, they could be limiting the number of people I meet for security reasons, so as not to expose the network."

"Possible or else it means they're a small unit that's growing but doesn't yet want to go public."

"The chap who got a bullet in his head a few months ago at the Royal Exchange might disagree with you if he could," Brett replied with feeling.

"He was another Visconti. That's all."

"What do you mean by public?" Brett asked.

"Exactly that – challenge the old Al-Qaeda group that's perceived as weak, particularly since Osama Bin Laden's death."

"If that's the case, The Sheik feels pretty secure and in control."

"Do you think he's a Brit who has returned after fighting the Jihad?"

"You're the expert." Brett took a mouthful of water and looked at the cab driver. It felt uncomfortable to talk in the back of a taxi. "I'd say almost certainly. His manners, his spoken English – he's well educated I'm afraid."

Both men remained silent, pondering on what they knew might validate Steve's view.

Brett kept casting an eye at the streets the taxi was taking them through. Steve noticed. "It's safe. Better than another meeting at your club."

Brett locked eyes with Steve. "If Henry Crowne was one of

the people who needed 'transportation' would it confirm that a new terrorist group is about to be formed?"

Brett enjoyed the result of his question. Steve's eyes darkened, his lips tightened into a straight line. He stopped his furious chewing.

"Being a smart arse isn't always a good idea in the world we inhabit."

Brett ignored him. "Perhaps, but looking for a financier with experience of organising money laundering for terrorist organisations like the IRA would validate your view. This splinter group as you call it needs and wants to get the money side of things right so it can fight its war."

"Brett, I've told you before. You're rather smart for a toff; however this time, take my advice, don't get involved."

Brett raised an eyebrow. "Thanks for the tip but, unfortunately, I am involved."

Steve grumbled a pain-in-the-arse answer and gave Brett a new set of instructions. The world of art trafficking was morphing into the trafficking of things Brett did not care about, people.

* * *

The big hand of the wall clock was moving towards the top of the hour. In one minute, it would pass that important point and Henry would make the call. The room was empty. Nancy had left. Pole was nowhere to be seen which told Henry something was up.

The clock struck 1pm. Henry stopped playing with his pen, running it over the back of his thumb and catching it as it came around, a clever little move very few managed. A smart arse, always a smart arse, Henry sighed.

He tested the phone he had been given by placing a call to Mossack Fonseca, the law firm in Panama. The notepad he had arranged in front of him was more for show than note taking. It had reassured Nancy who now walked everywhere with her yellow legal pad. He smiled at the thought.

Henry dialled the number he had memorised so many years ago. Many phone numbers had changed but he was certain that this one, his emergency number, would still connect. The phone rang and the answer phone at the other end spewed its message.

"This is Henry; call me back."

He resumed playing with his pen, round and round it went. The saying "a watched kettle never boils" amused Henry. This particular burner phone was about to become too hot to handle.

It took his contact less than fifteen minutes to ring back, a record, Henry reckoned. He let the phone ring once, twice. Holding his nerve.

"Crowne." The person at the other end of the phone stayed silent. Henry's voice had sounded steady. He needed to close the deal. "Mac, this is Henry Crowne. Are you OK to talk? My phone can't be traced."

"OK."

"I need a name."

"Who for?"

"That is not relevant; you know that."

A small intake of breath at the other end of the phone and Henry carried on.

"You knew this call would come one day, right?"

"The IRA has decommissioned."

"But you are still in Panama to handle the winding down of some of its funds and because you have branched out – right again?"

"As cocky as ever, Henry."

"Yup."

"What's for me in the deal?"

"I keep your name out of it."

"For how long though?"

"If I haven't grassed you so far, why would I do it now? I'm serving my sentence, as I'm sure you know."

"I've heard."

"And if I had wanted a reduction, you would have been done by now."

The line stayed silent for a moment.

"You know that it's easy to trace this call."

"To where, Panama? Big deal. You are calling me from a location that has no relationship with your office or house there and Panama is not renowned for its CCTV camera network."

216

"Glad to hear you thought it through."

"I always do Mac; so what's it gonna be?"

"What do you want?"

"The name of the UBO that sits at the end of a long corporate structure that starts in Panama."

"Any idea who is at the top of the ownership chain? Are you looking for someone in particular?"

"You tell me. I've prepared a document; it's on its way to you."

Henry selected the image he had photographed earlier and attached it to a message. "You have all you need on that."

"Got it. This is your new emergency number." Mac repeated a string of digits twice.

"I'll call you tomorrow."

"Not enough time."

"Tomorrow Mac, end of your day. You know the ropes better than anybody else."

"Can't promise." Mac hung up. Henry slumped back in his chair, his entire body jolted, and he closed his eyes. Small beads of perspiration gathered on his upper lip. Had it worked?

He had a long twenty-four-hour wait to find out.

* * *

"I'm certain." Pole's voice had hardened as Agent Harris repeated his question. He worked for the Met, but he was not a goddamn idiot. "I don't do counterterrorism – it's Ferguson's pad – but my team can definitely trace a suspect."

"How far have you gone?" Harris had shifted his phone. Pole could hear him typing on his keyboard.

"You mean do we have an address? Not yet, but we're rather close."

"Have you spoken to Ferguson?"

"No, we agreed – you first."

"Thank you." Pole was surprised but did not let it show. Was it a way of gaining his trust?

"I can't hold back forever though. How long do you need?"

"'til the end of today."

"That might work. I'll ask my man on the case to dig around more before we release the information." Pole grunted.

"Let me know when you do."

"You have an asset on the ground?"

Pole heard the smile in Harris' voice. "No comment in the interests of national security."

"Before you go …" Time for Agent Harris to deliver. "How about your enquiry in China?"

"Ah, Mr Wu's possible demise? I have something for you, Inspector Pole; not much but the beginning of a trail."

"Good," Pole replied. "It would be even better if I could take a look at this trail's beginning before the end of the day."

Harris laughed. "I'll have an envelope dropped to your office – before you call Ferguson."

"Much appreciated."

"I like a hard bargain, Inspector."

"Glad to hear it."

"And Inspector Pole, call me Steve."

* * *

"Things are going to move fast." Pole had perched on Henry's desk. His tall body leaned forward, hands on knees.

"You've spoken to Harris?" Henry almost felt comfortable with Pole.

"I have but that's not where I got this from."

Henry considered Pole for a moment. He was playing with his burner phone.

"Why do you do it?"

Pole crossed his arms over his chest – a no-go area.

"OK. OK," Henry said raising his hands. "You're just keen for me to get the bullet I deserve."

Pole rolled his eyes. "You don't really believe that crap."

"I just don't like it." Henry pouted like a sulking child.

"I don't like it much either but I'm your MI6 go-between and that's that."

Henry stood up, taking a few steps in the boxy room he had learned to like. He leaned against the wall.

"Why the warning?"

"You are a pain in the butt, Henry. Let's say you are about to find yourself a little over your head if you're not careful."

"You're kidding. The IRA wasn't exactly a friendly bunch."

"Granted but you were a key operative and your roots were in Belfast. Here you're just a tool."

"So what's the plan?"

"Harris has not graced me with the details. You're his asset and if I were him, I know where I would want you."

"Which is?"

"Out." Pole locked eyes with Henry. For the first time since they had met, Henry felt concerned. He hesitated. "You mean?"

"Out, escaped, gone and I presume at his service to infiltrate whatever he thinks he needs to infiltrate."

Henry's face froze and grew a little paler.

"Don't worry. I have been told in the interests of national security etc, etc."

"And you are fine with that?"

"As long as it doesn't end up being a bloodbath, I guess I am."

Henry moved back to his chair, uneasy. Pole changed the subject.

"When are you expecting a reply from Panama?"

"Tomorrow, his evening, so late here – 10pm."

"I need to let Marsh know. We'll send a special dispensation request off to the Home Office and Belmarsh."

"Understood." Henry thought for a while and Pole let him be. The atmosphere was almost relaxed.

"You think I should accept," Henry's voice trailed. He was asking Pole for advice.

"What can I say Henry? But knowing you, you need a purpose."

Henry shook his head in disbelief. He had been waiting for this moment for years. It was perhaps just around the corner. He thought of Nancy. He pushed the swelling pain away; not now, not in front of Pole.

"Have you finished your day?" Pole asked, standing up to leave.

"Not yet, I just want to go through a few things on the Internet; read through the docs Marissa left me again."

"I'll speak to Marsh now. Any problem, I'll let you know."

"How?"

"You've got a mobile, haven't you?"

"But I thought with a range limited to Panama."

Pole tapped his nose with his index finger – who was the clever boy after all?

* * *

Marissa sat back in her office chair. It was not the request she had expected from Mark Phelps. Her hand hovered over her phone. She withdrew it in a slow gesture that gave her time to think.

Why did Mark really want to meet Henry?

To confront the monsters that had taken his wife? The idea felt strangely out of character. She certainly needed Mark to testify when the case came to court. As a protected witness she might be able to spare him an appearance in court.

She returned to Mark's request. She could not imagine him coming to blows with Henry. And how would Henry react? She needed them both on the case. Could she perhaps delay the request until it was too late, until Henry was no longer allowed to leave HSU Belmarsh?

She could then organise a meeting in the confines of the prison environment. But Mark was an intelligent man; he would see through this. She could not lose his trust. They were so close: this case would not go the way the BAE Systems case went.

She picked up the phone swiftly and dialled Nancy's number.

Nancy replied after a few rings, a little breathless.

"Marissa – is everything all right?"

"Yes, sorry, I should have told you myself."

"I mean over and above you being targeted, dealing with the case and —"

Marissa interrupted. "You need to convince Henry to meet with Mark."

The phone remained silent.

"I'm sure you are reading my thoughts," she said at last.

"I know how it may sound."

"Now that you're close to getting some answers, what would you say if Mark asked you to stop? If he wanted to pull out. You did say earlier you wouldn't want to push him – but what about now?"

Marissa took a deep breath, ran her tired hand over her eyes. Then she smiled; she had just been subjected to what had made Nancy such a formidable QC – the ability to ask the tough questions.

"You're right. I would find it almost impossible now," Marissa said. "You know why, don't you?"

"Because you do not want to have another disappointment."

"I can't hide anything from you." Marissa smiled faintly.

"You can't because you don't want to; you want to get to the truth. You don't want Henry to stop cooperating either." Nancy paused. "What is the chance of Mark pulling out if he doesn't meet Henry?"

"Very high."

"For what it's worth, I think Mark needs to make sense of what happened."

"A question for you, Nancy – how will Henry react?"

Nancy inhaled deeply. "I would lie if I said I was certain." She paused again. "Speak to Pole. He will have a view on the question." To her amazement she felt Pole was better qualified to answer than she was.

Chapter Twenty-Two

The brown envelope was sitting on his desk. Pole hesitated. He had been closing the door of his office quite a lot recently, rather uncharacteristic of him.

He looked around for the letter opener, an instrument he used to use regularly, now made redundant by email. Where was the damn thing when you needed it?

Pole considered the state of his office. He would never find the implement quickly. A pair of scissors would have to do. He looked around, twisting his tall body this way and that.

In the end he simply lifted the flap of the envelope which came unstuck without much damage. Pole peered inside – photocopied documents, official-looking papers and some photos too.

He carefully turned the envelope upside down until its contents lay on the desk. He took one of the photos out and gazed at it.

An elegant young man in his early thirties was looking back at him, slim and of medium build. Pole concentrated on the face: delicate cheekbones, high forehead, intelligent almond eyes and the smile – perhaps not a smile, more an expression of the lips, that was both uncertain and humorous.

Pole was shocked by the likeness; there was no doubt in his mind that the young man in the photo was Nancy's father, Li Jie Wu. Pole turned the picture over. A date had been stamped on it, April 1980.

A bunch of papers had been bound together with a clip. They were old travel documents. China was just coming out of the terrifying period that the Cultural Revolution had been. Chairman Mao was dead, and his wife and the Gang of Four had been arrested. Travelling to and through China still had to be authorised though.

Pole wondered how Agent Harris had managed to find these but why should he care? The address on one of the documents was in Chinese with a translation: Shanghai to start with, then Beijing, then Chengdu, the main city of the Sichuan province. Chengdu, the place where Li Jie Wu was born and raised; his place of ancestry too.

A timid knock at the door startled Pole. Andy was hovering in the doorway with a look on his face that Pole knew well. He had found something that might have escaped a less discerning mind.

"I did a lot more digging, Guv, and I managed to follow the women after they left the tube station."

"After they left Seven Sisters?" Pole cautiously replaced the documents he was reading in their envelope and sat down, waving for Andy to do the same.

"That's right, Sir. They were all chatting happily, but I had a feeling they were protective of one woman amongst them."

Pole had called up a Google map of the area on his computer screen. Andy dragged his chair towards Pole's desk to help him track their movements. He picked up a pen and moved it across the map.

"They crossed the street, went into Page Green Common, walked through and crossed the road on the other side, but when I looked more carefully, I could see that one of them was missing."

"Well done. Does she reappear later?" Pole's voice had a new ring to it, the edge it took when the chase was on.

"No, but a car, a black SUV, arrives on the Green ten minutes afterwards."

Pole nodded expectantly.

"It parks underneath the trees then it leaves very quickly, driving back towards Finsbury Park. Got the reg number and ran it through ANPR. The number plate does not exist."

Pole smiled. "But you managed to track it because …?"

Andy chewed his lip. "Traced it by creating a new number reg that can be tracked by the system. Then the system recognises it because —"

He stopped abruptly, judging that the minutiae of his handiwork might not interest Pole. "To cut a longer story short, Guv. It went to a garage, rent a car place in Finsbury."

"That's a brilliant job."

"And." Andy grinned. "I managed to pick up a similar-looking woman walking towards Wilberforce Road. She then entered a small hotel. After that nothing ... can't trace a woman in full niqab."

"But a few women came out just wearing a simple scarf."

"Correct. I'm following through."

"We're closing the net." Pole's voice had an edge again.

"Are you speaking to Commander Ferguson?"

"Why do you ask?" Pole felt put on the spot. Did Andy suspect he was holding something back?

"If you give me a couple more hours, I might be able to track down where she actually went."

Ambition is sometimes a good thing. Pole nodded. "Granted, then we can discuss what you find."

Andy walked out a little bit taller, his plump body shaking with trepidation – puppy turned bloodhound. Pole liked it.

He sat back in his chair, an eye on the MI6 envelope. He could indulge himself for a few more minutes. Pole let more documents slide out into his hand: reports of political and artistic activity it seemed. Names of art pieces that the authorities had classified as subversive, mainly paintings, but also some sculptures that embraced Western modern art trends.

Despite the poor quality of the images and the paucity of the vocabulary describing the pieces, it was evident that the art was executed with confidence and spoke, at least Pole felt, about social anguish, individuality and reform.

The documents were dated up to 1989, the year of the fateful Tiananmen Square protest that saw the tanks of the Red Army kill ten thousand people.

Pole replaced the contents in the package. The search for Nancy's father went cold after that date it seemed.

* * *

Nancy had unpacked the small sculpture and it lay surrounded by protective bubble wrap on her settee. She ran her fingers over the stone and smiled. It felt both smooth and coarse at the same time. The profile of the young woman had the angularity of a Modigliani, yet the affirmation of a contemporary piece.

Pole's instinct had been spot on. It would look striking in her newly redecorated lounge. She had done away with the mural on the far wall and allowed the area to be painted plain white, space for more art. The first purchase had been made with Jonathan, a new painting by one of her friends, the artist Susan Rosenberg. The hanging of the piece had been a celebration, accompanied by a glass of excellent champagne.

She moved closer to Susan's piece, a colourful abstract piece unique and uplifting. Pole had moved into her life effortlessly. Yet it had taken the trauma of the previous case they had worked on together to make it happen. She needed his company; no, more, his affection. Nancy stepped back from the piece. Why could she not speak the word that kept wanting to be heard but not acknowledged?

Love.

She shook with irritation at her own inability to face her feelings. She, so very able to ask the harsh questions when working on a case, could not bring herself to ask the simplest one when it came to emotions.

Was it why she had formed a friendship with Henry, understood him, two people wrestling with their feelings? Pole had never been jealous of Henry and he was right. Their affection was of a different kind. She admired Pole for being able to recognise this and never trying to oppose it, despite his reservations.

Nancy drifted away from her lounge, into her office at the far end of her apartment. She looked in, uncertain why she had moved to that room.

Pole. Henry. The Letter.

She moved a strand of dark hair away from her face, still on the threshold of her office. She had to speak to Pole about The Letter. The equivocal note Henry had slipped into her hand a few months ago, both ominous and hopeful.

Her BlackBerry's ringtone interrupted her deliberations.

"Jonathan?"

"*J'ai besoin de vous*," Pole said. "In a professional capacity." A small wobble of embarrassment in his voice. "Marsh is being difficult."

"Well, I do not mind you needing me in whatever capacity," Nancy teased. "I'll do my best to convince The Super, *mon cher ami*."

"And you will succeed, *je le sais*." Tease happily received.

The thought of China floated into Nancy's mind. But why ask? Pole would let her know as soon as he had received news that was worth relaying.

It was good to have utter confidence in someone. It was reassuring, a feeling Nancy rarely sought but that she discovered she enjoyed. The burden shared felt so much lighter.

Pole was showering her with instructions regarding Marsh. She didn't mind for once, carried by his silvery voice, a warm rich authoritative baritone that cared.

"Jonathan, Jonathan," she finally interrupted. "I'll be fine."

"Of course." Pole stopped abruptly.

"Is Henry still at the Yard?"

"Not for long. I thought it would mollify Marsh and the Belmarsh governor if we sent him back early today."

"Good thought." Nancy hesitated. Whilst talking to Pole her hand had started fumbling with Henry's letter, burning her fingers. But what could she say now? And would it mean Henry not being allowed out of Belmarsh again, so he would be unable to obtain for Marissa the information she so badly needed?

"Nancy, are you still here?" Pole's voice interrupted her thinking.

She pushed the letter away. "Yes, I'm just wondering when the best time is to see Marsh."

"I'd speak to Marsh's PA and grab a slot as soon as possible if I were you," Pole said. "Do you fancy a drink afterwards?"

"*Une proposition irrésistible*."

"I might be a little late."

"I'm in no rush. I'll wait for you with a good book."

The Super was behaving like a petulant child. She hung up and dialled Denise's number immediately. Marsh needed to be acknowledged as the important man he was. She did not mind putting on the charm as long as it bore fruit and it would.

* * *

Brett had taken the call. It was the first time Mohammed had spoken to him on his burner phone.

"The Sheik wants to know whether you are ready?"

The sharp answer that was on Brett's lips stayed there. "I'm working on it. I told him I don't —"

Mohammed interrupted. "I don't know the details." And it was obvious he did not want to know either. His job was not to argue with Brett but to deliver the messages.

Sly, Brett thought. The Sheik would no longer communicate with him directly but put pressure on him through Mohammed. Brett had to say yay or nay and nay was out of the question.

"I'll be ready by the end of today. Say at what time?"

"It's imminent." Mohammed's voice had lost its rich Middle-Eastern tone. It had become the flat voice of a scared man, hardly uttering his words for fear of saying the wrong thing.

There was no point in giving Mohammed a piece of his mind.

"What's the process?"

"I'll meet you tomorrow with a new burner phone. The instructions will be sent on that," Mohammed finished with a cough of relief.

"That's a little slim," Brett protested, again why bother but it was good to vent.

He drew a blank from Mohammed, predictably.

"Fine, and I presume as usual a text one hour before the meeting will tell me where to go?"

"Sorry, yes."

Brett killed the call. His hands shook a little. He no longer was in control of the trajectory in which his business and possibly his life were going.

"Fuck." Brett threw the phone onto a chair. It rebounded and almost crashed on the floor. "Fuck. Get a grip."

He pulled back the exquisite Hereke rug from the floor, pressed hard on a couple of boards and a small opening appeared. He took out his MI6 laptop and logged in. The five minutes it took to go through the security protocols lasted an eternity. He sent an email to Steve – *will be told details of transfer tomorrow.*

The response was almost instantaneous. Steve was tracking Brett's emails, unexpectedly. Brett almost wished he could go back to the time when Steve took a couple of days to reply.

Shall we meet at the club?

Not now. I will find another way of communicating with you. Back in touch tonight.

Brett walked to his Louis XV antique desk, took out the Highland Park bottle of whisky and poured a large glass. Hell, the bottle was still half full, and he might never get to finish it. He took a mouthful and let the amber liquid do its trick. He topped up the glass and walked back to his armchair.

Brett took a more reasonable sip, grabbed another mobile phone he had prepared. Time to call his Italian contact and prep him up: flattery, more money no doubt, more flattery, perhaps a few veiled threats he might have to take the business elsewhere.

Yes, it would work.

* * *

Ferguson was on his way. He was bringing two of his team to review Andy's findings. There was nothing Pole could do to prevent it and he was almost glad Ferguson was coming. Agent Harris could not stop that.

Nancy was with Marsh, no doubt getting The Super to where he needed to be. Henry had left for Belmarsh and arrived without incident. It all sounded perhaps a little too smooth.

Marissa's name flashed on the screen of his BlackBerry.

"What can I do for you, Marissa?"

"Mark Phelps would like to meet Henry."

Pole's eyebrows shot up. "A confrontation?"

"I don't think so," Marissa replied slowly. "He needs to understand. Make sense of what has happened."

"Victim meets perpetrator. Do you think it will help?"

"I spent a long time with him this afternoon. I think it is important and —"

228

"You're worried he will pull away otherwise."

"Mark could meet him at the Yard."

"I can clear this with Marsh but, Marissa, who will tell Henry?"

"Nancy could."

Pole was about to reject the idea. But it seemed Nancy was brokering every delicate situation and making a splendid job of it already. Pole grinned. It was good to be vindicated about involving her.

"Do you think he will accept?"

Pole moved around his office whilst thinking. "To be frank I'm not sure he is ready."

Pole turned towards the clock on the wall. Ferguson was late. Unusual.

Marissa stopped, alerted by Pole's lack of focus.

"Sorry Marissa. Nancy is probably the best person to speak to Henry but don't expect him to rejoice."

Pole terminated the call by wishing her good luck and moved to Andy's desk. He had not heard either. Pole returned to his office. He would give Commander Ferguson another fifteen minutes and call.

He did not have to wait too long. The door of his office closed abruptly. Ferguson stood in front of his desk, alone.

"We need to talk."

Pole pointed to the chair in front of his desk. Ferguson dropped the files covering it on the floor unceremoniously, his face like thunder.

"I received a call from MI6."

Pole nodded, a few sharp pins prickling his spine.

"It seems that your case involves one of MI6's assets." Ferguson moved his fingers giving the word assets an air quotation.

"I see." Pole did his best to look surprised. Ferguson was too incensed to consider his reaction closely.

"Which means that I have to delay any intervention with this bloody lot your chap has traced."

"Why delay?" Pole knew the answer and he did not like it.

"I don't know. It's not uncommon to launch an assault and isolate the MI6 insider but there is always a risk."

"What do you want me to do?" Pole asked, hoping the answer would be nothing.

"Stay put until I get MI6 onside. I have not said my last word. National security is as much my concern as theirs."

Pole agreed, giving a few words of support as Ferguson was leaving. "And make sure your chap does not speak to anyone about what he has found. I don't like leaving this hanging but I've no choice, so keep it safe for me."

Pole nodded again and watched Ferguson disappear into the corridor. Pole's usual sound judgement was about to be tested to the full, he feared.

* * *

Superintendent Marsh was walking out of his office when she arrived. His face was a little red and unwelcoming. He made an effort to greet her and apologised immediately.

"Emergency meeting I'm afraid. I'm so very sorry I have to cancel just as you are walking in."

"Don't worry, Superintendent. I understand the pressure you are under."

Marsh straightened up a little; a compliment would always go a long way.

"It is very kind of you. Unfortunately, I cannot delay, but walk with me and we can talk."

They both made their way towards the bank of lifts. Nancy spoke about the request from Mark Phelps. To her surprise Marsh was not in the mood to argue. He agreed with the request, would speak to the Belmarsh governor and did not foresee a problem as long as the meeting was organised at the Yard.

"Something on your mind, Superintendent?" A bold question from Nancy perhaps, but why not?

"National security is on everybody's mind," Marsh volunteered.

His BlackBerry was ringing. "Pole, I'm coming your way."

Marsh bade Nancy goodbye, with a rapid bow. She had never seen him so anxious. He was taking Pole with him to his meeting and that could not be a good sign.

230

Chapter Twenty-Three

Pole could hear him before he saw him. Marsh was coming his way and evidently also on the warpath. MI6 was throwing its weight around and intruding into the Met's operations. He did not like it.

Pole stood up in anticipation.

"Ah, Pole – glad you are still at your desk."

Obviously. Pole bit his lip. "How can I help you, Sir?"

"You've spoken to Ferguson I gather."

"Yes, he came in to talk about our latest findings." Pole waited for Marsh to say his piece. Marsh's face had the livid colour of anger, his dark eyebrows gathered in one straight line.

"You mean your team has been able to track the shooter?"

Blast, Ferguson had spoken to his superiors already. "Although I wanted to discuss with Ferguson in detail to make sure."

Marsh did not even bother to rebuke Pole. He was keeping his frustration stored up for someone else to feel.

"Right, I've asked the Home Office to call an emergency coordination meeting. The constant interference of MI6 has to stop." Marsh was playing politics but Pole had indeed noticed MI6 interference; he was at the centre of it.

"I wouldn't know, Sir."

"Of course, you wouldn't."

Perfect answer and Marsh was still not asking the right question – who had given MI6 the heads-up?

"When is the meeting taking place?"

"Now. We are expected in fifteen minutes. You can brief me in the car about the evidence you have gathered."

Pole shrugged his jacket on. Picked up a file Andy had been compiling. Marsh was rehearsing his arguments with him: interference – trust – cooperation.

Pole fell back a little when they reached the ground floor on their way to Marsh's car, enough to send Nancy a quick text.

With Marsh – will be late, *vraiment désolée.* Jx

He had pressed the send button before wondering whether the x was too much.

When they reached the Home Office, Commander Ferguson and the Head of CT Command in London had already arrived. The Home Secretary and his aide were in the meeting room, having a final conversation behind closed doors.

A couple of people, a tall wiry man and a Middle-Eastern-looking younger man, sat in a different corner. MI6 didn't mix. The aide to the Home Secretary opened the door and everybody walked in. Pole followed Marsh. They all shook hands and introduced themselves.

Agent Harris was not there. Pole breathed a sigh of relief until one of Harris' colleagues mentioned he could not attend as urgent matters required his attention.

The Home Secretary set the scene and the squabbling started immediately. Pole observed the people around the table. Ferguson and his boss were facing MI6. Marsh had positioned himself a little off-centre but on Ferguson's side. Pole found himself relegated far out, a place he felt comfortable with.

"What do you mean, your asset is irreplaceable?"

"Commander Ferguson," the lean-looking man interrupted. "Infiltrating these cells is not easy. You know that as well as I do, so yes, our asset is irreplaceable."

"This cell is posing an imminent threat to the public," Ferguson's boss cut in. "We need to take them down now."

"I would agree if my undercover officer was warning me of an imminent strike, but his very reliable intelligence does not say that there is one planned."

"Nothing planned. How about the attempted murder of a key witness and a prosecutor in a high-profile case?"

"You've done a pretty good job so far of stopping them." There was a hint of humour in the thin man's voice.

"This is preposterous. We need to see your intel now." Ferguson had raised his voice.

"I can't comment in the interest —"

"Don't give me that crap," Ferguson growled. "You're not the only one defending national security."

"Gentlemen, gentlemen," the Home Secretary had raised her hands to calm the situation down. "This is not helpful."

"We are monitoring them closely. We will know if they try something else. In the meantime, this operation has given us the opportunity to discover more about what we believe is a new terrorist organisation."

"You mean a new cell in London? We know that already." Ferguson's face only showed contempt.

"I don't think you heard me right, Commander. I said organisation not operation."

The room fell silent. Marsh looked at Pole, then at the Home Secretary. Ferguson and his boss exchanged a surprised look.

The Middle-Eastern looking MI6 agent took over.

"We still don't know whether this is a splinter cell and new offshoot of Al-Qaeda, but we are seeing fresh movement on social media, a new way of talking about the Jihad, more aggressive, more ambitious."

"And you think they are in the UK? Why?" Ferguson's boss's voice showed genuine interest and doubt too. This was far too big to ignore or rebuff.

"The tactics for recruitment are different. They are prepared to recruit outside the traditional Muslim community."

"Can you substantiate that?"

Both agents remained silent.

"What do you need CT Command to do? Sit on our hands?"

The Home Secretary intervened before anybody started arguing again.

"You need to hold back until we position our asset. After that they are all yours," the thin man said.

"And dispose of them, which is what CT Command will do." The Home Secretary left no room for argument. Ferguson and his boss exchanged angry looks.

The MI6 agents savoured their victory.

Marsh had not opened his mouth until this point, a wise move Pole had to admit.

"How can the Met help?"

"Let us have what you've got so far, and we can all be on the same page." The lean man had turned towards Marsh and Pole.

Marsh turned to Pole. "And what do you think?"

Seven pairs of eyes started scrutinising Pole. For a split second he felt like a rabbit caught in the headlights.

"Perhaps you can liaise with Inspector Pole and keep me in the loop?" Marsh said irritated at Pole's lack of an immediate reply.

Pole simply nodded an "Of course". They know already and they know I know. Pole caught the eye of the Middle-Eastern agent. The message had been received. A few moments to agree contact points and updates then people disappeared. The Home Secretary left first. She did not want to be cornered by anyone.

Before they separated Ferguson's boss turned towards Marsh. "I'd like to know how MI6 got wind of our operation so quickly."

Marsh shrugged it off. "That's their job."

"Going home?" Marsh asked Pole as they were walking out of the Home Office.

"Not yet, Sir. Going back to the Yard – a few things to tidy up."

"Right." Marsh stood for a moment on the pavement. "You were very quiet in there."

"It's really not my scene," was the best Pole could think of.

Marsh eyed Pole. "Ferguson's right, of course. How did MI6 get hold of the information?"

Pole raised his shoulders, hailed a cab and disappeared.

* * *

The smell of bacon made Henry's mouth water. He did not take his eyes off the monitors. It was almost too good to believe. He had

234

already started work on his Bloomberg screens. Pole was at his side in three long strides.

"Morning Inspector. Peace offering?" Henry nodded towards the bacon sandwich wrapped up in greasy paper. Henry had almost forgiven Pole for being his MI6 go-between. He had pondered long and hard over the choice and had to admit Pole was the ideal candidate.

Outsmarted. How annoying.

"Morning Henry." Pole handed Henry his breakfast. He took his usual position, half sitting, half leaning against the makeshift desk. He looked tired and perhaps nervous.

Henry waited for an update.

"What's new on the market?"

Henry cocked his head. "Really, Inspector. You're not going to ask for my advice, are you?

"Hey, I too have a pension."

"Equities. And more equities, in the US in particular. They are heading up for a new bull run and don't be scared about the odd market retreat." Henry grinned.

Pole nodded. "Sounds good." He put down his own coffee and took a longer look at Henry. "Any news at your end?"

"What do you mean?" Henry was genuinely puzzled until the penny dropped.

"You mean?"

"That's right."

Henry's face grew serious. It was true; he had not had direct contact with Kamal and the current regime imposed by Belmarsh made it difficult for him to see any inmate.

"Nothing. I am not allowed to join the others, even for dinner, and I leave before breakfast."

"But I am sure there are ways of communicating."

Henry remained silent. He recalled the message he had received two days ago.

"Something springs to mind?" Pole kept prodding.

"Not really. The food is as bland as ever although they have not thought of poisoning me yet."

"That's the Bolsheviks, Henry, not Jihadists. They prefer the knife."

"I know but, hey, the Irish like the knife too."

Pole withstood the punch. Henry regretted throwing it as soon as it was said.

"Where is Nancy?" Henry asked. He could do with someone to smooth the conversation between him and Pole.

"She'll be in soon."

Surely Pole could be more forthcoming.

"When are you calling your contact again?"

"I'll try at 8pm this evening. It's more likely the answer will come later though, but I'll try."

"You're sure of yourself, aren't you?"

"I know you think I'm an arrogant prick but yes, I am sure. I know too much about him so he has no choice."

A rhythmic knock at the door made them both turn their heads at the same time. Nancy's elegant silhouette appeared in the doorway. They were all smiles.

"*Messieurs*, I'm glad not to be walking into a match of fisticuffs."

"Never," Pole and Henry chimed together.

"Good news. The Super has decided that in the interests of the enquiry, ha ha, the SFO case being so high-profile etc etc, he will ask the Belmarsh governor and the Home Office to let you, Henry, stay at The Yard until midnight today."

"You're the best." Henry stood up but stayed back a little. Pole was in the way. He graciously moved back. Henry landed a small kiss on Nancy's cheek, almost shy.

"Marsh sounded a little frazzled, Jonathan. He gave me all I wanted with hardly any need to convince him."

Pole's face managed to convey astonishment. Both Henry and Nancy were waiting for specifics. But he moved his hand vaguely – a no-idea gesture that failed to convince.

"Shall we see where we've got to?" Nancy changed the subject.

"Sure." Henry called up a few documents he had saved in a protected folder specially created for him. "Aren't we waiting for Marissa?"

Nancy avoided looking at Pole. "She's coming later."

Henry called up on screen a complex diagram showing all the

layers of companies, trusts, foundations and partnerships that had accumulated, one on top of another.

Panama to start with, then a trip around the world of tax havens and finally a box with a large question mark, the Ultimate Beneficial Owner. No matter how complex a structure was, and this one could have won a prize, there had to be an individual or individuals involved at the end of the chain.

Nancy looked at the different boxes stacked together, and colour coded to indicate the type of legal relationships they had. She was suitably impressed, certainly with the structure itself, but also with Henry's grasp of the legalities surrounding the chain of ownership in this maze of international arrangements.

"I too was a lawyer once, remember." Henry smiled his naughty-yet-clever-boy smile.

"Of course, Chase and Case. Was law not interesting enough for you?"

"I was an Irish boy working in a very closed shop environment. They may eventually have made me partner, but it would have been long after all my peers and I was too good at structured products to wait that long."

Pole moved to Henry's side to look at the diagram as well. Henry nodded his approval. Pole had remembered that he did not like anyone standing at the back of his chair, a remnant from his days on the trading floor during which the head of investment banking would prowl the floor in search of a victim.

"I'm still puzzled. How could compliance at HXBK let this go through?" Pole asked.

"Because there was a disconnect. Some senior people, close to the Ultimate Beneficial Owner, did the review of the structure."

"If the UBO is linked to the state that bought shares in HXBK to support their capital during the 2008 crisis, then that is a problem. Circular transactions of that type are illegal." Henry tapped the screen where the empty box lay.

"My other question is what is this money being used for?" Nancy said.

"Exactly. That should have worried the senior management."

"They are too keen to do business with the big oil producers," Henry replied to Pole.

"Your guy will tell us who the UBO is?" Pole still sounded dubious.

"Yup. And he will tell me how we can track him down, too." Henry crossed his arms behind his head and stretched his long legs underneath the table. He loved this. It was almost as thrilling as concluding some of the ridiculously large transactions he had the reputation of closing in his previous career.

Almost.

Unfortunately, in a few hours' time, instead of celebrating his success in an expensive restaurant, guzzling vintage champagne, Henry would be heading back to Belmarsh.

But just now, sitting between Nancy and Pole, Henry was enjoying the moment.

Pole's BlackBerry rang. He frowned, gestured an apology and walked out of the room. Henry relaxed a notch. It was good to be alone with Nancy.

"What's going through that great mind of yours?" Nancy turned on her chair to look at Henry.

"I'm simply enjoying the chase." Henry sounded playful.

Nancy moved her hand to the side of her neck and rested her elbow on the back of the chair.

"You haven't answered my question."

Henry sat at his screens looking away from her. *Please let it not be the letter.*

"Nancy, you may not believe it, but I have learned to live for the moment and I am enjoying this particular one."

Nancy let it go. She was preparing a difficult question. Henry prayed again, please let it not be the letter.

"I know you are expecting me to ask a difficult question."

"If it's about that stupid letter?"

"It's not. It's an unusual request."

Henry turned to face her. What could be so unexpected that he had not thought about it already?

"Mark Phelps would like to meet you."

The bolt of fire that punched him in the gut drew a small intake of breath from Henry. Lost for words, Henry stared at Nancy. The sudden numbness in his limbs became unbearable.

Henry opened his mouth, unsuccessfully. Was it a joke? Was Mark Phelps insane?

Nancy let him be. She gave Henry space to understand the request was real. She got up, poured two glasses of water, and handed one to Henry. He finished the glass in a couple of gulps.

"Is this why – I'm not?" Henry closed his eyes, fighting back tears he thought he no longer had.

"He needs to understand, to find some peace – and in order to carry on with the case, this is his request."

Henry dropped his head in his hands. He stayed silent for a while.

"What can I say that will make a difference? That I'm a bastard of a terrorist, that I regret what I did?" Henry's voice oscillated between pain and anger.

He stood up, walked to the wall. He spread his hands over it, his forehead resting against its cold surface; he was fighting emotions, despair and …

Shame.

"And if I say no?" Henry spoke, still facing the wall.

"He will almost certainly no longer be a witness in the case."

Henry turned his head slowly.

"Does he want to …?" Henry was searching for the word.

"I don't think he wants to make you feel …" Nancy tried to find the word Henry was looking for. "Inhumane. He is not that sort of person." Nancy had stood up as well. He felt her move in his direction. But he did not want to be approached. He moved to another corner of the room.

"Let him, then. Let him tell me what a monster I have been. Yes, let him."

Nancy froze. Her kind eyes were on him, trying to soothe his torment.

"You know this isn't true. You are not a monster."

"To you Nancy perhaps, but others – and who could blame them?"

Nancy was about to continue but Henry lifted a hand.

"We don't need to speak about this any longer. I will see him. Please go and tell him."

He needed to be on his own to prepare for what would be the most difficult conversation of his life.

Chapter Twenty-Four

The underpass smelt of urine and rotting food. Pole looked at his watch again. He had arrived a little early. He kicked a beer can that lay on the ground, the sound of it rolling on the rough asphalt reverberated along the walls. Almost too loud to bear.

Hurried footsteps were coming his way, a man's shoes. Pole was on his guard. Agent Harris turned the corner and broke into a slow jog.

"Ferguson's boss is wreaking havoc at the Home Office," he chuckled.

"You're not concerned?"

"Nope. What we've got is too big."

"I suppose it is."

"You spoke to Crowne?"

Pole's jaw clenched. He nodded.

"Anything I should be aware of?"

"Such as?"

"Change of mind, change of mood – trying to contact other people in the old IRA world."

"I am his go-between, not his confidante."

"But you're talking to him to find out, right?"

"As much as I can; it's not my job to snoop."

Harris gave Pole a broad smile. He unwrapped a piece of chewing gum and popped it into his mouth. "Trying to stop smoking." He kept grinning.

"Is that it?" Pole looked at his watch again. He could not be away for long in the middle of this political minefield.

"Got a message for Crowne." Harris grew serious. His beady brown eyes darkened. It was time to do proper MI6 business. "My source tells me that it will happen in the next twenty-four hours."

"What if we don't get the information we need to keep bringing him back to the Yard?"

Harris shrugged. "Find a way."

Pole took a step closer to Harris. That was not the deal as he understood it. Harris carried on chewing his gum. Even in the shadow of a towering Pole he was relaxed.

"I know it's going to piss you and a lot of other people off, but things are in motion and I don't decide on the timing. I can only give you the heads-up."

Harris was right but Pole stayed close for a moment longer, restraining the urge to stick his fist into the other man's face.

"Would do you little good, Inspector. It's not me you need to slam, is it?"

Pole pulled back.

"You and Ferguson will get the cell but first we need to let them do what they are planning to do with Crowne."

"People are going to get hurt," Pole snapped.

"We'll try to minimise that."

"How?"

"My problem, not yours."

"That's not good enough."

"But it will have to do. You and I know what we've got is too big for it not to go through."

"What if Ferguson finds out?"

"Why would he?" Harris had stopped chewing his gum and his eyes drilled into Pole – *don't even think about it.*

Pole turned around in one swoop, running one hand through his thick hair.

"If this thing goes wrong, I'll find a way to get to you," Pole spoke over his shoulder.

"Fair enough but you're underestimating what my team can do."
Pole kept walking away.

"Speak to Crowne and have a little faith in Her Majesty's Secret Service." Harris sounded surprisingly honest.

* * *

The day was going to be long and slow. Henry found himself looking at the wall clock yet again – a watched kettle. He needed to be doing something more than re-reading the file Marissa had left with him. Still, it was a welcome distraction from what had been haunting him since he had been told he would be meeting Mark Phelps.

He pushed away the thought of the meeting. He needed to concentrate on the task at hand, re-read the file, possibly spot something new and make the call to Mac in Panama.

But he had agreed to the meeting. It was the right thing to do. It was what the reformed Henry must do. Nothing had prepared him for the feelings that assailed him once Nancy had left him alone. He had gone to the wastepaper basket and nearly thrown up. His body was still feverish at the thought.

In the end, the idea of a meeting had given him greater resolve. He would see his plan through.

The sound of a text message delivered on his burner phone brought him back to the here and now. Mac had given him a time to call. The man had been busy all night. Henry breathed deeply. He could still make good on his commitment and the code he had used with Mac in their conversation still worked. The answer was ready for delivery and he would not have to wait until 8pm.

Henry deleted the text, stood up and poured himself a cup of water from the water cooler. It was all working towards the point of no return from which there would be no turning back. Henry was pouring a second cup when the door opened. Pole came in, eyebrows knitted, an expression that had seldom left his face in the last few days.

"Next twenty-four hours; get ready."

Henry's cup wobbled, spilling a little water at his feet. "Shit," he blurted.

"Leave it," Pole said.

Henry walked to his chair and slumped into it, cup in hand. He squeezed it so hard he heard the crunch of the plastic ready to split. His throat had closed. He could not swallow anything.

Pole moved a chair, turned it around and straddled it. "Harris is certain."

"But how?" Henry lifted his eyes and scrutinised Pole.

"He did not care to elaborate."

Henry put the cup down, slowly, not trusting his movements. He rubbed his hand over his face, pulling it down to form a strange grimace.

"The Belmarsh lot won't be able to communicate. I can't meet anyone until I'm back for good."

"Think about what happened in the last two days; there might have been a sign." Pole had crossed his arms, resting them on the back of his chair. He too wanted to validate Harris' information.

"It has always been very vague." Henry picked up the plastic cup. He hesitated, froze and finally lifted the cup to his lips, drinking in small gulps, hoping Pole had not noticed.

Pole stood up. "Let me know if something comes to mind."

Henry nodded – and both men knew MI6 was right.

* * *

Her back was turned to him when Pole entered the open-plan space. Nancy was talking to Andy. Pole slowed down his pace. Nancy had pulled her jet-black hair into what looked like a complicated bun. Her slim figure was twisted into an elegant pose, hand on Andy's desk partitioning, hips at an attractive angle. Pole forced himself out of his state of languorous admiration.

Andy must have told Nancy he was approaching since she now swirled around. Her smile was courteous, but her eyes relished their contact with Pole's.

"I spoke to Marissa. She will let Mark Phelps know Henry has accepted."

Pole's office phone rang. Andy picked up.

"It's Commander Ferguson."

Pole pulled a sorry face.

"Don't worry, but Jonathan, *j'ai besoin de vous parler.*" Nancy's eyes conveyed an urgency that surprised Pole.

"*Bien entendu.*" He disappeared into his office, door closed. Nancy was still speaking to Andy. Pole hoped Andy would not talk about the shooter. He had been clear with Andy; no one must know, no one – but Nancy had her ways with young men and come to think of it with a number of not-so-young men too.

Ferguson was raging on the phone. MI6 was not budging and would Pole at least give him something; he almost said please.

Pole clenched a fist. He did not enjoy keeping essential information from CT Command and yet Harris had been clear. He sat down and kept talking to Ferguson: options, who to call next. Pole gave some snippets of information as he spoke.

What if he was wrong? Pole stood up again. He had not felt so unsure of his instincts or his analysis of a situation for a very long time. Even the protracted case against Henry had not challenged his judgement as much.

Marsh's number appeared on another line.

"Ferguson, got to go; Marsh is calling me."

He ended one call and took the other. The bark of Marsh's voice irritated Pole. "I spoke to the Home Office again. They are reconsidering their position." Pole grunted. Marsh could certainly pull the strings of power, silent when needed, reaching out to the right people when necessary.

"You don't think it's a good idea?" Marsh snapped.

"We just don't have the full picture, Sir."

"Perhaps not, but we have a bunch of Jihadi on our streets that might attempt a terrorist act. I'm not happy to delay. In particular with the quality intel your team has dug up."

Marsh had a point. He failed to mention the enormous kudos he would derive were the Met at the centre of the arrest. Despite this Pole could see where Marsh was coming from.

"Shall I come your way to discuss strategy, Sir?" Always a good argument – the S word had a hypnotic effect on The Met's management and Marsh could never resist it. The meeting would give Harris a little more time to get organised.

Pole hung up, shook his head and walked off in the direction of Marsh's office. Nancy would have to wait a little longer before he could devote his attention to her.

* * *

Andy's voice sounded distracted as Nancy's eyes followed Pole's tall body moving swiftly towards the lifts. Something was up. She had felt it when Henry, Pole and she had been talking in the morning. The atmosphere was friendly, perhaps deceptively so, with no more sparring between Pole and Henry, she having to play the schoolmistress separating two rowdy boys.

Andy kept talking in the background, his voice suddenly more pressing. Nancy snapped out of her thoughts and forced her attention back to the young man. He was pointing at his screen. News alert. "I need to call Inspector Pole."

Nancy read the news alert on Andy's screen.

Prisoners have barricaded themselves in one of the wings of HMP Belmarsh. The prison is now in lockdown. Five anti-riot units and a negotiator have been dispatched.

Text kept coming.

Two prison officers have been seriously injured, one is in a critical condition. Hostage situation not confirmed.

"What's your mobile number Andy?"

Andy kept an eye on the screen whilst giving her the number.

"I'll give you a missed call so you know how to contact me."

She could not reach Henry on his burner phone.

The lifts were full. It was almost midday and employees were already going for their lunch trying to avoid the inevitable queues. She squeezed near the door, fighting the influx of people. Level 3, Level 2, Level 1, Ground Floor; almost everyone got out. She pressed Level -1 a few times; someone dashed in and the doors reopened. She tried to remain civil. As soon as they reached Level -1 she burst out of the lift and ran all the way to the room in which Henry was working.

One of the prison officers outside was on his mobile. The news about Belmarsh was spreading like wildfire.

Henry was typing furiously on his keyboard when she entered. The noise of the door made him jump.

"You've seen the news?" he said returning his attention to the monitors.

"Who are they?" Nancy had moved to his side, reading the information that was scrolling through Bloomberg news.

"Nothing on that yet." Henry responded, calling up another screen from the Reuters information platform.

"It only came up on the Met internal info line a few minutes ago."

"No time at all."

More data had started to appear.

Some of the prisoners have been heard shouting Allahu Akbar. Fear that a number of hardcore radicalised inmates have taken over Wing 2 at Belmarsh is growing.

Henry's body froze in a strange position, halfway towards the screen, his fingers in mid-air, immobile.

"What does it mean? Henry?"

No response came. She shook Henry by the shoulders.

"I don't know."

"Oh, come on," she almost shouted. "This can't be a coincidence."

Henry's eyes met hers and she could see hurt. "Sorry. I'm sorry. I shouldn't infer —" Nancy's phone rang. "I'm with him now." She mouthed Pole's name to Henry.

"Why?" she said. "This is ridiculous." Nancy felt the lump in her throat growing. "I will."

"What's happening?" Henry had turned his entire body sideways so that he could face her.

"The Belmarsh governor wants you back at HSU right away."

"This is ridiculous," Henry blurted. "I haven't finished."

"This is what Pole thinks too, and for once Marsh agrees."

"And that is what you have to convey to the prison officers outside."

"Correct." Nancy looked serious.

"Wow. I never saw you as a bodyguard but hey!"

"I may not look it but I sure can hold my ground."

"I don't doubt it and it seems you're going to be tested right away."
The door had just opened.

* * *

Mohammed was running his prayer beads through his fingers, thumb and index finger, rolling them one after the other. Brett could see him in the distance, eyes focused on the door. He half stood up and sat down again as Brett made his way over to him.

"Is The Sheik too busy to speak to me?" Brett's sharp tone sent a shiver of angst down Mohammed's round body.

"Shhh, not so loud."

Brett rolled his eyes and sat down. Mohammed half extended his arm in the direction of one of the waiters and tea materialised.

"Didn't know you were religious," Brett remarked after he had tasted his tea, a rather good and fragrant beverage, he had to admit.

"Who told you that I wasn't?" Mohammed's eyes darted around the room in fear.

"Relax. I've simply never seen you with prayer beads before."

"Helps the nerves."

Brett raised his glass in acknowledgement.

"You'll receive a text in the next twenty-four hours."

"And you got me here to tell me that?"

Mohammed did not reply. He waited for a couple of men to walk past their table and settle in another corner of the room.

"He has this for you." Mohammed handed over a large envelope. "To be opened when you are home."

"Obviously." Brett took the envelope. It was light and had no markings.

Brett finished his tea in a few gulps and left the tea shop without another word.

He walked down the large street, came to Seven Sisters tube and started walking down the stairs. He stopped to consult the tube map. Two people were following him, he was sure. He had seen their shadows when Mohammed had stopped talking.

Brett moved to the platform and sat down waiting for the next train. He leaned against the bench backrest, an eye on the people tailing him. He was pretty sure they were not supposed to be discreet. The Sheik had one message to communicate.

Remember Massimo Visconti.

* * *

"Crowne, Belmarsh governor wants you back to HSU now."

"On what grounds?" Nancy stood between the two prison officers and Henry.

The men looked at each other, incredulous. "Look lady," one of the officers started.

Wrong title.

"To begin with, young man," Nancy interrupted with eloquence. "You address yourself to me in the appropriate manner. Secondly, there is an understanding between the Home Office, the SFO, the Metropolitan Police and the governor that Mr Crowne needs to provide us with his assistance to gather vital information and that he will not be returned to Belmarsh until he has done so until late today."

"Perhaps but Belmarsh governor's just called us to tell us he wants him back at HSU."

"You mean Mr Crowne? May I remind you that since the 2004 Home Office reform inmates are called either by their first name or addressed as mister."

The second officer had said nothing so far. His calm contrasted with the irritability of his colleague, a puffed-up sparrow – all feathers and no weight.

"That does not change anything." The sparrow's face was turning crimson.

"I heard you the first time." Nancy was not budging.

"My colleague is right, Ms Wu. Perhaps you could check with Superintendent Marsh?" The polite yet determined tone of the other guard surprised Nancy.

"I will do so or, even better, speak to Inspector Pole."

"I think Superintendent Marsh might be the one deciding."

Hurried steps came down the corridor. Pole opened the door briskly.

"Shall we speak to Inspector Pole first?" Nancy's voice had taken on a relentless sharp edge. "These gentlemen are intending to take Mr Crowne back to HSU Belmarsh right away."

"Yes, I've been told and haven't had time yet to speak to Superintendent Marsh about it. For the time being, Henry stays put."

"But the Belmarsh gov —"

"I am aware." Pole snapped.

"Perhaps you should try him again?" The other officer said.

"Is this because of the riots?"

"We have not been told why; simply to bring Mr Crowne back to HSU immediately."

"It may not be safe."

"HSU Belmarsh is the safest prison in the UK, Inspector Pole."

Nancy liked the game Pole was playing. He too was playing the clock. If the riots escalated, Belmarsh might not be accessible and in complete lockdown.

"Not if the riots escalate into a complete lockdown."

"Mr Crowne is an HSU inmate. He must be returned to HSU. That is the procedure." The guard's calm was putting pressure on Pole. He shrugged.

"Still, I'm not comfortable with the risk that this entails."

"Let's see what Superintendent Marsh has to say."

Pole gritted his teeth and pulled out his BlackBerry. A text had arrived and he read it quickly. Pole pressed the recall button.

"Pole here. I am returning your —" Pole was interrupted by a flow of words. They sounded angry as they drifted out of his phone.

"Yes, Sir – if this has been agreed – understood, Sir."

Pole killed the call.

"You can have Henry."

Chapter Twenty-Five

It was happening.

The hairs rose on the back of Henry's neck when the two prison officers bundled him into the high security vehicle parked at the back of Scotland Yard. Nancy muffled a cry of anger with a quivering hand and Pole looked defeated.

It was not the sort of goodbye he had hoped for. Henry rested his head against the metal frame of the van and closed his eyes. He could feel the cuffs tight around his wrists. Not long now until they were off.

At Belmarsh, the breakfast they had brought him before he left for The Yard had angered him to start with: a bread roll roughly cut and already buttered, a glass of juice red in colour, a small lump of jam – must have been strawberry. He had drunk the juice and hardly touched the bread.

Henry had not thought about it until Pole had asked the question. But now he was in the van taking him back to HSU he was wondering. Was it a message? The events of the day kept intruding: the discussion with Nancy and Pole, the call with Mac and Pole's warning, the conversation he had agreed to have with Mark Phelps. He shook his head, opened his eyes. It had been there all day waiting for him to decipher, a subtle but perfect reference to his Catholic upbringing – a Last Supper allusion, bread and wine. Henry recognised Kamal's hand, subtle but to the point. The van had stopped. Henry braced himself, a few minutes elapsed, then the vehicle resumed its journey.

Henry moved his head a fraction to survey the two prison officers that sat close to the door. An odd pair he thought. The young chap was nervous, perhaps a newbie in his role as escort. The other officer seemed inscrutable, his calm almost eerie.

The van stopped again, this time at the side of the road. Henry could feel the movements of the van being reversed and driven into a parking bay. The walkie-talkie crackled and the young guard responded. The conversation was mostly happening at the other end with monosyllabic responses from the guard until finally he formed a complete sentence.

"That route won't delay us too much." He bent towards his colleague, informed him of the decision. The other nodded. "OK, let's do that."

Henry made his entire body let go. But what had he been expecting?

The van restarted with a jolt. Henry tried to ease off the tension that was building up steadily in his body. He rolled his shoulders, moved his neck, breathing deeply in the process.

He settled back against the cool metal. His mind drifted back to the case, to Mark Phelps. The fear he felt at having to face a victim who was not even his victim had startled him.

He had spent the time between working on the case thinking about it: what he would say, what the responses might be. Sorry was never going to be good enough even to start with. But maybe he could explain why he had followed the path he had taken, with honesty. That perhaps was all he had to offer.

He was not sure it would be sufficient, that it would fulfil the hope he nourished. The hope that something in his life was salvageable, that he was redeemable … The thought of perhaps escaping the meeting with Mark did not bring him joy or release. To Henry's greatest surprise he wanted to have this honest conversation with a victim.

The collision with the front of the van reverberates through its entire structure. The two prison officers brace themselves against the handlebars of their seats. Henry is thrown against the iron bars that separate his seating area from the guards'. The pain in his shoulder is searing, his mind takes him straight back to another van, to the explosion that marked his descent into hell. The walkie-talkie has fallen to the floor; it buzzes like a wounded insect – someone is calling urgently.

One of the guards grabs it.

"Is he hurt? I'll go and check."

"We shouldn't open the door until we're inside Belmarsh," the younger guard says, agitated.

"I need to check whether we killed this guy. Right, right."

Henry collects himself. His mind throws up images he does not want to see. He smells gasoline. He smells fire. He looks around in anguish but there are no flames to see.

The door of the van opens and shuts. People have congregated outside it seems: Henry can hear voices. The young guard is verging on panic. He stands up and peers through the protected windows. He cranes his neck but cannot see what he is looking for.

Banging on the door, the walkie-talkie crackles again.

"OK." He hesitates. More banging at the door again, not insistent; just a come-on-open-up-it's-only-me type of knock.

He complies and the cross of the M4 carbine strikes him square in the face. He has no time to pick himself up from the floor; the second blow crashes over his skull.

The older officer who went to check the incident has come back, his weapon in his right hand. He takes his keys and starts unbolting the door keeping Henry locked up. Henry looks at him, numb. He has been thinking about this moment for months and now he cannot move. The sound of a police siren yells in the distance. Henry steps away from the door.

The officer moves forward. "Cuffs," he says.

Henry moves in slow motion. He had not expected it to happen this way. He no longer knows what he was expecting. The cuffs are off. The guard turns around and throws a bundle of clothes at him. "Put these on." A dark hoodie, a pair of black waterproof trousers and jacket, a black helmet.

Henry's head is held in a vice. He could say no. He looks at the young man on the floor, blood already coagulating on his head wound. Who is he kidding – there is no turning back. A few final images and he knows – Liam, Nancy, his father.

He is putting the clothes on quickly now, hoodie, waterproofs. The guard is impatient, even suspicious. The look of fanatical hatred smacks Henry in the face. Hesitation has been swept away from him. He puts on the helmet and gets down from the van.

Outside, the motorbike that had slid under the front of the vehicle is still there. Two other men are pointing M249 sub-machine guns at the driver. Even locked in his armoured vehicle, the metal is no match for the penetration power of the ammunition.

The driver is holding his hands up over his head. Two motorbikes are parked either side of the van. There is no traffic in this side road they diverted into. One car has driven past, accelerating.

It seems that in the middle of Deptford no one wants to know about a police van under attack. The guard fires up one of the bikes. A loud moan comes out of the van.

Impossible.

Henry snaps his fingers in the direction of the gun that sticks out of the belt of one of the bikers. The guard hesitates. Henry snaps up the visor, his face has grown cold. What is he waiting for? Henry grabs the gun the guard has handed to him, walks back to the van.

Two loud firearm discharges and Henry straddles the bike that is waiting for him.

* * *

Nancy was still on her call to Marissa. Pole was on his way to his office. He knew what was coming next. Assailed by doubts, he could not bring himself to speak to Andy who had received yet another call from Ferguson's team. Henry had been gone barely an hour when a text pinged on Pole's burner phone. Pole closed the door of his office and leaned against it.

Call me now.

He felt the urge to throw the phone against the wall.

He pressed the call button instead.

"Crowne is out."

Pole remained silent, his throat dry, incapable of speech.

"Are you there?"

Pole grunted. "Casualties?"

"Not sure but you need to be on your way to the scene."

"Marsh?"

"I'll deal with him."

"Ferguson?"

"Ditto."

"I'll call you when I'm there."

"Good."

Pole's siren let him blaze through the traffic, the longest twenty-minute drive of his career. He had just let an ambulance overtake him.

He parked his car in the middle of the road and walked quickly towards the officers already on the scene. He showed his badge. "Any casualties?"

One of the officers moved his head towards the van without a word. Pole's gut tightened as he looked inside.

"Hello Sir. What's your name? Can you hear me, Sir?"

Pole recognised the young man who had been so keen to take Henry back to Belmarsh. His face had started turning blue and the force of the impact had no doubt crushed some bones.

"I need to speak to him please." Pole flashed his ID again.

"And I need to assess him first." The paramedic held her ground. The tall woman had turned back to the patient.

"We may have some extremely dangerous people on the run and an abduction."

She hesitated. Her colleague had kept asking questions and the young man was coming around. He recognised Pole.

"Where is Crowne?"

"Gone."

"The other guard?"

"Gone."

The young man closed his eyes and for a moment Pole thought he had passed out. The paramedics moved Pole out of the way but the young man fluttered his eyelashes in an effort to focus.

"But – did not." His mouth was dry and the paramedics helped him with a damp tissue. His eyes moved towards the side of the van.

"Did not – kill —"

"They did not kill you?" Pole asked.

The young guard batted his eyelids, yes. "Crow —"

"They did not kill Crowne?"

Frustration flashed in his eyes. "Me, me."

"That's enough Inspector. I need to take him to hospital."

Pole let the paramedics do their job. He moved to the side of the road. The driver of the van was wrapped in a blanket, sitting sideways in the police car that had arrived first on the scene.

"Are you OK?" Pole asked. He meant it.

"Fine. I didn't see it coming."

"Can you tell me what happened?"

The driver took a sip from a water bottle and started his story. He did his best to give a fair account and Pole did his best to take coherent notes.

"I thought he was dead – the boy," he finished.

"You mean because of the beating?"

"No because of the gunshots – two of them. I thought that's it."

"He was shot at?"

"As I said two shots."

Pole finished taking notes and headed back to the van.

He bent forward in the direction the young guard had indicated. Two bullets had penetrated the metal. Pole stood up, hands on hips, thinking the unthinkable.

Someone had fired two shots at the young guard at point-blank range and missed.

The paramedics were loading the stretcher onto the ambulance. Pole ran to them. He lunged forward for one last question.

"Who shot at you?"

"Crowne."

The woman was about to be rude to him but Pole managed to add, "Crowne missed you?"

A look of relief went through the young man's eyes. He had delivered his message. He moved his head slightly and the stretcher disappeared into the van. The female paramedic closed the door forcefully in Pole's face.

Pole walked away from the scene and found the recessed entrance of a small building. Harris had to know.

"You're certain?" Harris asked after Pole had told him what he knew.

"Certain, I checked the van – two bullet holes. He could not have missed him, not unless he did it on purpose."

Harris grunted. "Why the fuck did he have to get involved?"

"To save a life," Pole shot back.

Harris did not reply immediately but Pole sensed he was holding his tongue.

"Leave it with me. Send me the names of all the people on the scene: police, paramedics —"

"Got that already," Pole replied irritated. Who the hell did he think he was?

"Good man – shoot me a text. We need to make sure the story that comes out on the news is the right one."

"What else do you need from me?"

"I'll let you know."

Pole sent the text and replaced the burner phone in his inside pocket.

His sole consolation for the events of the day was that Harris would soon be dealing with Henry directly.

Henry Crowne had not gained the reputation of being the smartest of arses for nothing as Harris was about to find out.

* * *

The bike was using the back streets of Deptford. The other bike had disappeared. No doubt to avoid identification.

The bike stopped. Another man, also dressed in black, visor down, was waiting for them in a small alleyway.

"Ahmed is going to take you to where you need to go."

Henry nodded. Ahmed pointed to a bag on the floor. "You need to change clothes."

Henry slammed the visor up. "On the side of the road? Why?"

"It's good enough here."

"That's ridiculous." Henry glanced at the two men. There was no way he could make a run for it. And to go where? He removed his helmet, moved to the back of the alley and stripped out of his Belmarsh jogging pants. He grabbed what was in the sports bag. Another set of dark clothes.

"Underwear."

"No fucking way," Henry said. He had already put on the trousers and was not going to expose his manhood to these two in the middle of the street. He put on the jumper with ferocious determination.

The officer and Ahmed exchanged a few words in what Henry knew was Arabic. Ahmed relented, unhappy. Henry had already made a friend.

The ride continued through an area Henry knew nothing about. They hit a main road that seemed to be going towards the river.

The weather was overcast and a few droplets of rain started hitting Henry's helmet. The downpour came in a wave of unexpected strength. It was pelting down on Henry's shoulders, seeping through to his back like a glacial drip. People were hurrying out of the way.

The bike stopped at a set of traffic lights. Henry cursed. He wanted to be somewhere dry. In the distance he thought he recognised the skyline. When the bike turned left he knew where he was – the Cutty Sark.

They were near the Thames but Henry could not recall a bridge over the water in that direction. The bike turned again into an open space. Henry was about to tap the driver on the shoulder when they stopped in front of a strange construction. It looked last century, round and squat – similar to the Greenwich Observatory.

Ahmed and Henry alighted. Ahmed made his way towards a set of lifts, pushing the bike. Henry read the name Greenwich Foot Tunnel. The lift was empty. Ahmed pushed the bike into it and they rode to the bottom of the tunnel. Ahmed fired up the engine again and they started their journey underground and underwater. The noise of the bike was deafening, bouncing off the walls of the tunnel. Henry looked back. But there was no one coming out of the lifts.

Minutes later the bike had reached the other side. Ahmed loaded the bike yet again into the lift and when they emerged on the other side Henry recognised the unmistakable shape of Canary Wharf. A cold piece of ice dropped into his stomach – his old life was gone forever. He straddled the bike again. They made their way north.

* * *

Nancy and Andy were reading the news that had started rolling onto Andy's screen when Pole arrived. Her body no longer showed a relaxed nonchalance but complete tension.

Nancy was fidgeting with one of the buttons of her jacket. Pole could not hear what she was saying but Andy had turned his face towards her and looked concerned.

Nancy's face was pale and her eyes shone with the fever of anxiety.

Had Henry been taken?

"Guv – did you get my call?"

"I did."

Andy looked puzzled. A question was forming on his lips but Pole cut it short.

"Speak to Ferguson; matters might have changed."

"Let's go into my office." He tried to sound reassuring. Nancy had not uttered a word. "How come —"

"I was called as soon as the van hold-up was reported." That was not entirely wrong. Nancy sat heavily in the chair in front of Pole's desk.

"Wasn't there anyone closer?"

"We are talking Henry Crowne."

"But still?" She lifted her head towards him. "Can't you tell me?"

Pole breathed in. "A couple of police cars had arrived before me but I am The Met contact."

No, he could not tell her.

Nancy grew even paler.

"The van was held up. They took Henry. Whoever they are."

Nancy's focus on him was a mixture of fear and scrutiny. Her almond eyes had changed shape, a little narrower perhaps. It could not be the whole story and she knew it. Pole ached.

He wanted to tell her all he had seen, to use her skills openly and comfort him he had made the right decision … but he wanted to protect her too.

Nancy bent forward unexpectedly, placing her head in her hands.

"I need to speak to you about a letter," Nancy said slowly. She hesitated and lifted her head. She was looking straight ahead, to the place where Pole should be sitting. A sense of unease had settled in the room. She was working out how best to explain. Her face told him so. He had seen the same line of her eyebrows and the frown on her forehead before. But today he was not certain he liked her need to gather herself before speaking to him.

"Is it about Henry?"

"Who else but Henry Crowne," Nancy's tone had an edge Pole did not recognise. "Henry gave me a letter. She was still looking at Pole's empty chair. "Not a letter really, more like a note, handwritten – when he was last allowed out of Belmarsh."

"You mean after the Bank of England hostage situation?" Pole's voice was incredulous.

"That's right. I don't know when he wrote it but he gave it to me just before he left for Belmarsh."

Pole stayed where he was, leaning against the wall and its large window. He could not bring himself to sit on his chair, behind his desk – too official.

"It was a strange sort of note. I mean the tone was strange." Nancy shook her head. "I'm not describing this right." Her hand tightened, frustrated. "It felt out of character; someone who had had a revelation. I took it seriously but perhaps not seriously enough." The words were excruciating.

"Did he mention escaping?" Pole cursed his bluntness.

"No, of course not," Nancy had finally turned to face him. Her protestation felt unconvincing.

"But it was implied?" Pole was surprised by his own calm. Perhaps aided by the fact that he too already knew.

"It was – a possibility." Nancy agreed. She had turned paler again.

Her hand had risen to her throat in a protective gesture. "I'm sorry, Jonathan." Nancy's eyes had lost a little of their spark.

Pole left the window and came to lean against his desk close to Nancy's chair. He pushed his hand through his hair and left it there for a moment.

"Why did you not say?" Pole's gaze rested on her hands.

"Because it looked impossible – HSU Belmarsh – and he needed some hope. I thought it would all dissipate eventually."

"Is that all?"

Nancy pulled a quizzical face. "You mean I'm his legal brief – that too of course."

Pole did not reply, and Nancy looked stunned. "You don't think …?" Her voice wobbled. "He is a friend, maybe a bad choice …"

"And what am I? A friend too?"

"Jonathan you are much more, so much more than that —"

The buzzing noise of a mobile phone interrupted. Pole's BlackBerry was still on his desk where he had left it. Pole pressed his hand to his jacket pocket.

"I must take this."

He walked out of the office and through the open-plan space in long strides, finding a small corner where people went to have coffee.

"Spoken to Ferguson – they have the go-ahead to mount an assault." Harris was uncommonly serious.

"Where is Henry?"

"Just been delivered there."

"What do you mean – the address Andy mapped?"

"I know what you are thinking," Harris carried on. "But it will work and also get Ferguson off my back."

"Does he know?"

"That Crowne is there? No – and it will stay that way."

"How?"

"That's my business." Harris shot back. "Ferguson will ask you to be there; act surprised."

Pole stood in the corner, burner phone still in hand. A few people had tried to join Pole, but his glare had told them to find another spot.

What was the idiot doing? Catching Henry again after his escape.

260

For what – sending him back to Belmarsh with a more credible story. Perhaps it was time to speak to Nancy about all of this. She had levelled with him. Her last words had rung true and he had not been able to tell her he believed her, that he had pushed too hard with his last question.

He had never doubted her. It was friendship with Henry on her part although he had often wondered what Henry's true feelings were.

Pole walked back to his office to find it empty.

"Shit." He dialled her mobile – engaged.

Call me. This is URGENT. PLEASE. Pole sent the text.

Where had she gone?

* * *

Nancy had been saved by her own BlackBerry ringing, showing Marissa was calling. She too had been told of Henry's disappearance. She had no details either. Was it an abduction? What was Henry thinking of if he had masterminded this? But it was HSU Belmarsh. Had she facilitated?

"What an absolute idiot I've been," the words stuck in Nancy's throat. Had she been played all along?

She was walking fast, on her way to meeting Marissa. Nancy accelerated her pace further. She was fleeing Scotland Yard and the scene of her mistakes. She could still see Pole's face, his controlled anger and perhaps even his disappointment. The last words she had spoken she would have wanted to deliver differently. She was not even certain she was ready to utter them in the first place.

Curse Henry. She shook her head – idiot, you bloody idiot.

Nancy tried to focus on what there was to salvage. She slowed down. *Where was Henry's burner phone?*

She found herself in front of the SFO building near Trafalgar Square. She fumbled with her BlackBerry to let Marissa know she had arrived. A text flashed on the screen. "Call me". It was from Pole. She hesitated. She might not want to know what the rest of the text said.

Marissa was pacing up and down the SFO lobby when she saw Nancy outside looking at her mobile. She dashed out.

"Do you have fresh news?"

"Very little." Nancy shook her head.

"Pole?"

"Not much on his side either." Nancy's voice wobbled a little. She cleared her throat.

They walked back into the lobby in silence and found a couple of large chairs. Marissa flopped down into one of them.

"I can't even start to think about what this means for the case." Nancy sat down. *Was there hope?*

"We need to find out what happened to Henry's burner phone."

Marissa leaned her head against the back of the chair. "It will only give us a number."

"Perhaps, but his contact is still expecting a call; we could try to speak to him." She refused to be beaten.

Marissa looked at her surprised. "I doubt ..." She did not need to elaborate further. "And then there is Mark Phelps."

Nancy stood up. This was unbearable. She needed to find a way, a solution to this mess. She needed to make the feelings that were slowly creeping into her heart go away.

Anger and shame.

Despite her brilliant legal mind, she could not see a way out of the impasse.

Chapter Twenty-Six

They entered through the back yard. Henry could hardly make his way amongst the piles of objects covered in plastic that had been left lying there. He suspected he might not want to know what was being stored underneath them.

Ahmed opened the door. Another man was waiting for them inside, solid build and thick neck, black leather jacket. Not the Jihadi look Henry was expecting. But Henry recognised in his eyes the same determination he had seen in some of the IRA men he had known well, and in Bobby's.

The door shut behind him. Ahmed removed his helmet and the three of them stayed silent for a long moment.

Was he up for it?

Too late.

The black leather jacket man gestured with his head. Henry followed him into a large room with flaking paint and rising damp on the walls. A young man was already sitting on a low bed covered with a thick blanket.

A few rugs had been thrown on the floor, some cushions. "As-salaam Alaykum," the man said with a smile, exposing a row of perfect white teeth that matched the whiteness of his robe and crocheted hat.

"Wa Alaykum As-salaam." Henry did not hesitate, laying the palm of his right hand against his heart.

"Sit Henry." The Sheik gestured towards another low bed that looked old and tattered. "We have much to discuss."

Henry removed his shoes and sat down, fighting the urge to identify a way out of the room.

"Abu Maeraka has told me you should join us," The Sheik carried on. He stopped as the door opened and a woman in full niqab entered. The tray she carried was laden with food and the delicious smell made Henry's mouth water. She poured some tea into two glasses and left without a sound.

"But you must tell me about yourself."

The educated accent of The Sheik amazed Henry. This was not an ignorant thug. He had been schooled in the UK and his fluency indicated higher education.

Henry nodded and drank some tea. He thought about apologising for perhaps looking aloof. After all he had just escaped from prison, but he changed his mind.

This was a job interview; no mistake about it. This one would not end with a simple handshake and a "will call you later" if it had not been successful. The parting words would be a bullet in his head or a knife through his throat.

A challenge – at last.

Henry was factual. Ireland, the IRA funds, investment banking and most importantly the fact that he had been caught not because of his carelessness but the vengefulness of his enemy, Anthony Albert.

The Sheik was silent. Henry saw from his relaxed face that he was doing well. Henry bent down to take the glass that had been refilled with tea.

The lights went down.

* * *

Pole is standing at the door of a large vehicle parked one street away from the target. Harris is speaking to SO19, Ferguson is all rifled up, balaclava rolled up on his forehead, raring to go. Harris is passing two photos around the assault team.

"These are my agents – do *not* shoot them." Harris keeps repeating. Each officer looks at the photos and nods.

Pole knows that one of the photos is Henry's. He hasn't been shown the other one. Harris is too preoccupied with his assets getting out of the op alive.

Pole knocks at the van door and enters the mobile control room. Two people are manning the screens: a man and a young woman who seems to be in charge.

She is checking whether properties within the perimeter have been evacuated. Ferguson is now standing behind Pole, pressing Control for quicker results. Time is of the essence and so is the element of surprise.

The young woman pulls her headphones down abruptly. "We're all clear."

"Roger that." Ferguson adjusts his earpiece, one final comms check and the balaclava comes down together with the night vision goggles.

"All right lads, let's go." He is already walking outside amongst his men. Harris has joined Pole in the van. "I hope they don't bollocks this up." Harris is chewing on his piece of gum furiously. Pole nods.

Pole hears the woman's voice give instructions. "Controlled evacuation complete on the North side; we are clear to breech."

The lights go down.

Both Harris and Pole are looking at the screens tracking SO19's progress in infrared light. The colour is a strange monochromatic sepia.

For the untrained eye it is not always easy to make out who is who. Harris is bending forward over the officer manning the screen, but the other man does not notice. All his attention focuses on the action unfolding in front of him.

The first phosphorus bomb goes off.

Pole can hear the shouts. "Armed Police – get down, get down." And the shooting starts, short bursts, screams, retaliation.

Harris pops another gum in his mouth.

"Fuck, they are shooting left, right and centre."

Pole feels his stomach tightening. He is powerless and he hates that sensation.

On the ground floor, a couple of targets are hiding in a room that controls the bottom of the stairs. The burst of sub-machine guns is incessant.

Ferguson has spread his men; three of them are looking for the back door. Another of Ferguson's team crawls on the ground and delivers another phosphorus bomb into the room. The cries become shrieks.

The three men dispatched to the back of the house find a way in. Ferguson and his team climb the stairs, cautious, guns at the ready. More gunshots and a body hits the wall at the top of the stairs.

"Where are you guys?" Harris is anxious. His people are in the middle of this shooting match and a stray bullet is all it takes.

Ferguson's team is doing a room by room sweep. Two women are screaming, hands in the air.

"Get down, get down."

They fall on their knees. It takes only a second for the smaller of them to pull a gun from underneath her dress and discharge it at one of Ferguson's men. The retaliation is ferocious. She will never pull the trigger again.

"Officer down. I repeat officer down."

"Shit." Harris swears as each room is cleared.

Pole has not uttered a word. He is used to violence but not of this intensity.

Ferguson's team is now on its way to the second floor. They ascend the stairwell without encountering resistance. The first door they check is locked.

The burst of a machine gun and the door explodes into splinters. The windows are open, a man in a white robe is about to jump, gun in hand. A burst of bullets stops him before he can escape through the window. His body hesitates and slumps back into the room.

Harris leaves the van before the officers can protest. He runs towards the backyard, pushing on his earpiece to keep it in place.

"They are in the backyard," he shouts. "Don't shoot them – my guys are in the backyard."

Pole turns towards the screens again. He can see the muzzle of several machine guns pointing at two men on their knees at the bottom of the fire escape.

266

Ferguson's men have pulled back. One of the silhouettes collapses on the ground. The other man stands up slowly and turns towards him helping him to stand up as well.

Henry is rising to his feet.

The blanket on his back is barely keeping him warm. He is chilled to the marrow. One of his hands is clinging to the rug. He can't quite recall how it happened, but he is also clutching a cup of tea. Harris is speaking to his other agent, Wasim, the officer who helped Henry escape. They are surveying the carnage again, accounting for who in the world of terrorism has been eliminated.

Pole has been barely listening. Henry knows what is on his mind. He wants to attract Pole's attention, to indicate he needs a word, but his body is not responding. He wants to rest and simply feel he is still alive.

Henry focuses on Pole's face in the distance. Now that he is looking at Pole, Henry notices he is strangely attractive. His personality speaks through his body. The way he holds himself. The way he talks or listens. He moves, assured and yet restrained. Henry envies him for a second, but the thought passes almost as quickly as it came.

Whatever Henry is, he is not a jealous man.

Pole finally moves away, extracting himself step by step from the conversation. The others don't notice.

"How are you feeling?" Pole has found a space next to Henry at the back of the van.

Henry gives a small nod. He tries to clear his throat, "Alive."

Before Pole can respond he summons all his strength.

"I have something for you – and Nancy." His voice sounds cloggy. His teeth start chattering. He inhales. He can do this.

Henry puts his tea down very slowly, each move costs him an enormous effort. His fingers fidget underneath the blanket. He is getting something out. He can feel it underneath his fingers.

Pole looks at Henry's hand. It cradles in its centre a small mobile phone SIM card.

"Take it."

Pole registers and he cannot help but smile.

"Everything is on it. I wrote notes as messages. Nancy should have all she needs."

"Including?"

"The UBO – yes."

Pole has taken the SIM card. Henry cradles his tea for comfort.

"But I thought …?" Pole doesn't need to formulate his question. He has the answer. "You didn't give us the correct time for the call to your contact in Panama."

"I was worried you would somehow track the calls." Henry is drinking in small gulps.

Pole shakes his head.

Harris and his agent have almost finished.

Pole has slipped the SIM card into the inner pocket of his jacket. Henry has almost finished his tea, his gaze remains on the empty cup.

"There is a lot I would like to say to Nancy but …" He stops and drinks the dregs. He cannot be shy. There will not be another occasion. "Tell her I wished I could have said goodbye and that …" He hesitates because he wants to get it right. "She has been the best friend I could ever have hoped for."

Pole nods. He understands and there is nothing equivocal about it. Henry has fallen silent. He feels the lump in his throat swelling.

"Are you sure you want to do this?" Pole's eyes are searching Henry's face.

Henry inhales and manages a smile.

"It's my path – chosen – the only way I can make sense of all the mistakes."

"Redemption?" Pole asks.

"Perhaps, one day."

They feel Harris' eyes on them. He approaches slowly. He is happy to let them have a few more minutes it seems. Soon Henry will disappear with the other agent, into the underworld of Jihadism – yes, he can have a few more minutes. Pole hesitates to leave but when he does it is with a *Thank you* that means much to Henry.

Harris has taken Pole's place at his side. "Ready?"

Henry let's his body slump, in a slow move against the metal frame of the van they are in. There is one more thing Harris needs to help him do, one final meeting he needs to have before he surrenders himself to MI6. It crushes him it won't be with Nancy. But the man he has in mind needs it more than she does.

* * *

It was way past midnight but she would not be asleep. Pole had called Nancy to tell her he was on his way. When the door of the lift opened on her floor, Nancy was waiting for him. She looked pale and almost fragile in a long woollen dress that hugged her body close. Her eyes searched his for an indication of what had happened but also to see how he felt. She waited for him to get close and slid her arms around his body, her head dropping against his chest. Pole felt the firmness of her embrace and he closed his arms over her, breathing in the scent of her hair.

"He is alive." He repeated. "Henry is alive."

Nancy nodded and lifted her face to his. "Tell me."

The SIM card was lying on the coffee table wrapped in a piece of tissue. She was looking at it without sadness or joy. She turned to Pole.

"It's all on there?"

"Yes. You and Marissa have all you need to pursue the case." Pole was sitting next to her on the sofa, one arm around her waist.

"It may sound ridiculous but I always assumed I would be the last person to see him if something happened," Nancy's voice trailed. "I don't even know what I really mean by that. I would never have allowed him to …"

"This is what he wants; perhaps, rather, what he needs."

"Henry fighting for Queen and Country?" Nancy said.

"No, he is fighting for himself – no one will ever own Henry Crowne and if they think they do they will be bitterly disappointed."

"*C'est vrai.*" Nancy pushed her body back into the comfort of Pole's embrace.

She rested her head on his shoulder.

"I am sad, Jonathan; he had become a friend. There was something good striving to come out but somehow I don't think the

confrontation with Mark would have given either of them closure."
She shut her eyes.

Pole took her hand and placed his lips on her fingers.

"And he valued your friendship above all." Pole kissed her fingers once more.

Nancy opened her eyes and gave Pole a gentle smile.

"And you, *mon cher* Jonathan, know that you are much more than a friend."

* * *

The head grip is brutal. An arm is locked around his neck in a nutcracker choke that is strangling him – in a few seconds he will lose consciousness. His hands try to grab the attacker's limb with little success. He summons all his strength and shoots his elbow into the man's stomach, his fingers into the man's eyes, the grip loosens. Henry rolls around and twists with vicious strength the arm that has choked him. Wasim falls and slaps the floor. Henry releases him and collapses next to his instructor. It is intense training.

"That was the best you've done so far." Wasim throws a bottle of water to him.

Henry nods. He opens the bottle slowly and drinks, surveying his surroundings yet again. The place he has been moved to with Wasim is almost derelict. They left London after the shooting a few weeks ago and arrived in Manchester late at night. He has only come back to London once since then. Harris almost gave him up, when he set his conditions to join MI6.

"You're not in a position to ask yet, mate."

"But I'm your best bet to infiltrate these people in Syria."

"Shit, I knew you were going to be a pain in the arse to handle …" Harris has grumbled. But he has delivered.

Henry is standing in the garden of Mark Phleps' parents. He is wearing the red uniform of a postman and has been given a bundle of post. He has one hour to talk to the man who has so wanted to speak to him. MI6 has spotted a reoccurring window in Mark's routine. It's Henry's only chance.

His breath is shallow, and his mind fuzzy ... does he always have to push himself to the limits?

Henry knocks on the glass bay window and holds up the letters in his hand. Mark looks up from his book. He is a little startled, but he stands up with a wince and moves towards the door. Henry drops the items to the ground and steps back in a reassuring gesture.

Mark opens and asks a question, bending down to grab the post. Henry doesn't catch what he says ... it doesn't matter. He takes a deep breath and with a slow but clear voice begins.

"My father was an IRA man."

Mark is frozen on the spot. His eyes have widened and there is more disbelief than fear in them.

Henry removes his red cap, revealing his face so that Mark is in no doubt about his identity.

"Now ... Why?" is all Mark manages to say. Henry's escape from HSU Belmarsh has been all over the news.

"Because you wanted that conversation ... and I need to explain ..."

"Don't expect forgiveness ..." Mark spits out.

"I have made many mistakes, but I am not that much of a fool."

Mark steps back and returns to the seat he occupied earlier. His face has sagged. In the deem light of the lounge he looks much older than the picture Henry has been shown ... Henry walks in. He hasn't been invited but he knows this is what Mark wants ... what he needs.

Henry sits down in front of a man whose life has been devastated and simply tells him about what made him who he had become.

As he remembers the London meeting, Henry can feel Wasim's eyes on him. Wasim has learnt to let Henry return to that moment without interruption. A moment of intense truth Henry is still wrestling with. And Henry is grateful for his patience. Henry nods his appreciation.

Wasim Khan is the other man infiltrating the new terror group for MI6 but unlike Henry he is a Muslim. Henry suspects Wasim Kahn is not his real name and that he is working under legend. What were the chances he'd have a name exactly matching that of a famous cricketer?

Henry stands up. He snatches the towel that has been thrown on an old set of pipes. It has seen better days and has started to smell. Still, he wipes the sweat from his face. Wasim is waiting for Henry to sit down next to him.

"I have made contact again." He moves a cloth over his thick neck. His manners are strangely considerate for such a powerfully built man.

"Are they ready?"

"They are."

Henry never speaks about Agent Harris or MI6 with Wasim. He has been told very clearly on his way to Manchester. He does not initiate conversation. He does not take risk. Wasim knows when they can talk safely.

Wasim has checked the cameras he has set up around the perimeter. They are alone. The sympathisers who come to bring supplies won't come during the day, but it pays to be careful.

Henry is burning to ask the question *Am I ready?* but it would sound weak. He also knows that the only person who can convincingly answer is himself.

"How?" Henry asks instead.

"Boat across the Channel to France. After that, I have not been told."

"Why haven't they told you if you are coming too?"

"They have alternative routes and will decide at the last minute; more secure that way."

"Have you made the trip to Iraq before?"

"No, but I've been to other places …"

"Such as?"

Wasim does not reply immediately Henry must learn that he can't ask all the questions he wants. "Pakistan," he volunteers.

Henry nods. He is learning fast from his trainer about the way of the jihad. The training camps, the brutality towards those who cannot make the grade.

"They want you safely delivered," Wasim carries on.

"Are you coming back to the UK after that?"

Wasim grins. "*Inshallah.*"

"Sorry, a no-go area," Henry replies with raised hands.

Henry stands up, walks to the broken windows that have been patched up with mismatched wooden planks. Nancy's image springs into his mind and she feels far away, not only a few hundred miles, but as if she now belongs to another world. He turns back, away from the window, and as he does, Wasim nods.

"You're ready."

SPY SHADOWS

The most wanted INTERPOL fugitive,

The most destructive Terror Group in the world,

The most impossible British Intelligence Services' mission...

Henry Crowne, disgraced financier and former IRA operative
has escaped London's top high-security prison with the
unexpected help of MI6.

His mission...infiltrate an emerging terror group that has
already claimed many lives in the West and threatens to
destabilise the Middle East further. Henry's perilous journey
leads him to the group's centre of power in Syria and Iraq. His
aim, to meet the elusive man who runs a merciless war against
those who oppose him.

But Henry decides to help Mattie Colmore, a war reporter
hostage. Can he still hide in plain sight, bring back the
information the West desperately need to defeat Islamic State
and save Mattie at the same time?

* * *

SPY SHADOWS is a political and espionage thriller, the fourth
in the "Henry Crowne, Paying The Price" series. If you liked Rob
Sinclair's SLEEPER 13, L.T Ryan's NOBLE BEGINNINGS or the
TV series MacMafia or Spooks, you will enjoy the twists and turns
of Freddie P Peters' latest fierce-paced thriller.

Discover it now...

Dear Reader,

I hope you have enjoyed reading **NO TURNING BACK** as much as I have enjoyed writing it … Perhaps I can now ask for a small favour? Please take a few minutes to write a review on Amazon, Goodreads or BookBub. Thank you so very much!

Don't forget FREE access to the genesis of **NO TURNING BACK** as well as FREE chapters, or receive information about the next book in the series.

Join Freddie's book club at <u>www.freddieppeters.com</u>

Looking forward to connecting with you…
Freddie

Acknowledgements

It takes many people to write and publish a book ... for their generosity and support I want to say thank you.

Cressida Downing, my editor, for her no-nonsense approach and relentless enthusiasm for books ... mine in particular. Lucy Llewellyn for her expertise in design and for producing a super book cover, yet again and her team Catriona, Aimee and Melanie. Helena Halme, an author in her own rights, for giving me her help in marketing my books.

To the friends who have patiently read, reread and advised: Kate Burton, Alison Thorne, Elisabeth Gaunt, Helen Janececk, Prashila Narsing-Chauhan, Geraldine Kelly, Malcolm Fortune, Tim Watts, Gaye Murdock, Kathy Vanderhook, Kat Clarke.

Finally, a special thanks to ARCADE Gallery for providing plenty of fantastic contemporary art, and to my artist friends Bernard McGuigan and Susan Rosenberg for providing plenty of inspiration.